When the sun sets, these handsome, hot-blooded Spaniards rule the night!

Hot nights with a
SPANIARD

Three sizzling novels from Carole Mortimer, India Grey and Lynn Raye Harris

Hot nights with an
AUSTRALIAN

EMMA DARCY   NICOLA MARSH   LINDSAY ARMSTRONG

Hot nights with a
SPANIARD

CAROLE MORTIMER   INDIA GREY   LYNN RAYE HARRIS

Hot nights with a
GREEK

MICHELLE REID   SARAH MORGAN   NATALIE RIVERS

Hot nights with an
ITALIAN

SARA CRAVEN   HELEN BIANCHIN   LUCY GORDON

Hot nights with a
SPANIARD

CAROLE MORTIMER

INDIA GREY

LYNN RAYE HARRIS

Mills & Boon, an imprint of Harlequin (UK) Limited,
Eton House, 18-24 Paradise Road, Richmond, Surrey TW9 1SR

HOT NIGHTS WITH A SPANIARD
© Harlequin Enterprises II B.V./S.à.r.l. 2012

Bedded for the Spaniard's Pleasure © Carole Mortimer 2009
Spanish Aristocrat, Forced Bride © India Grey 2009
Spanish Magnate, Red-Hot Revenge © Lynn Raye Harris 2009

ISBN: 978 0 263 90194 8

25-0812

Harlequin (UK) policy is to use papers that are natural, renewable and recyclable products and made from wood grown in sustainable forests. The logging and manufacturing processes conform to the legal environmental regulations of the country of origin.

Printed and bound in Spain
by Blackprint CPI, Barcelona

Bedded for the Spaniard's Pleasure

CAROLE MORTIMER

Carole Mortimer was born in England, the youngest of three children. She began writing in 1978, and has now written over one hundred and forty books for Mills & Boon. Carole has four sons—Matthew, Joshua, Timothy and Peter—and a bearded collie called Merlyn. She says, 'I'm happily married to Peter senior; we're best friends as well as lovers, which is probably the best recipe for a successful relationship. We live in a lovely part of England.'

CHAPTER ONE

'CAN I help— You!' Cairo's pleasant query broke off in a gasp, and she came to a startled halt in the driveway as she easily recognized the man stepping out of the car a short distance away.

No!

This couldn't be!

This man could not be here, of all places!

Cairo had been lazing beside the pool, sunbathing, when she'd seen the silver car slowly moving up the winding, narrow road with access only to this villa in the South of France. She had already been on her feet and pulling on a thigh-length black T-shirt over her bikini when she'd heard the car stop outside. Forcing down her irritation at this intrusion, she had hurried towards the driveway to tell the driver that they had obviously lost their way.

But nothing—nothing!—could have prepared her for the man who now stood beside the car, sunglasses pushed up into the dark silkiness of his hair, as he looked across the car's bonnet at her through narrowed lids.

If she was surprised to see him, then he looked no more pleased to see her, his mouth tightening grimly even as he lifted a hand to move the sunglasses back into place over those eyes of sky-blue.

'Cairo,' he greeted her with a terse nod of his head.

Cairo couldn't speak. Couldn't move. In fact, this whole situation felt completely unreal!

'Cat got your tongue, Cairo?' he taunted in his huskily familiar transatlantic drawl, dark brows quirked above those sunglasses. 'Or maybe it's just been so long that you don't remember me?' he taunted.

Not remember him…?

Of course Cairo remembered him!

It might be eight years since she had so much as set eyes on this man, but what women ever—truthfully!—forgot her very first lover? No, Cairo had never completely forgotten Raphael Antonio Miguel Montero. How could she have, when Rafe Montero was the half-American, half-Spanish A-list actor who had been known all over the world for the last fifteen years, and more recently as director of the Oscar-winning film *Work of Art*?

He regarded her coldly now. 'Do you really have nothing to say to me, Cairo?'

'I said all that I needed to say to you the last time we met!' she snapped, even as she desperately tried to make sense of the fact that Rafe was here at all, at this remote villa situated in the hills above the picturesque town of Grasse.

Rafe grimaced as he moved to the back of the car. 'It's been so long I've forgotten,' he drawled before lifting up the boot of the car to begin taking bags from inside and placing them beside him on the driveway.

Cairo could only stand and stare at the man who had once filled her twenty-year-old heart, as well as her bed.

Now aged in his late thirties, if anything Rafe was even more devastatingly—sinfully!—handsome than he had been eight years ago. He was well over six feet tall, his dark hair was brushed back from his face, the natural swarthiness of the skin he had inherited from his Spanish father adding density to those mesmerizing sky-blue eyes set in a ruggedly chiselled face. His long aquiline nose and curved lips were set above a square jaw that had what most women called either a cleft or a dimple in its centre—but all agreed was sexy as hell. And the black polo shirt and faded denims he wore emphasized the muscled width of his shoulders, tapered waist and lean powerful thighs above long, long legs.

Cairo shook her head. All of this was very well, but none of it explained what he was doing here, taking luggage from the boot of his car! 'What do you think you're doing?'

He straightened. 'Moving in, of course. Grab a bag, hmm, Cairo?' He slung the bag containing his laptop over his shoulder and picked up the two small suitcases, leaving only a holdall sitting on the driveway.

'Grab a—? Rafe, you can't just— What do you mean, you're *moving in*?' she repeated incredulously.

'Exactly what I said.' He shrugged those broad shoulders as he strode towards her.

Cairo instinctively took a step back. 'I— But—You can't!'

'Why can't I?' he asked calmly.

'Because—because—'

'Stop babbling, Cairo, and bring the bag in.' He didn't so much as pause in those long strides that were rapidly taking him towards the villa.

Towards Cairo's haven of tranquillity after months, years, of never knowing a moment's peace. A peace that Rafe Montero had destroyed the moment he got out of his car!

She hurried to catch up with him and then struggled to match her strides to his much longer ones. 'Rafe, what are you doing here?'

'I could ask you the same question,' he countered without so much as glancing at her. 'Where are Margo and Jeff?'

'They aren't here,' she replied.

Although Cairo was beginning to wish they were—her sister and her husband might have some explanation as to what Rafe Montero was doing here at their holiday villa!

'No?' He arched those dark brows again. 'Have they gone out for the day or just shopping locally?'

'Neither.' Cairo shook her head exasperatedly. 'Rafe, will you just stop and tell me what's going on?' Her voice rose in agitation as she came to a halt, her hands clenched tightly in frustration on the narrowness of her hips.

Rafe slowly placed his luggage inside the front door of the villa before pushing his sunglasses up into his hair once more to look across at Cairo through narrowed lids as he tried to come to terms with her being here.

It had been eight years since he had last seen this woman.

Eight long years.

It was a hell of a shock to suddenly find himself face to face with her again after all that time—

A shock?

Dammit, he was still reeling!

If anything, Cairo Vaughn was even more beautiful. Perhaps a little too thin, he allowed with a slight frown, those almost six feet of curves very willowy now. But her hair was still that long tumbling red, and her legs were still long and shapely beneath the black thigh-length T-shirt. Her face was thinner, too, emphasizing the delicate curve of high cheekbones beneath chocolate-brown eyes, her nose small and straight, but her lips were as full and pouting above the stubborn set of her small, pointed chin as they'd ever been.

Although her cheeks were healthily flushed with temper at the moment, those chocolate-brown eyes looking ready to shoot flames! It made her look more like the famous actress she was than the pale woman whose photograph had been on the front page of the newspapers for months during her very public divorce.

It was none of his business, Rafe told himself grimly. Just as Cairo herself was none of his business, either.

'So where are Margo and Jeff?' he asked again. He had a few things he would like to say to the other couple concerning the fact that neither of them had warned him that Cairo was going to be here!

'I told you, they aren't here,' Cairo repeated exasperatedly.

Rafe's eyes narrowed. 'At all?'

She shook her head. 'Margo's doctor has ordered complete bed-rest for the last four weeks of her pregnancy.'

Margo and Jeff weren't here.

Only Cairo was.

And neither Margo nor Jeff had bothered to let him know that little fact!

What was he supposed to—?

'Uncle Rafe! Uncle Rafe!'

Rafe just managed to turn in time to catch the small golden-haired bundle dressed in a pink bathing costume as she came hurtling out of the villa and launched herself in his general direction.

Daisy.

Margo and Jeff's six-year-old daughter.

If Cairo had brought Daisy with her, that probably meant she didn't have a lover with her, as well. *Probably*…

'Mummy said you'd be arriving today!' Daisy beamed at him excitedly even as he swung her up to hold her in his arms.

To Cairo only one part of Daisy's statement was relevant. 'Margo *knew* you were coming here?'

'Of course,' Rafe confirmed as he moved Daisy into the crook of one arm to look across at Cairo with guarded blue eyes.

Cairo could barely breathe. Could barely think.

After the last stressful weeks, months, she had desperately needed to get completely away for a while, to be somewhere where she wasn't being constantly photographed wherever she went. Which was why she had been only too happy to accept the suggestion her sister Margo had made, when she'd pointed out that as she and Jeff were unable to go on their usual May holiday to the South of France this year, Cairo might like to make use of the villa in their stead.

It had been Cairo's own idea, with Margo eight months into what was turning out to be a precarious second pregnancy, that as six-year-old Daisy was on half-term holiday anyway, she could take the little girl with her.

It had all gone so smoothly until now, too. None of the press that had hounded Cairo so doggedly the last ten months had been looking for a woman travelling with a little girl of six. Neither had they recognized the actress Cairo Vaughn behind the dark sunglasses and the baseball cap she had worn to hide the fiery length of her hair as she drove onto the train that would take them through the Eurotunnel into France.

It had been a long drive, of course, but the villa, set high in the hills above Grasse, had been a pleasant surprise, a large, sprawling single-storey building that maintained its rusticity at the same time as providing all the amenities they could possibly want, including a huge pool on the lower terrace, and a number of small shops in the local village that would see to their daily needs.

And Daisy had proved a delightful companion, as only a gregarious six-year-old could, as she kept up a constant stream of chatter on the journey here, and then yesterday threw herself into the pool with enthusiasm once they'd finally reached the villa.

In fact, the simplicity of it all had been a wonderful relief to Cairo after so many years of knowing exactly what she would be doing next week, next month, next year!

But never, during any of Cairo's plans to come to France, had Margo so much as mentioned Rafe Montero. In fact, Cairo hadn't even known that her sister and brother-in-law were still friends with him.

She gave a puzzled shake of her head. 'Margo didn't say anything to me about your coming here.'

'If it's any consolation, she didn't say anything to me about your being here, either,' Rafe retorted sharply.

'It isn't,' Cairo assured him impatiently. 'I appreciate that Margo hasn't been too well recently, but—'

'Perhaps it might be better if we continued this conversation later,' Rafe cut in with a pointed glance at Daisy before he turned his blue gaze warningly on Cairo.

A warning Cairo took absolutely no notice of. 'I really feel we should sort this situation out now, Rafe—'

'Your feeling is noted, Cairo,' he acknowledged brusquely.

Noted, and dismissed, Cairo realized indignantly. Had Rafe always been this infuriating? So arrogantly sure of himself and his surroundings that he totally ignored—or just didn't see or hear!—what anyone else wanted?

Probably, Cairo thought wryly. She had just been too naïve eight years ago, too enthralled by him, too much in love with him, to see it.

Well, she wasn't now and she wouldn't let him get away with it.

'And obviously ignored,' she snapped. 'Rafe, I have absolutely no idea what your arrangement was with Margo and Jeff.' But she certainly intended finding out when she telephoned her sister shortly! 'But as they're obviously still in England, there is no way you can expect to continue with your own plans to stay here.'

He quirked dark brows. 'And just where would you suggest I go instead?'

The hardness in his eyes told her she'd do better to hold back on the reply that she really wanted to make. So instead, Cairo replied, 'To a hotel, of course.'

'You really expect me to be able to do that in the week of the Cannes Film Festival?' he taunted.

'I— The Cannes Film Festival?' she repeated slowly.

'It's the reason I'm in France at the moment,' Rafe explained. '*Work of Art* has been put up for several awards.' He shrugged. 'As director, I'm expected to make an appearance.'

The Cannes Film Festival, Cairo berated herself in her head. Of course Rafe's film had been nominated for an award; it had virtually wiped the board at the Oscars earlier in the year.

'But Cannes is miles away,' she said stubbornly.

'So?'

'So there must be a hotel there where you could stay. It would be much more convenient than being all the way out here, anyway,' Cairo reasoned firmly.

Rafe's mouth tightened. 'I'm sure it's very kind of you to attempt to rearrange my plans for me in this way, Cairo,' he bit out sarcastically. 'But I've been travelling for hours now, and certainly have no intention of discussing this any further until I've at least taken a swim. What do you say, Daisy-May, shall the two of us go for a swim?' He smiled affectionately at the little girl as she gave an excited squeal of approval. 'It would appear you're outnumbered and out-gunned, Cairo,' Rafe drawled as he put Daisy down on the tarmacked drive and she instantly took hold of his hand to begin pulling him down towards the swimming pool on the lower terrace.

'But—'

'Outnumbered and outgunned,' Rafe repeated softly as he released his hand from Daisy's to begin pulling his polo shirt over his head, revealing a broad golden expanse of naked chest and shoulders.

Cairo's mouth went dry and her breath caught in her throat as she found herself unable to look away from the sight of Rafe slowly peeling the shirt from his body.

Eight years ago, she had been intimately familiar with every hard, muscled, beautiful inch of Rafe's body, from those wide shoulders, across that muscled chest and flat stomach and down to thrusting thighs.

The time since then had only honed that body, with not an ounce of superfluous flesh on his muscled torso. Rafe's dark hair rested rakishly on his shoulders as he looked across at her with challenging blue eyes. He looked every inch a Spanish conquistador with that mocking smile playing about those chiselled lips. He seemed fully aware that he had rendered Cairo momentarily speechless.

The bastard. He had done that on purpose. Had deliberately—

'Rafe!' she gasped as his hand moved with slow deliberation to unfasten the top button of his denims and slowly slide down the zip.

He arched mocking brows. 'Something wrong, Cairo?' he taunted.

Something was very wrong!

Eight years ago, the two of them hadn't exactly parted the best of friends. In fact, the two of them hadn't seen or spoken to each other again in all that time.

But just to look at him now made Cairo feel breathless, her face hot and flushed. No, *all* of her felt hot and flushed as she found herself unable to look away from those unfastened denims and the deep V of dark hair that disappeared beneath them.

She moistened dry lips. 'Daisy, would you pop into the villa and get us some lemonade to drink by the pool?' She gave her niece what she hoped was a reassuring smile; the muscles in her face didn't seem to be working properly!

'You won't be long, Uncle Rafe?' Daisy paused to ask wistfully.

'Two minutes, Daisy-May,' he promised huskily.

There it was again. That gut feeling that something wasn't quite right about this situation.

And Cairo knew exactly what it was!

Uncle Rafe.

Daisy-May.

It was obvious from Rafe's arrival that Margo and Jeff had kept up their friendship with him, but for how long and how well did Daisy know Rafe that the affection between them was so obvious and the little girl addressed him by the honorary title of 'Uncle'?

And only the family and really close friends ever called Daisy by the affectionate Daisy-May...

Admittedly Cairo had lived mainly in America the last eight years, her visits home infrequent to say the least, but still she would have thought that she would at least have had some idea that her sister and brother-in-law had remained such close friends with Rafe all this time.

Rafe could almost see the disagreeable thoughts racing through Cairo's head. She was undoubtedly annoyed with Margo and Jeff for putting her in this position in the first place.

He could only guess as to the other couple's motives for their actions; Margo and Jeff had never made any secret of the fact that they regretted that he and Cairo had parted eight years ago.

That they 'had parted'! Such simple words to describe such a catastrophic event.

Their last meeting had consisted of a pretty one-sided conversation as Cairo had told him their relationship was over, followed three days later by the announcement of her engagement to Lionel Bond.

A marriage that had now also come to an end.

But Margo and Jeff were whistling in the wind if they thought that little fact was going to make any difference to how Rafe and Cairo felt about each other. Although her obvious determination now to see him leave only made Rafe stubbornly want to do the opposite!

'Lemonade, Cairo?' he commented with a grimace. 'My own preference would have been a glass of wine on the terrace while we gazed out at the view down the valley to the bay of Cannes.'

She glared at him. '*We* aren't going to be *gazing out* at anything together, Rafe,' she snapped. 'In fact—'

'I said let's save the explanations until later, Cairo,' he reminded her forcefully. 'For the moment I intend taking a swim with Daisy.' To prove his point he deliberately slid the zip on his denims the rest of the way before slowly pushing the heavy material down his thighs.

And watched as Cairo's eyes widened, and then widened even more as she realized his intent, her protest only dying on her lips as she saw that Rafe actually wore black swimming trunks beneath the jeans he had now completely removed.

But that momentary lapse in her protests had shown that she wasn't as immune to him as she would have him believe, Rafe noted consideringly. Although he had no doubt, as he saw her shoulders straighten with new determination, that if challenged, she would vehemently deny that awareness.

She drew in a deep breath. 'Rafe, how many times do I have to say it? You are *not* staying here!'

'Sure I am,' he came back easily. 'We'll spend the afternoon swimming and sunbathing with Daisy, then later this evening we can all cook dinner together, and then when Daisy is in bed, the two of us can—'

'We can *what*, Rafe?' Cairo cut in sharply, brown eyes glittering in dark warning as she gave an exasperated shake of her head, having thankfully now regrouped after being completely thrown seconds ago when she had believed Rafe was going to strip off to his underpants.

He usually wore the very briefest of underpants, if her memory served her correctly. And she was pretty sure that it did! Not that the swimming trunks were much better, as the thin material clearly outlined every powerful inch of his hips above long, tanned legs.

Her mouth thinned as she looked up and determinedly met his mocking blue gaze. 'I repeat, Rafe, that the two of us are not going to be doing anything together—not later on this evening when Daisy is in bed, or at any other time!'

'Do I take it from that remark that you aren't pleased to see me again, Cairo?' he murmured throatily.

How had he moved so fast? Cairo wondered slightly dazedly as she suddenly found Rafe was standing only inches away from her, so near she could actually see the pores in the skin of his face. So close that she could actually feel the heat of his body, and smell that clean male smell that was totally Rafe: tangy soap, a lightly elusive after-shave, and a pure animal scent that acted on a woman's senses like a drug. On her senses like a—

No!

This man had broken her heart eight years ago. He hadn't just broken it—the womanizing rat had trampled all over it!

Cairo stood her ground as she refused to be intimi-dated by the close proximity of his near-nakedness, almost eye to eye with him as Rafe was only a couple of inches taller than her own almost six feet. A compatibility in height that had once given them both incredible pleasure as they—

This was *not* the time to remember that compatibility! What she *should* be recalling was that in every other way that mattered they had been totally *in*compatible.

Her mouth tightened. 'I have no idea what gave you the impression I might be— What are you doing?' She flinched her head back sharply when he would have reached out and touched her cheek.

Rafe's gaze narrowed as he saw her purely instinctive response to the move, his hand dropping slowly back to his side. He wondered just what Cairo's eight-year marriage to Lionel Bond had been like to have caused her to flinch in that way at the merest hint of physical contact.

Unless it was just him that she didn't want to touch her…?

It was a definite possibility, Rafe acknowledged grimly. The last time he and Cairo had spoken together she had left him in absolutely no doubt that, although she had enjoyed their relationship while it had lasted, she now had other plans for her life that most certainly did not include him.

Cairo had taken Hollywood by storm when she'd moved there with her movie-producer husband eight years ago, but even so, she and Rafe had never met again until now. Cairo was a member of the partying set that Rafe avoided at all costs.

Rafe stood unmoving now, his gaze steadily holding Cairo's more wary one as he noted other changes in her beside that ethereal slenderness.

Her eyes, those chocolate-brown orbs that could melt a

man's soul, were guarded now rather than glowing as they used to do.

There were dark shadows beneath those eyes, too, as if she hadn't slept well for some time. And there were small delicate lines on either side of the fullness of her mouth, as if a smile had been grimly set there far too often and for far too long as a shield to the inner unhappiness she had no intention of allowing anyone to see or even guess at.

A veneer that had been totally exploded when Cairo had first separated from, and then divorced, her very powerful husband.

On the surface, their marriage had seemed idyllic. A myth that Rafe, along with everyone else who had ever seen or read anything about the couple, had totally believed in until their separation ten months ago....

'Let's all just go for that swim, hmm, Cairo, and talk about this later?' he encouraged softly now.

Cairo stepped away from him. 'You're many things, Rafe, but I never thought stupid as being one of them—' She broke off with a frown as Rafe gave her a derisive smile. 'You find something about this situation amusing?' she bit out irritably.

Yes, Cairo was definitely still in possession of that fiery temperament that had once attracted him so strongly and that made her so electrifying to watch on the big screen.

'Only the way you keep insisting that I have to leave.' He shrugged. 'Even if I could manage to find an available hotel room in the middle of the Cannes Film Festival, I wouldn't,' he admitted.

'Why wouldn't you?'

'Firstly, because I much prefer the peace and quiet to be found here—'

'I agree—it *was* quiet and very peaceful!' Cairo gave him a pointed glare, letting him know clearly that he was the reason that was no longer the case. 'Rafe, you must know I have absolutely no intention of letting you stay on here.'

'Ah.'

'What do you mean, "ah"?' she prompted warily.

'The thing is, Cairo, that brings me to the second reason I have no intention of leaving, either now or in the immediate future,' he told her firmly.

'Which is…?' she challenged.

Rafe couldn't help laughing out loud. 'That I'm not the guest here, Cairo—*you* are. This is my villa,' he added dryly when she continued to look at him blankly.

Cairo stared at Rafe unblinkingly.

Rafe was the 'friend' who let Margo and Jeff stay at his villa in the South of France every year?

CHAPTER TWO

No one looking at Cairo's calm expression, as she relaxed in her bikini on a lounger beside the pool, would ever have guessed at the emotions seething inside her.

Except Rafe, of course.

The cause of those seething emotions!

But he was apparently too busy playing with Daisy, in the pool he had dived into immediately after announcing he owned the villa, to even seem aware of Cairo's presence there, too. Other than physically dragging him out of the pool—which, considering Rafe weighed twice as much as she did, was a non-starter—and demanding he leave, Cairo had little choice but to join the two of them down on the lower terrace.

Dark glasses shielded her eyes from prying eyes, as well as the glare of the sun as she contemplated her options.

Rafe owned this villa in the South of France.

A little fact that Margo had apparently forgotten to mention for the last eight years, seven of which she and Jeff had been coming to stay here for a couple of weeks every spring!

Or perhaps Margo had simply felt it more diplomatic not to mention that the villa belonged to Rafe....

Cairo had absolutely refused to discuss, with anyone, the reason for the end of her relationship with Rafe Montero. In fact, not only had she refused to talk about him, she had also forbidden Margo to talk to her about him, too. Which would, admittedly, have made it extremely difficult for Margo to tell Cairo that she and Jeff had remained friends with him all these years!

However, there was no way she could stay on here now that she knew Rafe owned the villa, so that meant Cairo had two options.

She could either return to England and the publicity, which, although it was nowhere near as unrelenting as it had been in the States, still dogged Cairo's steps every time she so much as stepped out of the apartment she had bought in London and moved into six months ago.

Or alternatively she could find somewhere else for herself and Daisy to stay in this beautiful area of France.

The latter option was the obvious one, of course. For one thing, Daisy was sure to be very disappointed if they had to cut their holiday short. For another, Cairo really didn't want to return to England yet, seeing as she had actually been enjoying this first proper holiday she had taken in years.

Dammit, why had Rafe Montero had to turn up and disturb their tranquillity in this way?

Also, having turned up, and discovered Cairo here instead of Margo and Jeff, what was he *still* doing here? He had to know how awkward this situation was for her. He also had to know that the two of them couldn't remain here alone—apart from Daisy—together!

He just didn't give a damn.

But then, he never had....

Cairo looked across at him from behind her sunglasses, watching the droplets of water glistening on his face and shoulders as he stood up in the deep end of the pool playing a ball game with Daisy, his dark hair wet now and slicked back from his face as he grinned mischievously at the little girl. That ruggedly handsome face had once made Cairo's heartbeat quicken just to look at it...

She turned sharply away, her hands clenching at her sides as she fought back those painful memories.

Here and now was what mattered.

But here and now Cairo felt completely at a loss to know what to do next. Rafe, on the basis that this villa was actually his, was quite rightly refusing to leave, but the logistics of finding another villa for Daisy and herself to move into seemed overwhelming to Cairo.

And this indecisiveness was Rafe's fault, too!

Because Cairo had allowed herself to relax during the last twenty-four hours, to just let herself be, to exist, to let herself revel in the fact that, after years of making films back to back, she had no pressing work pressures for the next two weeks, when she was due to begin rehearsals for the lead in the London play she had agreed to appear in.

Now Rafe, with his unwanted presence here, was forcing her into once again making decisions, when it was the last thing she felt like doing.

She desperately blinked back the tears of frustration. She wouldn't cry. She would not!

So if she wasn't going to be 'sad,' then she would just

have to get 'mad'. And Rafe Montero was the obvious person for her to get mad at!

'Are you coming in for a swim or not?' Rafe leant his arms on the side of the pool as he looked across at her.

He had been totally aware of Cairo the last hour or so as she lay so still and silent on a lounger beside the pool, not reading a book or magazine but just staring off into the distance.

She looked even more slender now that she had removed the overlong T-shirt to reveal that she wore only a brief black bikini beneath; there didn't seem to be an ounce of superfluous flesh on those long silky limbs.

Long, silky limbs that had more than once been entwined with his…

'No, I'm not coming in for a swim,' she answered him tersely now. 'Rafe, you must see that we have to talk about—about the awkwardness, of this situation…?'

Yes, of course he knew the two of them had to talk. Dammit, he was no more happy about finding himself practically alone here with Cairo—young Daisy apart—than she obviously was at having him here.

But neither did he think it was a good idea to have Daisy witness an argument between her aunty Cairo and her 'uncle' Rafe, especially when—as it was sure to!—it resulted in the two of them saying things it would be much better for Daisy not to hear.

His mouth thinned. 'Cairo, how does Daisy seem to you?'

'Seem to me?' she repeated with a frowning glance at the little girl playing at the other end of the pool by throwing a coin into the water before diving in to collect it.

'Dammit, Cairo.' Rafe quickly ascended the steps that

led out of the pool. 'How long is it since you've seen or cared about anyone but yourself?' he demanded as he stood beside her to pick up a towel and begin drying his hair.

Cairo gasped at his accusing tone. 'That is totally unfair, Rafe!' It was also totally unfair what his semi-nakedness was doing to her heart-rate as he leisurely dried himself off with the towel!

'Is it?' he challenged grimly as he moved to sit down on the lounger next to hers. 'Tell me what you see when you look at Daisy,' he ordered.

Cairo stared at him rebelliously for several long seconds before turning her attention to her young niece. 'I see…a little girl having fun playing in the pool,' she said.

'Look again, Cairo. Closer,' he insisted as she would have protested.

Cairo bit back her resentment at his arrogant tone as she turned her attention back to Daisy. Tall for her age, with shoulder-length golden hair and blue eyes, Daisy looked to her like any other healthy, happy six-year-old on holiday.

Or did she…?

Now that Cairo thought about it, before Rafe's arrival earlier, Daisy hadn't been as chatty this last twenty-four hours. Oh, her niece had played in the pool yesterday and, this morning, had helped Cairo prepare their meals, but she had been less gregarious than usual, less spontaneous, less inclined to do anything, and had refused absolutely to go to the local shops with Cairo this morning so that they could restock on food. Cairo had put this uncharacteristic lack of cooperation down to tiredness after their journey, but what if that wasn't the reason?

Cairo turned frowningly back to Rafe. 'You think she's worried about Margo?'

His mouth twisted derisively. 'What do you think?'

Not knowing how much Daisy actually knew about Margo's condition, Cairo wasn't really sure how to answer that question.

Maybe Rafe was right. Maybe Cairo had been too wrapped up in her own problems just recently to give anyone else's a thought. Although she certainly didn't thank Rafe for being the one to point that out—until now she hadn't even known he liked children, let alone understood Daisy's moods.

She sat up on the lounger. 'Perhaps I should sit down with her and calmly explain that Margo just needs to rest for a few weeks because her blood pressure is a little high—'

'And you think a little girl of six will be reassured by that explanation?' Rafe said sarcastically.

Colour warmed Cairo's cheeks at his intended rebuke. 'I think it might be worth a try, yes!'

He scowled. 'If that's the extent of your knowledge of children, perhaps it's as well that you and Bond never had any!'

Cairo gasped incredulously at his scorn, the fact that she had thought exactly the same thing following her separation from Lionel not important at that moment; Rafe certainly hadn't meant it in the same way she did.

'Look at yourself, Cairo.' Rafe's gaze ran over her with scathing dismissal. 'Perfect hair. Perfect skin. Perfect teeth. Too-perfect body. Perfect damned everything! At least you looked human eight years ago; now you just look like every other *perfect* Hollywood actress!'

Cairo felt her cheeks pale at his deliberately insulting tone. It was too much on top of everything else she had gone through the last eight years.

She stood up. 'When I want your opinion, I'll ask for it— Let *go* of me, Rafe!' she instructed between gritted teeth as he reached out to curl long fingers about her wrist.

A too-slender wrist, Rafe decided even as he felt the creamy softness of her skin beneath his fingers, his gaze moving down to her hand now, the long, slender fingers completely bare of rings. Although there was a slightly whiter band of skin on the third finger of her left hand where her wedding ring and that huge rock that Bond had bought her as an engagement ring used to be....

'I don't think so,' he challenged softly, even as his fingers tightened about her wrist.

Dark sunglasses hid the emotion in her eyes, but the pallor of her cheeks and the unhappy curve of her mouth were evidence of her rising anger.

She was angry? After years of deliberately blocking any memory of Cairo from his mind, Rafe had been forced to relive every single one of them during the last hour. It hadn't improved his temper at all.

His mouth compressed into a thin line. 'How's your career, Cairo?'

Her eyes narrowed with suspicion. 'The last time I looked it was just fine, thank you.'

'Really?' Rafe taunted.

'Yes—really!' she grated.

Rafe shrugged. 'You can't live on the publicity of the divorce for ever, you know. At some time in the not too distant future you'll have to get back to work.'

Cairo's palm itched, her free hand actually aching from the effort it took to stop herself from slapping that arrogant smile from Rafe's mockingly curved lips.

He grimaced. 'I'm just trying to be helpful—'

'When I want your advice, I'll ask for it!' Her eyes flashed an unmistakable warning.

He quirked dark brows. 'Which would be never—right?'

'Right!'

'I'm just interested, Cairo. Relocating yourself to London after your separation doesn't exactly seem like a good career move, does it?' Rafe's gaze was fixed on her face.

'Mind your own damned business!'

'Fine.' He released her abruptly to hold his hands up as he stepped away from her.

Cairo glared at him for several more seconds before giving an abrupt nod. 'If you'll excuse me…'

'Running away, Cairo?' Rafe taunted her as she turned away.

Cairo paused to look back at him, her chin raised stubbornly high. 'I believe you said earlier that you would enjoy a glass of white wine…?'

His brows rose. 'And you're about to go and get me one?'

'If it means I get to spend a little less time in your unpleasant company, yes!' she bit out. 'But, of course, if you've changed your mind—'

'You should know by now that once my mind is made up about something—or someone—then it rarely changes,' he said pointedly.

'Luckily, neither does mine,' she came back just as pointedly.

They continued to look at each other for several long,

tense seconds, a battle of wills that was totally matched in intensity, with neither of them willing to back down.

It had always been like this between them, Rafe recalled ruefully. Cairo might only have been a twenty-year-old actress just starting out in her career eight years ago, but even then she'd had a definite mind of her own, had known exactly what she wanted and how to get it. And eight years ago, she had decided she wanted to become the wife of multi-millionaire movie producer Lionel Bond and un-ashamedly used her relationship with Rafe as a stepping stone to achieving that goal.

He moved to lie back on the lounger as he looked out over the terraces of orange trees that surrounded the pool. 'White wine sounds good,' he said curtly.

He felt Cairo continue to look at him frowningly for several more seconds before she turned sharply on her heel and continued up the steps to the villa.

Rafe waited until he was sure she had left before turning to look at her, his hands clenching at his sides as he watched that red hair cascading wildly down a back that seemed endless and almost sensuously feline, a bottom smoothly curving in the black bikini, and legs that were long and shapely.

Dammit, even after all this time, after all that had happened between them, Cairo was still one of the most seductively beautiful women Rafe had ever laid eyes—or hands—on.

Not a comfortable realization for a man who made a point of never becoming involved with a woman. Not any more!

He looked across at Daisy playing in the pool. 'Sweet-heart, do you want to go inside and get changed now? It'll be time to eat soon.'

'Okay, Uncle Rafe.' Daisy obediently got out of the pool and went inside the villa.

Cairo's movements were agitated as she collected wine from the fridge and glasses from the cupboard, not forgetting to get some more juice for Daisy, too, in case she fancied a drink.

How dared Rafe even presume to offer her advice?

Rafe had callously broken her heart eight years ago, leaving her completely vulnerable to the face-saving offer of Lionel's marriage proposal—

Cairo came to an abrupt halt in the middle of the kitchen, her eyes closing as she swayed dizzily.

It was the first time she had ever admitted, even to herself, that Rafe's actions were the real reason she had married Lionel….

She shook her head as she once again fought back the tears.

No matter what her reasons might or might not have been for marrying Lionel, despite the fact that she hadn't loved him, she had tried to be a good wife to him, had accompanied him to numerous parties and premieres, always the glamorous and smiling asset. Her work schedule had also been horrendous in recent years, more often than not for Lionel's own production company.

Yes, she really had tried to be the 'perfect' wife to Lionel.

The fact that she had ultimately failed still haunted her….

'Cairo, exactly what are you doing?'

Cairo was so startled by the harsh sound of Rafe's voice behind her that she dropped the carton of juice she was holding, staring down as it seemed to fall in slow motion before landing with a very liquid splat on the tiled floor to spray the juice high into the air.

She gasped as most of that cold juice landed on her bare legs, stepping back quickly, only to come up against a hard, immovable object.

Rafe's body...

Cairo froze as her back came into contact with the searing heat of Rafe's bare chest and thighs, her spine stiffening as she immediately tried to move away from that contact.

It was too much, Rafe decided grimly. Having an almost naked Cairo pressed against him, her bottom nestled neatly against his hardening thighs, was just too much on top of coming face to face with her again so unexpectedly earlier on.

He grasped her arms to turn her round to face him, knowing by her sudden gasp, the widening of those dark brown eyes as she looked up at him, that she had read the intent in his eyes.

That she knew Rafe was going to kiss her.

Not gently.

Not searchingly.

Certainly not with the slow sensuality with which they used to kiss.

Rafe was hungry.

Very hungry.

So damned hungry for the taste and feel of Cairo that he wanted to strip those two scraps of material from her body, push her against the wall, and take her where she stood!

He held her gaze with his as his arms moved about her like steel bands, moulding her willowy curves against the lean length of his own body before moving his eyes down to look at the parted softness of her lips.

Cairo had always had the most erotic mouth he had ever

seen, her lips full and pouting, slightly moistened now, as if inviting and ready for his kiss.

And he was more than ready to kiss her!

Cairo was held mesmerized by the fierceness of Rafe's gaze, but her breath stopped completely as his head swooped and his mouth forcefully claimed hers, deeply, fiercely, demanding a response from her rather than asking for one.

A response Cairo was unable to deny him as her lips seemed to part of their own volition. Her arms moved up and her hands clung to those wide, powerful shoulders, Rafe's skin feeling like steel encased in satin beneath her fingertips.

Heat exploded between them, a fierce, burning heat.

Everywhere were licking flames of complete awareness, of fierce arousal, as her body curved more intimately against Rafe's and she returned the hunger of his kiss.

It had been so long—too long!—since Cairo had felt so stingingly, vibrantly alive!

Rafe's hands, his large, evocative hands, moved caressingly across her back as that devouring kiss continued, Rafe's tongue now thrusting into the moist heat of her mouth, and all the time those hands seeming to burn as they caressed her from hip to breast in restless demand.

Muscles rippled along Rafe's spine as Cairo touched him there, his silky skin feeling hot, hard, and so wonderful.

Cairo was so lost to reason, so totally aroused, that she offered no protest as she felt Rafe unfastening the single hook at the back of her top before one of his hands moved round unerringly to cup the nakedness of her breast.

Cairo melted completely as the soft pad of his thumb moved caressingly across the thrusting pout of her nipple, rivers of pleasure engulfing her—

'Uncle Rafe…?'

Cairo barely had time to register Daisy's presence in the kitchen before Rafe pulled sharply away from her, eyes darkly—briefly—accusing as he thrust Cairo impatiently behind him before turning to face the little girl.

Rafe breathed raggedly. 'Aunty Cairo and I were just—'

'It's okay, Uncle Rafe, Mummy and Daddy kiss each other all the time,' Daisy told him in that patronizing tone of voice that only a precocious six-year-old could possibly use when talking to an adult. ''Course I didn't know that you and Aunty Cairo kissed, too, but I suppose it's all right.' She shrugged.

'That's very—adult, of you, Daisy,' Rafe told her dryly.

'Grown-ups are always kissing and stuff,' Daisy assured him with a total lack of interest.

Cairo was hastily dealing with her bikini top—not having as much luck fastening it as Rafe had done unfastening it because her fingers trembled so much!—but even so she was aware of the muscles rippling in Rafe's back as he suppressed a chuckle at Daisy's bored dismissal of the scene she had just witnessed.

Cairo certainly didn't share his humour concerning this totally embarrassing situation. Rafe had only been back in her life a matter of hours and already she was allowing him to kiss her!

Well…no, she hadn't exactly allowed him to kiss her—being Rafe he had just taken the opportunity to kiss her.

And he wasn't 'back in her life', either—something she intended making very plain to him the next time they were alone together.

So far today Rafe had mocked her, taunted her and insulted her—he certainly wasn't going to get away with making love to her whenever he felt like it!

Cairo drew in a controlling breath as she stepped out from behind Rafe, her bikini top now firmly back in place. 'What would you like to do first, Daisy, cook dinner or phone Mummy?'

Daisy's face instantly brightened. 'Phone Mummy!'

'We'll go and do it right now,' Cairo promised, determinedly keeping her gaze averted from Rafe's as she crossed the kitchen to take the excited Daisy's hand in her own.

'Don't worry about me,' Rafe drawled behind them. 'I'll just stay here and clear up this sticky juice from the floor, shall I?'

Cairo turned back to give him a mocking smile. 'That's very kind of you, Rafe,' she accepted lightly. 'I'm sure you'll find everything you need in the cupboard under the sink,' she added.

His eyes glittered dangerously. 'Not everything that I need, Cairo,' he ground out harshly.

She gave him a censorious frown. 'Just do your best, hmm?' she snapped.

'I usually do,' he stated deliberately.

Cairo shot him a silencing glare before leaving the kitchen, Daisy's hand still tucked trustingly in her own.

CHAPTER THREE

RAFE had showered, dressed, already had the barbecue alight and ready for cooking the steaks for their dinner, and was sitting on the terrace drinking another glass of white wine by the time Cairo and Daisy rejoined him outside. Daisy looked very cute in her blue corduroy skirt and pink T-shirt, and Cairo looked even better in flat sandals, her tanned legs bare, and a dark green, knee-length, strappy silk dress that clung in all the right places.

Or—depending on your point of view—all the wrong ones, Rafe allowed wryly as his gaze lingered on the bareness of her tanned shoulders and the tops of her breasts.

It had been a mistake to kiss Cairo earlier, he acknowledged now. But it was simply the most recent of the many mistakes he had made where she was concerned—allowing himself to fall for her eight years ago having definitely been the worst one of them all….

His mouth tightened as he raised his gaze to hers. 'Help yourself to a glass of wine,' he invited as she moved to sit down at the other end of the marble-topped dining table. 'How was Margo?'

'Very well,' Cairo answered distantly as she poured

some of the white wine into a second glass—and having absolutely no intention of telling him what her sister's reply had been when Cairo had challenged her over Rafe's arrival earlier today.

'Get over yourself!' had been Margo's unhelpful comment.

It wasn't herself Cairo had to get over—it was Rafe's mockery of her and her resentment towards him!

'It's high time the two of you got over that, too,' had been Margo's response to that claim.

Not exactly helpful advice when even now Cairo could feel the antagonism between Rafe and herself burning beneath the surface of this polite exchange.

Not that Rafe looked particularly concerned by it. In fact, he looked altogether too disturbingly handsome in faded denims and an open-necked, short-sleeved shirt the same shade of blue as his eyes, the dampness of his hair brushed back from those hard, aristocratically chiselled features inherited from his Spanish father.

Cairo had chosen her own dress for this evening with care, knowing she would need all her self-confidence to face Rafe again after that heated exchange in the kitchen. She had also swept her hair up and secured it loosely on her crown, leaving her neck and shoulders bare, her face already lightly tanned and requiring only a peach gloss applied to her lips.

The lips that still felt tinglingly sensitive and slightly bruised from the force of Rafe's kiss!

'Mummy said to say hello, Uncle Rafe,' Daisy told him happily.

'Did she, now?' he drawled.

'Yes.' The little girl nodded. 'And she hopes you do well at the film festival.'

'That's very thoughtful of her,' Rafe accepted dryly— he had a few things he intended saying personally to Margo once Daisy was safely tucked up in bed! 'Can your aunty Cairo make a salad, do you think?' he teased gently as he stood up to turn the steaks on the barbecue.

Daisy gave a giggle. 'Aunty Cairo cooked omelettes last night.'

'Did she now?' Rafe quirked dark, mocking brows. 'She's obviously a woman of many talents!' he added with a taunting sideways glance at 'Aunty Cairo'.

Daisy seemed completely unaware of the intended insult to her aunt, singing quietly to herself as she began to lay the table outside for the three of them.

But Cairo certainly wasn't, the narrow-eyed glare she gave Rafe letting him know in no uncertain terms that she wasn't amused.

Rafe returned Cairo's look for several long seconds, his smile derisive, before he turned his full attention to cooking the steaks. The problem was that Cairo was just too beautiful for him—or any other man!—to look at for too long without wanting to take her to bed.

Which was something that was never going to happen ever again, Rafe told himself grimly, in spite of the fact that he had enjoyed kissing her earlier. No, he'd more than enjoyed it—he had been wanting to repeat the experience ever since.

Eight years, dammit—and within hours of seeing her again Rafe's body ached with the desire that had been aroused earlier and remained unfulfilled!

'How is Margo, really?' he asked once Daisy had gone into the kitchen to collect the cutlery.

Cairo shrugged those delectably bare shoulders. 'She believes that the specialist is thinking of admitting her to the clinic tomorrow if her blood pressure hasn't gone down by then.'

Rafe could hear the underlying concern in Cairo's voice. 'She wasn't ill like this with Daisy, was she?'

'Not as far as I'm aware, no.' Cairo frowned. 'I haven't spent a great deal of time in England the last few years, Rafe,' she explained sharply as he raised questioning brows.

His lip curled scornfully. 'Too busy making a name for yourself in Hollywood, I expect.'

'That's where Lionel lived, Rafe,' she said defensively as she heard the censure in his tone. 'And where he worked. It was only natural that I should mainly work there, too.'

Really, this man seemed to think that everything she did, everything she said, was suspect—especially if it allowed him to make some cutting comment about it!

'I seem to remember that you once said your main love was the stage,' he said huskily. 'I even talked of moving to England for a while so that I could be with you when you accepted the part you had been offered in *The Graduate*.'

Cairo gave a pained frown. Yes, Rafe had talked of staying temporarily in England. But that had been before he'd become bored with their relationship and had an affair with another woman!

Her mouth tightened. 'So you could be with me *and* all those other adoring females panting at your bedroom door!' she dismissed scathingly. 'If you'll excuse me, Rafe,' she added, standing up abruptly, 'I need to go and make the salad.'

* * *

Dinner hadn't exactly been a relaxed meal, Cairo acknowledged ruefully as they cleared everything away a couple of hours later. Thankfully Daisy, reassured after her earlier chat on the telephone with her mother, was back to her normal, talkative self, and her chatter had filled in the silence that had existed between Rafe and Cairo. The two of them had barely addressed a word directly to one another—'could you please pass the salt?' really didn't count as conversation!

Rafe excused himself to make a telephone call while Cairo put Daisy to bed, delaying as long as she possibly could in her niece's bedroom before rejoining Rafe on the terrace. She finally came outside to find him watching the last rays of sunset gleaming redly in the rapidly darkening sky, dozens of lights on in the houses dotted in the valley below.

Cairo stood hesitantly in the doorway, not altogether comfortable with the air of intimacy that surrounded him.

'Sit down, Cairo,' he ordered without turning.

She gasped. 'How did you—?'

'Your perfume,' he elaborated as he turned to look at her. 'Stop hovering over there in the doorway, Cairo, and come and sit down.'

Her eyes widened indignantly at his autocratic tone. 'You always were arrogant, Rafe. I'm sure that as a director you wield a lot of authority, but I can assure you—'

'For God's sake, *sit down*, Cairo!' He turned to look at her, blue eyes glittering brightly in the semi-darkness. 'I want to talk to you about Margo,' he added impatiently as she remained unmoving in the doorway.

'Oh. Fine.' She moved to sit in the chair furthest away from his own. 'That's who you were talking to on the telephone just now?'

'It's good to know that all those years of marriage to Lionel Bond didn't completely dull your intelligence!'

'Rafe—'

'Will you just shut up and listen for once, Cairo?' He stood up to move restlessly to the edge of the terrace. 'I spoke to Jeff, as it happens. Apparently Margo, for obvious reasons, was deliberately keeping the situation light when she spoke to you and Daisy earlier.' His expression was grim. 'They're concerned about the baby now, as well as Margo, and the doctor's intention is to admit her tomorrow and perform a Caesarian section.'

Cairo stood up abruptly. 'I'll make arrangements for myself and Daisy to return home immediately—'

'That's the last thing Jeff wants you to do!' Rafe turned to her swiftly. 'Cairo, he has no idea how the operation is going to turn out, for either Margo or the baby, and the last thing he wants is for Daisy to go back to England and get caught up in the middle of that uncertainty. Even if the operation is a success, Margo and the baby will have to stay in hospital for several days, so there'll be plenty of time then for you to arrange to get back for her homecoming.'

'Even if the operation is a success' was the only thing in Rafe's last statement that registered with Cairo....

She swallowed hard. 'Is there— What do they think the chances are of them both being okay?'

Rafe wasn't enjoying this conversation at all. He knew that the two sisters, having lost both parents in a car accident ten years ago, had remained emotionally close, even though they had lived on different continents for years. It was because of the sisters' closeness that Rafe had got to know Margo and Jeff in the first place....

'Cairo—'

'Just answer me, will you, please, Rafe?' she said tautly, her eyes gleaming brightly with unshed tears, her hands clenched at her sides as she faced him tensely.

Under other circumstances—with any other woman—Rafe knew he would have taken her in his arms and comforted her. But after what had happened between the two of them earlier, Rafe didn't dare touch Cairo again!

Instead he remained where he was, several feet away, his expression remote. 'Jeff believes there's a good chance that both Margo and the baby will be fine—'

'Thank God!' Cairo breathed her relief, some of the tension relaxing in her shoulders. 'But...?' she added shrewdly, as if she sensed that Rafe hadn't told her everything Jeff had said.

Rafe grimaced at her perception. 'He also asked if the two of us would remain here with Daisy until he knows exactly what's happening.' And if Cairo thought he was any happier about that request than she was, then she was completely mistaken! 'The idea being that, between the two of us, we keep Daisy so busy, at least over the next couple of days, that she doesn't have too much time to telephone or think too much about what's going on at home.'

Cairo blinked. 'Jeff wants the two of us to stay on here *together*?' she repeated incredulously.

Rafe's mouth tightened at her tone. 'I can be civilized about this if you can, Cairo.'

As far as Cairo was concerned it wasn't a question of either of them being 'civilized'. She had been hoping, once Daisy was in bed, that she and Rafe could finally have a sensible conversation about one of them leaving. Preferably Rafe. And preferably this evening!

But Jeff's request had quashed that idea and instead her brother-in-law was asking her to stay on here with Rafe. Well, obviously not just with Rafe—if Daisy weren't here, then Jeff wouldn't have needed to make the request in the first place.

Cairo knew perfectly well it would be Rafe who would be the dominant presence over the next couple of days; it was obvious the two of them couldn't even be in the same country without arguing.

As indicated by this conversation alone!

But at the same time she recognized that Jeff did have a point; after only a few hours Cairo could see the rapport between Rafe and Daisy, and that being with him had already lightened the little girl's introspective mood. That those same few hours had been absolute purgatory for Cairo really shouldn't come into the equation when it was Daisy's peace of mind they were all concerned about.

Nevertheless…

She frowned. 'Do you actually have to stay here at the villa for us to do that?'

'*I* own it, Cairo!' Rafe reminded her irritably.

She shrugged. 'Then maybe I should be the one to move to a hotel—'

'Will you stop being so childish!' Rafe interrupted forcefully. 'Or is it just that you don't trust yourself to be alone here with me even for a couple of days?' he jeered.

Her eyes glittered with anger as she instantly responded with all the sarcasm of which she was capable. 'Don't flatter yourself, Rafe!'

'Oh, yeah, I forgot.' His mouth twisted with distaste.

'You've had so many lovers the last few years you were probably looking forward to a break for a few weeks!'

'I didn't have any lovers during my marriage!' Cairo protested vehemently.

He shrugged. 'That wasn't what Bond said ten months ago.'

'He was angry at the time, making things up,' Cairo defended herself a little shakily.

'Sure he was—'

'Don't use that patronizing tone with me, Rafe!' she blazed at him. 'I did *not* have an affair during my marriage to Lionel!'

Rafe's brows rose. 'Aren't you protesting a little too much, Cairo?' he taunted softly.

She shook her head. 'I'm merely trying to explain that Lionel was upset when he made those accusations, because I had left him.' Her chin rose. 'Besides, your own numerous relationships over the years haven't exactly been a well-kept secret!' she challenged.

As his clandestine relationship eight years ago with his co-star Pamela Raines hadn't remained the secret he had hoped, either…

'The difference being that I'm not married,' he pointed out.

'No, you've never made that commitment, have you, Rafe?' she scorned.

'Not if it meant I was ultimately going to end up with an unfaithful wife like you, no,' he rasped.

'Haven't you been listening to a word I've said?'

'Oh, I listened, Cairo,' he snarled. 'I just have great difficulty believing your claim of innocence!'

Cairo swallowed hard. 'You take delight in insulting me, don't you, Rafe?'

No, dammit, Rafe didn't take any delight in talking about the other men Lionel Bond had claimed Cairo had been involved with during their marriage. As far as he was concerned, if the glitter to her marriage had worn off, if Cairo had been unhappy with Bond—and it now appeared that she had been—then she should have just got out, not taken a string of lovers to compensate for that unhappiness.

Rafe's mouth thinned. 'Our being here isn't about you or me, Cairo,' he growled. 'This is about a six-year-old little girl that we need to keep distracted so that Jeff can feel free to concentrate on Margo and the baby.'

He was right. Cairo knew he was right. Rafe had just shaken her by talking of the things Lionel had said in anger when she'd told him she was leaving him, accusations he had later privately apologized for. Too late, of course, for the press had already gleefully printed the lies and were not inclined to print a retraction.

It was also disconcerting to realize that Rafe's affection for her niece was such that he was even willing to stay on here with Cairo when he would obviously rather not. Cairo had never thought of Rafe as being in the least paternal, and yet his obvious feelings for Daisy clearly disproved that....

Again posing the question as to why Rafe had never married and had children of his own. Today had at least shown Cairo that he would make a wonderful father.

It was his role as a faithful husband that would be in question!

'You're right,' she admitted. 'I'm willing to—to try and put our differences aside, if you are.'

Rafe's teeth gleamed whitely in the darkness as he gave a humourless smile. 'Call a truce, you mean?'

'Call a halt to the insults and accusations, I mean,' Cairo told him determinedly.

He shrugged. 'I'll behave if you will.'

'Then we're agreed. For Daisy's sake, we will try to give every outward appearance of getting on together for at least the next two days.'

Rafe inclined his head in acquiescence. 'For Daisy's sake.'

Cairo hesitated in the doorway. 'And there will be no repeat of—of what happened in the kitchen earlier,' she added huskily, still not completely reconciled inside herself to how easily—how fiercely!—she had responded when Rafe had taken her in his arms earlier and kissed her.

No doubt a lot of soul-searching was in order once she reached the privacy of her bedroom!

'Ah. Now that's something else, Cairo.' Rafe folded his arms across the width of his chest as he regarded her with mocking eyes. 'After all, it may just turn out that you can't keep your hands off me.'

'In your dreams, Rafe,' she scoffed.

'Maybe. We'll see, won't we…'

No, they would not 'see', Cairo determined as she stormed off, making her way to her bedroom at the front of the house.

A couple of days, that was all this was going to be. And surely she could avoid finding herself in any compromising situations with Rafe for that short length of time?

CHAPTER FOUR

'Don't forget your mobile phone— Cairo, what the hell are you wearing?'

Cairo, about to push her sunglasses up onto the bridge of her nose, instead paused in the movement to look at Rafe over the top of them as he stared at her with a scowl on his face.

She knew it wasn't the sunglasses he was referring to, or the white T-shirt and skirt she was wearing with flat sandals, so that left…

'A baseball cap, of course,' she snapped dismissively as she adjusted the peak of the white cap further down her forehead, her hair gathered up and looped through the fastening at the back to hang down in a loose ponytail. 'An item of headgear that originated in your mother's country, I believe,' she added dryly.

'So did the Stetson, but that doesn't mean I'd ever wear one,' Rafe retorted.

The three of them had spent most of the morning down by the pool until Rafe had suggested a trip out to collect more food supplies from the local supermarket. Daisy had then added her own idea that after they had brought the food back to the villa they could all go down into Grasse and have lunch in one of the many restaurants there before going on to one of the beaches along the coast.

A suggestion Rafe said he was more than happy to go along with, and meaning that Cairo was once again 'outgunned and outnumbered'!

But that didn't mean she was willing to go out without the disguise of her baseball cap. 'I tend to freckle in the direct sun,' she explained mendaciously.

His mouth quirked. 'And we mustn't let a freckle ruin that perfect complexion, must we?'

Her eyes narrowed. 'Rafe, why don't you—'

'Actually, Uncle Rafe, Aunty Cairo is famous,' Daisy informed him airily. 'She wears the hat because she doesn't want people to recognize— I'm sorry, Uncle Rafe, I didn't hear what you said…?'

Daisy might not have been able to discern Rafe's mumbled response, but Cairo certainly had, and she didn't appreciate his comment of '*infamous* more aptly describes it'!

'I'm nowhere near as famous as your uncle Rafe, Daisy,' she assured the little girl lightly even as she shot Rafe a quelling glance before adjusting the sunglasses onto the bridge of her nose.

And completely hiding the expression in those dark brown eyes, Rafe noted—although it wasn't too difficult to imagine what it was!

'Come on, Daisy-May.' He ruffled the little girl's golden curls. 'We'll wait outside in the car while your aunty Cairo finishes putting on her disguise.'

'Very funny, Rafe,' Cairo drawled as she fell into step

beside them. 'Make sure you bring a bag out with you later, Daisy—your uncle is something of a sex-symbol, and we may need to beat off his female fans before the day is out,' she warned her niece conspiratorially.

'Now who's being funny?' Rafe raised dark brows as he opened the back door of the car so that Daisy could climb inside.

Cairo gave him a sweetly mocking smile. 'I'm only stating the obvious, Rafe,' she jeered.

Rafe grimaced. 'A sex-symbol?'

She shrugged narrow shoulders as she moved round to the passenger side of the car. 'I seem to remember reading somewhere that you were voted the sexiest man in America last year.'

Not a title he was particularly proud of.

As, no doubt, Cairo was well aware!

'I'm surprised, with all that was going on in your own life this last year, that you could find the time to read about mine, as well,' he jibed.

The teasing smile faded from her lips. 'It made a pleasant change from some of the other trash that was being printed at the time!'

Rafe quickly moved round the car to where she stood. 'Cairo—'

'We really should be going, Rafe,' she told him brittlely as she opened the car door herself to get inside and close the door firmly behind her.

Leaving Rafe standing in the driveway feeling like a heel. They had called a truce last night, for Daisy's sake, and for most of the morning he had kept to that truce, as had Cairo. His present lapse was due, he knew, to the fact that he hadn't slept at all well last night and that lack of sleep was catching up with him.

But how could he sleep when he knew that Cairo was in another bed just down the hallway? Probably as awake as he was, if for different reasons.

He hadn't been able to forget how good Cairo had felt when he'd touched her earlier, but Cairo would have been worrying about Margo, something Rafe knew he hadn't taken too much into consideration during their conversation. But hell, at the time Jeff had just asked him to stay on here and take care of Cairo and Daisy. A request, for Daisy's sake, Rafe had known he couldn't refuse.

But that didn't mean he had to like being here with Cairo.

Any more than Cairo had to like being here with him, perhaps?

'I'm sorry,' Rafe muttered as he got in the car beside her and switched on the engine.

Cairo gave him a startled look. 'What?'

Rafe drew in a sharp breath. 'I said I'm sorry,' he repeated more clearly. 'It was a cheap shot.'

'Yes, it was,' she agreed huskily—although an apology was the last thing she had been expecting!

He gave a wry smile. 'I guess I deserved that.'

'I guess you did.' She nodded.

Rafe scowled. 'Were you always this—opinionated?'

'Probably not,' she conceded softly. 'I guess time changes all of us. And not always for the better.' She shrugged.

Cairo knew she had changed over the last eight years, that her life with Lionel had brought about subtle if not major differences in her. For instance, she no longer trusted even affection, let alone rakishly attractive men like Rafe Montero!

Rafe gave Cairo several sideways glances as he drove them down into the village, Daisy exclaiming in the back of the car as she pointed out several of her favourite haunts from previous holidays taken here.

At one time, Cairo would have been almost as happy as Daisy was by a trip to the shops and then into town for lunch. But not now, Rafe realized. It wasn't so much that she had grown cynical as that her emotions were hidden away behind a wall of indifference that seemed almost impenetrable.

Or perhaps she was just bored, Rafe conceded ruefully. After all, this holiday with a six-year-old was probably a bit tame for her after the exotic life she'd led in Hollywood with Lionel Bond.

The sort of life Rafe avoided for the main part.

Oh, he couldn't escape attending some of the parties or award ceremonies—like the one in Cannes this week. But given a choice Rafe preferred to be at his house on the beach, well away from the falseness and artificiality of the majority of the social scene in Hollywood itself.

But it was a life that Cairo, photographed at numerous glitzy parties over the years, had obviously thoroughly enjoyed.

'How about we go to St Moritz for lunch instead of Grasse?' he suggested once they had finished shopping in the local supermarket and were waiting beside the car for Daisy to come back from returning the trolley.

'St Moritz?' Cairo echoed guardedly.

He nodded. 'We can either drive down the coast or get a boat across from—'

'I know how to get there, Rafe, I've been there before,'

she cut in before shaking her head. 'I just don't see the appeal for a six-year-old girl.'

Of course she had been there before, Rafe acknowledged self-derisively. No doubt Cairo had been to all the fashionable in-places during her marriage, which meant she probably wouldn't be interested in a trip to the sophistication of Monte Carlo, either, which was down the coast from Cannes in the opposite direction from St Mortiz.

So much for Rafe's decision to try to make up for being so awful to her earlier on today.

'I just thought a twenty-eight-year-old woman might be missing the shops on Rodeo Drive!' he drawled.

Delicate colour warmed Cairo's cheeks at the deliberate taunt. Shortly after her arrival in Los Angeles Lionel had opened accounts for her in all the exclusive stores on Rodeo Drive, and Cairo had to admit that for the first few months of their marriage it had been fun to go into any of those shops and buy anything that caught her eye.

But the novelty of shopping, like the gloss of her already failing marriage, had soon worn off, and she had been relieved to get back to work.

'I don't miss anything about my life in Los Angeles,' she told Rafe flatly.

'Nothing?' he scorned.

'Absolutely nothing,' she echoed coldly.

'I find that very hard to believe,' he commented. 'I seem to recall that never a week went by when your photograph didn't appear in the newspapers or some glossy magazine as one of the "beautiful people" attending some party or premiere.'

'Which I hated,' Cairo told him stiffly. 'It was

Lionel's way of life, not mine,' she added as Rafe raised sceptical brows.

'No?'

'No— What is it?' she asked as she saw Rafe's attention had become distracted by something, or someone, across the car park.

She turned to follow his line of vision, but there was only a man unlocking and getting into his car, one of the ubiquitous long loaves of freshly baked bread under his arm.

'Rafe…?' she prompted with a frown as she turned back to him.

He shook his head. 'Sorry, what were we talking about?'

Nothing of any importance, Cairo acknowledged heavily, knowing that Rafe had no reason to believe her claim that she hadn't enjoyed the glamorous Hollywood party circuit. And why should it matter to her anyway? Except that it did….

'Nothing important.' Cairo gave him another searching look before turning away to smile at Daisy as she returned and got into the back of the car. 'Do up your seat belt, poppet.' Her voice warmed affectionately as she slid into the passenger seat.

Rafe remained distracted as he drove back to the villa, occasionally checking in his driving-mirror for that blue car and its driver.

He didn't see it, but that didn't mean it wasn't there….

He had first noticed the car behind them on the drive from the villa to the supermarket, had taken note of the fact that it had followed them into the car park, but had dismissed the coincidence when the driver got out to go to the stall in front of the supermarket where the fresh bread was being sold.

But they had been in the supermarket for at least half an hour, and the man had still been hanging about when they had come out again, supposedly reading a newspaper, although he had sauntered across to his car while they were loading their shopping in the boot.

He was becoming paranoid, Rafe decided as he turned up the lane to the villa and the little blue car was still nowhere in sight.

Paranoid or just hypersensitive after unexpectedly meeting up with Cairo again after years of avoiding her. She was right when she pointed out he hadn't lived like a monk the last eight years, and those years had fooled him into believing himself well over her. But since he had kissed and caressed her yesterday afternoon in the kitchen he knew that he wasn't over her at all.

There was no doubt Cairo was different now, sleekly so, her clothes all designer-label, everything about her more sophisticated and self-assured than the bright-eyed twenty-year old he had met while filming on the Isle of Man.

But he would be lying if he claimed that the attraction, that fierce ache to make love with her, wasn't still burning beneath their thin veneer of civility.

Extremely dangerous.

And it was a danger Rafe needed to get away from, if only for a few hours!

'For obvious reasons I have to go down into Cannes this evening,' he told Cairo as the two of them put the shopping away while Daisy collected her swimming things from her bedroom.

'Fine,' Cairo accepted without interest as she continued to put cereals away in a cupboard.

'You and Daisy can come with me if you like?' Rafe heard himself offer—in complete contradiction to his thoughts of a few minutes ago…

His only excuse was that Cairo's complete lack of interest in his plans for this evening had annoyed the hell out of him!

Cairo stiffened before slowly turning to face Rafe. 'Why on earth would I want to do that?' she prompted incredulously while inwardly shying away from the thought of going anywhere near all that glitzy artificiality again after she had so enjoyed avoiding it the last ten months.

As Rafe had pointed out earlier, she had attended numerous award ceremonies with Lionel over the years, both as an actress in her own right and as Lionel's wife, had even been nominated for and won an Oscar herself three years ago.

Which meant Cairo knew exactly what the party in Cannes this evening would be like, everyone really there to see and be seen rather than to actually meet up and chat with old friends and just enjoy themselves.

Rafe leant back against one of the kitchen units to study her through narrowed lids. 'You haven't worked in almost a year, Cairo.'

She blinked. 'Sorry?'

His mouth thinned. 'You haven't made a film in over ten months.'

'So?'

'So, as I pointed out yesterday, the world of acting is a fickle one.' He shrugged. 'Too long out of the limelight, and the industry, as well as the public, tends to forget you exist.'

'Your point being?'

He frowned. 'My point being, you need to get back to work!'

Cairo gave a humourless laugh. 'As I told you yesterday, I really don't see what business it is of yours—'

'You can't hide away for the rest of your life, Cairo,' he pointed out.

Her eyes widened. 'I'm *not* hiding—'

'What else would you call it?' he attacked her impatiently. 'You're staying in a villa miles from anywhere, and you wear sunglasses and a baseball cap to disguise your appearance when you do go out. I'd call that hiding, wouldn't you, Cairo?'

'No,' she bit out. 'What I would call it is taking a well-earned holiday after years of constantly working my—' She stopped and drew in a controlling breath. 'I can't remember the last time I was able to just relax and lie in the sun.'

'You'll freckle, remember?' he taunted.

'I'll risk it!' she snapped. 'And I really don't see what any of this has to do with my not wanting to come to a party in Cannes with you this evening.'

'There will be directors there. Producers, too. The people who will give you your next job, Cairo,' Rafe explained patiently as she made no response.

'I don't need anyone to give me my next job, Rafe,' she assured him.

He studied her carefully. 'You already know what you're going to work on next, don't you?'

Cairo gave a mocking inclination of her head. 'Yes, Rafe, I already know what I'm going to work on next.'

'Which is?'

'None of your business!'

'Are the two of you arguing?' Daisy asked from the kitchen doorway, her expression curious rather than concerned.

'Of course not, poppet,' Cairo hastened to reassure her. 'Uncle Rafe and I were just—having a discussion about something unimportant.' She shot Rafe a warning glance.

'Oh.' Daisy nodded. 'Because Mummy and Daddy always kiss and make up when they have an argument.'

Cairo snorted at the thought of her and Rafe ever being able to 'kiss and make up'. There was simply too much history between them for them ever to be able to do that!

A sentiment Rafe obviously agreed with as he answered the little girl. 'As Aunty Cairo said, Daisy, we weren't arguing,' he said dryly. 'So, who's hungry?' he added enticingly, Daisy's shout of agreement completely overshadowing the fact that Cairo said nothing.

She was too irritated with Rafe to speak, that was why!

She had spent years being persuaded, cajoled and pushed by Lionel into taking one film role after another, usually for his production company, of course, and she wasn't about to be railroaded by anyone else—least of all the arrogant Rafe Montero—into doing anything, or going anywhere, she didn't want to go.

She certainly wasn't going to allow Rafe to goad her into going to Cannes with him this evening!

But he seemed no more interested in pursuing the subject as they found a place to park in Grasse before walking through to the shops and restaurants. In fact—thankfully!—Rafe seemed decidedly distracted again, leaving Cairo to enjoy the aromas and atmosphere of the town whose main industry was its wonderful perfumes.

* * *

Rafe hadn't been being paranoid earlier about the blue car and its driver…

He was pretty sure of it now, the little blue car having come out of a side road as Rafe drove down from the villa and out onto the main road. It had then stayed a two-car distance behind them on the drive to Grasse, and followed them into the same car park once they got into the town. Although the driver, definitely the same man as before, noticing Rafe's narrow-eyed interest across the car park as he got out of the blue car, had quickly locked the doors before disappearing in the opposite direction to the one Rafe, Cairo and Daisy took.

Admittedly Rafe hadn't seen the man since, but a sixth sense, a tingling sensation at the back of his neck, told him that the man was still around somewhere.

Was he just an avid movie fan who had maybe recognized Rafe when he arrived at the supermarket?

Or—worse!—a reporter?

Several people had given Rafe a second glance as the three of them strolled through the busy streets of Grasse, as if they thought they recognized him, only to look at Cairo and Daisy and decide they must be mistaken; Rafe Montero wasn't married, let alone father to a six-year-old girl.

But the man in the blue car seemed more dogged than that, and he had obviously been waiting at the bottom of the access road in the hopes of being able to follow the next time Rafe left the villa.

Or Cairo did….

Rafe gave her a frowning glance. She was still wearing the baseball cap and dark sunglasses, but otherwise seemed relaxed, and was obviously enjoying herself as she and Daisy looked at scented candles as a present to take home to Margo.

Something Rafe doubted she would continue to be if the man following them should turn out to be a reporter hot on her trail!

'Is everything all right, Rafe?' Cairo queried once the three of them were seated at a shaded table in the square where they had decided to have lunch.

He raised dark brows. 'Why shouldn't it be?'

Cairo frowned. 'You seem—preoccupied, that's all.'

'I get that way when I'm hungry,' he dismissed, before pointedly turning his attention to reading the menu.

Cairo continued to look at him for several more seconds before looking down at her own menu; after all, she had no reason for complaint as long as Rafe continued to help keep Daisy entertained.

Besides, he was probably as worried about Margo as Cairo was.

She had spoken briefly to Jeff on the telephone this morning, her brother-in-law promising to call her later today once he had any news about Margo and the baby. Cairo's mobile was turned on in her shoulder-bag for just that reason.

It was very pleasant sitting here in the sunshine, Cairo decided as she relaxed back in her chair once they had given their order to the waiter and Daisy and Rafe were busy discussing the merits of the beaches in the area, something they were both familiar with if the friendly argument that ensued was anything to go by.

Cairo watched the two of them from behind dark sunglasses, appreciating how good Rafe was with Daisy, talking to her as an adult rather than a child as he considered the merits of her suggestions, Daisy obviously equally enthralled with him.

Again Cairo asked herself why he had never married and had children of his own…

Rafe was thirty-seven now, at the very top of his profession, a successful director, as well as one of the most sought after—and sexy—actors in the world: the most sexy according to that American poll last year!

There had been plenty of women in Rafe's life over the years, too, photographs of him with those beautiful women often appearing in the glossily expensive magazine that she occasionally read while waiting in her trailer to be called on set.

Yet he had never married, had remained one of the most elusively eligible bachelors in the world…whom Cairo knew herself to be completely physically aware of!

It would be futile to claim otherwise when she was sensitive to everything about him, from his silkily dark hair that brushed the collar of his black polo shirt, down to the bareness of his slimly elegant feet casually thrust into black deck-shoes.

He was as sexy as hell, Cairo acknowledged achingly. Even more so than he had been eight years ago, maturity having added another dimension to his already many-faceted personality, lines of experience now beside the deep blue of his eyes, his rare smile one of mocking challenge.

'She's a great kid, isn't she?' Rafe said as Daisy excused herself to go to the ladies' room inside the restaurant.

'Er—yes, she is,' Cairo agreed abruptly even as she wrenched her gaze away from the moulded perfection of Rafe's sensually curving mouth and her thoughts from the memory of how forcefully that mouth had claimed hers yesterday afternoon.

Rafe's gaze narrowed on her flushed cheeks. 'Have you ever wondered that if we had made it together, we might have had a daughter of Daisy's age by now? Maybe a couple more, too?'

'Certainly not!' she denied firmly.

Rafe shrugged. 'Just a thought.'

Thank goodness she hadn't become pregnant during their three-month affair—that really would have complicated a situation that had ultimately proved heartbreaking enough when Rafe had become bored with her naïve adoration and secretly turned his attentions to another, much more experienced, woman.

But she couldn't deny that at one time, in her naivety, she had inwardly, deliciously thought about becoming the mother of Rafe's children….

'I think I'll just try giving Jeff a call while Daisy isn't here.' She took her mobile from her bag and put the call through to her brother-in-law, effectively putting an end to that conversation.

But if nothing else, it had served as a reminder that Cairo hadn't been enough for Rafe eight years ago, and despite her earlier thoughts of how wonderful he was with Daisy—of what a good father he would make to his own children someday—Cairo knew that she wouldn't be enough for him now, either.

Rafe took advantage of Cairo's preoccupation to sit back and run a lazily sweeping glance over the busy square, aware that he still had that uncomfortable prickling sensation at the base of his nape, as if he was being watched.

Not that he had actually seen the driver of the blue car again.

But perhaps that wasn't surprising after Rafe had shown him so clearly in the car park that he was aware of the other man's interest?

Or maybe Rafe was wrong and it really was coincidence that he had seen that particular man in that particular car twice in one day?

Maybe…

He just didn't happen to believe that strongly in coincidences—

'Dammit!' Rafe grated harshly even as he surged angrily to his feet and turned to stride towards where he had just seen Daisy emerge from the ladies' room in the restaurant.

To where a man—the same man who had earlier been driving the blue car, Rafe was sure of it—had stopped her and engaged her in conversation!

CHAPTER FIVE

'FOLLOW him, Rafe!' Cairo cried anxiously behind him as the man saw Rafe's approach and quickly broke off his conversation with Daisy to turn on his heel and hurry out through the back entrance of the restaurant.

Rafe didn't need any encouragement—he had every intention of going after the other man.

'Take care of Daisy,' he instructed grimly, before hurrying out the back entrance himself.

But no matter how hard Rafe looked both ways up the street and in several shops, he couldn't find him, the other man having apparently disappeared. He knew where the man's car was, of course, and debated whether or not he should just go straight to the car park and hope to get there before the other man did.

But Rafe's first concern had to be Daisy and Cairo, so he returned to the restaurant.

'I lost him.' Rafe scowled as Cairo looked at him, her face having taken on a greyish tinge, her hands trembling as she held Daisy tightly against her. 'I'm pretty sure it isn't what you think, Cairo,' he added more reassuringly. 'I'll explain later.' He shot Cairo a warning look before going down on his haunches beside the little girl. 'Okay, Daisy-May?' he prompted gently.

'Can we have lunch now, Uncle Rafe?' she asked hopefully.

He gave an appreciative chuckle. 'Sure we can. Okay with you, Cairo?' He looked up at her.

Cairo felt too sick with reaction to answer him immediately.

She hadn't even realized there was anything wrong until Rafe had stood up and rushed into the restaurant and she had seen the man talking to Daisy.

A man who had seemed strangely familiar….

'Fine,' she answered distractedly, knowing from Rafe's warning expression that he didn't want either of them to alarm Daisy when she seemed to have taken the incident in her six-year-old stride.

Unlike Cairo.

It was every parent's nightmare!

They had only taken their eyes off Daisy for a minute or so. What if—

'It really isn't what you think,' Rafe assured her quietly, taking a light hold of her arm as they followed Daisy back to their table. 'At least, I'm pretty sure that it isn't,' he added grimly.

'You'll have to give me a better explanation than that, Rafe.' She gave an involuntary shudder. 'What if he had taken Daisy? I would never have forgiven myself if—'

'Don't even think about it.' Rafe squeezed her arm. 'I would never have let that happen.'

Cairo believed him.

After all that had happened between them, the way Rafe

had proved so unfaithful as a lover, Cairo still believed him implicitly when he assured her that he would keep Daisy safe....

Rafe wished he could be as sure of being able to keep his promise to Cairo as he sounded! But until he found out who the man in the blue car was, and why he had been following them most of the day, he really had no idea whom he was actually supposed to be protecting.

Daisy...or Cairo?

Daisy was the one to give him part of the answer. 'I think that man was one of your fans, Uncle Rafe,' she told him once she had eaten a piece of pizza.

'Why do you think that, Daisy?' he asked, at the same time aware that Cairo was picking at her salad rather than eating it, obviously still very shaken by what had happened. Even so, Rafe couldn't help but admire the fact that she was trying to appear as if everything were normal.

'He asked me if you were Rafe Montero,' Daisy explained happily before picking up another piece of her pizza.

Rafe shot Cairo a frowning glance before answering the little girl. 'And what did you say, Daisy-May?'

'I said you were.' She nodded. 'Because you are, aren't you?'

'Yes,' Rafe agreed with a smile. 'For my sins, that's exactly who I am.'

Daisy nodded. 'Then he asked me the name of my mummy.'

'Your...mummy?' Rafe repeated slowly with a quick glance at Cairo.

'Mmm.' Daisy gave a mischievous grin. 'I told him that her name was Margo. Because it is, isn't it?' she added with satisfaction.

'Daisy—'

'Don't you see, Uncle Rafe, that man thought Aunty Cairo was my mummy?' She giggled at the joke she had played on the other man.

Yes, Rafe did see—better than Daisy, in fact. As he knew that Cairo must.

'He was a reporter!' Cairo spoke for the first time since they had returned to the table, anger starting to replace her emotional turmoil as she realized Daisy hadn't been in danger, after all; she had simply been pumped for information about Cairo and Rafe.

'I had a suspicion that he might be, yes,' Rafe admitted grimly.

Cairo's eyes widened. 'You had a—? He was at the supermarket this morning!' she breathed incredulously as she suddenly remembered why the other man had seemed so familiar to her a few minutes ago. She also remembered Rafe's distraction earlier as he'd watched the reporter getting into his car!

Her mouth tightened. 'How long have you known he was following us?'

'Not now, Cairo!' he snapped, a nerve pulsing in his tightly clenched jaw.

'But—'

'I said not now,' he ordered harshly.

Cairo clamped her lips together as she continued to glare at him from behind her sunglasses.

Rafe had known that man was following them. He had known, dammit, and he hadn't so much as warned her....

* * *

'For God's sake, calm down,' Rafe told her impatiently an hour or so later as the two of them sat on the golden-white sand amongst the rocks in a relatively private cove, Daisy off building sandcastles nearer the water.

'Calm down!' Cairo repeated furiously as she turned to face him. 'You knew that man was following us. You knew, Rafe, and yet you said nothing!' She breathed agitatedly.

'Because I knew you would react like this,' he retorted. 'Look, don't worry about it, okay? I'll make a couple of calls when I get back to the villa, and—'

'Oh, you'll make a couple of calls,' Cairo repeated sarcastically. 'That's all right, then. The arrogant Rafe Montero will just "make a couple of calls" and everyone can once again sleep safely in their beds—'

'Not everyone, Cairo,' he cut in.

She scowled at him. 'I'm really not in the mood for your innuendos just now, Rafe.'

'Then what are you in the mood for?' he challenged softly.

Her eyes widened as she saw the intent in his. 'Don't even think about—' She broke off abruptly as Rafe reached out to remove her sunglasses and throw them down on the towel before his mouth came down fiercely on hers.

Cairo kissed him back just as fiercely.

Furiously.

All the emotions of the last couple of hours were in that kiss.

The absolute terror when she had seen that man talking to Daisy.

The relief when she'd reached Daisy's side and was able to hold the little girl to her protectively.

Followed by this burning, almost uncontrollable rage towards Rafe for not even telling her he had thought they were being followed.

How dared he?

How *dared* he!

She wrenched her mouth free of his to put her hands against his chest and push him away from her. 'I thought I told you there would be no repeat of—of this sort of thing!' she snapped fierily.

'What sort of thing would that be, Cairo?' he jeered.

Cairo drew in a ragged breath. 'I'm sure your lethal charm usually silences a woman, Rafe,' she scorned, her cheeks flushed, eyes fever-bright. 'But—'

'Is my charm really lethal, Cairo?' he interrupted.

'Not to me!' she denied, continuing to glare at him as she sat with her arms wrapped protectively about her knees.

His devilish smile said otherwise. 'All evidence to the contrary, my dear Cairo.'

'I'm not your "dear", anything,' she came back vehemently. 'And I don't care what promise you made Jeff yesterday.' She shook her head. 'Now that we know a reporter has tracked you down—'

'Or you.'

Her eyes narrowed. 'It was *you* the reporter recognized—'

'If that's what he is.' Rafe shrugged.

'Whatever,' Cairo snapped. 'He's following *you*, Rafe. Which means you're the one who will have to leave—'

'I've already told you I'm not going anywhere,' Rafe retorted firmly.

He hadn't meant to kiss Cairo again just now. Hadn't meant to. But he had been unable to stop himself. She had looked so damned beautiful as she'd glared at him so fiercely. So achingly desirable.

Cairo was right; he should leave. He should get himself as far away as possible from the temptation she still—incredibly!—represented.

But after the incident at the restaurant Rafe knew he had even more reason to stay. If the man who had been following them this morning did turn out to be a member of the paparazzi, then a little thing like Rafe chasing him off earlier wasn't going to shake him. The man knew exactly who Rafe was now, and, despite what Daisy might have told the man about her 'mummy', Rafe knew that if the other man was any good at his job, then it wouldn't be long before he found out who Cairo really was, too.

But he was sure Cairo must already know that....

His mouth twisted wryly. 'It's just one reporter, Cairo—'

'Who will no doubt quickly be followed by others!' she pointed out, her voice rising with her agitation. 'Daisy and I were doing just fine before you arrived.'

'Sure you were,' Rafe said sarcastically.

'And just what is that supposed to mean?'

Rafe's gaze ran over her with slow deliberation. 'Daisy is a great kid, but you—you're too thin, Cairo. You have dark circles under your eyes because you don't sleep properly. You're as nervy as hell.' He heaved a disgusted sigh. 'I wouldn't call that "doing just fine", would you?'

'I believe I've already told you before that when I want your opinion, I'll ask for it—'

'No, Cairo, you'll get it whether you want it or not,' he told her forcefully as he dropped down onto the sand beside her to take her chin in his grasp and turn her face towards his. 'What happened to the Cairo Vaughn I knew and loved?'

'*Loved*, Rafe?' She laughed incredulously. 'You don't even know the meaning of the word!' Her gaze was challenging.

Rafe continued to look at her wordlessly for several seconds before abruptly releasing her, knowing he wasn't going to reach her this way. If there was any of the old Cairo left to reach…

Cairo glared at him with frustrated anger. Rafe hadn't loved her. If he had loved her, then she wouldn't have gone to his hotel suite that day eight years ago and found a naked woman in his bed!

'This beach is slightly different from the one we once walked on together at midnight, isn't it?' he said huskily now.

Cairo eyed him warily, not quite sure how to reply to that comment.

She knew exactly which beach Rafe was referring to, of course. Just as she clearly remembered what had happened at the end of that walk. She was just surprised that Rafe remembered it, too, after all this time….

'I seem to remember I ruined a pair of perfectly good shoes walking across the pebbles and rocks,' she said coolly.

'It was worth it,' Rafe murmured softly.

Yes, it had been, but—

'Have you ever been back there?' Rafe asked, quirking up one eyebrow to signal his interest.

'To the Isle of Man?'

She had only vaguely even heard of the Isle of Man, a small island located between England and Ireland, before she had been there on location during the filming of *A*

Love For All Time. The island's old-fashioned quaintness had been a perfect spot for the post-war love story, in which Rafe had had the role of male lead and Cairo had had the supporting actress role to Pamela Raines's female lead.

A situation that had, unfortunately, become echoed in real life!

'I try not to dwell on past mistakes,' she dismissed in a deliberately offhand tone of voice.

'It was damn cold on the beach that night, wasn't it?' he said, ignoring her supposed lack of interest in the topic.

Until they'd found the ideal way to keep warm, yes....

'Rafe—'

'Life seemed a lot simpler then, too,' he continued wistfully as if she hadn't spoken.

Her eyes widened. 'Simpler?'

He nodded. 'There was just you and me—'

'And Pamela,' Cairo put in dryly. 'Let's not forget the beautiful and rapacious Pamela, shall we?'

Rafe's mouth tightened. 'I forgot about her years ago.'

Cairo gave a derisive smile. 'How convenient to have such an—accommodating memory!'

His eyes narrowed and his voice turned positively icy. 'Pamela meant nothing to me.'

'Has *any* woman ever meant anything to you, Rafe?' Cairo enquired hotly.

How could he sit and claim Pamela had meant nothing to him?

The other woman had been naked in his hotel room that day, her hair all tousled, that look—that look of sleepy satisfaction on her face the result of Rafe's lovemaking that

Cairo had seen so often on her own face when she'd looked in the mirror.

His gaze became hooded now. 'Just the one,' he murmured, his meaning obvious as he steadily held her gaze.

'Oh, please!' Cairo muttered in disgust as she stood up and moved away from him. 'I'm not that naïve twenty-year-old any more, Rafe. So don't even think about trying your seduction routine on me again—'

'It isn't a routine, dammit—'

'Of course it is!' She turned on him angrily. 'You sailed into Douglas Bay that day looking like a Spanish pirate captaining his ship and completely swept me and every other woman on the island off their feet!'

Cairo could remember it as if it were yesterday, standing at the window of her hotel room, watching as the three-masted sailing ship came round the headland and anchored in the bay, a small launch leaving the ship minutes later, the man at the wheel—looking every inch that Spanish pirate!—clearly the darkly handsome Rafe Montero.

Cairo had lost her heart to Rafe's dark and rugged wildness before she was even introduced to him an hour later.

And she wasn't going to fall for it again.

Ever.

'I'm going for a swim,' she told Rafe abruptly as she took off her T-shirt before peeling her skirt down over her hips and legs and revealing that she wore a brief white bikini beneath.

Rafe stood and watched Cairo as she ran down the golden sand to wade thigh-deep in the water before diving smoothly beneath its surface, his hands clenching at his sides as he appreciated how the white of her bikini emphasised the golden tan of her skin. Smooth, silky skin he could still feel against the palms of his hands.

Cairo was right; she was no longer a naïve twenty-year-old. Just as he was no longer twenty-nine and bowled off his feet by her beauty the moment he was introduced to her.

But a part of him wished that he were….

CHAPTER SIX

'I THINK you're being absolutely ridiculous, Rafe,' Cairo told him coolly as she hung their wet costumes and towels on the line strung between two trees at the back of the villa. Daisy was inside watching a cartoon channel on the television.

They had all showered and changed since returning an hour ago, Cairo now wearing a loose cream-coloured blouse over fitted jeans, the dampness of her long hair twisted into a knot and secured at her crown, her face completely bare of make-up.

She looked about eighteen, Rafe decided impatiently. Although that in no way stopped her being so damned stubborn he wanted to shake her until her teeth rattled!

His gaze narrowed on her warningly. 'If you won't agree to come down to Cannes with me this evening, then I'm not going, either,' he repeated evenly.

'Scrap my previous statement—your behaviour is positively juvenile!' Cairo glared at him. 'I won't if you won't,' she mocked as she reached for another of the towels and began to hang it on the line. 'You have to go to Cannes this evening, Rafe—I don't!'

'I don't have to go anywhere until I've managed to find out the identity of the man who spoke to Daisy at lunchtime,' Rafe assured her just as stubbornly.

Rafe had called several people he knew in the newspaper business, but as yet none of them had been offered a story about himself and Cairo. They would call him back when, or if, they did.

Admittedly his own temper was slightly frayed around the edges after those memories earlier of their time together on the Isle of Man. But Cairo's adamant refusal to even think about reconsidering her decision not to go down to Cannes with him tonight was only increasing Rafe's frustration, which was already exacerbated by a sexual tension that was becoming more unbearable by the minute.

She sighed. 'So much for your "couple of phone calls".'

'If he's a reporter, then we'll know by tomorrow morning, anyway,' Rafe pointed out. 'I only said *if* he's a reporter, Cairo,' he said as she gave a pained groan.

She shook her head. 'We both know that he is. Do you think he has photographs, too?'

'If he's any good at his job then, yes, of course he has photographs.' There was no point in even attempting to lie, Rafe knew, when tomorrow morning's newspapers would tell their own story, no doubt including wild speculation about their relationship.

He could see it now, photographs of himself and Cairo shopping for food, of them walking through Grasse with Daisy, of the three of them laughing together as they sat down at the table in the square outside the restaurant.

All very cosily domestic.

Deceptively so.

Anyone who had ever listened to a single conversation between himself and Cairo would know differently—they couldn't even discuss the weather without getting into an argument about it!

'I don't see anything in the least funny about this situation, Rafe!' Cairo snapped as she saw his rueful smile. 'The reason I'm annoyed is pretty obvious after the publicity following my divorce from Lionel.' She grimaced. 'But I'm sure there must be someone in your own life who isn't going to be amused, either, by photographs of the two of us together.'

Cairo hadn't spent long, boring hours in her trailer waiting to be called on set for months now—that was the only time she flicked through the glossy magazines that contained those sorts of gossipy articles—so she had no idea whether or not Rafe was involved with anyone at the moment. But he probably was....

His mouth twisted mockingly. 'I doubt any of my family will be concerned.'

Cairo sighed. 'I wasn't talking about your family and you know it.'

Rafe had occasionally talked about his family when they were together. Of his Spanish father who had visited America as a student and fallen in love with the blonde-haired, blue-eyed daughter of a Texas rancher, the two of them marrying once they finished college, and now working that ranch in Texas themselves, along with Rafe's younger brother, Pedro, and his wife and young family.

Rafe grinned. 'I'm well aware of that, Cairo,' he drawled. 'And, no, I very much doubt that photographs of you and I together are going to bother anyone but the two of us.'

'What a shame,' she came back insincerely.

Rafe sobered. 'Cairo, I would never have kissed you last night if I was involved with someone else.'

She raised sceptical brows. 'Really?'

'Dammit, Cairo—'

'Rafe, I have no intention of getting into yet another argument with you,' she told him wearily. 'Just accept that I am not going to Cannes with you tonight—'

'Why the hell not?'

'One, I don't want to go. Two, I didn't bring anything suitable to wear. Three,' she added simply, 'I'm still waiting for Jeff to return one of my calls.'

She had made two so far. One at the restaurant when she had reached his answering service, and hadn't bothered to leave a message as she had quickly rung off to be with Daisy. And another one at the beach when she had returned from her swim and had left a message asking Jeff to call her back as soon as possible to let her know how Margo was.

She had brought her mobile outside with her now in the hopes he would call back soon.

Rafe scowled. 'One, I don't give a damn what you want; I'm not going out and leaving you and Daisy here alone this evening. Two, you can go naked for all I care. And three, that's what mobile phones are for!' he all but snarled.

'There's no need to shout—and I told you not to touch me again, Rafe!' Cairo's eyes flashed a warning as she looked down at the fingers that had reached out to curl like steel bands about her arm.

Rafe breathed unevenly as he looked down at her for several long seconds. 'You would try the patience of a saint, Cairo!'

'You should be just fine, then, shouldn't you?' she baited him. 'I told you to let go of my arm, Rafe.' She looked up to meet his gaze unflinchingly.

The very air seemed to have stilled about them, not a sound to be heard except their own breathing as they continued that silent battle of wills, their faces only inches apart as blue eyes held brown.

Cairo felt as if the whole of her insides were melting as Rafe stood far too close to her, those fingers encircling her arm sending waves of awareness to her breasts and thighs.

Only Rafe had ever been able to make her feel like this with just a look. Only Rafe had ever been able to make her want him with just the touch of his hand against her flesh.

A hand he now let drop back to his side even as his gaze continued to hold hers captive. 'Do you know what I want to do to you right this minute?' he murmured.

Cairo moistened dry lips, unable to speak or look away from that mesmerizing gaze.

'If you won't let me touch you, then let me tell you all the things I've been imagining doing with you,' Rafe said gruffly. 'Wild, wonderful things—'

'Rafe—'

'Erotic beautiful things,' he continued mercilessly, his eyes gleaming with the desire he no longer held in check. 'You see that wall behind you…? Yes, that wall,' he confirmed softly as Cairo gave the low stone wall a quick glance. 'I want to slip off your jeans and panties before sitting you on top of that wall and kneeling in front of you. I want to slowly unbutton your blouse to bare your breasts to the sun so that I can touch them, kiss them, lick your nipples, suckle them into the heat of my mouth—'

'*Rafe*…!' Cairo's intended groan of protest instead came out as an aching entreaty for him to continue, her skin becoming sensitized just by his words, by the evocative image he was creating, her nipples hard against the soft material of her blouse, and a moist heat pooling between her thighs.

His eyes were dark. 'Then I want to kiss my way—slowly—down to your navel.' His voice was low, hypnotic. 'Dipping my tongue, tasting you, before I go lower, parting your legs even as I part your glossy curls and find the very centre of you with my lips and tongue. I still remember the taste of you there, Cairo. So sweet and hot…' He groaned.

'Rafe, you have to stop this now!' she choked, all of her feeling on fire now, aching with a need for the things he had described so eloquently.

'Why do I, Cairo?' His gaze still held hers. 'I'm only talking, telling you of the things I would like to do with you.'

Cairo could feel every single one of them! Could feel his hands and lips against her breasts, suckling her nipples, his mouth hot and liquid across the flatness of her stomach as he moved lower, tasting that pool of moisture there, licking her, sucking ever so gently on her arousal and taking her over the edge into wild oblivion. She could feel all of that just as strongly as she felt the sun beating down on them.

Just as she could imagine touching Rafe, her hands gliding lovingly over the broadness of his bare shoulders and torso, her lips following that same path, kissing him, caressing him as she slowly made her way down to the hard thrust of his arousal, lips and tongue tasting him as she took him in her mouth and felt his response to those caresses, hearing his groans of longing, his need for release…

Why had everything gone so wrong between them eight years ago? she wondered achingly. Why, when she had loved him so much, given so much—when they had been able to give each other such physical pleasure—hadn't she been enough for him?

They were questions Cairo had asked herself many times over the years. The answers were all too obvious.

With the prospect of a month's filming on the Isle of Man—a beautiful unspoilt island but nevertheless one that offered very little in the way of entertainment for a man as rakish as Rafe Montero—Cairo must have been an easy conquest, a diversion in what might otherwise have been a tedious time for him when he wasn't actually filming.

Admittedly the relationship had continued for a while longer once they'd all returned to London to complete the filming, Cairo more often than not spending the night in Rafe's penthouse suite at his hotel with him, the two of them even occasionally going out to dinner with Margo and Jeff.

But somewhere along the way Cairo had missed the signs that Rafe was tired of the relationship. She knew why she had missed them, of course; her own love for Rafe had made her completely blind to anyone and everything else!

She had certainly been blind to the fact that Rafe's attention had moved on to someone else, that it was now his co-star, Pamela Raines, who interested him, and whom he wanted to share his bed. As it had turned out, Rafe had been so determined the actress would share his bed that he hadn't even had the time to tell Cairo to vacate it before moving Pamela Raines into it...

Cairo certainly couldn't allow herself to be seduced into becoming Rafe's South of France 'diversion', too!

What thoughts were going through her head, Rafe wondered as he looked at her searchingly. Whatever they were, they were making her frown.

'Were you and Bond happy together?' he suddenly rasped harshly.

Her eyes widened. 'I don't think—'

'It isn't going to hurt you to tell me that much, surely, Cairo?' Rafe pressed, knowing the moment of intimacy was over. For now…

She shook her head. 'Haven't you been reading the newspapers the last ten months, Rafe?'

He shrugged. 'In my experience they rarely report the truth.'

She gave a laugh of pure cynicism. 'That's been my experience, too!'

'Well?'

'I haven't asked you about any of your relationships the last eight years, so why on earth should I answer any of your questions about my marriage to Lionel?' she retorted indignantly.

'Ask away,' Rafe invited.

'I—' Cairo broke off as her mobile began to ring. 'That could be Jeff,' she pointed out huskily.

'Then you had better answer it, hadn't you?' he bit out curtly, before turning away to thrust his hands in his pockets.

Dammit, every time he and Cairo came even close to understanding each other, something, or someone, interrupted them!

Why the hell he wanted answers to these questions after all this time was beyond him. Maybe it was because of those memories this afternoon of when they'd met on the Isle of Man, when the connection between them had seemed so instant and exclusive....

As it had seemed to be just now, too....

Or maybe it was because the abrupt end of his relationship with Cairo three months later had always seemed like unfinished business to him....

One day they had seemed to be totally together and the next she had told him it was all over, using empty phrases like 'we both need our own space' and 'it was fun while it lasted but now it's over' as she'd walked out of his life.

Phrases that had only made sense to Rafe when that very same evening Cairo had gone out to dinner with the producer of the film, and only weeks later she had married him!

To add insult to injury, the 'happy couple' had even invited him, and the rest of the crew from *A Love For All Time* to the wedding! Rafe had excused himself from that invitation and spent the afternoon in bed with his co-star Pamela Raines instead.

But being here with Cairo like this, talking to her, touching her again, imagining making love with her, seemed to have released all those old memories, the good, as well as the bad.

Half of him had wanted to punish her just now as he told her of how he would make love to her, the other half punishing himself for still wanting her. He was still hard from those imaginings, his arousal a low throb that he had no control over—

'Margo's had the baby,' Cairo spoke huskily behind him. 'A little boy,' she added as Rafe turned in sharp enquiry. 'Margo is fine,' she continued emotionally. 'The baby—

Simon Raphael—is in an incubator, but Jeff seems very hopeful that he's going to be okay, too—' She broke off to bury her face in her hands as she began to cry.

'But that's good, isn't it?' Rafe frowned, this time having no choice but to take her in his arms.

Cairo had no idea why she was crying. Relief, probably. She had been so worried about Margo and the baby.

But it wasn't just that, she knew. The strain of being here with Rafe, talking to him, having him describe what it would be like making love to her, feeling every caress and touch of his lips on her body, was also taking its toll. Finding herself in his arms certainly wasn't helping her dispel the effect!

She straightened, avoiding his searching gaze as she wiped the tears from her cheeks to step away from him. 'It's much better news than I'd hoped for,' she agreed.

His eyes narrowed. 'Does Jeff want you and Daisy to go back to England now?'

'Not for a few more days, until he's absolutely sure…' Cairo shook her head. 'I have to go in and tell Daisy the good news,' she said as she turned away.

'Cairo?'

She closed her lids briefly before turning back to look at him with guarded eyes. 'Yes?'

Rafe's gaze was mocking. 'Now there are only two reasons why you can't come to Cannes with me this evening….'

She drew in a sharp breath. 'Rafe, you have no idea of the avalanche of publicity we would be bringing down on ourselves by appearing in public together!'

Rafe gave a rueful smile. 'I think I have a pretty good idea. Besides, with the appearance of tomorrow's newspapers, the chances are we're going to be presented with a fait accompli, anyway.' His mouth tightened grimly. 'Personally I would rather spike the bast—the guy's guns, by appearing in public with you tonight and so ruining his chances of an exclusive tomorrow.'

He had a point, Cairo realized unwillingly.

She was weakening in her resolve not to accompany him, Rafe noted with satisfaction as she hesitated. And he was determined that she would, meant it when he told Cairo she couldn't go on hiding like this. Yeah, her divorce had been messy and very public, but she needed to get some perspective back in her life.

With their past history, why the hell should he care what Cairo did, either now or in the future?

He shouldn't.

And yet he knew that he did....

He should never have given into the temptation of telling her all the things he would like to do to her.

'Well?' he prompted tersely.

Cairo sighed heavily, knowing that he wasn't going to give up.

'Okay, I—I'll ask Daisy what she wants to do—'

'Coward,' Rafe told her softly.

Her chin came up, her eyes flashing darkly. 'You know nothing about me, Rafe. Nothing!' she snapped angrily.

He shrugged. 'Then prove me wrong, Cairo, and come with me tonight.'

Her mouth twisted into a derisive smile. 'I guarantee you'll regret your insistence more than I will.'

He raised an eyebrow. 'I'm willing to take that chance if you are.'

Was she? She could see the logic of what Rafe was saying concerning spiking the guns of the reporter who had followed them today. The two of them appearing together in public this evening would certainly diffuse the exclusivity of any story he might have written. Except the very idea of appearing in public with Rafe as her partner for the evening, so totally aware of him as she now was, was Cairo's idea of a nightmare!

'I'll ask Daisy,' she repeated firmly. 'If *she* wants to go, then we will.'

Rafe could tell by the finality in her tone that it was the best answer he was going to get for now.

'Okay.' He sighed. 'Go and talk to Daisy now so that I know whether or not I have to call and make my excuses for this evening, after all.'

Rafe made no effort to follow Cairo into the villa, instead moving to sit on one of the chairs on the terrace, needing these few minutes' respite to bring his throbbing need for her under control.

Impossible when he could practically taste her....

CHAPTER SEVEN

'YOU have to believe me, Cairo, when I tell you I had no idea Bond had been invited this evening!'

Cairo knew by the grimness of Rafe's expression as he looked down at her so intently that he was telling the truth.

Not that she had ever thought otherwise; the two of them might have had their differences in the past, Rafe uncaring of her feelings for him, but she had never found him to be a vindictive man.

Believing what he did, to have deliberately brought her to this party in Cannes knowing Lionel was going to be here, too, would definitely have been vindictive on Rafe's part!

Until now it had been a surprisingly pleasant evening. Cairo had met up and chatted with several old acquaintances as she sipped the freely flowing champagne, and Daisy was absolutely enthralled with the whole thing as she pointed out people she recognized from films and television.

There had been the usual barrage of photographers outside, of course, an experience Cairo had also found less of an ordeal than she had expected. Rafe had kept a firm hold of her arm and smilingly fended off most of the more personal questions while at the same time keeping an eye out for the man who had followed them earlier today. He wasn't there, Rafe had informed her as they went into the huge white marquee on Cannes beach where the party was being held.

No doubt the man believed he had enough of an exclusive for one day!

Which he probably did....

Cairo had decided to put him firmly from her mind—along with that earlier, erotic, conversation with Rafe!—once she realized she was actually enjoying herself, having reacquainted herself with several friends that she hadn't seen since her move to London.

Until she chanced to glance across at the entrance of the marquee and see Lionel making a belated appearance!

'Maybe he wasn't invited.' She sighed, knowing that Lionel was quite capable of inviting himself if he had learnt that Cairo was here, seeing as she had so far evaded all of his previous efforts to see or speak to her.

'Do you want to leave?' Rafe asked.

Did she?

Admittedly, seeing Lionel again like this so unexpectedly had been a shock, but if she left now, it would look as if she was running away from an awkward situation. Worse, she would feel as if she was running away!

'No, I don't want to leave,' she answered Rafe firmly. 'Let's just continue to circulate, hmm?' she suggested tautly as she slid her hand into the crook of his arm.

'Fine with me.' Rafe nodded as he looked down at her with approval.

Despite her claim that she had nothing suitable to wear,

Cairo looked stunningly beautiful this evening, the simple black sheath of a dress she wore giving her a classically elegant appearance when compared to all the glittering gowns being worn by the other women present. Her red hair was loose and silky about her shoulders, her eyes dark and luminous in her lightly tanned face, her lips glossed a challenging red.

Warpaint she might need before this evening was over, Rafe acknowledged heavily as he saw Lionel Bond making his way determinedly towards them.

Her ex-husband came to a halt in front of Cairo, his smile smooth and self-assured. 'I had no idea you were going to be here this evening, Cairo,' he greeted lightly. 'I seem to recall your telling me you hated this sort of thing?' he added quizzically.

Cairo returned that smile even as her grip tightened on Rafe's arm and her nails dug into the sleeve of his dinner jacket. 'I've made tonight an exception,' she replied coolly.

Rafe's gaze narrowed as he saw the way Bond was looking at Cairo with such warmth. Not entirely surprisingly, he found his own feelings towards her ex were far from friendly.

He could see why she'd been attracted to the man, of course. For not only was Lionel Bond incredibly rich and powerful, he was also six feet tall, still athletically fit in his late forties, with a boyishly handsome face and blond hair tinged a distinguishing grey at the temples.

Yes, Rafe could see the reason Cairo had once been attracted to this man. That she might still be attracted to him, in spite of their recent divorce…?

Cairo was sure that her knees were shaking so much

they were actually knocking together! It hadn't even occurred to her that Lionel might be here this evening. She definitely wouldn't have come if it had.

And yet…

This first meeting since their divorce, a meeting she had steadfastly avoided in spite of Lionel's repeated efforts for it to be otherwise, had to have happened at some time, so why not get it over and done with?

The guilt she had carried with her for so long where Lionel was concerned, unable to love him and yet unable to leave him, either, because of that guilt, along with the fear that she might be the reason for his gambling addiction, no longer seemed like quite such a heavy weight as she looked at him now. Lionel looked surprisingly fit and well, and was obviously surviving quite well without her.

Perhaps he really had finally been able to stop the addiction that had for so long threatened to ruin him….

'I wonder why you've made tonight an exception?' Lionel turned to look at Rafe, his pale grey gaze wide with speculation.

Cairo turned to include Rafe in their conversation. 'You know Rafe of course…?'

'Of course.' Lionel nodded briefly in the younger man's direction, neither one making any attempt to shake hands.

Cairo couldn't help but appreciate the differences she could see in the two men as they stood so close together, Rafe so dark and compellingly attractive, Lionel a golden blond and all that was suave and handsomely self-assured.

But the expression of dislike on both men's faces was identical as hard blue eyes clashed with steely grey!

'I must say that I would have expected you to be a little

more—original, shall we say—in your choice of lover, Cairo,' Lionel challenged as he looked at Rafe. 'I had rather hoped I'd taught you to be a little more discerning in your tastes over the years.'

Cairo's breath caught in her throat at the deliberate insult, and she could feel Rafe's tension in his arm beneath her hand as he also recognized the directness of Lionel's attack.

Lionel had never been happy about her previous involvement with Rafe eight years ago, had considered Rafe one of the 'wild' set that had dominated Hollywood at the time. But Rafe had matured into a formidable and dangerous opponent in the intervening years, and he looked every bit as suave as Lionel this evening in the tailored black evening suit, snowy white shirt and red bow tie.

She gave her ex-husband a confident smile. 'There has never been anything wrong with my taste.'

'Really?' The intensity of Lionel's gaze seemed to look for some inclusion of himself in that statement.

'Yes—really,' Cairo echoed softly. 'Now if you'll excuse us—'

'You're looking rather beautiful this evening, Cairo,' Lionel told her warmly.

'I— Thank you.' She gave him a censorious frown.

'I'm sure Montero agrees with me, don't you, Montero?' he added with a mocking glance.

Rafe had never felt so much like hitting another man as he did at that moment. Not that he was going to. For one thing, it would achieve nothing except to relieve his own anger towards this man for even looking at Cairo so warmly. For another, he wouldn't give Bond the satisfaction of knowing how much it bothered him.

Rafe also doubted that Cairo would appreciate it if he laid her ex-husband out cold at her feet!

He released his arm from Cairo's hand to curve it about her waist, effectively pulling her to his side. 'In my experience, Cairo looks beautiful whatever the—occasion,' he drawled provocatively.

This conversation was spiralling out of control, Cairo decided impatiently. Ridiculously so, seeing as she and Lionel were already divorced, and she didn't have any relationship at all with Rafe!

'Enjoyable as this conversation is—' her tone implied the opposite '—I think I would like to go outside for some air, Rafe.' She looked at him compellingly.

Rafe gave a terse inclination of his head. 'Of course—'

'Uncle Lionel?'

Cairo had completely forgotten—not surprisingly!—Daisy's presence until that moment, her young niece rejoining them now that she had finished speaking to the young actor they had introduced her to after she had asked to meet him so she could tell the other girls about it when she returned to school next week!

'Daisy?' Lionel raised surprised brows as he turned to look at his former niece.

Daisy grinned up at him unabashedly, looking absolutely adorable in a lemon sundress and white sandals. 'Aunty Cairo didn't say you were going to be here, too!'

'No, I don't suppose she did,' Lionel said with a rueful glance in Cairo's direction. 'I had no idea this was a family gathering. Can I expect to see Margo and Jeff this evening, too?'

Cairo gave him a quelling glance, Margo and Jeff never

having made any secret of the fact that they didn't particularly like or approve of Lionel. 'No, there's just the three of us,' she answered pointedly.

'Hmm,' he murmured enigmatically. 'It's really is good to see you again, Cairo,' he added huskily. 'The two of us need to talk—'

'I don't think so, Lionel,' she cut in firmly; she and Lionel had absolutely nothing left to say to each other. They had spent months, years, trying to sort out the problems between them, all to no avail.

He reached out and grasped her arm. 'Tell me where you're staying, Cairo, and I'll—'

'Take your hand off her, Bond!' Rafe snarled between clenched teeth.

Lionel shot him a look of pure dislike. 'Butt out, Montero—'

'I'll give you until the count of three—'

'And then what?' Lionel challenged. 'This is absolutely none of your business—'

'I'm making it my business,' Rafe said in a lethal tone.

'Please don't, Rafe.' Cairo put her hand on his arm, her look one of pleading before she turned back to her ex-husband. 'We both know we have nothing left to say to each other, Lionel, and I certainly don't appreciate the way you're drawing attention to all of us,' she added as she became aware of the many curious gazes turned in their direction. 'I believe it's time that we left, Rafe.'

'I'll call you,' Lionel called after her.

Rafe turned to give the other man an icy glare, his hands clenching at his sides as he saw the almost desperate look on Bond's handsome face as he gazed after Cairo.

'Do we really have to go?' Daisy frowned her disappointment. 'I'm not in the least tired,' she assured them, widening her eyes as if to prove the point, and looking absolutely adorable as she did so.

Rafe chuckled softly as he released his hold on Cairo's waist to swing Daisy up into his arms. 'Aunty Cairo needs her beauty sleep,' he told her teasingly.

Daisy turned to look at her aunt. 'Aunty Cairo can't be any more beautiful than she already is,' she informed him proudly.

No, she couldn't, Rafe acknowledged heavily. She was absolutely gorgeous. Assured. Desirable.

'Then maybe it's me who needs my beauty sleep,' he said ruefully.

'You're much better looking than Uncle Lionel,' Daisy confided with innocent candour.

Rafe looked at Cairo over Daisy's head, wondering how she was taking the comparison, but unable to read anything from her composed expression as she coolly met his gaze.

'I like you better than Uncle Lionel, too,' Daisy continued with that same innocence. 'He never played with me like you do.'

Cairo thought this conversation had gone far enough. Even if she did completely agree with everything Daisy had just said!

Rafe's rugged handsomeness was much more appealing than Lionel's suave urbanity. And, despite their differences, like Daisy, Cairo liked Rafe much better than she did Lionel, too....

'All the flattery in the world isn't going to stop us from leaving, young lady,' she teased her niece, although it was still several minutes before they got outside as people engaged them in conversation as they made their way towards the exit.

Daisy was fast asleep in the back of the car within minutes of their leaving the bright lights of Cannes. 'So much for her not being tired,' Cairo murmured wryly as she turned from making the little girl more comfortable within the confines of her seat belt. 'Phew.' She sighed deeply. 'I can't say I'm sorry that's over!' She leant back wearily against the headrest and closed her eyes.

Rafe gave her a brief glance, a frown creasing his brow when he turned back to the road as he was once again struck by Cairo's air of fragility. 'Is that the first time you and Bond have met since the divorce?' he asked.

'Yes.'

'I'm sorry it had to be in such a public way.' Rafe grimaced.

'I'm not.' Cairo turned her head to look at him. 'Thank you for being so—supportive,' she told him huskily.

Rafe's mouth tightened as he once again wondered how she really felt about seeing Bond again....

He shrugged. 'Bond didn't really give me any choice in the matter.'

'No,' Cairo accepted ruefully. 'But I thank you, anyway.'

Rafe couldn't think of a single thing to say in answer to that comment as they made the rest of the drive back to the villa in silence.

A tense, almost expectant silence, as even the air between them seemed to crackle with a taut, nerve-tingling tension that was electric in its intensity.

'I'll carry her inside,' Rafe offered as he parked the car in the driveway of the villa to get out and lift Daisy from the back seat.

'Thank you,' Cairo murmured, barely able to look at the broadness of Rafe's back as she followed him through the villa to Daisy's bedroom.

What had happened between them in the car just now?

Because something had. Something so tangible Cairo felt she could almost reach out and touch it. Could reach out and touch Rafe.

As she knew he wanted to touch her....

'I'll be waiting outside on the terrace when you've finished putting Daisy to bed,' he breathed softly as he straightened after laying Daisy down on the cool sheets.

Cairo looked at him wordlessly, her gaze searching the hard, unreadable arrogance of his face. 'Rafe—' She broke off, her eyes wide, as Rafe moved to stand so close to her their bodies almost touched, that crackling tension she had been so aware of in the car intensifying as their gazes met and held.

Cairo could barely breathe. Rafe made no effort now to hide the desire burning in the luminous depths of those deep blue eyes, the same desire that had been there earlier this afternoon when he'd told her of all the things he would like to do to her.

He lifted his hand, his palm cupping her chin as the pad of his thumb moved gently across her bottom lip. Cairo instinctively parted her lips at the softness of that caress even as she felt her nipples harden and swell beneath her dress.

Time seemed to stand still.

Not a sound, not a movement of air disturbed them.

All there was at that moment was Rafe and this wild, singing awareness that heated the blood in Cairo's veins and made her skin burn with the need for the caress of his hands upon it, stroking, cupping, arousing.

She didn't move—couldn't move as Rafe began to lower his head towards hers, her breath catching in her throat as his lips moved softly, enticingly, against hers. He was no longer touching her in any other way but held her captive there with just those arousing lips as he slowly sipped and tasted her.

How long that kiss lasted Cairo had no idea. Nor did she care as she responded with everything that was in her.

Cairo tasted wonderful, Rafe acknowledged achingly. Warm. Silky. Intoxicating.

He felt the hardening of his thighs even as he became drunk on the heady pleasure of kissing her. Nothing else. Just the softness of her lips against his as they drank their fill of each other.

Eventually it wasn't enough, of course. Rafe wanted more. So much more.

Rafe lifted his head to look down at Cairo, knowing from her flushed cheeks and the glow in the deep, dark brown of her eyes that she was as aroused as he was. 'I want you so much, Cairo,' he groaned throatily. 'Don't keep me waiting outside too long, hmm?'

Don't keep him—!

Rafe thought that the two of them—? That they were going to—?

Rafe believed her response to his kiss was an invitation for the two of them to go outside together and make love in the way he had described earlier? Then what? A few more days of the same, before he returned to his world and she returned to hers?

Reality washed over Cairo like the shock of a blast of cold air, and she could only stare up at him as something withered and died deep down inside her. Some hope… Some remembered dream of long ago…

But this was Rafe Montero, she reminded herself. The same man who had claimed her heart eight years ago and then cast it aside when he became bored and moved on to another conquest. As he would become bored with her again once he had made love with her!

Not again, Cairo told herself firmly. Never again would she allow her heart to rule her head.

'I'll be outside,' Rafe whispered, running a slow, caressing finger down the hollow of her cheek before turning and quietly leaving the room.

Cairo stood as still as a statue.

She felt like one, too, at that moment.

A figure of cold marble in which no emotion, no sensation existed.

Not even pain….

CHAPTER EIGHT

'WHAT the hell do you think you're *doing*?'

Cairo was sitting up in bed reading a book—or, at least, appearing to!—when Rafe burst unannounced into her bedroom. A quick glance at the face of the slender gold watch on her wrist showed her that it was now half an hour since he had told her he would be waiting outside for her on the terrace.

She had considered actually lying down in bed with the light off and pretending she was asleep when he came in search of her—as she had known that he would—but had decided that would be too undignified; Rafe wasn't the type of man to just turn and leave again and was more than capable of switching on the light before dragging her from the bed kicking and screaming!

So instead she had removed her make-up and taken a leisurely shower before donning a pale cream nightgown of the sheerest silk, only a band of matching cream lace across her breasts preventing it from being completely transparent. She'd then stood in front of the mirror brushing her hair until it shone straight and sleek over her shoulders and down her spine.

Her tools of war, she decided angrily as she arranged her pillows before getting into bed to sit and wait, her tension increasing with each tick of her wristwatch.

However, none of that tension showed as she looked over her book at Rafe where he stood in the doorway glowering across the room at her. He was no longer wearing the jacket to his suit or the red bowtie, and the top two buttons of his shirt were open to reveal the silky black hair on his chest.

Cairo suppressed an inward shiver as she acknowledged how dark and dangerous he looked. Instead, she gave him a bright, enquiring smile. 'I'm reading a book, of course.'

Rafe's scowl deepened as he advanced into the room, his movements predatory before he came to an abrupt halt beside the bed. 'I've been waiting outside for you for the last half-hour,' he growled.

Cairo could almost feel his anger, knew by the nerve that pulsed in his clenched jaw just how near to the surface that anger was.

She gave a shrug as she lay the book face down beside her on the bed. 'I decided I was just too tired for any more conversation tonight, Rafe.'

'You—!' Rafe bit off what he was going to say and instead drew in a deep, controlling breath. Like his father before him, Rafe had a volatile Spanish temper. A temper that Rafe rarely, if ever, lost. Only Cairo, it seemed, had the power to stretch his control to its very limits.

He very carefully reached down and plucked the book from beside her and placed it on the bedside table before sitting down on the edge of the bed. 'We both know conversation was the last thing I had in mind when I asked you to join me outside once Daisy was in bed,' he said softly.

'Really?' She continued to meet his gaze unblinkingly.

'Yes,' he acknowledged pleasantly. 'Good book?' He nodded towards the bedside table.

'Very good,' she confirmed slowly, no longer quite as composed as Rafe saw a slight frown appear between the clear brown of her eyes.

'What's it about?' Rafe reached out and picked the book up so that he could read the back cover. 'Strange,' he said as he put it back down. 'I would never have tagged you as a reader of murder mysteries.'

She smiled. 'This one's about a woman who kills her lover after she finds out he's been cheating on her.'

'Really,' Rafe commented, easily holding her gaze with his. 'But I bet she gets caught in the end. They all do.'

'Not all of them,' Cairo said dryly. 'If you wouldn't mind, Rafe…? I really am very tired.' She raised one auburn brow.

Rafe wanted to reach out, grasp her shoulders, and shake her. Anything to put some spark of emotion back into her!

He had become more irritated by the minute as he'd stood outside waiting for her to join him, knowing that earlier Cairo had wanted him as much as he wanted her.

But as he looked at her now he saw none of that softly desirable woman he had kissed such a short time ago. Instead he saw a woman whose barriers were so firmly back in place it was impossible to tell what thoughts were going through her head.

He gave her a narrow-eyed look. 'Did seeing Bond again tonight reawaken a spark of emotion for him? Is that it?'

She blinked in surprise. 'You're being utterly ridiculous, Rafe.' She gave him a pointed look. 'Now, if you wouldn't mind leaving? I really am very tired—'

'Cairo.' Rafe spoke her name quietly, but it was enough to silence her.

Cairo's gaze became less certain on his as she became aware of how dangerous it was for them to be alone together in her bedroom.

Very dangerous.

Not that she thought for one minute that Rafe would use force to get what he wanted. Why should he when he knew he only had to touch her to ignite a passionate response from her?

Perhaps she should have turned the light off and pretended she was asleep, after all!

'Lionel and I are divorced, Rafe,' she reminded him.

'That doesn't mean you can't still be in love with him!'

She sighed. 'You obviously know nothing about me if you believe that. But, then, you never did know anything about me, did you?'

'I thought I did,' he muttered.

Her eyes flashed. 'And you thought wrong, didn't you?'

Yes, he had been wrong about Cairo eight years ago, Rafe acknowledged grimly. So very wrong.

Then.

And now…

He stood up abruptly. 'You're right, Cairo, this was a bad idea. I'll leave you to get back to your book.'

'Thank you,' she snapped.

Rafe paused to look back at her as he stood in the bedroom doorway, his smile self-derisive. 'I should probably be thanking you for preventing me from making yet another mistake where you're concerned.' And yet the ache of his body told him that gratitude was the last thing he really felt….

Cairo's eyes glittered darkly. 'I'll take it as said!'

'Goodnight, Cairo.'

'Goodnight, Rafe.'

Rafe gave her one last lingering glance before leaving the bedroom and the villa, stepping outside to take deep breaths of the perfumed night air, his gaze drawn to the swimming pool as the moonlight shimmered invitingly on the water.

He didn't even hesitate, throwing off his clothes as he reached the lower terrace before diving smoothly into the coolly refreshing water.

She was crying, Cairo realized numbly. Tears that burnt her skin as they tracked down the paleness of her cheeks.

She wiped those tears away impatiently as she got out of bed, too restless to even think about sleep now as she began to pace the confines of her bedroom.

She had to get out of here!

She needed air.

Space in which to breathe.

The villa was in darkness, not a sound to be heard as she trailed through the comfortable sitting-room and out onto the terrace, the silence there broken by a sound she had come to associate with this area of France: hundreds of frogs croaking in the moonlight.

Somehow that familiar sound comforted her, calmed her, a smile curving her lips as she walked down the steps to the lower terrace to where the sound of the frogs became even louder.

Rafe floated in the shallow end of the pool, watching Cairo as she approached. She looked almost ghostly in the moonlight, her feet bare, her cream nightgown transparent against the nakedness of her body, her face a pale oval. The eerie light gave her long hair the appearance of cinnamon touched with silver.

That she was unaware of his presence in the water was in no doubt, a smile curving her lips as she held out her arms and turned her face up to the moonlight, long lashes shadowing her cheeks as she closed her lids.

She was Aphrodite.

Goddess of love.

Rafe's breath caught in his throat as he looked at her, her breasts full and pert against the sheer material of her nightgown, her waist narrow, hips gently curving, a shadowed triangle visible between her thighs.

His body hardened in response to that beauty, his earlier resolve crumbling into dust as he knew that, despite everything, he still wanted to make love with her.

Cairo raised her lids as she heard another sound besides the croaking of the frogs, turning slowly to the source of that sound, her eyes widening as she watched Rafe stepping slowly up from the pool.

A completely naked Rafe, water dripping down his body, his thrusting arousal obvious as he walked slowly towards her. His gaze held hers as he took her in his arms, his body wet and cold from the water. Then his head lowered and his mouth claimed hers.

They kissed hungrily, deeply, lips and tongues seeking, drinking, devouring, as Cairo's fingers became entwined in the silky darkness of Rafe's hair, their legs entwined, bodies pressed closely together.

Cairo groaned as she felt Rafe slip the thin straps of her nightgown down her arms. She felt his cool hand against her heated flesh, her back arching in invitation when, as he had described this afternoon, he cupped one of her breasts to run the soft pad of his thumb caressingly across that sensitized tip, engulfing her in a warmth that reached from her toes to her fingertips.

Rafe kissed her lingeringly on the lips, tasting her, his hand still caressing her as he raised his head to look down at her. Her eyes were half closed, her breathing soft and shallow, a slight flush to the hollows of her cheeks.

His gaze darkened as he lowered it to where his hand cupped and held her, the small, perfect roundness of her bared breasts tipped with nipples of deep coral, full and tight as they pouted towards him in tempting invitation.

Rafe lowered his head to run his tongue moistly around that roused nipple, closing his lips about its coral-pink tip and suckling deeply as he heard her moan. His tongue lapped and rasped over it as his long, slim fingers continued to caress the arousal of that other deep rose tip.

Then Rafe's hands spanned the slenderness of her waist and he lifted her up into him so that he could feast on those breasts, licking, sucking, feeling the spasms that rocked her body as he gently nibbled her roused flesh before once again suckling her deeply inside the warmth of his mouth.

He moved one of his hands from her waist to slide the silk nightgown up the smoothness of her legs and thighs as he sought and found the centre of her arousal.

She was already moist, her thighs parting as she allowed him to touch her there, to stroke and caress her before his questing hand moved lower and he gently probed that moistness with one finger, and then two, entering her, claiming her as he felt her rush of dampness against the rapidly increasing thrusts.

He gave the hard pebble of her nipple one last lingering kiss before moving lower, kneeling at her feet as his lips and tongue moved over the creamy silk of her waist and stomach, lightly probing her navel before he moved lower still. Cairo's hips arched in a silent plea as his tongue moved unerringly against the hard nub nestled amongst the silky dampness of her red-golden curls and he felt her response, tasting her, sucking that nub into his mouth until she gasped.

Cairo was lost.

She had been lost from the moment Rafe's mouth had touched hers and his hands had caressed her, his clever tongue and lips now driving her heatedly, relentlessly, towards a climax that claimed her so quickly, so fiercely, she could only cling mindlessly to his shoulders as the pleasure began deep inside her, her breath now coming in weak, gasping sobs. That pleasure swelled and grew, consuming her, flinging her into a maelstrom of feelings, sensations that seemed never ending as Rafe continued to suckle her and his tongue lapped against her in greedy hunger.

Her fingers clenched in the thickness of his hair, holding him to her as he drained every last vestige of pleasure from her totally acquiescent body.

And still she wanted more, ached for more, wanted to know that pleasure again as much as she needed Rafe buried deep inside her, groaning her disappointment as he stood up and she felt him moving away from her.

He couldn't leave her now!

She reached out and touched him, watching Rafe's eyes

close as her fingers curled around him. He was steel encased in velvet and she ran her fingers down the long length of him, her other hand cupping and holding him as she caressed rhythmically, hearing Rafe's groan as her lips trailed moistly across his chest on a downward path to the centre of his arousal.

Rafe's knees almost buckled as Cairo knelt before him and he felt her lips close about him before she oh-so-slowly drew him deep into the heated moisture of her mouth, his hands tightly gripping her shoulders before he held her away from him as he felt himself losing control.

'Not yet, Cairo,' he murmured throatily even as he lifted her up and away from him.

Not because he didn't like her mouth on him, or that velvety caressing tongue lapping and tasting the hard length of him. Truth be told, he liked it too much, was in danger of just letting go and spilling himself like some inexperienced boy. And he hadn't drunk his fill of Cairo yet. Hadn't touched her, kissed her, caressed her nearly enough to assuage eight years of hungry need.

She stood perfectly still as he lowered the nightgown completely to let it fall down about her feet, her breasts small and firm as he lowered his head and kissed each of them slowly in turn before holding her away from him to feast his eyes on her nakedness. She was the most beautiful woman he had ever known. So tiny and yet so totally, femininely perfect, her skin soft and silky, and the colour of magnolia, with those rosy tipped breasts so pert and thrusting it made him feel hungry for her just looking at them.

Rafe swung her up into his arms and sat down on the lounger, her legs straddling him, the warmth between her thighs reaching out to tempt him as his hard arousal moved restlessly against that heat.

'Take me into you, Cairo...' Rafe groaned. 'Deep, deep inside you!'

'Soon,' Cairo promised as she rubbed herself against him, wetting him, giving herself pleasure, as well as him, as her own arousal mated with his, her aching nipples a caress against the soft hair on Rafe's chest as she raced towards another climax.

Rafe's hand moved between them and she cried out as he found her hardened nub, thumb caressing even as his fingers slid smoothly inside her, those thrusts becoming harder, faster, Cairo almost sobbing as her climax peaked again and again.

'Now, Rafe,' she moaned. 'I want you inside me now!' she begged as she raised herself slightly to curl her hand about him and rub the tip of his hard shaft against her wetness, hearing Rafe's groans as she teased them both until they could wait no longer. She opened herself to him and took him inside her slowly, her gaze holding his as he entered her inch by pleasurable inch.

Rafe felt as if he were almost going insane as Cairo slowly wrapped herself about his engorged arousal. He felt the quivers of her recent pleasure, longed to thrust deep inside her, hard and fast, needing to assuage his own burning need for release, but at the same time wanting this moment to last for ever.

He groaned again, his eyes closing, as Cairo slowly began to ride him, her knees placed on the lounger beside him to give her purchase as she raised almost to his tip before plunging down again. Again. And again. Riding him steadily faster. Harder. Her hips thrusting, drowning him in sensation, until he felt the first surge of his own release, his hands moving instinctively to her hips as he began to pump deep inside her, grasping her, holding her as he thrust into her in ever-increasing wildness, falling weakly backwards as she continued to milk every last drop from his body.

The fog of desire faded as the cool night air stroked the aroused heat of Cairo's body, and she groaned low in her throat as she realized exactly what she and Rafe had just done.

This wasn't real, she recognized achingly as she stared down at him in the moonlight. This madness with Rafe, the two of them being intimate like this, it wasn't real. It never had been.

Not eight years ago.

And not now, either.

'Cairo…?' Rafe questioned huskily as he obviously felt her withdrawal.

This wasn't real, she told herself again as she began to tremble in reaction.

She shook her head. 'We can't ever do this again, Rafe.' Her voice broke emotionally.

'Why the hell not?' he rasped his disappointment.

'I— We just can't!' Cairo cried, not even knowing how she was going to escape from this with dignity.

Minutes ago, she had been in ecstasy, totally lost to reason, but now she could see this for exactly what it was. A purely physical attraction—at least, on Rafe's part. Cairo was very much afraid that for her—as it had been eight years ago—it was something totally different.

She stared at Rafe, at his dark beauty, her eyes widening

with horror as she realized that, despite everything, she was still in love with him.

Had she ever really stopped loving him?

No, she hadn't, Cairo acknowledged heavily. Rafe had been her first love and he was also her last love. But he hadn't been able to love her in return when they were together before, and it wasn't love he felt for her now, either. She had made a lot of mistakes in her life, but she wasn't about to make the biggest one of them all by deceiving herself into believing it could ever be otherwise!

She moved up and away from him to turn and pick up her discarded nightgown. 'I think it's time I went inside. Alone,' she added abruptly so that Rafe should be left in no doubt about her intentions.

'Cairo?' Rafe stood up to reach out and grasp her arm, turning her to face him as he looked down at her searchingly.

What the hell had just happened?

Minutes ago, he knew Cairo had been as wild for their lovemaking as he had, and now she was just going to walk away? He gave a puzzled shake of his head. 'What's going on, Cairo? Why are you so hot, so wild, one minute and then back to being the ice-maiden the next? Was I just a quick lay? Is that it?'

She gave a pained frown. 'It wasn't like that—'

'It sure as hell seems like it to me!' he grated.

She shrugged. 'I—I was curious, that's all.'

'You were *curious*?' he repeated in a dangerous tone.

She nodded. 'To see if that physical attraction really was still there.'

Rafe's eyes narrowed ominously. 'And?'

'Obviously it still is,' she acknowledged dryly. 'But that doesn't mean we have to do anything more about it.'

His mouth twisted derisively. 'Your *curiosity* has been satisfied. Is that it?'

'I— It was a mistake. A mistake that's better not repeated, don't you think?' Her face was very pale in the moonlight.

No, Rafe certainly did not think that!

Nor did he believe that Cairo was as coolly dismissive of what had just happened between them as she wanted him to believe. He just had no idea why she was behaving like this. With any other woman he would have said she was running scared from the depth of their response to each other, but he knew it couldn't be that because it had always been this way between them. From their very first night together their passion had been just this out of control.

'No, I don't think it was a mistake, and it's not what you really believe, either, Cairo,' he bit out.

She looked momentarily taken aback and then she gave an incredulous laugh. 'Strangely, Rafe, I find I don't actually give a damn *what* you think!'

'No?'

'No,' she insisted as she calmly slipped her nightgown back over her nakedness. 'It's only your own arrogance that makes you say differently.'

'You—' Rafe swallowed an angry expletive. 'You're playing with fire, Cairo,' he warned harshly.

'But that's my point, Rafe; I have played, and I don't want to play any more.' She shrugged. 'Maybe Lionel was right, after all, and my tastes have become more— sophisticated, over the years. I certainly hope I've learnt never to make the same mistake twice,' she added.

Rafe drew in an angry breath. 'Let's hope you've learnt the same sense where Bond is concerned, then,' he snarled.

'What's this got to do with Lionel?'

Rafe's mouth twisted humourlessly. 'Unless it escaped your notice earlier, the man obviously wants you back.'

'It isn't me Lionel wants, Rafe,' she contradicted.

'What do you mean?' he prompted sharply.

'Never mind.' Cairo gave a weary sigh. 'It really is very late, Rafe, and despite her late night I'm sure Daisy will still be awake bright and early in the morning.'

Rafe looked at her searchingly for several long seconds, a gaze that Cairo returned unblinkingly. Unemotionally. The passionate woman he had held in his arms such a short time ago had completely disappeared behind that façade of cool indifference.

But to Rafe it was obvious now that it *was* just a façade and he was more determined than ever to penetrate it. For now, though, he knew Cairo had had enough. Of Lionel Bond. And of him. If he tried to push her any more tonight, she would just retreat even further behind that barrier she had erected around her emotions.

He forced the tension from his shoulders and smiled slightly. 'Okay, Cairo.' He nodded. 'Sleep well, hmm?' he added ruefully—knowing he wasn't going to be as lucky!

She looked a little less certain as she eyed him guardedly. 'I— Yes. And you.'

He grimaced. 'I think I'll go for another swim and cool off.'

'Goodnight, then.'

''Night, Cairo,' he echoed huskily.

Rafe stood and watched her as she glided up the steps before disappearing inside the villa.

He stood there for several more minutes and mulled over this last conversation with Cairo, wondering exactly what she had meant by that last remark about Lionel Bond....

CHAPTER NINE

'NICE of you to join us,' Rafe drawled dryly as Cairo stepped onto the terrace where he and Daisy were eating breakfast.

'Good morning, Daisy.' Cairo completely ignored Rafe's jibe as she sat down next to her niece and poured herself a cup of coffee. 'I knew you were up,' she told him as she sat back in her chair cradling her mug of black coffee. 'I heard you and Daisy talking hours ago.'

'Was that before or after we went out and got breakfast?' Rafe taunted as he helped himself to another of the freshly baked croissants.

'Does it matter?' Cairo asked airily.

She had been woken by Daisy's overloud whispers at least two hours ago, Rafe's equally audible replies telling Cairo that her niece wasn't alone, and so she had simply pulled the duvet back over her head and gone back to sleep!

She gave a contented sigh as she gazed out at the tranquillity of the valley. 'It's another lovely day.'

'We're going home today, Aunty Cairo!' Daisy could obviously contain her excitement no longer.

Cairo raised questioning brows at Rafe before giving her niece a quizzical smile. 'We are…?'

Daisy nodded, her eyes glowing and her cheeks flushed. 'I wanted to come and wake you hours ago so I could tell you, but Uncle Rafe wouldn't let me disturb you.'

'What I actually said, Daisy, was that women of your aunt's advanced age need all the beauty sleep they can get!' Rafe corrected mockingly.

Cairo had wondered just how she and Rafe were going to face each other again after the incident down by the pool last night—now she knew! Sarcasm was obviously the order of the day....

She gave him a saccharin-sweet smile. 'And I thought we had agreed last night that, at the advanced age of thirty-seven, it's you who needs your beauty sleep?' That Rafe looked very lean and dangerously attractive in a white T-shirt and faded jeans gave lie to that statement!

Daisy turned to look at Rafe, her eyes wide. 'Are you really thirty-seven, Uncle Rafe?'

Rafe gave a rueful nod of his head in Cairo's direction as he heard the note of awe in Daisy's voice. 'Daisy, honey, when you're older, you'll realize that men are like a fine wine—they just get better as they mature.'

'Or they become as sour as vinegar,' Cairo put in lightly.

And not exactly honestly, where Rafe was concerned, she acknowledged inwardly. He did have at least one thing in common with a fine wine, as last night testified only too well—the last eight years had just made him more headily potent!

He looked across at her with teasing blue eyes. 'I think your Aunty Cairo is—confusing her wines,' he drawled.

That was quite enough of that conversation, Cairo decided firmly. 'So, we're leaving later today…?' she prompted in a pointed attempt to change the subject.

Rafe continued to hold her gaze challengingly for several more seconds before nodding. 'Jeff telephoned earlier; Margo and baby Simon are going to be discharged tomorrow morning.'

Cairo's face lit up and she put her coffee mug down on the table so that she could give Daisy a hug. 'That's wonderful news!'

Rafe took advantage of Cairo's momentary distraction to take in her appearance. She looked sleek and tanned this morning in a knee-length cream sundress, her legs bare and silky. She had cream flip-flops on her feet, and her face was bare of make-up, too, apart from a peachy gloss she had applied to her lips.

The lips that still looked slightly bruised from the force of their lovemaking the previous evening….

His stomach muscles clenched. Dammit, he had promised himself he wouldn't think about last night! At least, not until after he had safely delivered Daisy back to Margo and Jeff, anyway….

Cairo was still smiling as she looked across the table at him. 'What travel arrangements have you made for Daisy and me?'

'For all three of us,' Rafe corrected.

Cairo's smile faded. 'But you can't leave yet—'

'I can do what I please, Cairo.' Rafe scowled.

'But what about the film festival?'

'What about it?'

Cairo shrugged. 'I assumed you needed to be there to collect your award.'

'*If* I win an award, my assistant director can pick it up,' Rafe dismissed without concern. 'It's more important to get you and Daisy back to England.'

'I'm quite capable of getting myself and Daisy back to England, thank you very much—'

'I have a private jet organized to fly us out this afternoon,' he cut in abruptly in a tone that brooked no argument.

Cairo frowned as she slowly released Daisy. 'But I came over in my car....'

'I've also made arrangements for your car to be collected and driven back to England.'

Her brows rose at his arrogance. 'I really would rather drive my own car back, *if* you don't mind.'

'I don't mind in the least,' Rafe drawled. 'But you might want to look at these before making a definite decision on that...' He pushed a pile of newspapers across the table towards her.

Cairo glanced down at the newspapers, her eyes widening as the very first one in the pile, an English publication, had a front-page photograph of herself and Rafe smiling at each other as they sat at the table together in the square in Grasse.

Cairo became very still as she pulled the tabloid newspaper further across the table. Although that hadn't been necessary in order to be able to read the three inch headline above the photograph: CAIRO AND RAFE FIND LOVE IN THE SOUTH OF FRANCE!

Not exactly subtle. But, then, were any of the tabloids?

'More photographs and story on page three' was the smaller announcement beneath that damning photograph.

What story? Cairo wondered incredulously. Until she and Rafe returned to the villa last night there hadn't been a story—

Oh, no…!

No!

Cairo could feel herself paling even as she quickly turned to page three, her breath leaving her in a relieved gasp as she saw that the 'story' actually only consisted of half a dozen more photographs of herself and Rafe together yesterday in Grasse.

'That man didn't take a single photograph of me, Aunty Cairo,' Daisy told her indignantly.

'Didn't he, love?' she answered distractedly as she moved on to the next newspaper in the pile.

This one, and the other four, all had photographs of herself and Rafe as they arrived at the party in Cannes together the previous evening.

Not a single one of those reporters had been enterprising enough to follow them back to the villa last night in the hopes of taking intimate photographs of her and Rafe together. Thank goodness!

She and Rafe looked good together, she realized with a fierce frown. With her wearing three inch heels they were of a similar height, Rafe's dark hair and swarthy skin a perfect foil for her own fairer colouring as they stood close together, Rafe's hand resting lightly beneath her elbow, a confident smile curving his lips.

Looks can be deceptive, Cairo decided firmly as she pushed the newspapers away to look across the table at the man himself. 'Your point is…?'

God, she was beautiful when she was being haughty, Rafe acknowledged admiringly. If a little lacking in perception! 'Surely it's obvious? You turn up anywhere today expecting to travel home by public transport and you're going to be mobbed by yet more reporters.'

'Damn!' She grimaced. 'Damn, damn, damn!'

Rafe relaxed back in his chair as he regarded her mockingly. 'Are you sure that's appropriate language to use in front of Daisy?'

'Daddy says *damn* isn't swearing, Uncle Rafe,' Daisy told him brightly. 'And neither is—'

'I think your daddy is using a lot of poetic licence, Daisy,' Rafe teased. 'Still not want to come on the plane with us this afternoon, Cairo?' He arched quizzical brows.

Cairo didn't want to go anywhere with Rafe, not this afternoon or at any other time! But neither was she stupid enough to turn down the offer when the alternative was sure to turn out to be the nightmare Rafe had just described.

She sighed with resignation. 'What time do you want us to be ready to leave?'

His eyes gleamed with satisfaction. 'Two o'clock should do it. We— Who the hell is that?' He scowled darkly as he stood up to glare down at the car driving up the private road to the villa.

Cairo stood up to stand beside him, a sinking feeling in the pit of her stomach as she thought she knew exactly who it was.

Either another enterprising reporter.

Or, more likely, it was Lionel…

He had left three messages on her mobile during the night. The first had been pleasant as he told her how nice it had been to see her again yesterday evening.

The second one had started out pleasant enough, too,

with him asking her to meet with him so that they could talk. Unfortunately, as so often happened, it had deteriorated into insults after that as Lionel, obviously the worse for champagne, accused her of having been involved in an affair with Rafe all the time they had been married. As if! Cairo hadn't even been able to bear being on the same continent as Rafe for the last few years, let alone share the same bed after what he'd done to her.

Also predictably, the third message had been Lionel apologizing for the previous abusive one!

Cairo hadn't returned any of those calls. What was the point? She might still feel a certain amount of guilt where Lionel was concerned, had always felt that her lack of love for him had contributed to his addiction for gambling, but all the guilt in the world couldn't change the fact that they both knew their marriage was over.

'Do you want me to deal with this if it's another reporter?' Rafe asked grimly, turning to look at Cairo as she made no response.

She was staring intently at the car as it slowly came up the service road, her dark eyes shadowed above hollow cheeks.

'Cairo…?' he prompted.

She drew in a ragged breath before turning to look at him. 'I— Would you mind taking Daisy down to the pool or something?' she muttered.

'Why on earth would I—'

'Because I think our visitor is Lionel, that's why,' she explained wearily.

Lionel Bond was coming *here*?

Rafe turned his attention back to the car, his gaze narrowed as he tried to identify person behind the wheel. Yep. It was Bond, all right.

He glanced down at Cairo. 'Do you want to speak to him?'

'Not particularly.' She grimaced.

'Then don't,' Rafe rasped.

She gave a wistful smile. 'It isn't as simple as that, Rafe.'

'Yes, Cairo.' Rafe nodded. 'It really is.'

She looked up at him quizzically. 'Maybe for you it is, Rafe.' She sighed. 'But I've never been able to be quite that cruel.'

He shrugged. 'Sometimes you have to be cruel to be kind,' he said curtly.

'Like you were with me eight years ago?' she challenged.

Rafe's mouth thinned at the accusation. 'I don't believe we were talking about you and me.'

'No, of course we weren't,' Cairo said immediately. 'Forget I said that.'

Rafe wasn't sure he wanted to forget it. He had been so stunned when Cairo had ended things between them so unexpectedly, quickly followed by her announcement of her engagement to Bond, that the two of them had never got to talk about the abrupt end of their own relationship.

Now probably wasn't the best time to have that talk, either….

'Okay, Cairo,' he acquiesced. 'Talk to Bond if that's what you feel you have to do. But at the first sign of trouble I'm coming back up here to knock his teeth down his throat!'

Cairo stared up at him for several seconds before she gave an incredulous laugh. 'I really don't think that will be necessary, Rafe, but thanks for the offer!'

'Believe me, it will be my pleasure.'

How strange that Rafe, of all people, should offer to be her protector, Cairo mused as she walked over to meet with Lionel in the driveway. Not that Cairo would ever ask for his help, but she could still appreciate the irony of the situation.

However, her rueful smile quickly faded to one of weary resignation as she approached Lionel. 'How much do you need this time, Lionel?' she asked heavily.

'So what did he want?'

Cairo turned from packing the suitcase open on top of her bed, her expression becoming guarded as she looked at Rafe as he leant against the door frame.

She straightened. 'I really don't think that's any of your business, Rafe.'

He raised an eyebrow. 'I think you'll find, Cairo, that I don't really care what you do or don't consider my business.'

Rafe had spent the last fifteen minutes beside the pool watching from behind dark sunglasses as Cairo and her ex-husband talked together on the terrace, trying to gauge from their body language exactly what was going on. But Cairo's ultra-calm demeanour and Bond's animated one hadn't really told him an awful lot.

He had expected Cairo to join him and Daisy beside the pool once the other man had got back in his car and left, but instead she had disappeared inside the villa.

To pack, it seemed…

'Well?' he prompted impatiently.

Cairo frowned. 'I'm sorry, Rafe, but I'm not telling you anything—' She broke off, her eyes widening as Rafe crossed the room in three long strides to stand just inches away from her. She swallowed hard. 'Shouldn't you be outside with Daisy?'

'Daisy's too excited about going home to swim any more and has gone to her room to dress, instead.'

Cairo had no intention of telling Rafe the reason for Lionel's visit. It was awkward enough that Lionel had tracked down the reporter from yesterday in order to find out where she was staying with Rafe, without going into the details of their conversation.

'Shouldn't you be packing, too, if we're leaving for the airport in a couple of hours?' she pointed out, inwardly wishing Rafe wouldn't stand quite this close to her; his proximity was totally unnerving her!

Rafe shook his head. 'I find Bond's visit much more interesting than packing.'

'Really?'

'Yes—really,' Rafe drawled. 'You made an intriguing comment yesterday evening…'

'Just the one?' she came back in mock disappointment. 'And here I was deceiving myself that I'm much more interesting than that!'

Rafe gave an admiring smile as he appreciated the way Cairo was trying to change the subject. But Rafe had no intention of letting her succeed.

'Oh, don't worry, you are *extremely* interesting,' he assured her throatily. 'But you implied last night that it isn't you Bond is interested in. So if it's not you, what is it?'

Her smile faded as her gaze became guarded. 'I really can't discuss this with you, Rafe—'

'Oh, but you really can, Cairo,' Rafe insisted softly, his own gaze compelling.

She shook her head. 'Not without breaking a confidence, I can't,' she told him determinedly.

Rafe's eyes widened. 'A confidence with *Bond*?' he murmured disbelievingly. 'You divorced the man three months ago!' he reminded her.

'Yes, I did,' she acknowledged stiffly. 'But that doesn't mean I have to actually hate him, does it? Or discuss his private business with someone he regards as—' She broke off, frowning.

'"He regards as"…?'

'Never mind,' Cairo said hurriedly. 'Lionel and I may be divorced, but I don't hate him,' she insisted.

Rafe grimaced. 'In my experience that's what usually happens when two people divorce.'

'Well, it isn't true in my case,' Cairo assured him firmly.

How could she possibly hate Lionel when she still felt so responsible for what had gone wrong between them? She couldn't. But without telling Rafe the whole sorry story of her marriage, of the fact that she had married Lionel while still in love with *him*, she couldn't even begin to explain her feelings of guilt…

'I can see that,' Rafe grated harshly. 'Why bother to divorce him if you're going to come running every time the man crooks his little finger?'

Her eyes glittered darkly. 'It isn't like that!'

'Then what the hell *is* it like?' Rafe demanded incredulously. 'Last night you gave every impression that meeting Bond again was an ordeal for you, and yet today the two of you seem to have shared a pleasant conversation together!'

Cairo had found meeting Lionel again an ordeal because she had hoped—prayed—that when she ended their marriage, it might finally snap him into doing something about the mess his life had become. Those telephone calls last night, his visit today to ask her for money—yet again—told her that wasn't the case....

But without revealing everything to Rafe—which she had no intention of doing!—she was never going to persuade him of that. Lionel had managed to hide his gambling addiction from everyone for years, and Cairo certainly couldn't be the one to betray him now. Not even to convince Rafe that there was nothing between herself and Lionel.

Especially not in order to convince Rafe that there was nothing between herself and Lionel! Last night had shown her all too clearly just how dangerously susceptible she still was to Rafe....

'I really would prefer it if you stayed out of my life, Rafe.'

'And what if *I* would *prefer* to remain in it?' he challenged.

'This is ridiculous—'

'I agree,' Rafe interrupted.

Cairo scowled at him. 'Can we just stop playing word games?'

He raised dark brows. 'What other sort of games did you have in mind?'

She gave an impatient snort. 'I've never particularly liked playing games of any sort,' she snapped. 'Even as a child I was always the one that landed on the snake!'

Rafe gave an appreciative grin. 'I like you in this feisty mood, Cairo.'

'I don't want you to like me, Rafe!' she insisted as she moved away from him to resume her packing, but not as neatly as she had earlier, instead throwing things haphazardly inside the suitcase.

Rafe continued to look at her through narrowed lids for several long minutes.

She didn't seem overly upset by Lionel Bond's visit. More resigned than anything else.

But resigned to *what*?

CHAPTER TEN

'HE's absolutely gorgeous, Margo!' Cairo told her sister warmly as she stood up to hand baby Simon back into his mother's arms.

They had left the villa and the South of France without further incident, arriving back in England in the early evening, with a car waiting there for them. Rafe had driven them all to the clinic to visit Margo. The proud father was there, too, of course, Jeff looking and sounding much more relaxed now that the danger was over for both Margo and the baby.

It certainly wasn't the time for Cairo to remonstrate with either of them for failing to tell her of Rafe's ownership of the villa and his subsequent surprise arrival!

Rafe had brought in Daisy's small suitcase so that the little girl could return home with her father, leaving Cairo with the uncomfortable feeling he was going to insist on driving her to her flat. A feeling that was confirmed a short time later as he took his leave of Margo and Jeff at the same time as Cairo did, his hand firmly on her elbow as they walked down the carpeted corridor together.

'I'm sure you have somewhere else to go, Rafe, so—'

'Don't even think about trying to get rid of me just yet,'

Rafe warned softly as he pushed the door open for her to go outside into the early evening sunshine. 'In fact, why don't the two of us go out to dinner? You weren't expecting to be back in England for several more days, so you won't have anything in your apartment for us to eat,' he reasoned.

Cairo frowned up at him as he unlocked the doors of the sporty black car. 'Despite what you seem to have assumed to the contrary, it was never my intention to have dinner with you this evening, either at my flat or anywhere else!'

He gave a mocking smile as he opened her door for her. 'That isn't very friendly of you, Cairo, after I've gone to the trouble of transporting you back to England so quickly and efficiently.'

'It wasn't just me, Rafe, you also transported yourself and Daisy back….'

'Ah, but as you pointed out earlier today, I really needed to stay in Cannes. I don't even have a hotel reservation for tonight yet…' He quirked dark brows at her.

Cairo glared at him. 'That's your problem, Rafe, not mine.'

'I'm sure you could make it yours, too, if you really wanted to….'

She stared at him in disbelief. Was Rafe actually *flirting* with her? It certainly seemed as if he was!

'But I really don't want to,' Cairo told him dryly. 'So could you either give me my suitcase from the boot of the car so that I can get a taxi home, or drive me there yourself?'

'I'm driving you there myself, of course,' Rafe stated.

Cairo continued to eye him suspiciously as she slid into the passenger seat, not trusting him in this mood at all.

But what could he do, really? She didn't even have to invite him into her flat if—

There was no 'if' about it—she wasn't going to invite Rafe into her flat at all!

'Very nice,' Rafe murmured approvingly as he stood in the hallway looking at the simplicity of the sitting-room in Cairo's apartment, liking the cream carpet and terracotta-coloured suite, the paintings on the walls all bright and cheerful, too.

Cairo stood firmly in the doorway blocking his entrance to the room. 'Okay, Rafe, you've delivered my suitcase, as you insisted on doing,' she bit out, still irritated that she had lost that particular argument. 'Now it's time for you to leave.'

He put the case down. 'You could show your gratitude by offering me a glass of wine....'

Her foot tapped impatiently. 'I was quite capable of carrying my own suitcase!'

'I'm sure you're quite capable of doing most things yourself, Cairo, but my father brought me up to be a Spanish gentleman. And carrying a lady's bags for her is one of the things a Spanish gentleman does.'

Cairo wasn't fooled for a moment by this explanation; Rafe had been determined to wangle an invitation into her flat from the start. She just wasn't sure why....

'Very well.' She sighed heavily. 'Would you care for a glass of wine, Rafe?'

'How kind of you to offer, Cairo,' he accepted sarcastically, before stepping past her into the sitting-room.

Leaving Cairo no choice but to follow him! 'Red or white?' she offered, more than a touch disgruntled.

'Red would be fine, thanks. Have you lived here for very long?' he asked as he made himself comfortable in one of the armchairs.

'Six months or so,' Cairo answered distractedly as she took a bottle of red wine from the rack and uncorked it before pouring some of the wine into two glasses. 'Here.' She thrust one under Rafe's nose.

Blue eyes glinted with mockery as he looked up at her before taking the glass, his fingers lightly brushing against hers as he did so....

Cairo made no effort to sit down herself but instead walked over to look out of the window high above the London skyline as she slowly sipped her own wine, all the time aware of that intense blue gaze on the rigidity of her back.

'For goodness' sake, relax, Cairo.' Rafe finally sighed into the tense silence.

How was she supposed to do that when Rafe was in her flat?

This was *her* space, the first place she could completely call her own for over eight years. And Rafe's presence was a definite intrusion on that solitude.

'Nice view.'

Cairo almost dropped her glass of wine at the close proximity of Rafe's voice, turning to glare at him as he stood beside her, his tread having been so soft on the carpet she hadn't realized he had joined her in front of the window. 'I like it,' she snapped irritably.

'I'm not sure it's a good idea for you to be drinking on

a relatively empty stomach,' Rafe commented; Cairo hadn't eaten any breakfast at all, and only a sandwich for lunch.

'The wine was *your* idea—'

'For you to offer me a glass,' he corrected. 'You know what happens if you drink wine and you haven't had enough to eat,' he reminded her huskily.

'I know what happened once, Rafe. Just once,' she re-iterated firmly, the blush on her cheeks telling him she remembered the incident only too well.

'Hmm.'

'And what's that supposed to mean?' she challenged.

Rafe had forgotten what fun it was to tease Cairo. How she got that light of battle in her eyes. The angry blush to her cheeks. Her mouth set in that stubborn line.

He took the remaining half-glass of wine from her fingers and placed it on a bookshelf with his own. 'Come out to dinner with me tonight, Cairo,' he invited gruffly.

She blinked up at him uncertainly. 'Why on earth would I want to do that?' she breathed huskily, but with much less conviction in her voice.

Rafe held her gaze with his as he gave her a quizzical smile. 'Because I'm a stranger in town—'

'You're Rafe Montero—you could ask any woman to have dinner with you and she would drop anything else she had planned just to be there!'

'The one I'm asking right now doesn't have anything else planned—and yet she's refusing.'

'Rafe—'

'Cairo?'

'You really are—' She broke off frustratedly. '*Why* do you want me to have dinner with you?'

He shrugged. 'Because we both have to eat this evening and we may as well do it together.'

She shook her head. 'If you think, because of what happened last night, that I'm going to sleep with you later, then—'

'Cairo, the invitation was for dinner, not bed,' he cut in firmly.

'Yes…' She eyed him suspiciously.

'Although I doubt I would be averse to the idea later on if you were to—'

'I won't!'

He raised an eyebrow. 'Then I guess I'll settle for dinner.'

She sighed. 'Okay, Rafe, I'll come out to dinner with you. But only,' she continued as he would have smiled, 'if you promise me never to mention that embarrassing incident with the wine ever again.'

'You mean, the incident where you threw off all your clothes and—'

'Yes—that incident!' she glared.

'Fine.' It was difficult for Rafe to hold the smile back this time. 'I promise I'll never—ever—mention that night we had dinner in my hotel room eight years ago and you stripped off and tipped cream all over your—well, all over you—and then offered yourself as dessert—' He broke off, laughing now when Cairo began to pummel his chest with her fists, and was still grinning even as he held both her hands in his. 'It was the best dessert I ever had,' he told her throatily.

It was very hard to remain annoyed with him when he gave her that heart-melting smile, Cairo thought in despair. Especially when she also remembered the night in question—how could she ever forget it? It was the most wildly erotic night....

Which meant it also wasn't a good idea to let Rafe continue to hold her hands in his. Or to look into those sky-blue eyes that seduced her with only a glance. Or to allow him to draw her, slowly, purposefully, towards him—

'No, Rafe!' She broke that seductive spell as she straightened away from him, pulling her hands out of his grasp as she did so. 'I said dinner and I meant just dinner!'

'Pity,' he murmured lazily.

She gave him a reproving look. 'If you would like to sit here and finish your wine, I just need to go to my room to freshen up before we go out.'

Although she'd agreed to the lesser of two evils—going out to a restaurant with Rafe rather than having him stay on here—it still wasn't a good idea, Cairo told herself as she shut her bedroom door firmly behind her and leant back against it.

What game was Rafe playing now?

Whatever it was, she couldn't allow it to continue!

'How on earth did you manage to get a table here at such short notice— No, don't tell me.' Cairo gave a wry smile. 'You're *Rafe Montero*.'

Rafe studied her across the table in what was a very exclusive London restaurant. 'I really wish you wouldn't say my name as if it's some sort of expletive,' he drawled ruefully. 'Besides,' he continued lightly, 'there has to be some compensation to losing every vestige of your privacy just because you chose acting as a career.'

Cairo gave him a considering look, coolly beautiful in

the green figure-hugging, knee-length dress she had changed into after freshening-up, her red hair long and silky. 'I never realized it bothered you.'

He shrugged. 'It wasn't a problem when we were on the Isle of Man. Since the film studio opened up there in the late nineties the islanders have become used to celebrities walking down Strand Street, and they pretty well take it in their stride. Most other places it can be a problem, though. That's the reason exclusive restaurants like this one are so popular with people like you and me. Everyone's a celebrity, so no one stares.'

No, Cairo acknowledged, no one was staring. Now. But the two of them had caused quite a stir when they'd arrived together half an hour ago, probably because of all the publicity about them in the English newspapers this morning….

Rafe gave her a quizzical glance. 'Do you ever regret becoming so well known?'

Did she? She could quite well have done without all the publicity that had surrounded her separation and divorce the last ten months. But otherwise…? No, probably not.

'It goes with the job, I suppose,' she said, before taking a sip of the pink champagne Rafe had ordered. A drink he had first introduced her to on the Isle of Man…

'And do you enjoy the job as much as you thought you would?'

'Sorry?' It was impossible for Cairo to miss the slight edge that had entered his tone.

Rafe shrugged. 'When you were twenty, you were pretty determined to make a name for yourself. At any price, apparently,' he added bitterly.

She put her champagne glass carefully back down on

the table. 'Rafe, if you're going to start being insulting again, then I shall have to leave.'

'I've always assumed your ambition was the reason you married Bond so quickly and moved to the States with him.' He sat back in his chair, his gaze hooded as he looked across the table at her. 'Although I still have no idea why you agreed to talk to him when he came to the villa...' he added speculatively.

Cairo's mouth tightened. 'Rafe, you either desist in pursuing this subject or I *will* leave!'

'I'm just interested, Cairo,' he said. 'After all, we have to talk about something while we eat,' he added lightly as their first course was brought to the table.

Cairo waited until the waiter had left before answering Rafe. 'I do not want to talk about Lionel. Not his visit to the villa yesterday or anything to do with my marriage and divorce.' Unless Rafe wanted her to end up with indigestion! 'Why don't we discuss why it is you've never married, instead?' she added challengingly as she picked up her fork and began to eat her prawns.

Rafe smiled. 'I already told you, that's much less interesting.'

'Because you've never met the right woman,' Cairo taunted. 'And do you really believe that there's a right woman or right man for everyone?'

'Don't you?' Rafe had believed at one time that he had found the right woman for him. But, as it had turned out, he obviously hadn't been the right man for her....

Cairo shook her head. 'I think it's probably wiser—safer—to opt to be with someone of a similar background, career and interests.'

'Like you and Bond, you mean?'

Colour warmed her cheeks. 'Rafe—'

'Or you and me,' he added softly.

No, *not* like her and Rafe! As Cairo had learnt to her cost, she and Rafe had ultimately had absolutely nothing in common. Except a physical awareness that Cairo could feel even now….

Because no matter how she might try to deny it—to ignore it!—last night had only increased her awareness of everything about Rafe, from the silky glossiness of his hair down to the slender elegance of his feet.

She put her fork back down on her plate, her appetite having completely deserted her. 'No, not like you and me,' she denied huskily. 'I think it's time that I left, Rafe—'

'Run away, you mean?' he bit out caustically.

Her eyes flashed darkly. 'I'm *not* running away.'

'Sure you are. It's what you do—it's what you've always done,' he said grimly.

Her throat tightened painfully. 'I should have known your earlier pleasantness wouldn't last.'

'Because you obviously prefer a man with no ba—'

'How dare you?' Cairo gasped.

'How dare I?' Rafe repeated harshly. 'Oh, I think you'll find that where you're concerned I *dare* to do a lot of things— No, Cairo!' He sat forward to place his hand firmly over hers as she went to pick up her evening bag from the table before leaving. 'If you leave now, the headlines in tomorrow's newspapers are going to read, "Cairo and Rafe split up after only two days together".'

'We've never been together—'

'I remember a time when we were *very* together,' he growled.

'I—'

'Don't even think about denying what we once had, Cairo,' he warned.

'What I thought we had,' she corrected tightly.

'I thought we had it, too,' he rasped. 'You must have realized this last two days that I still want you—'

'Rafe, please don't—'

'And you still want me,' he added softly.

'I most certainly do not!' Her face blushed revealingly even as she spoke the lie. For how could Rafe ever doubt that she still wanted him after their lovemaking last night?

His mouth twisted humourlessly. 'Don't make me prove it, Cairo.'

The passionate heat in the blue of his eyes held her captive, the tension between them unbearable. She was barely breathing. Couldn't think. Couldn't speak. Was held in the glitter of that blue gaze like a fawn mesmerized by the headlights of an approaching car.

Because, amazingly, Rafe *was* approaching her! Completely unconcerned with their surroundings, and the other diners, he stood up, reached across the table and curved a hand beneath her chin to tilt her face up to his and place his mouth forcefully down on hers.

To claim.

To possess.

To totally steal Cairo's breath away as she felt herself responding to the hard demand of Rafe's mouth on hers.

Rafe's eyes glittered with emotion when he finally raised his head to look down at her. 'I want to sweep ev-

erything off this table before laying you down on it and—'
He broke off suddenly as they were surrounded by a soft
round of appreciative applause, closing his eyes briefly before straightening to turn and give a brief, ironic bow to
the diners who were smiling at the two of them indul-
gently. 'Scrap that previous headline,' he muttered as he
resumed his seat. '"Cairo and Rafe can't keep their hands
off each other" would probably be more appropriate!'

Cairo was dumbstruck, totally stunned by the unexpect-
edness of Rafe's kiss.

And by her own aching response....

Because for the time that Rafe's mouth had possessed
hers she had totally forgotten their surroundings, would
probably have helped him sweep the plates and glasses
from the table-top before pulling him down on it and making love with him!

'How could you?' she finally gasped shakily, a brief, embarrassed glance around the restaurant telling her that the
other diners—having obviously enjoyed the show!—had
now gone back to their own meals and conversation. 'That
was absolutely— Rafe, how could you?' she said again.

It was more a question of how could he not, Rafe realised as he picked up his glass and took a much-needed
swallow of the champagne. The challenge thrown down,
he simply hadn't been able to stop himself.

The problem was that Cairo made him forget everything
else but her.

Being with her.

Making love with her.

And he still did want to make love with her—
desperately; his body was hard and aching with that need

right now. But one glance at Cairo's pale, accusing face told him that was as likely to happen, following that very public display, as snow in August!

Although surely it had to snow somewhere in the world in August....

His mouth twisted into a humourless smile. 'Perhaps we should just put it down to your own fatalistic allure.'

Cairo glared at him. 'And perhaps we should just put it down to your need to humiliate me!'

Rafe winced. 'Cairo—'

'Don't bother trying to deny it, Rafe, because you know that's exactly what you did.' She picked up her bag, her face flushed with anger now, and her eyes glittering darkly. 'I think we'll just stick with the original headline, hmm?' With one last fiercely scathing glance she stood up and left the table, her head held high as she made her way through the restaurant to where the maître d' held the door open for her leave.

Well, that certainly went well, Rafe, he congratulated himself dourly as he threw the rest of the champagne in his glass to the back of his throat before refilling it. The chances of Cairo now letting him anywhere near her again, let alone making love with her, were once more as likely as that snow in August!

Not good enough odds, Rafe decided as he threw some money down on the table to pay for their meal before following Cairo, his expression grim.

CHAPTER ELEVEN

RAFE caught up with Cairo as she stood on the pavement outside trying to flag down an available cab, something apparently not that easy to find since the new regulation banning the use of private cars from the inner city roads had increased the demand.

'Would it help if I apologized?'

Cairo glanced round sharply at the sound of Rafe's voice behind her, then glared at him in the semi-darkness. 'Not in the least,' she informed him coldly, before turning back to look for a taxi with its light on, at the same time completely aware of the fact that Rafe had moved to stand beside her.

'Cairo, at least let me drive you home—'

'And give you the chance to humiliate me yet again?' she snapped. 'I'd rather walk!' She began to do exactly that.

Rafe fell into step beside her. 'Cairo, you still haven't had hardly anything to eat—'

'And whose fault is that?' she accused as she came to an abrupt halt, positively bristling with anger at him. 'I went out to dinner with you in the first place completely against my better judgement—and look how right my reservations proved to be!' She gave an impatient shake of her head. 'Just face it, Rafe, you and I have absolutely nothing left to say to each other.'

Rafe totally disagreed; the amount of things they had never said to each other would fill a football stadium!

He drew in a ragged breath. 'We used to be able to communicate without words—'

'Is that what all this is about, Rafe?' she challenged. 'If all you want is to go to bed with me again, then why don't you just say so?' Her breasts quickly rose and fell in her agitation.

Because it *wasn't* all he wanted, dammit! But quite what he *did* want Rafe wasn't sure of, either—yet. The only thing he did know, now that he had spent time with Cairo again, was that he wasn't willing to let another eight years pass before he saw or spoke to her again.

'And if it is?' he rasped.

She stared at him for several tense seconds. 'Fine,' she finally said. 'Let's go back to my flat and have sex, then, shall we?' She turned back in the direction Rafe had parked the car.

Rafe stood unmoving, a frown creasing his brow.

He did want Cairo. He wanted to make slow, leisurely love to her again. But not like this. Never like this.

She stopped several feet away to turn back and face him, auburn brows raised in mocking query. 'Changed your mind, Rafe?' she taunted.

He shook his head. 'This isn't like you, Cairo—'

'I thought we had agreed that you don't really know me!' she scorned. 'Last chance, Rafe,' she added. 'A once-in-a-lifetime offer!' Her eyes glittered.

Not with anger, but with tears, Rafe recognized with horror.

Cairo knew she was almost at breaking point. That much more of this conversation and she was going to end up blubbering like a complete idiot. Which was ridiculous. She was a twenty-eight-year-old recently divorced woman, for goodness' sake; most women in her position would have been only too happy to be offered a night of uncomplicated sex with Rafe Montero!

Except Cairo wasn't 'most women' and, loving Rafe as she now knew she still did, it wouldn't be just uncomplicated sex to her, either....

'Time's up, I'm afraid,' she announced with faux brightness as Rafe still made no response to her offer. 'You had your chance and you—' She broke off suddenly as Rafe stepped forward to wrap his arms about her and hold her against him with a gentleness that was completely her undoing.

A sob caught at the back of Cairo's throat as she allowed her head to drop forward onto Rafe's shoulder and the tears began to fall hotly down her cheeks. Then his arms tightened about her as she began to cry in earnest.

'I'm sorry, Cairo,' he groaned into her hair. 'I am *so* sorry!'

Rafe's apology—for what exactly...?—just made her cry all the harder, deep, racking tears that she hadn't allowed to fall during the last ten months. Probably because she had known that once she started she wouldn't be able to stop!

The tears fell like a river now, completely drenching the front of Rafe's shirt as he continued to hold her.

She cried for the loss of Rafe eight years ago.

She cried for her years of being married to Lionel.

She cried for the end of that marriage.

She cried for the loneliness that was so deep inside her it threatened to completely overwhelm her.

But finally there were no more tears left, and instead Cairo became aware of exactly where she was—and in whose arms she was crying.

Rafe Montero's.

The man who had so cruelly broken her heart eight years ago, and had so unwittingly—uncaringly?—shaped those intervening years....

She began to extricate herself from his arms, brushing the tears from her cheeks as she straightened, her gaze avoiding his as she pushed her hair back behind her ears. 'Well, that was a little—embarrassing, wasn't it?' She gave a broken laugh, frowning as she saw the lip gloss smeared across the front of Rafe's now very damp white shirt. 'I'm sorry about that.' She brushed ineffectually at the smear before stepping back. 'If it doesn't come out in the wash let me know and I'll replace the shirt—'

'Cairo.'

'It's silk, right?' Cairo continued. 'Although you'll have to tell me your size, I'm afraid—'

'Cairo.'

'I've never been very good at guessing a man's shirt size. I remember I once—'

'Cairo, just *stop*, will you?' Rafe cut in forcefully, a dark scowl on his brow.

Her gaze was guarded as she looked up at him, her eyes red and puffy from the tears she had cried, her cheeks blotchy and her nose slightly red for the same reason.

She had never looked more beautiful to Rafe....

After an interminable pause, she finally murmured warily, 'Unless it's escaped your notice, Rafe, I have stopped now.'

He gave a rueful smile. 'I noticed.'

She frowned slightly. 'And…?'

'You really do need to eat this evening, so how about we pick up a Chinese takeaway on the way back to your apartment?' He shrugged. 'It's the least I can do after behaving so badly I made you miss dinner,' he added persuasively as her eyes widened. 'We can make it a Chinese takeaway for one, if that's what you would prefer?' he offered as Cairo continued to look at him suspiciously.

'If we make it a meal for two, what happens afterwards?'

Rafe's mouth tightened. 'Afterwards I'll leave,' he said curtly. 'Hell, Cairo, just because I don't have someone in my life at the moment doesn't mean I spend my every waking hour trying to devise ways of getting you into bed!' he added as she still hesitated.

Well, not his *every* waking hour…but Rafe had to admit—to himself, at least!—that he hadn't thought of too much else since arriving at the villa two days ago and finding Cairo there, and it had got even worse since their stormy lovemaking the previous evening.

'I didn't imagine that you did,' she said dryly.

He quirked dark brows. 'No?'

'No!'

'Okay, then,' Rafe said. 'So do we get Chinese food for one or two?'

She needed her head examined, Cairo knew, to even be thinking of prolonging this evening with Rafe. And yet she *was* thinking about it….

No doubt the two of them would end up arguing again before the evening was over. They seemed to do little else nowadays. And yet Cairo still felt a certain reluctance to say a final goodbye to him….

'Two,' she decided at last. 'I'll probably have cause to regret that, too, but—'

'You never did know quite when to stop talking,' Rafe remarked as they began to walk back to the car.

Her eyes narrowed. 'I'm already starting to regret it—'

'Please just get in the car, Cairo,' he instructed as he opened the passenger door for her, having no intention of arguing with her again before they had eaten.

No doubt it would be another matter afterwards!

'So you're going back to work, after all? And in the theatre?' Rafe couldn't hide his surprise as the two of them sat on the carpeted floor in the sitting-room of Cairo's apartment using chopsticks to eat the Chinese food directly from the cartons, and finishing off the bottle of red wine Cairo had opened earlier.

Cairo had suggested warming plates and laying the table, but Rafe had vetoed the idea, opting for this less formal way of dining once Cairo had changed into comfortable worn jeans and a green cashmere sweater so that she could sit cross-legged on the floor.

'I start rehearsals in a little under two weeks and open in three.' Cairo nodded as she reached over to pick up a prawn.

Rafe found himself watching as she lifted the chopsticks and deftly popped the food into her mouth, her lips bare of gloss—well, they would be, as most of it was still on his shirt!

He had always loved Cairo's mouth. The fullness of her lips. The way they tilted slightly at the corners. Their pouting softness when he kissed them....

'I'm really looking forward to it,' she added, before licking the sauce from those delectable lips.

Rafe dragged his gaze away, aware that it was only the way he was also sitting cross-legged on the carpet that prevented Cairo from seeing his purely physical response to the provocation that was her mouth.

He nodded. 'I remember you saying years ago that it was your first love. But it's hard work, and there's no money in it—'

'I'm not interested in the money, Rafe.' Cairo turned to him impatiently. 'I want the immediacy of the theatre. The audience response as each performance is just slightly different. The adrenalin rush each night just before you step onto the stage for the first time.' She shook her head, her eyes glowing. 'There's nothing quite like it.'

Rafe could see that for Cairo there wasn't.

His own years of performing off-Broadway, before he was 'discovered' by a movie producer, seemed like a lifetime ago, but he did still remember that adrenalin rush.

He was just surprised, that after years of starring in increasingly popular box-office hits—the millions Cairo was paid for each performance increasing as a result—she was actually going back to the gruelling demand of theatre work with very little monetary reward.

'Maybe I'll come to your opening night…' he murmured.

Cairo gave him a sharp glance. 'What on earth for?'

He tensed. 'Why not?'

Admittedly this last hour of just sitting on the floor, eating informally and chatting about everything and nothing—mainly nothing, as it was less controversial!—had been very pleasant after the previously fraught forty-eight hours.

But the last thing Cairo needed was to know that Rafe

was sitting out in the audience on the first night of her return to the theatre after a break of almost eight years.

What if she was awful?

Making films was totally different from working on stage—no retakes for one thing!—and Cairo was nervous enough already without the added pressure of knowing Rafe was sitting beyond the footlights watching her.

'I would really rather you didn't, Rafe.' She grimaced.

He frowned his irritation. 'Why the hell not?' he repeated harshly.

Well, Cairo supposed it would have been too much to expect 'very pleasant' to last for too much longer!

She sat back. 'Why would you want to bother? Just so that you can see me fall flat on my face?'

'That's damned unfair, Cairo, and you know it!' Rafe protested.

'No, I don't know it, Rafe.' Cairo shook her head. 'We aren't really even friends any more, so why on earth would you want to come to the theatre to watch me on my opening night?'

His eyes were glacial. 'Maybe I would just like to wish you well?'

'A bouquet of flowers would do that, don't you think?'

No, Rafe didn't. He found himself annoyed far beyond reason by Cairo's dismissal of his suggestion. Dammit, he wanted to come to London in three weeks' time and watch her opening performance!

She looked about eighteen again, sitting there in her tight jeans and that soft green sweater, her face almost bare of make-up, her hair pulled up into a band at her crown, leaving the long arch of her neck vulnerably bare.

Rafe's anger faded as quickly as it had flared into life. 'Are yellow roses still your favourite flowers?' he asked huskily.

Cairo gave him a startled look. 'I— Yes. Yes, they are.'

His mouth twisted self-derisively. 'You thought I'd forgotten.'

'I—' She broke off to once again moisten the pout of her lips with the tip of her tongue. 'It's been eight years, Rafe,' she pointed out.

Eight or eighty, Rafe hadn't forgotten a single thing about this woman's likes and dislikes. Either in bed or out of it!

She gave him a teasing smile. 'A lot of other women have passed through your—'

'Cairo,' Rafe bit out warningly.

'—life, since then,' she continued ruefully.

Rafe held her gaze with his as he reached over and plucked the chopsticks from her unresisting fingers. 'And I couldn't tell you the favourite flower of a single one of them,' he admitted softly.

Cairo blinked, totally disorientated by the way the atmosphere between them had once again changed from being charged with anger to sexual tension instead.

She shook her head as she nervously moistened her lips—

'Don't *do* that, Cairo!' Rafe groaned.

'Don't do what?' She was barely breathing as Rafe's head slowly bent towards hers.

'This,' he murmured throatily as his tongue stroked softly against her lips, lightly, erotically, igniting a warmth deep in the pit of Cairo's stomach as Rafe continued the caress.

Cairo closed her eyes as she gave herself up to the sensation, to that heat spreading to her thighs and causing her breasts to swell in tingling awareness as Rafe's tongue now dipped temptingly between her parted lips.

She groaned low in her throat as Rafe's lips slowly sipped and tasted hers and he pulled her closer against the hardness of his chest. Cairo's hands moved up of their own volition so that she could entangle her fingers in the dark thickness of his hair as he deepened the kiss to one of hungry demand.

Rafe had no idea how long he and Cairo kissed, deeply, hungrily, her breasts pressed against him as one of his hands moved beneath the softness of her sweater to caress the length of her spine from her nape to the dipping hollow at its base, her skin like silky velvet beneath his touch.

But it wasn't enough; he needed to kiss that velvety skin, too, wanted to cup her breasts in his hands and worship them with his lips and tongue until he heard those little noises in Cairo's throat that told him she was about to explode.

Dammit, he wished at that moment that he had the petals of dozens of yellow roses to scatter over the carpet before laying Cairo's naked body down on them as he parted her thighs and plunged his aching arousal inside their moist heat!

But instead, as Rafe attempted to lie down on the carpet with her, he found himself—and Cairo—surrounded by the smell and cartons of half-eaten Chinese food!

His mouth left hers and he raised his head to look at the offending cartons. 'Hell!' he muttered in frustration.

'I don't suppose chicken chow mein has the same appeal as whipped cream, does it?'

Rafe turned slowly back to look at Cairo, a smile curving his own lips as he saw the gleam of laughter in her eyes. 'We could try it, I suppose…'

'No, we could not!' Cairo protested laughingly as she turned on her side away from the food, taking Rafe with her so that she now lay on his chest. 'That's disgusting!' She shuddered just at the thought of those rapidly cooling noodles against her skin, slowly sobering as she found herself now looking down at Rafe, his eyes warm with intent. 'I'm not sure this is a good idea, Rafe,' she breathed.

He raised a hand to curve it about her cheek as his thumb moved caressingly against her lower lip. 'Live dangerously,' he encouraged.

That maybe wasn't such a good idea, either, when she had just spent the last eight years living with the repercussions of the last time she had acted so impulsively!

'Cairo, you think too much…' Rafe groaned as he obviously saw her uncertainty.

'First I talk too much, and now I think too much, too?'

'Sometimes you do, yes—'

'Well, one of us needs to, don't you think?' she asked tensely.

'You're deliberately trying to provoke an argument,' he said slowly. 'Why is that, Cairo? Why do you need to keep putting me at a distance?'

'You're hardly at a distance at this moment!' Her breasts were pressed against the hardness of his chest, her legs lying between his, the hardness of his arousal straining against her own heated thighs….

But the mood was broken, along with that tenuous link between them that had temporarily allowed Cairo to forget all the reasons why she should not allow herself to be here like this with Rafe.

'I'm not trying to provoke an argument.' She rolled away from him to sit up with her arms wrapped about her bent knees. 'I just don't want to make another mistake where you're concerned,' she explained.

Rafe sat up slowly, his gaze deliberately holding hers. 'I don't believe we were a mistake the first time around.'

She shrugged. 'You're entitled to your opinion, of course.'

His eyes narrowed. 'Exactly why did you finish things between us before, Cairo?'

She gave an impatient shake of her head. 'Isn't it a little bit late for the two of us to be having this conversation?'

'It's certainly long overdue, I would have thought,' he grated.

She sighed. 'You know exactly why I stopped seeing you.'

'You wanted to marry Bond—'

'You and I had parted before I so much as went out to dinner with him!' she defended herself heatedly.

'You broke up with me at lunchtime and went out with Bond the same evening!' Rafe's voice rose, too. 'I went shopping that morning and when the two of us met up for lunch, you told me that you didn't want to see me any more, that you needed to be free to concentrate on your career!' He scowled. 'Considering you went out with Bond that same evening, got engaged to him three days later, and then married him three weeks after that, your concentration must have been incredible!'

Cairo gasped at the insult. 'Don't try and turn this around on *me*, Rafe.'

'Who else am I supposed to blame?'

'I should try looking at your affair with Pamela Raines, if I were you!' she accused as she stood up to pace the room restlessly. 'You even spent the afternoon of my wedding in bed with her!'

Rafe scowled darkly. 'Well, I was hardly going to attend the wedding and wish you well, now, was—' He broke off to give her a narrow-eyed look. 'How the hell do you know how I spent that afternoon?'

Cairo glared at him. 'How do you think I know?'

'I have no idea—' He stopped and looked at her disbelievingly. '*Pamela* told you?'

Cairo nodded. 'It was the excuse she gave when she arrived extremely late and dishevelled to the wedding reception, yes.'

Rafe shook his head. 'I can't believe she would— Why on earth did she do that?'

For the same reason the other woman had told Cairo three weeks previously that she and Rafe had been having an affair for weeks—because it was the truth!

That morning Rafe claimed to have gone shopping, Cairo had finished filming early and decided to go to Rafe's hotel suite, only to have the door opened—shockingly!—by a completely nude Pamela Raines, her hair rumpled, the bedclothes in disarray on the bed in the room behind her. Pamela's sympathy had been unbearable as she'd told Cairo that Rafe had been trying to tell her about the two of them for days now, but that he knew she was in love with him and was worried about how she would react if he told her about himself and Pamela, that he feared she might do something stupid.

Cairo had saved him the trouble and broken things off with him instead!

Calmly.

Coolly.

And then she *had* done something totally stupid!

Lionel had been asking Cairo to have dinner with him for several weeks, ever since his arrival in London to see how filming was going, and when he'd asked Cairo out again later that same afternoon, she had accepted. Still in the same reckless 'I'll show Rafe' state of mind, she had also accepted Lionel's whirlwind marriage proposal only three days later....

Cairo frowned now. 'I would really rather not talk about your affair with Pamela any more, Rafe—'

'There was *no* affair, dammit!' he rasped. 'I did spend the afternoon of your wedding in bed with Pamela, yes, but it was the first and last time—'

'It had been going on for weeks before my wedding!' Cairo accused, her voice rising agitatedly.

'What? Cairo, I categorically did *not* have an affair with Pamela Raines before your wedding!' Rafe scowled.

'She tells a completely different story!'

Rafe eyed her uncertainly now. 'She does?'

'Yes! Now will you please leave, Rafe?' she requested tautly. 'This whole conversation is giving me a headache.'

Rafe looked at her searchingly. The frown between her eyes, the strain he could see in reflected those dark brown eyes, the hollows of her pale cheeks, and the thin, unhappy line of her mouth, confirmed that she did indeed have a headache.

But he couldn't just leave it there. 'Cairo, you have to believe me—'

'Rafe, I don't *have* to do anything where you're concerned,' she cut in. 'I make it a policy never to talk about the past,' she added firmly as he would have spoken again. 'It serves no purpose but to open up old wounds—'

'What if those wounds never healed in the first place?' he asked.

She gave a derisive smile. 'I'm sorry to disappoint you, Rafe, but I was over you long ago.'

'I wasn't referring to *your* wounds, Cairo….'

Cairo became very still as she now looked at Rafe as searchingly as he had looked at her seconds ago.

He looked grim and determined, with an underlying impatience—he certainly didn't look anywhere near as devastated, or broken-hearted, as she had been that morning eight years ago when she'd discovered he was having an affair with Pamela Raines.

And all the talking in the world couldn't change that!

'It's far too late for the two of us to talk about this, Rafe,' she insisted. 'I have my own life now, and you have yours—and those lives have no common ground,' she said with certainty.

'We still want each other—'

'You're talking about sex again, Rafe,' Cairo interrupted. 'And, yes, I admit, having met you again, that it's interesting to realize the sexual attraction is still there,' she conceded. 'But the truth of the matter is I don't want any sort of relationship in my life right now, sexual or otherwise,' she added coldly.

The absolute certainty in her tone told Rafe that Cairo meant exactly what she was saying.

Which left him precisely where?

As far as Cairo was concerned, obviously nowhere.

But that didn't mean Rafe didn't intend finding out for himself exactly what had happened to the two of them all those years ago. Because one thing this conversation with Cairo had definitely told him was that there were things about that time he had been completely unaware of. Not that any of that was going to change how Cairo now felt about him, but *he* wanted—no, needed—to know, dammit!

He drew in a deep breath. 'This is goodbye, then, Cairo.'

'It would appear so, yes,' she clipped.

He gave a rueful smile. 'Friends usually kiss each other goodbye, don't they?'

Cairo gave a tight smile. 'I thought the one thing we had just agreed on was that the two of us can never be friends.'

Rafe shook his head. 'You can't seriously believe that I mean to never see you again?' Just the thought of that happening made his stomach muscles clench.

Her laugh sounded forced. 'You survived without seeing me for eight years, Rafe. How do you suppose we managed that, anyway?' she mused. 'With us both living in Los Angeles and mixing with the same crowd of actor friends and acquaintances?'

Rafe knew exactly how they had avoided meeting each other—whenever he had known Cairo and Lionel were going to be at a party or an awards ceremony, he had avoided going himself, the thought of seeing the two of them together enough to turn his stomach.

'Incredible to believe, isn't it?' he acknowledged dryly.

A miracle, was how Cairo would have described it!

She had lived in nervous trepidation for the first year of her marriage to Lionel just at the thought of accidentally finding herself face to face with Rafe again. But as the months, and then years, had passed without that happening, she had put the idea of it from her mind.

Only for it to happen eight years later at a villa in the South of France, of all places!

'Incredible,' she echoed, before giving Rafe a pointed look.

He nodded. 'It's time I was leaving,' he said. 'But I'm sure it isn't going to be another eight years before the two of us meet again, Cairo,' he promised huskily.

She gave him a startled look. 'You are?'

Rafe shrugged. 'If not before, then we will most certainly see each other again at Simon Raphael's christening.'

Cairo had completely forgotten that Margo and Jeff had earlier asked if the two of them, along with Jeff's brother Neil, would be Simon's godparents.

'Of course,' she acknowledged stiffly. 'I'll—' She broke off the polite adage—she would not look forward to seeing Rafe again, either at the christening or before! 'I'll see you to the door,' she said instead, before crossing the room to open the door for him to leave.

Rafe paused in the open doorway. 'It really has been good to see you again, Cairo.'

'Of course it has,' she came back dryly.

His mouth twisted. 'Cynicism doesn't suit you.'

She shrugged. 'It's a little difficult to be any other way when— Never mind,' she dismissed brightly. 'Have a good flight back to Cannes tomorrow,' she added politely.

Rafe had no intention of going ahead with his original plan of returning to the Cannes Film Festival tomorrow. Not when Pamela Raines, the person he was now determined to talk to, was in Los Angeles....

'Thanks,' Rafe accepted noncommittally.

'You're welcome.'

'Cairo—'

'I'm sure it doesn't usually take you this long to say goodbye, Rafe!' Cairo snapped, her nerves stretched to breaking point. This evening had already been difficult enough without the added strain of this lingering goodbye!

'No,' he acknowledged. 'But, then, this really isn't goodbye, Cairo,' he said, running a single finger down the warmth of her cheek before finally taking his leave.

Cairo hastily closed the door behind him before leaning weakly back against it.

She accepted that there was no way she could get out of being her new nephew's godmother without actually hurting Margo and Jeff's feelings. Nor could she hope that Rafe would change his mind about being godfather to his namesake. But the christening was sure to be weeks, possibly months away—plenty of time for Cairo to have built back her crumbling defences where Rafe was concerned.

She hoped....

CHAPTER TWELVE

'WHO are these roses from?' Cairo asked Josie, the wardrobe lady, as she entered her dressing-room at the theatre on opening night and saw a huge vase of yellow roses in pride of place amongst the other half dozen bouquets that had been delivered.

'There is a card, I believe,' Josie told her distractedly as she examined Cairo's costume for any last-minute problems.

But Cairo didn't need to read the card to know who the yellow roses had come from! Did that mean, despite her having asked him not to, that Rafe was out there in the first-night theatre audience, after all?

Oh, God…!

She sat down abruptly on the chair in front of the dresser, her hand shaking slightly as she picked the card out from amongst the beautiful yellow blooms and read the words printed on it: 'I believe the correct term is break a leg, but I would really rather you didn't break anything. Will you have supper with me afterwards?'

There was no signature beneath the message, but after their conversation three weeks ago Cairo knew that only Rafe could have sent her the yellow roses.

But why had he?

And why, after Cairo had made it so clear to him that she didn't want to see him alone again, was he inviting her to have supper with him after the play ended?

She wouldn't go, of course.

She couldn't go.

Because, as hard as she had tried, Cairo's response to the arrival of these yellow roses told her that she hadn't managed to rebuild her defences against Rafe in the last three weeks at all!

That perhaps she never would....

'You were wonderful, Cairo!' Lionel took her in his arms to beam at her proudly once he had managed to make his way to her side through the crowd in her dressing-room.

'Thank you.' Cairo glowed, still too excited by the triumph of the evening to question what her ex-husband was actually doing here.

As she had stood in the wings earlier waiting to make her first entrance a complete calm had come over her, and she had forgotten everything—and everyone!—else as she had concentrated on the performance ahead.

The spontaneous applause, followed by numerous curtain calls, and then the director coming onto the stage to present her with a huge bouquet before hugging and kissing her, had been more than enough to convince her she had succeeded.

'You were right, Cairo, this is where you belong,' Lionel told her ruefully. 'It's a little mad in here right now.' He laughed softly as more people tried to crowd into her dressing-room. 'Will you meet me for lunch tomorrow? I

have something important to tell you,' he added persuasively as Cairo started to refuse.

She didn't want to meet with Lionel tomorrow; she had
even less to say to him than she did to Rafe, but the genuine
appeal in his face was more than she could withstand.
'Okay, Lionel, I'll have lunch with you tomorrow,' she
agreed reluctantly.

He grinned his satisfaction. 'One o'clock at Gregory's?'
He mentioned the name of the restaurant she'd had dinner
at with Rafe three weeks ago.

'One o'clock at Spencer's,' she corrected, opting for a
restaurant in which she and Lionel had occasionally dined
in the past when they had been in London.

But not so often that it had become 'their' place…

Whatever Lionel had to tell her, she didn't want him to
get the wrong idea about her acceptance of this luncheon
invitation.

'I really do have to go now, Lionel,' she said, laughing
at the loud pop of several champagne bottles being opened.

'Sure you do.' He nodded. 'This is definitely your night.
But I'll look forward to seeing you tomorrow.' He gave her
another hug before kissing her lightly on the lips.

Suddenly Cairo became aware of the deadly silence that
had fallen over a room that seconds ago had been full of
laughter and loud conversation. She stepped back slowly
to release herself from Lionel's arms and glanced over towards the door.

Rafe!

He stood in the doorway holding another bottle of
champagne, very tall, his dark hair silky, and looking incredibly handsome in a black evening suit, snowy white

shirt and black bow tie—and with an expression on that ruggedly arrogant face that was enigmatically unreadable.

The room was full of other members of the cast, the director and backstage crew, as well as family and friends—and all of them, without exception, were staring at the famous actor standing in the doorway of Cairo Vaughn's dressing-room!

'Everybody out, and give Cairo some space,' Paul, the director, called authoritatively even as he began to shoo people out of the room.

'Please don't leave on my account,' Rafe drawled politely.

But it was a politeness that no one, not even Margo and Jeff—the traitors!—took any notice of as Rafe stepped aside and they filed out of Cairo's dressing-room, leaving only Cairo, Lionel, and Rafe—and an awkward silence.

'Time I was going, too,' Lionel remarked, giving Cairo a wry smile before strolling over to the door. He stopped in front of Rafe, the two men looking at each other in silent challenge for several seconds before he spoke again. 'She's too good for both of us, Montero.'

Rafe gave a slight inclination of his head. 'I'm aware of that,' he grated harshly.

'I hope that you are.'

'Lionel—'

'It's okay, Cairo,' Rafe said, before turning back to the older man. 'I'm glad we understand each other,' he said quietly.

Cairo couldn't even begin to understand what had just transpired between the two men, what underlying message their brief conversation had carried—a message that excluded her while somehow being about her.

Men!

'I'll see you at one o'clock tomorrow, Cairo,' Lionel called back, before closing the door behind him as he left.

Cairo was instantly aware of the fact that she was still in the slinky black dress she had worn for the final scene, and that her stage make-up was much too harsh, too over-emphasized in the confines of her dressing-room.

'I look a mess.' She turned away to take one of the cleansers from the packet on her dresser before bending down in front of the mirror to begin wiping the make-up from her cheeks. She looked at Rafe's reflection in the mirror. 'Did you see the play? Or have you just arrived?'

'You do not look a mess,' he assured her as he stepped further into the room. 'And, yes, I saw the play. You were magnificent. Wonderful. Electrifying! I doubt a single person took their eyes off you the whole time you were on the stage.'

Pleasure warmed her cheeks. 'I—received the roses, too, thank you.'

He held up the bottle of champagne. 'Do you have any glasses left in here for this or did they take them all away with them?' he asked lightly as he deftly popped the cork on the bottle.

'I have some in here.' She opened the cupboard beneath the dresser. 'What would you have done with this if I'd bombed?' she teased as she held the glasses out for him to pour the champagne into.

'Then I would have collected the second bottle I've got in the car and made sure you became very, very drunk!' Rafe said.

'I think I'm already drunk on success,' she admitted glowingly.

Rafe held up his own glass of champagne. 'To you,' he toasted her huskily. 'You were an absolute triumph tonight, Cairo.' He sipped the champagne, his gaze not leaving the flushed beauty of her face.

He had literally been mesmerized by Cairo the moment she had stepped on the stage earlier tonight, the complete hush that had fallen over the theatre for the whole of her performance, followed by all those curtain calls, telling him that he wasn't alone in his admiration.

He had always known Cairo could act, but tonight, in the setting that she loved best, she had far outshone any of her previous performances on screen.

'I don't want to keep you from the party…' He smiled wryly as he heard the sounds of the rest of the cast and crew still celebrating outside in the hallway.

She laughed. 'It will go on for most of the night, I'm sure.'

'I'm sure of it, too.' Rafe nodded. 'Did I see Margo and Jeff in here a few minutes ago?'

'You did,' Cairo confirmed. 'Rafe, I doubt I'm going to be able to get away for supper for several more hours yet,' she told him apologetically as the noise outside became louder still.

He had already guessed that. But this was Cairo's night and she deserved to enjoy every moment of it.

He smiled reassuringly; at least Cairo hadn't said she didn't want to have supper with him, only that she couldn't right now… 'I thought maybe I would go and have a drink with Margo and Jeff, and the two of us could meet up at my hotel for supper later.'

She grimaced. 'I may not be in any condition to eat supper later!'

'Then I'll just put you to bed and we can have breakfast together in the morning.'

Cairo became very still, sipping her champagne as she thought over what he had just said. Rafe's intention was for them to have supper together at his hotel? Or breakfast! She gave him an overbright smile. 'You could just stay and join in the party?'

'You saw what happened just now…' He shook his head. 'This is your night, Cairo—you don't need Rafe Montero muscling in on the act.'

Her smile widened. 'No doubt it would add to my kudos if he did!'

Rafe threw his head back and laughed. 'Cairo Vaughn doesn't need any added kudos,' he teased.

He seemed different, Cairo realized, frowning at him slightly. Less harsh. With none of that sarcasm and scorn that had been such a part of him when they had met again three weeks ago. But he unnerved her just the same—still making her feel totally aware of him and the response of her own body to his proximity.

Not a good idea!

She deliberately changed the subject. 'Congratulations on winning the Best Director award at Cannes, by the way.' Although, strangely, Cairo had read in the newspapers that Rafe hadn't been there to collect the award himself, after all, that his assistant director had collected it on Rafe's behalf….

'Thank you.' He inclined his head in acknowledgement, the intense blue of his gaze not leaving her face. 'Will you have supper with me later, Cairo? There are some things I need to say to you,' he added gruffly even as Cairo would have made a polite refusal. 'To explain.'

He was hard to resist in this softer, less accusatory mood. More like the Rafe she had known eight years ago. Or the Rafe she had thought she knew, Cairo reminded herself firmly.

She shook her head. 'I really don't think that's a good idea, Rafe.'

He stepped forward to take one of her hands in his and raise it to his lips, his gaze once again holding hers as he pressed a lingering kiss to the back of it. 'Just do this one last thing for me, Cairo,' he begged. 'After that— well, it will be up to you whether or not we see each other again.'

Cairo was totally unnerved now, her hand tingling from the touch of his lips against her skin, every part of her completely aware of him, her breasts feeling full and aroused, the beginnings of warmth between her thighs.

It was the adrenalin, the excitement of a successful opening night, and not Rafe who was the cause of that, she told herself impatiently as she pointedly removed her hand from his. 'Perhaps we could meet some time tomorrow instead?'

He raised an eyebrow. 'I believe you already have a luncheon engagement at one o'clock.'

Cairo had wondered if he had overheard all of her conversation with Lionel. Now she knew.

'We could meet later in the afternoon,' Cairo offered briskly. 'I don't need to be back at the theatre until seven o'clock in the evening.'

'If that's the best you can do.'

He couldn't exactly blame Cairo for her reluctance to meet and talk with him again. Not after the way he had treated her three weeks ago!

She looked at him searchingly. 'Rafe, what's all this about?'

Rafe debated how much to tell her now. This was hardly the time or the place for the conversation he wanted to have with Cairo, and he should have realized that before writing the message on the card he'd had delivered with the yellow roses.

He straightened. 'Redemption, Cairo,' he admitted huskily. 'It's about redemption.'

Her eyes widened, her expression wary. 'Now you really have intrigued me, Rafe,' she said slowly.

'Enough to change your mind about supper?'

She hesitated. 'Maybe,' she finally allowed cautiously.

Rafe smiled. 'I have a suite at The Ritz if you should decide to join me later, after all…'

She would be stupid to do so, Cairo knew. Stupid, as well as certifiably insane. But then, her feelings for Rafe had never been exactly sane in the first place!

'We'll see,' she answered noncommittally. 'Although it could be very late,' she added as the revelry outside seemed to become even louder.

'Any time will be fine.'

Cairo really was intrigued by this conversation, couldn't even begin to imagine what Rafe wanted to talk to her about. But the question was, was she intrigued enough to put herself in the position of joining Rafe at his hotel later on tonight—or tomorrow morning?

Her brain told her a firm no.

But her heart—and every other tinglingly aware part of her—said yes!

'As I said, we'll see,' she repeated. 'Now, if you wouldn't mind, I have to change before joining the others….'

It was the best he could hope for, Rafe knew. In fact, in the circumstances, it was more than he had hoped for!

He knew now that he bore a large part of the blame for Cairo having been hurt enough eight years ago to end their relationship. Pamela might have been the instrument of that hurt, but Cairo had only been twenty; he'd been sophisticated enough in the ways of women, had known Pamela well enough, to have foreseen what had happened and stopped it before Cairo had become involved, too. Then getting drunk and sleeping with Pamela on Cairo's wedding day had only confused matters even more—he should never have done that as it had given Pamela even more ammunition against Cairo.

'Of course,' he accepted lightly. 'Enjoy the rest of your party, Cairo—you deserve it.'

But Cairo didn't enjoy the party, or the club they all spilled out to once they had left the theatre; instead she remained totally distracted by her earlier conversation with Rafe and could think of little else.

Why did Rafe need redemption?

Or perhaps it wasn't his own redemption he had been referring to…?

CHAPTER THIRTEEN

IT WAS almost three o'clock in the morning when Rafe opened the door of his hotel suite to Cairo, although the challenging expression on her face as she swept past him and into the sitting-room wasn't exactly encouraging.

She looked gorgeous, of course, her hair loose down the length of her spine, the green off-the-shoulder, knee-length dress clinging to all of her beautiful curves, the sheerness of the material clearly outlining the firm thrust of her breasts. Her legs were long and silky smooth, her feet thrust into matching green high-heeled sandals.

Gorgeous and very self assured—and not a little annoyed, Rafe acknowledged ruefully as he saw the flush of anger in her cheeks and her glittering eyes as she stood facing him across the room.

'Would you like to sit down?' he invited.

'I'm not staying,' she snapped.

She was very annoyed, Rafe realized regretfully. Mainly with him, but a little with herself, he would guess—for having come here at all....

'Have you had enough champagne or would you care for some more?' He indicated the bottle he'd had cooling in an ice-bucket on the table for the last two hours, along with two fluted glasses.

Cairo eyed Rafe impatiently, most of that impatience directed at herself as she felt herself responding to how devastatingly handsome he looked.

His overlong dark hair was slightly tousled, as if he had been running his fingers through it before she arrived, and he had removed his dinner jacket and bow tie, the white silk evening shirt fitting perfectly over his wide shoulders, the black trousers tailored to powerful hips and the long length of his legs.

'No, thanks,' she refused. 'As I said, I'm not staying.' She looked at him narrowly. 'You made an intriguing remark earlier, Rafe—something about redemption?—and I want to know what you meant by it.'

He grimaced. 'Do you mind if I have some?' He indicated the champagne.

'Knock yourself out.'

This was going to be harder than he had imagined, Rafe thought as he moved to uncork the bottle and poured some of the pink champagne into a glass, taking a slow sip before turning back to face her.

At twenty Cairo had been very young, as well as very naïve and trusting; now she was eight years older and looked as if she trusted very little any more—especially anything to do with him!

'It's very late, Rafe,' she pointed out as she moved to do what she had said she didn't want to do, and sat down in one of the armchairs. 'And I really am very tired.' She gave a weary sigh, leant her head back against the chair and closed her eyes.

Rafe could see the truth of that now that her cheeks were no longer flushed and he couldn't see her eyes sparkling with temper. Also, that air of vulnerability he had noticed about her three weeks ago was back in evidence.

An impression that was instantly dispelled as she opened her eyes and straightened in the chair, ready for the attack. 'So, what did you want to say to me, Rafe?'

So much. And yet so little. The whole sum of what Rafe wanted to say to Cairo could be said in three words. Just three little words. But he was getting ahead of himself, he cautioned; Cairo would probably laugh in his face if he said those particular words to her now without bothering to explain....

He moved to sit in the chair opposite hers. 'First of all we have to go back eight years—'

'Why do we?' She tensed. 'It was all so long ago, and surely has no bearing on our lives now?'

'It has every bearing on here and now,' he insisted. 'Cairo, when I left you three weeks ago, instead of returning to Cannes, I flew back to the States.'

So that was why he hadn't been in Cannes to collect his award himself, Cairo realized guardedly. But what of it? What possible interest could it be to her what Rafe had done three weeks ago, or at any other time, for that matter?

Rafe's mouth was a thin, uncompromising line. 'Cairo, I went back to Los Angeles to see Pamela Raines—'

'Rafe, I don't want to know who you went to see!' Cairo told him forcefully as she stood up in an immediate reaction to hearing that name. 'You are unbelievable, do you know that?' She glared at him. 'Not content with having interrupted my holiday with Daisy, you've now ruined my first night back at the theatre, too, with your enigmatic requests to talk to me! Why don't you go and ruin someone else's life, Rafe, and just stay out of mine?' She was breathing hard with the strength of her emotions. 'Damn you,' she finally bit out furiously. 'How *dare* you come here and talk to me about Pamela Raines?'

He sat forward in his chair, his expression grim. 'Cairo, I'm trying to tell you that I did not, nor did I ever, have an affair with Pamela Raines. I only ever slept with her that one time on your wedding day—'

'That's a lie, Rafe,' she interrupted angrily.

'No. No, it isn't.'

'You were having an affair with her while you were still seeing me, dammit!'

'I know now that *you* thought I was—'

'I didn't *think* anything, Rafe. Nor did I imagine it,' Cairo assured him icily. 'I finished filming early one morning and came to your hotel suite. She— Pamela answered the door. She was stark naked— The bed was a mess— Her clothes were all over the floor—'

'But where were *my* clothes, Cairo?' he put in softly.

'I—well—wherever you were, you were obviously wearing them!' she dismissed with a wave of her hand. 'What does it matter where your clothes were, Rafe?' She scowled at him darkly. 'What matters is that you were obviously *not* wearing them a short time before I arrived so unexpectedly, because you and Pamela had been— God, it still makes me feel ill to know that you—that you were sleeping with both of us at the same time!'

Rafe gave a parody of a smile. 'Now probably isn't the right time to point out that what you thought I was doing with both of you had nothing to do with *sleeping*....'

Cairo's eyes narrowed to livid slits. 'Not unless you want me to hit you over the head with that champagne bottle, no!'

Rafe's smile became a little more genuine. 'Perhaps you should have done that after you thought you had caught me out with Pamela? At least that way we could have talked this through when I woke up!'

'I could no more have sat down and talked with you about your affair with Pamela then than I can now—'

'There was *no* affair, Cairo,' Rafe repeated firmly. 'Not then. And most certainly not now.'

'You—'

'Not now. And certainly *not* eight years ago,' Rafe reiterated evenly, his gaze steadily holding hers. 'Pamela had made it more than obvious that was what she wanted, but I wasn't interested.'

His mouth twisted self-derisively. 'I was only interested in the red-haired witch who had knocked me off my feet the very first moment I looked at her…You, Cairo,' he added so that there should be absolutely no doubt in her mind.

Cairo looked at him searchingly for several long seconds, seeing only sincerity in his expression. Sincerity and a plea for her to believe him.

'So you didn't go to bed with her that morning?'

'I didn't,' Rafe said patiently. 'In fact, until you mentioned it three weeks ago, I'd had no idea that that was what you had always believed.'

'But I know what I saw, Rafe,' Cairo pointed out. 'So how do you explain it?'

He stood up restlessly. 'It was only when you insisted that I had been involved with Pamela for weeks that I even suspected— Don't you understand, Cairo? What you saw in my hotel room was totally engineered by Pamela!'

Cairo shook her head in denial. 'Don't think you can make a fool of me again, Rafe—'

'I assure you I'm not trying to do that.' Rafe sighed. 'That morning at the hotel Pamela charmed one of the housemaids into letting her into my suite before throwing off all her clothes and just sitting there waiting for me to return, absolutely sure that once I did, I wouldn't be able to resist her.' He grimaced. 'Unfortunately, you came to my hotel suite before I did. But, never one to lose an opportunity, Pamela rethought her plan and deliberately turned the situation to her advantage by giving you the impression that she and I had spent the morning in bed together and that I'd been cheating on you with her for weeks!'

Cairo stared at him, sure that what Rafe was saying was too fantastic to be true. And yet, at the same time, it was too fantastic to have been made up, either!

She swallowed hard. 'Why would she do something like that?'

'Pamela is well known for wanting—and getting—her own way. For having any man she wants. When she made it obvious that she wanted me, I tried to let her know I wasn't interested. But I should have known—should have guessed— that Pamela wouldn't just accept that, that she would do something. I had absolutely no idea what had happened that morning at the hotel, Cairo, which is why I was so totally stunned when we met for lunch and you told me it was over between us. If I'd been thinking more clearly, I should have realised immediately that something was wrong—that you must have had a reason for doing what you did.'

It was incredible!

So incredible it just might be true…?

But if Rafe hadn't been involved in an affair with Pamela Raines eight years ago, after all…

Cairo looked across at the man she had once loved. At the man she still loved! She moistened her lips with the tip of her tongue. 'Is all of that really true, Rafe?'

'I swear that it is,' he breathed raggedly. 'The only time I ever stupidly slept with her was because I had already drunk myself practically into insensibility on your wedding day.'

'What a mess,' she groaned.

'Yes,' Rafe agreed. 'We've wasted *eight years*, Cairo. Eight long years!'

They had been just as long for Cairo, most of them spent married to a man she could no longer trust, let alone love.

'Where do we go from here?' Rafe asked as she continued to stay silent. Why didn't she say something?

Anything!

Because her silence, now that she knew the truth, was killing him….

She gave him a sad smile. 'I don't see that we go anywhere, Rafe.'

He frowned darkly. 'Why don't you?'

She shrugged. 'Obviously Pamela Raines's lies precipitated the end of our relationship, but I very much doubt that it would have lasted much longer anyway—'

'How can you say that, Cairo?' Rafe rasped fiercely, his hands clenching at his sides. 'How can you possibly *know* that?'

'Well, I don't, of course,' she allowed. 'But I think it's

safe to say that our lives were as different then as they are now. You're the famous Rafe Montero—'

'You're the equally famous Cairo Vaughn!'

Cairo grimaced. 'It's taken me years to become her, Rafe. When we first met, I was only just starting out, was a relative unknown. It's only been through hard work that I've made a name for myself.'

Rafe looked at her searchingly. 'Why did you work so hard, Cairo? Why have you made one movie after another, back-to-back sometimes, never seeming to take a break, and always on show, your photograph constantly in one magazine or another?'

Her expression became guarded. 'You seem to forget that I've taken a break the last ten months,' she reminded him stiffly. 'Besides, didn't *you* tell me three weeks ago that I needed to get back to work in order that the public didn't forget me?'

Yes, he had told her that. But the coincidence of her taking a break from her career following her parting from Lionel Bond was too obvious to pass without comment....

'Was your marriage to Bond all you hoped it would be, Cairo?' Rafe pursued.

'Obviously not, as we've recently divorced,' she commented unhelpfully.

'But you were married to him for over seven years—'

'Rafe, I'm—happy, to have learnt what really happened eight years ago, but that doesn't entitle you to know anything about my marriage to Lionel,' Cairo said defensively as she bent to pick up her evening bag from where she had earlier placed it on the arm of the chair. 'In fact, I think it's probably time I left—'

'Cairo, that morning I had gone out shopping to buy you an engagement ring!'

Cairo froze.

Absolutely froze.

Rafe couldn't really have just said—he *couldn't* have—

'It's here, Cairo,' he continued raggedly as he picked up his discarded evening jacket to take a small ring-box from one of the pockets. 'There's even the receipt here to show you the date that I bought it.' He held up a neatly folded piece of paper.

Cairo straightened abruptly to eye him in complete shock. Rafe had bought her an *engagement ring* eight years ago?

'That day—' He broke off, briefly closing his eyes before opening them again to look at her. 'I had intended asking you to marry me when we went out to lunch that day, and I had the ring in my pocket to give you if you said yes. But before I could do so, you told me it was all over between us!' He shook his head. 'I was too stunned—was hurting too badly—to even question why you were doing it. By the time I had recovered my senses enough to need those answers, you were already going out with Bond. Then when you announced your engagement to him so quickly, it made, as I thought, any explanations between the two of us completely unnecessary.'

Cairo stared at him, unmoving, almost not breathing.

Rafe's mouth twisted. 'Don't worry, I haven't carried the ring around with me for years like some lovesick puppy— in fact, if we had still been in the Isle of Man at the time I would probably have hurled the damn thing into the Irish Sea! But I did keep it, Cairo,' he added huskily. 'If only as a reminder to myself of just how fickle love can be.'

Cairo swallowed, the blood pounding through her veins so loudly it almost deafened her. '*Love*, Rafe…?' she finally managed to ask faintly.

His expression softened. 'I was completely, deeply in love with you, Cairo. I knew that I wanted to spend the rest of my life with you.'

And instead only weeks later Cairo had married another man!

Because she had believed Pamela Raines's lies.

Because Cairo had been so young and unsure of herself that she had believed the other woman when she'd taunted her that she could never hope to hold the interest of a man like Rafe Montero.

She moistened her lips with the tip of her tongue. 'That—that's simply unbelievable, Rafe.'

'It's the truth, dammit!' Rafe barked forcefully, his eyes gleaming fiercely. 'Look at the ring if you don't believe me, Cairo.' He snapped the box open and thrust it towards her, revealing a huge emerald surrounded by six only slightly smaller diamonds. 'You once told me that emeralds were your favourite stone,' he added gruffly.

Yes, she had. But she had never thought—never believed—Rafe had been in love with her eight years ago! Or that he had been going to ask her to marry him!

'It's beautiful,' she whispered emotionally.

'I thought so,' he agreed, before closing the lid of the box and throwing it down on the table. 'At least now perhaps you can understand some of my more—bitter accusations, concerning your sudden marriage to Bond.'

Cairo understood only too well.

But what did she do next?

These explanations about the past were all very well, but they gave her no clues as to how Rafe felt about her now!

'To answer your earlier question, Rafe—no, my marriage to Lionel wasn't anything like I had hoped it would be,' she told him woodenly.

Rafe eyed her guardedly, not wanting to read more into her statement than was intended. The problem was, he had no idea what Cairo intended! But she had deserved to know the truth about eight years ago. All of it, including the fact that Rafe had been in love with her and wanted to marry her.

Cairo shook her head. 'How could it possibly be a happy marriage when I had married him while still in love with another man?'

Rafe felt his heart lift. 'Cairo—'

'No, let me finish, Rafe,' she told him with quiet firmness. 'I told you three weeks ago that I couldn't tell you any of this without breaking a confidence, but I believe, after what you've just told me, that I at least owe you some explanation in return. I married Lionel because he asked me to, and because I was still absolutely devastated by what I had thought was your betrayal. It wasn't a bad marriage. Lionel and I got on well enough to start with, neither of us making demands that the other couldn't give.' She shrugged. 'I'm sure that lots of marriages have survived with less,' she added ruefully.

Rafe wasn't sure he wanted to hear all of this now that Cairo actually wanted to tell him. Just the thought of her being with Lionel Bond, of her marriage to him, had tied Rafe up in knots for months, years, afterwards, to the point that he had never been able to fully trust or love another woman.

Cairo continued, 'We would probably have continued to survive if I hadn't learned of Lionel's gambling habit. More like an obsession, really,' she corrected heavily. 'I'd had no idea when I married him, but only months later I discovered that he gambled every dollar he could spare. A couple of years into our marriage he was so hooked that he began to gamble dollars he didn't even have.' She sighed. 'It didn't really matter, of course, because I had started to earn big money by that time, and by working almost exclusively for Lionel's production company I also put more money back into his bank account, too.'

'*That's* the reason you've been working so hard all these years?' Rafe realised furiously.

She nodded. 'I blamed myself, you see, because although I liked Lionel I—I simply couldn't love him.' She avoided Rafe's searching gaze, determined to finish this now that she had started. 'When Lionel realized how deeply he had become addicted, we were still friends enough for him to feel he could come to me and confess all.' She shook her head. 'He promised me that he would stop.'

'But he didn't,' Rafe said slowly.

'No.' She sighed. 'He just became more secretive about it. Maybe I should have realized sooner, I don't know. But it's very hard to maintain a balanced relationship in a marriage when you have to constantly watch your partner in case he lapses back into a destructive habit. As it turned out, I didn't watch Lionel nearly close enough. Part of my trusting him was having a joint bank account with him, and—about a year ago—I discovered that he had been secretly taking money out of that account, too, and using that to gamble—and lose—with.'

'Leaving you broke, too?' Rafe asked shrewdly.

She gave a sad smile. 'Not quite. I wasn't stupid enough to put all that I earned in our joint account, and I have worked very hard over the last few years, Rafe. I really tried to save our marriage, too, but after the incident with the joint bank account I realized that nothing I did or said was going to make Lionel stop. There was also the hope that by putting an end to our marriage I might shock him into stopping,' she admitted.

'And did it?'

'It would appear not,' Cairo said flatly. 'When he came to the villa that day it was to ask me for money—'

'That's what you meant when you said it wasn't actually you that Bond wanted back?' Rafe interrupted.

'Yes.'

'You didn't give him any more money, did you?' he burst out angrily.

All these years—all this time, he had thought Cairo was at least happy with the choice she had made! Now it seemed she had no more been happy than he had!

'No, I didn't,' she confirmed heavily. 'It was hard to say no to him, because—because I've always felt that it was because I didn't love him, couldn't love him, that his obsession with gambling intensified after our marriage—'

'That's ridiculous, Cairo,' Rafe cut in harshly.

'Is it?' She frowned. 'I became a workaholic in order to paper over the cracks in my marriage, so why shouldn't it have increased Lionel's obsession with gambling?'

'Because we're all ultimately responsible for our own actions,' Rafe reasoned. 'Hell, I lost the woman I loved, and that made me extremely unhappy, and very wary of ever falling in love again, but it certainly didn't turn me into a workaholic or an obsessive gambler!'

'No.' She smiled wryly. 'But you're a much stronger man than Lionel.'

'You think?' Rafe bit out.

'I *know* you are, Rafe,' she said softly.

'What else do you know about me, Cairo?' he said emotionally. 'For instance, do you know that I still love you? That in all these years I've never stopped loving you? Not even for a moment?'

'You still love me…?' Cairo stared at him in shock as the full force of what Rafe had just said hit her like a physical blow.

Rafe nodded. 'I always have. From the very first moment I saw you.'

'But you never said—you didn't tell me!'

'I was a fool,' he rasped. 'You were perfect, unbelievable, and for three months it all seemed too good to be true. We had an incredible physical chemistry between us, but I thought it was too much to hope that you might feel more for me than that, that perhaps you might come to love me in return. But then I decided to hell with it, I would tell you anyway, and then ask you to marry me; the worst thing that could happen was that you would turn me down.'

'I would have said yes!'

He closed his eyes briefly. 'Don't tell me that, Cairo, it only makes it worse!'

'But I loved you, too, Rafe,' she admitted huskily. 'I loved you so much!'

'Loved, Cairo?' he said painfully. 'Past tense?'

Her own tears were blinding her, and her legs felt decidedly shaky. Trying to swallow past a huge lump in her throat, for a moment Cairo couldn't speak.

'Cairo, will you please at least answer me?' Rafe ordered.

She drew in a trembling breath, knowing by the almost defensive expression on Rafe's face that he actually feared what that answer might be. 'I still love you, too, Rafe,' she admitted, her gaze steady on his. 'I've never stopped loving you. Not for a single moment of the last eight years!' she choked even as she threw herself into his arms, her hands cupping each side of his face as she kissed him over and over again. 'I love you, Rafe!' She smiled shakily, her eyes glowing with the emotion. 'I love you! I love you!'

Those same three little words that Rafe knew he should have said to her long ago but hadn't! The same three words that would now bind them together for a lifetime. Because he never intended letting anything, or anyone, come between the two of them ever again!

'I still love you, too, Cairo,' he groaned as his arms clamped about her like steel bands and he held her tightly against him. 'I've never stopped loving you, either.'

'Never, Rafe?'

'Never,' he repeated fiercely. 'I used to see photographs of you in magazines, newspapers, usually with Bond, and each time I did it was like a twist in my gut, an agony I couldn't bear.'

Cairo shook her head. 'That was the life Lionel wanted us to lead, not me. I put up with it, felt it was the least I could do when I had so little else to give him, but really I hated all that artificiality. Parties. Premieres.' She gave a shudder. 'I didn't enjoy it at all. The only consolation was that I never had to actually meet you at any of them,' she admitted.

'Deliberately so,' Rafe told her huskily. 'I stayed away on purpose, Cairo,' he explained as she looked up at him with an obvious query in her eyes. 'I just couldn't stand the thought of seeing you and Bond together,' he acknowledged heavily.

Cairo's gaze became searching as she saw the truth of his words in his face. 'Oh, Rafe, what fools we've been!' she groaned achingly.

'But no more,' he vowed. 'I love you, Cairo, and I know without a doubt that I always will,' he promised. 'Will you marry me?'

'Oh, yes,' she breathed raggedly. 'Yes, yes, *yes*!'

Rafe gave a shout of triumphant laughter as he gathered her even closer in his arms, and then his mouth claimed hers.

Cairo, the woman he had loved, did love, would always love...

'We're getting married as soon as we can get a licence,' Rafe told her determinedly a long time later. They were lying in bed together, Rafe's arms wrapped tightly around Cairo as her head rested on his bare shoulder, her fingers played teasingly with the dark hair on his chest, both of them flushed and satiated from making beautiful love together.

Cairo smiled dreamily. 'You won't hear any arguments against that idea from me,' she murmured.

Mrs Rafe Montero.

Mrs Raphael Antonio Miguel Montero.

It sounded wonderful!

It would *be* wonderful.

She and Rafe had been through too much, had loved each other for so long in spite of everything, and Cairo had no doubts that they would continue to love each other for the rest of their lives. Which reminded her...

She raised her head to look down at him with clear brown eyes. 'I love you very much, Rafe.'

'Never, ever doubt that I love you,' he responded forcefully, blue eyes glittering with the emotion. 'Never, Cairo!'

She never would, for she knew now that the love she and Rafe felt for each other was a love for all time....

EPILOGUE

'NOT giving you ideas, is it, Mrs Montero?' Rafe teased huskily as Cairo handed four-month-old baby Simon back to Margo as they all left the church following the christening.

'And if it is?' Cairo gave him one of those enigmatic smiles that always made Rafe want to take her to bed.

As did her laugh. And her rare—nowadays—frown. And her thoughtful look. Hell, Rafe just enjoyed taking Cairo to bed, no matter what her expression!

The two of them had made their lifetime vows two and a half months ago, with only Rafe's parents, his brother and his family, and Margo, Jeff and the children in attendance.

It had been ten lovely weeks of being together constantly whenever Cairo wasn't at the theatre. Now Cairo's very successful run was over, the two of them intended to return next week to Rafe's house at the beach.

Rafe slid his arm possessively about Cairo's waist. 'I can't imagine anything I would enjoy more than to see you growing big with our child,' he admitted throatily.

Cairo leant into him to murmur, 'Then stop imagining it, Rafe.'

His eyes widened as he looked down at her. 'You mean— Cairo, are you—?'

She chuckled softly at his dumbstruck expression. 'I do. And I am. Seven weeks, according to Margo's doctor.'

Cairo had never felt so happy in her life as she had been this last three months with Rafe, ten weeks of it as his wife, and the knowledge that she now carried their child was almost overwhelming.

Even the shadow of Lionel had been removed from her life, the 'important' thing he had wanted to tell her over lunch that day turning out to be his decision to book himself into a clinic, a condition of his engagement to the movie director Sarah Wallis. Cairo knew Sarah slightly, had worked with her in the past, and knew her to be tough and single-minded; if Sarah had decided that Lionel wouldn't gamble any more, then Cairo had no doubts that he wouldn't.

As the two of them were to be married next month, it seemed that Sarah had got her way!

Cairo shot Rafe a teasing look now. 'Of course, it means I may have to take a few months off work once we've finished filming *Forgiveness* together...' For the first time in years, the two of them were to work together again, Cairo in the lead role, Rafe as director, something they were both looking forward to immensely.

'Cairo, I don't give a damn whether you ever work again,' he told her happily.

'But the public might forget me,' she teased him.

'You belong to me—and our baby—not the public,' he stated arrogantly.

Cairo chuckled. 'I love you very much, Rafe Montero.'

'And I love you, Mrs Rafe Montero,' he murmured huskily as he turned to take her in his arms. 'Till my dying breath,' he promised gruffly as his mouth claimed hers and the two of them forgot everyone, and everything, but each other....

Spanish Aristocrat, Forced Bride

INDIA GREY

A self-confessed romance junkie, **India Grey** was just thirteen years old when she first sent off for the Mills & Boon® writers' guidelines. She can still recall the thrill of getting the large brown envelope with its distinctive logo through the letterbox, and subsequently whiled away many a dull school day staring out of the window and dreaming of the perfect hero. She kept those guidelines with her for the next ten years, tucking them carefully inside the cover of each new diary in January, and beginning every list of New Year's Resolutions with the words *Start Novel*. In the meantime she also gained a degree in English Literature from Manchester University and, in a stroke of genius on the part of the gods of romance, met her gorgeous future husband on the very last night of their three years there. The last fifteen years have been spent blissfully buried in domesticity, and heaps of pink washing generated by three small daughters, but she has never really stopped daydreaming about romance. She's just profoundly grateful to have finally got an excuse to do it legitimately!

CHAPTER ONE

THE shadow of the helicopter fell over the lush velvet lawns of Stowell Castle, stirring up the hot August air and ruffling the canopies of the great trees in the parkland.

Tristan Romero de Losada Montalvo glanced down. Below him the party was already well under way, and he could see waiters carrying trays of champagne circulating between the groups of outlandishly dressed guests scattered across the emerald grass. Dispassionately he noticed that people were looking up, emerging from the marquees placed at opposite ends of the lawn and shielding their eyes from the sinking sun to watch his arrival.

It was set to be the party of the year, because Tom Montague's Annual Charity Costume Ball always was. This was the event that drew the glitterati and the aristos back from their Malibu beach houses and Tuscan palazzos to indulge in twenty-four hours of lavish hedonism in the idyllic setting of Stowell Castle's gardens.

It was also the event that had drawn Tristan Romero back from the jaws of hell some two thousand miles away, for reasons that had nothing to do with indulgence or hedonism.

He was here for Tom.

Sighing wearily, he circled the helicopter round over the lawn so that the roofs of the marquees snapped and strained like galleons' sails. Tom Montague was the seventh Earl of Cotebrook and one of the most genuinely good and generous people imaginable; a combination which Tristan felt was particularly dangerous—especially where women were concerned. Tom only ever looked for the good in people, even when it was invisible to the rest of humankind. Which was why they'd been friends for such a long time, Tristan thought acidly, and why he now felt duty bound to come and make sure that the girl that Tom had talked about incessantly over the past few weeks was worthy of him.

But, of course, he would be dishonest as well as emotionally bankrupt if he tried to pretend that that was his only reason for coming.

Ultimately he was here because the tabloid press and the paparazzi and the gossip columnists expected him to be. It was part of the deal he had made when he sold his soul to the devil. Grimly he swung the helicopter round, following the path of the river that looped around Stowell and marked its northern boundary. As he came lower his eyes raked the trees along the river bank, looking for the telltale glitter of sunlight on a long lens.

They would be there, of that he was sure. One of the hardened group of paparazzi elite, who were dedicated enough to go the extra distance for a picture and ruthless enough not to question the ethics of getting it. They would be there somewhere, watching and waiting.

He would be almost insulted if they weren't. Many people in a similar position to him complained endlessly about press intrusion, but to Tristan that was missing the point. It was a game. A game of strategy and skill, in which the truth was an irrelevance and a lapse of concentration could cost you your reputation. Tristan didn't like the paparazzi, but neither did he underestimate them for a second. It was simply a case of use or be used. Be the manipulator or the victim.

And Tristan Romero would never be a victim again.

Down below Lily Alexander slipped through the crowds of people in their spectacular costumes as if in a dream. The champagne in her hand was vintage, the silk Grecian-style dress she wore was designer, and the stretch of grass beneath her bare feet was at that moment just about the most enviable place to be on the planet.

So why did she feel as if something was missing?

There was a saying on the London modelling circuit: 'There are three things that money can't buy: love, happiness and an invitation to the Stowell Annual Costume Ball.' *Magical* was the word people used to describe it, in tones of wistful reverence. Lily was unutterably privileged to be here, as she told herself for about the fortieth time that evening, blotting out the dissatisfied little voice that answered, *But where's the magic? Surely there has to be more to life than this...*

A shadow passed across the dipping sun, darkening the extravagant pink and gold evening. Walking across the lawn in search of Scarlet, Lily was aware of a throbbing in her head; a steady, rhythmic pulsing, like a second heartbeat, which only seemed to intensify her edginess.

This year the theme of the party was Myths and Legends, and as the sun cast long shadows across the grass silken-clad girls with elaborate, shimmering fairy wings were mingling with Greek gods and screen icons. Several large marquees stood around the fringes of the lawn, with a space in the centre where, according to Scarlet, a troop of semi-naked stunt riders were going to perform later.

On unicorns, apparently.

A warm breeze was stirring the leaves of the stately horse chestnut trees, making them bend and sigh. By this time tomorrow she would be half a world away in the arid heart of Africa, and all of this would seem more like a dream than ever, if that were possible. Perhaps it was normal to feel like this just before a trip like the one she was about to embark on? She was branching out from the safe confines of the shallow, superficial life and plunging straight into the depths of a world that until now she had only read about in the papers and seen on TV news reports. Being nervous was probably completely understandable. Except that nervous didn't quite describe the feeling she had…

Restless.

The word flashed into her head from nowhere, echoing round it, amplified by the throbbing that was growing louder all the time. She tipped her head back, suddenly aware that the evening air held a kind of tension; a pulsing energy that resonated inside her, filling her with a sense of anticipation. A helicopter was suspended high above and, mesmerised, she watched its blades slicing through the soft apricot sky as it circled like some dark, powerful predator.

Suddenly she jumped as the mobile phone she was clutching tightly in her hand rang, breaking the spell. She answered quickly, pressing it tightly to her ear so that the shrieks of laughter and the sporadic bursts of ear-splitting music from the rock band that was tuning up in the marquee couldn't be heard on the other end of the line by the director of the African children's charity with which she was going to be working.

'Yes, fine, thank you, Jack. All ready for tomorrow, I think….'

The noise persisted, all but drowning out Jack Davidson's voice, and Lily walked quickly across the lawn away from the party in the hope of finding somewhere quiet to talk.

'Yes, I'm still here…' she said loudly. 'Sorry, it's a bad line.'

She kept her head down, focusing all her attention on the voice in her ear. Jack was running through the itinerary for the trip, and the words 'orphanage' and 'feeding station' seemed utterly incongruous in her present luxurious surroundings. She kept walking, rounding the corner of the castle with its massive stone turret and heading out across the open ground beyond. She had left behind the lush greenness of the formal gardens and was now crossing an area of rough, parched grass behind the castle. The sounds of the party were muted here, but the noise of the helicopter blades was getting louder, pulsing insistently through the honeyed afternoon, whipping up the heavy air until Lily felt as if she were standing in the eye of the storm.

High above, Tristan Romero smiled as he watched her.

The reason he hadn't seen her earlier, he realised, was that her pale golden colouring had made her melt perfectly into the drought bleached grass of the field. She was like a goddess of the harvest, he thought with a stab of curiosity as he hovered above her. She was wearing some kind of delicate crown of golden leaves on her head, but this didn't stop her long, wheat-coloured hair rippling out in heavy streamers in the wind from the rotor blades. She stood still, struggling to hold down her dress as it billowed up around her, but her efforts were hampered by the fact that she was holding a mobile phone to her ear with one hand and a glass of champagne in the other, and simultaneously trying to control her wind-blown hair.

He came down just in front of her and couldn't resist keeping the blades going for a minute longer than was necessary, so he could enjoy the delicious spectacle of her long, long brown legs beneath the flyaway dress, which was being flattened against the most incredible body.

There was something familiar about her, he thought as he pulled off his headset and jumped down from the cabin. In the sudden stillness she had shaken back her heavy hair and as he walked towards her he got a proper look at her face. He wondered whether he'd slept with her before.

No. With a body like that he would almost certainly have remembered. She was tall, but there was a slow grace in her movements that told him that bedding her would be an unforgettable experience. Tristan felt desire uncurl somewhere low down in his exhausted body. She was still on the phone, her head bent, clearly totally preoccupied with the conversation she was having. As he got closer he heard her say, 'Yes, yes, don't worry, I know it's important, but I'm writing it all down. I've got all the details here in front of me.'

A beautiful girl with an outrageous disregard for the truth. How intriguing, he thought as she finished her conversation and looked up at him.

He felt a small shock jolt through his body, as if he had just touched a live wire. Against the golden tones of her hair and skin and dress, her eyes were a cool, clear silver; the colour of the mist that hung over the lake first thing in the morning.

'Eight-thirty,' she said out loud. Her voice was slightly breathless, and she was looking straight at him, but almost as if she weren't seeing him. 'Eight-thirty, tomorrow morning. Heathrow Terminal One.'

He smiled, quirking an eyebrow as he carried on walking towards her. 'I'll remind you when we wake up,' he said dryly.

It was a joke. A throwaway remark. He had made it without even intending to stop walking, but the moment the words left his lips two things happened.

Firstly, he heard it: the quiet cicada whirr of a camera shutter, and from the corner of his eye caught the glint of a lens in the shadow of the trees. And secondly, he saw the instantaneous darkening of those extraordinary silver eyes.

Tristan Romero had many skills. Heading up the list had to be seducing women and manipulating the press. He didn't even have to think about it. Before she could utter a single word of protest he had put his hand around her waist and was pulling her towards him.

The first thing she had noticed about him was his eyes.

His dark hair was cut close into his perfect neck, a couple of days of stubble emphasised sculpted cheekbones and his skin was tanned to a deep, even gold that made the blue of his eyes seem almost shocking. Looking up into them, desperately trying to imprint on her memory the instructions she'd just been given for meeting the rest of the African expedition tomorrow, Lily felt her throat tighten as sharply as if someone had wrapped a cord around her neck and pulled it. Hard.

Blue.

Blue you could float in.

Drown in.

She'd spoken out loud because she knew that all the information that she'd just been given was in danger of evaporating from her brain like water hitting hot stone. His answering remark was clearly a joke, but her body didn't seem to get the humour. The world stopped and time vanished into a vortex of cinematic, freeze-frame intimacy as the blueness pulled her down. In the deep underwater world of his eyes everything slowed. Lily could hear nothing but the drumming of her pulse in her ears, feel nothing but the bloom of heat beneath the surface of her skin, the prickle of awareness low down in her pelvis.

And then he'd pulled her against him and she wasn't drowning any more. She was *burning*. His kiss was pure magic. Firm, expert, and shockingly tender. Lily felt as if the sinking sun had slipped from the flame-streaked sky and set the world on fire, and that she were standing in the midst of the leaping flames with no desire to be rescued. His arm was around her waist, his hand resting in the small of her back. Lily felt herself arching helplessly towards him, her hands—still holding the phone and the champagne glass—hanging uselessly by her sides as her lips opened for him and the darkness behind her closed eyes glittered and glowed with blistering lust.

'He's here!'

It was just a distant shout, but suddenly he was lifting his head, pulling away slightly so that his blue eyes met hers. For a second Lily caught a look that was almost like despair in their depths, but then it was gone and he was letting her go.

Dazedly she turned round. From the direction of the party Scarlet and Tom were walking towards them, hand in hand, and behind them came a drift of girls dressed as fairies and mermaids and wood nymphs in shimmering silks and floaty chiffons.

'Finally!' Tom shouted, his kind face breaking into a grin as he walked up to the man who had just fallen out of the sky like some avenging angel and kissed her to within an inch of her life. With his pale, romantic English looks Tom looked absurdly at home in his St George costume, and oddly pure and noble next to the dangerous glamour of the beautiful stranger. 'I see you've already met Lily,' he said easily.

'Lily…' The devastatingly sexy mouth that moments ago had been caressing hers now twisted into an ironic, mocking smile as that blue gaze swept over her, taking in the coronet of golden laurel leaves in her hair and the Grecian pleated silk dress. 'That makes it easier. I wasn't sure if you were meant to be Helen of Troy or Demeter, goddess of the harvest.'

Lily felt the colour flood her cheeks. The dress was one she had worn in a shoot a couple of years ago when the Gladiator look had been at its peak. Suddenly she wished she'd taken the time to plan something a bit more interesting, like Scarlet, who was stunning in a little black dress and diamonds as Coco Chanel.

'I was kind of thinking Helen of Troy…' she said awkwardly, not meeting his eye.

'Of course. The face that launched a thousand products. You're the girl from the perfume advertisements?'

Lily nodded, jumping like a startled deer as he reached out and took hold of her wrist, raising it slowly. Her first thought was that he was going to kiss her hand, but he turned it palm upwards and his thumb brushed the blue-veined skin of her wrist. Then he bent his head and breathed in.

'Every time I see one of those adverts I wonder if the perfume smells as good as you make it look,' he said thoughtfully. 'But I never actually imagined it would be possible.'

His voice seemed to reach down inside her and caress her in places she'd never been touched before. His English was perfect, but the Spanish accent ran through it like wine through water. Lily had to force herself to focus on his words. To reply to them.

'I'm not wearing it,' she stammered. 'Not tonight. I'm not wearing anything.'

Oh God. Had she really said that?

'Really?' His mouth curved into a smile that would have melted ice caps, and yet didn't quite manage to warm those cool blue eyes. 'What a very appealing image that conjures up.'

For a heartbeat he looked at her, and then he turned away.

And that was how he did it, Lily thought as heat and liquid excitement cascaded through her, drenching her body from within while her logical mind switched off and shut down. Whoever he was, he had a way of drawing you in with one hand and then slamming the door in your face with the other. It wasn't nice, but, God, was it effective. She felt disorientated, unhinged by what had happened, as if he had kidnapped and brainwashed her, and then thrust her back out into ordinary life.

Lily was aware of Scarlet desperately trying to catch her eye, but then Tom pulled her forward and was saying, with mock formality, 'Scarlet, I want you to meet Tristan Romero de Losada; Montalvo, Marqués of Montesa, and my oldest friend.'

Lily's heart gave a violent jolt, as if electrical pads had just been pressed to her chest.

Tristan Romero de Losada Montalvo?

Oh, God. How could she not have recognised him?

But the truth was that none of the grainy, long-lens photographs in the tabloids or close-up red-carpet shots in the glossy magazines could have prepared her for the impact of seeing the Marqués of Montesa in the bronzed and beautiful flesh.

Introductions over, Scarlet came over to her and Lily seized her arm and dragged her a little way away, back towards the castle and the rest of the party.

'Tom's *best friend* is Tristan Romero de Losada? From the uber-aristocratic Spanish banking family?'

Scarlet looked amused. 'That's right. They've been best friends even longer than we have, since they were locked up together in some grim Dickensian prep school as little boys.'

Lily's head was spinning. The lingering pleasure from his kiss mixed with shock and shame that she could have been so easily taken in. 'But Tom's so nice,' she faltered, 'and he's… he's…*wicked.*'

'Lil-y,' said Scarlet reproachfully. 'You should know better than most not to believe everything you read in the papers—or at least to understand that it's never the entire story. Tom won't hear a word against him—apparently Tristan practically saved his life on more than one occasion when Tom was bullied at school. Anyway,' she said, turning to Lily with a speculative look, 'how come you seem to know so much about him? Since you'd rather read Nietzsche in the original than a tabloid newspaper, you seem very well informed.'

'Everyone knows about him,' Lily muttered darkly as they walked back towards the castle. 'You don't even have to read the tabloids. The broadsheets and the financial pages mention the Romero name pretty regularly too, you know.' Most reporters were torn between disapproval and awe at the breathtaking ruthlessness that had ensured that the Romero bank had ridden out all the economic storms of modern times and remained one of the most significant players in global finance, and the Romero family one of the richest and most powerful in the world.

'Anyway,' she said, aware that she sounded like a sulky child, but unable to stop herself, 'what's he come as? James Bond? He's hardly a myth or a legend.'

'Darling, he hasn't come as anything. He's the one person for whom Tom makes an exception to the fancy dress rule. He's come as himself—legendary Euro Playboy, mythical sex god. He'll have left some party on a yacht in Marbella or the bed of some raving beauty in a chateau in the Loire and come straight here.' She gave a gasp of laughter, which she quickly stifled, and leaned closer to Lily's ear. 'In something of a hurry, I'd say. Check out his shirt. It's buttoned up all wrong.'

Glancing backwards, Lily's eyes went automatically to his chest. Scarlet was right. Beneath the dark, slightly crumpled jacket of his perfectly tailored suit, his white shirt was untucked, the collar open, lopsided, showing an expanse of deep golden flesh and one sculpted collarbone.

She wasn't sure which was worse: the instant rush of hot indignant anger that the kiss that had turned her inside out with longing had been given so casually, so randomly by a man whose body was barely cold from another woman's bed.

Or the low down ache of desire, and the shameful knowledge that she didn't care. That she just wanted to kiss him again.

'Everything OK?' said Tom out of the corner of his mouth. They had walked back across the field to the party and were now striding across the lawn towards the marquee where the bar was.

Tristan gave a curt nod. 'Sorry I'm late. I couldn't get away.'

'Not a problem. For me, anyway, although your extensive collection of female hangers-on have been getting increasingly restless. I was running out of answers for where you could be.'

'A house party in St Tropez is the official story.'

Tom threw him a swift grin. 'It must have been some party. Perhaps you'd better do your shirt up properly, old friend, or we might have a riot on our hands.'

Tristan glanced down with a grimace. Dressing quickly when he'd landed his plane at the nearby airfield, he'd been so tired he'd hardly been able to see straight. Hardly the ideal circumstances to get ready for what was always dubbed the social event of the year. The mild air pulsed with music from one of the marquees around the lawn, an insistent reminder that yet another sleepless night lay ahead of him.

'So that's the official story,' said Tom soberly, 'but what's the truth?'

'Khazakismir,' Tristan replied tonelessly, looking straight ahead and unbuttoning his shirt as they walked across the lawn towards the tented bar.

Tom winced at the name. 'I hoped you weren't going to say that. News coverage here has been patchy, but I gather things are pretty grim?'

The name of the small province in a remote corner of Eastern Europe had become synonymous with despair and violence in the course of a decade-long war, the original purpose of which no one could remember any more. Power rested in the blood-stained hands of a corrupt military government and a few drugs barons, who quashed any sign of civil unrest quickly and ruth-lessly. Reports had filtered through in the last week of a whole village being laid to waste.

'You could say that.' A door in Tristan's mind swung open, letting the images flood back into his head for a moment before he mentally slammed it shut again. 'One of our drivers was caught up in it. His family were killed—everyone apart from his sister, who's pregnant.' His mouth quirked into a bitter smile. 'It seems that the military were keen to make use of the brand new cache of weaponry they have courtesy of funds from the Romero bank.'

Pausing at the entrance to the marquee, Tom laid a hand on his arm.

'Are you OK?'

'Fine,' he said tersely. 'You know me. I don't get involved in the humanitarian side. I'm just there to help out with prac-ticalities. Redress the balance.'

He didn't meet Tom's eyes as he spoke, looking instead over his shoulder and into the distance, where the lake lay in its hollow of shadows, the tower in the centre wreathed in mist. A muscle flickered in his jaw.

'Anything I can do?' Tom said quietly.

Tristan flashed a brief, ironic smile as they moved into the damp, alcohol-scented warmth of the marquee. 'I haven't been seen anywhere for a while, so I could do with giving the press their pound of flesh. If any word got out tying me to activities over there it would be a security nightmare.'

Tom's smile didn't waver as he shouldered his way through to the bar, nodding a welcome to his guests. Speaking quietly, he said, 'That's easily arranged. The usual tame photographers are here, the society event ones who have progressed slightly further up the evolutionary scale from the paparazzi, but if you pick someone high profile and enjoy a little bit of public affection, I'm sure they'll regress into mindless savages who'll sell your picture to every glossy magazine and sleazy gossip rag by Monday morning.' He took two glasses from the tray on the bar and handed one to Tristan. 'Cheers, old chap. So—who's it going to be?'

'Lily.' Tristan tossed back the dark coloured liquid in the shot glass, feeling it burning a path down his throat as he watched Tom's open face fall. He was gauging his reaction before admitting what had already happened. It wasn't positive.

'No. No way. Not a good idea.'

'Why not? She's high profile.' And beautiful, there was no doubt about that. Even Tristan, tired and jaded, had been jolted by it, which had surprised him. It was more than that, though. For a moment back there when she was in his arms he had found himself looking into her slanting, silvery grey eyes and felt almost…

Almost human?

'She's also Scarlet's best friend,' Tom said firmly. 'You screw her up—which let's face it, you certainly will—and you screw things up for me.'

'Why would I screw her up?' Tristan picked up another shot glass and looked restlessly around. 'She's a model, Tom; hard as nails and, judging from what I just saw, not really all there. She'll end up with something shiny and expensive from Cartier, and a whole raft of publicity, and I'll feed the press appetite to portray me as a pointless playboy and throw them off the scent. Everyone's happy.'

Tom looked worried. 'I don't think she's like that.'

'You're too nice, Tom, my friend,' Tristan said grimly, draining his glass. 'They're all like that.'

CHAPTER TWO

As TWILIGHT fell it brought with it a kind of enchantment. Paper lanterns glowed palely in the trees and the scattering of diamond stars that glittered in the purple heavens looked as if they'd been placed there purely for the delight of the guests.

Lily wouldn't have been surprised. Nothing was impossible here tonight.

Earlier, as waiters had circulated with cool green cocktails that tasted of melons and champagne, masked girls dressed as dryads and wood nymphs had appeared from the shadowy trees that fringed the lawn on white horses, with delicate, spiralling unicorn's horns on their foreheads. To the haunting strains of a full orchestra headed by a stunning girl playing an electric violin they had performed a display of equestrian dance, weaving around each other, making the horses rear and pirouette, until Lily wasn't sure if she was dreaming. Once, through the writhing, stamping figures of the unicorns, she found herself staring straight into the eyes of Tristan, standing opposite, his shirt half unbuttoned and his arm around a well-known young Hollywood actress dressed as Pocahontas. A shock, like a small electrocution, sizzled through her.

The next time she looked he was gone.

She had hardly touched her cocktail. She didn't need to. Already she felt heavy and languid with tiredness, but beneath that there was an edge of restlessness, a throbbing pulse of desire and impatience and wild longing that alcohol would only exacerbate. The riding display finished and the unicorns melted back into the darkness that had gathered beneath the trees. Lily turned to say something to Scarlet, but she had moved away slightly and was standing with Tom. His arms were looped around her waist and as Lily watched he pulled her into him and spoke into her ear.

Lily felt a beat of pain, of anguish, deep inside her chest and turned away.

She and Scarlet had been a team for so long. All through school at a fairly rough comprehensive in Brighton it had been the two of them—united by both being tall, skinny and teased for it—until the day when Maggie Mason had spotted them shopping together in The Lanes and invited them both up to London for an interview at her famous modelling agency. Lily had been so set on going to university, if it hadn't been for Scarlet there was no way she would have even taken Maggie's card. But they had been in it together, two halves of the same whole—as different as it was possible to be. But always together.

Which was, she told herself firmly, why she was so pleased for Scarlet. Tom was lovely, and when she thought of some of the unsuitable men that her friend could have fallen in love with…

Tristan Romero de Losada Montalvo, for example.

The violinist was playing solo now, a gentle, haunting melody that echoed across the mist-shrouded fields and gentle hills enfolding the castle. Another horse cantered into the ring, this time with the most fantastic pair of wings attached to its saddle. A murmur of delight ran around the crowd, which quickly turned to a gasp of surprise as the scantily clad girl rider opened the lid of the basket she carried.

There was a flurry of feathers, a whispered beat of wings and a flock of white doves spiralled upwards into the sky. In the smudged violet light their wings were almost luminescent. For a moment they seemed to hang motionless in the air, as if uncertain what to do with their unexpected freedom, and out of the corner of her eye Lily caught a movement in the crowd opposite. She turned her head, and was just in time to see a man in a Robin Hood costume raise his bow and arrow and take a shot.

A macho jeer went up from the group around him as one of the doves faltered, losing height for a minute in a ragged tumble of feathers. Lily could see the arrow, hanging tenuously from the bird's side, seeming to drag it downwards. Miraculously the bird didn't fall but, with an odd, lopsided flapping, flew down towards the lake.

Rage exploded inside her. The display was over and the crowd began to drift away towards the next entertainment, but Lily began to run, down the sloping lawn to the water. The grass was cool and damp beneath her bare feet and as she got near the lake the ground grew softer. Heart hammering, she pushed her way through the thick tangle of undergrowth and looked around, across the glassy surface of the water to the island in its centre.

The ruined walls of the stone tower were dark against the faded lilac sky behind, but in the stillness she could hear the agitated beating of wings. Doves rose from the broken ramparts at the top, and she strained her eyes into the gloom to see if the injured one was amongst them. What if the arrow was still there, lodged in the bird's flesh?

Her eyes stung and frustration drummed in her head as she peered up into the nebulous sky, but it was impossible to make anything out clearly. With a gasp of exasperation she was just about to turn back when she noticed a wooden walkway at the back of the tower leading across the stretch of water to the island. Hurrying round, she felt the brambles snag at the hem of her dress and the damp grass cling to her legs. The walkway was narrow, the boards old and very smooth, but stepping tentatively onto them Lily could feel that it was sturdily made.

From across the lawn she could hear more yells of hilarity above the bass beat of the music as the party escalated, which only strengthened her resolve and refuelled her fury. The sound of the doves at the top of the tower was a soft murmur, but it was comforting as she stepped onto the dark island.

In spite of the warmth of the evening she shivered. Everything was inky, insubstantial; layers of grey that melted into each other until it was impossible to say what was real and what was shadow. The air was heavy with the scent of roses and through the indigo dusk Lily could see their pale globes clustered around a small door in the tower.

Her heart was knocking so violently against her ribs that she could feel it shaking her whole body as she went towards the door. Hesitantly, almost hoping that it would be locked, she put her hand against the blistered wood.

It sprang open, without her even pushing. Lily gasped; a sharp indrawn breath of pure fear as a figure appeared in the doorway, white shirt ghostly in the opaque light. She leapt backwards, pressing her hand to her mouth, choking with fear as the man reached out and caught her, pulling her back towards him.

'Helen of Troy.' The voice was very deep, very scathing, very Spanish. He gave her a little shake. 'You followed me, I suppose?'

Lily's heart was almost beating out of her chest, but the arrogance of his words penetrated her shocked haze. '*No!* I came to look for a bird…an injured dove. Some…*idiot* with a bow and arrow took a shot at it when they were released and it flew in this direction. When I came to look for it I saw that they'd flown up to the roof of the tower, but I didn't know that you were here—' She stopped suddenly, as the most likely explanation for Tristan Romero to be discovered on a secluded island in the middle of a party popped into her horrified mind, and then tried to take a hasty step backwards. 'Sorry. I'll go.'

His hand tightened around her arm. 'No. Don't let me stop your mission of mercy,' he drawled. 'There's a dovecote on the roof. Go up and look for it.'

She hesitated, remembering the Pocahontas girl. 'Are you here alone?'

'Yes.' Against his white shirt his skin looked very dark, and the hollows beneath his hard cheekbones were inky. Apart from that it was impossible to see his face in any detail, but his voice was like sandpaper and when he laughed there was no humour in it. 'I take it Tom's warned you off. Perhaps you'd prefer to come back with a chaperone?'

His fingers were still circling her wrist. She could feel her rapid pulse beating against his thumb. 'Don't be ridiculous,' she said, with a brave attempt at scorn. 'I just didn't want to *interrupt* anything, that's all. Now, if you'd like to tell me where to go?'

He let go of her, stepping back into the shadows with a sweep of his arm. 'Up to the top of the stairs.'

Inside the tower the air was chill and damp. A stone staircase spiralled above them, and Lily's bare feet made no sound on the ice cold stone as she began to climb up. The staircase opened onto a small landing halfway up, where a narrow, arrow-slit window spilled soft light onto a closed door. Lily stopped outside the door, but Tristan walked past her, leading the way up another twisting staircase.

At the top he pushed open another door and stood back to let her through first. Lily stepped out and turned around slowly, letting out a low exhalation of awe as she did so.

From below it looked as if the tower were half ruined, the stone walls crumbling and uneven, but now she could see that this was a deliberate illusion. The platform she now stood on was paved with smooth stone flags, and all around the insides of the thick stone walls that looked so dilapidated from the other side of the lake were recessed ledges where birds could nest. But this hardly made an impression. It was the view that stole her breath. Over the lowest part of the wall she could see the pink stained sky beyond the trees that fringed the far side of the lake. At the front of the tower the wall was higher, but a narrow gothic-style arched window framed a view over the lake to the gardens and the castle and the fields beyond, making it possible to look out without being observed. Lily walked over to it.

'It's amazing. I thought this was a ruin; an empty shell.'

'That's the idea,' said Tristan from the doorway. 'It was commissioned by one of Tom's more inventive ancestors, and intended to appear decorative but functionless. In reality it's an incredibly cleverly designed gambling den. Where you're standing now is a lookout post, so that anyone approaching could be seen long before they had any chance of getting here.'

Lily shook her head and laughed softly, tilting her head back and looking up at the violet velvet sky, feeling suddenly light and breathless. Tristan levered himself away from the low doorframe where he'd been leaning, and came slowly towards her.

Her pulse quickened, and she felt the laughter die on her lips as electricity crackled through her. In the hazy half-light his eyes were dark blue, his face grave, and she sensed again that weary despair she had glimpsed in him earlier. Suddenly she found it impossible to reconcile this achingly beautiful man who wore sadness like an invisible cloak with the sybaritic playboy whose libertine lifestyle so fascinated the gutter press.

'You're right.'

Lily gave a small, startled gasp, wondering how he'd managed to read her mind, but then he raised one hand, gesturing to a recess in the wall beside her.

'The injured dove,' he said tonelessly. 'There it is.'

'Oh…' She frowned, stooping down and letting her hair fall across her face as she felt heat spread upwards. The bird was huddled in the back of the nesting recess, its wing held up awkwardly. The white feathers were stained with crimson at the place where the wing joined the body. 'Poor thing…' Lily crooned gently. 'Poor, poor thing…'

Tristan felt his throat tighten inexplicably. Her voice was filled with a tenderness that seemed to slip right past his iron defences and go straight into the battered, shell-shocked heart of him.

Usually he slipped between lives with the insouciant agility of an alley cat, letting the doors between the two halves of his world swing tightly shut behind him. But tonight—*Dios*—tonight he was finding it hard to leave it all behind. The raucous revelry of the party had grated on his frayed nerves like salt in an open wound, which was why he'd had to get away. But this…

This gentle compassion was almost worse. Because it was harder to withstand.

'I think its wing is broken,' Lily said softly. 'What can we do?'

He looked out over the lawn to the glittering lights of the party. 'Nothing,' he said, hearing the harshness in his voice. 'If that's the case it would be best to end its suffering quickly and kill it now.'

'No!' Her response was instantaneous and fierce. She stood up, placing herself between him and the bird, almost as if she were afraid he was going to grab it and wring its neck in front of her.

'You couldn't. You wouldn't…'

'Why not?' he said brutally as images of the place he had been earlier flashed into his head with jagged, strobe-lit insistence. This was just a bird, for God's sake. An injured bird; a pity, not a tragedy. 'Why not end its suffering?'

'Because you don't have the right to play God like that,' she said quietly. 'None of us do.'

Standing in the last light of the fading day, she looked remote and almost mystically beautiful. Not of this world. What did she know about suffering? He could feel the pulse beating loudly in his ears, but her words cut through it, exploding inside his head. *No?* he wanted to say. *Then who will? It's not power that makes men behave like God, but desperation.*

He turned away abruptly, walking back towards the door to the stairs. 'It's not about having the right,' he said bleakly. 'It's about having the guts.'

'Wait!'

He heard her come down after him, and the blue twilight darkened as she shut the door at the top of the stairs again. Tristan stopped on the landing, his shoulders against the closed door, and watched her come down the stairs, melting out of the shadows like something from a dream.

Slowly she came down the last couple of steps and stood in

front of him, shaking her head. 'I don't,' she said in a low voice. 'I don't have the guts to kill it. What shall I do?'

He shrugged. 'Sometimes you just have to accept that there's nothing you can do.'

'But that's—'

'Life,' he said flatly. 'That's—'

But he didn't finish, because at that moment the dusk was shattered by two loud explosions that detonated a chain of nightmarish images and sent an instant tide of adrenaline crashing through him. He saw her start violently, her head snapping round to the window, her eyes wide with shock. Pure instinct took over. Without thinking he reached for her, pulling her into his body, against his crashing heart as he shouldered open the door behind him and dragged her into the room beyond.

The next moment the sky beyond the two tall, arched Gothic windows was lit up with showers of glittering stars.

Fireworks. It was fireworks. Not bombs and mortars. Relief hit him, followed a heartbeat later by another sensation; less welcome, but every bit as powerful as he became aware of the feel of her breasts beneath the silk of her dress, crushed against his chest. As another volley of blasts split the sky she pulled away from him, laughing shakily.

And then she looked around her at the hexagonal room, with its pale grey walls and its arched windows and the bed with the carved wooden posts at its centre, and suddenly she wasn't laughing any more.

'Yours?' she whispered.

He nodded briefly. Over the years he'd lent Tom more money than either of them bothered to keep track of. The tower was a token return for his investment. 'It's where I come when I want to be alone.'

Their gazes locked. Time hitched, hanging suspended. Her full lips were parted, her breathing was rapid and her grey eyes shone with shimmering colour from the fireworks that exploded above them. Then she blinked and looked away.

'Oh. I see, I'm sorry—I'll go.'

She moved towards the door, but he got there first, slamming it shut and standing with his shoulders against it.

'Tonight I don't want to be alone.'

CHAPTER THREE

ADRENALINE was pulsing through Tristan, making the beat of his heart hard and painful. It vibrated through his whole body as the explosions continued outside—audacious reminders of the things he had travelled around half the world to forget.

In the grainy, blurred light Lily's luminous beauty had an ethereal quality. Her eyes were still fixed on his, and as he gazed into them he felt the panic recede a little, washed away by the warm, anaesthetising tide of desire. Rationality slipped away, like sand through his fingers. For a moment he battled to hold onto it, to anchor himself back in the world of reason, but then she moved forward so she was standing right in front of him and he could see the spiked shadows cast by her lashes on the high arc of her cheekbone and feel the whispering sigh of her breath on his skin as she exhaled shakily.

'I don't want to be alone, either,' she said in a low voice. 'But I don't want to go back to the party.'

Slowly, almost reluctantly, he reached out and touched the gleaming curve of her bare shoulder with his fingertip. He felt her jerk slightly beneath his touch, as if it had burned her, and an answering jolt of sharp, clenching desire shot through him.

With deliberate slowness he bent his head, inhaling her scent as he brought his lips down to her shoulder. 'You don't like parties?'

'I don't like crowds. I prefer...' she breathed, then gave a soft, shivering gasp as his mouth brushed her skin '…privacy. I don't like being looked at.'

'You're in the wrong job,' Tristan said dryly.

'Tell me about it.'

There was a wistful ache in her voice that made him lift his head and look into her face. For a fleeting moment he glimpsed the bleakness there, but then she was tilting her head up to his, her lips parting as they rose to meet his, and the questions that were forming in his head dissolved like snow in summer.

He didn't want to know anyway. He didn't want to *talk* to her, for pity's sake. This was purely physical.

Not emotional.

Never emotional.

Her hands came up to cup his head, her fingers sliding into his hair, pulling him down, harder, deeper. He sensed a hunger in her that matched his own. The silk dress hung loosely from her shoulders and he knew that simply slipping the narrow, gathered straps downwards would make it fall to the floor, but he forced himself to wait, to take it slowly, to suppress the naked savagery of his need.

Above all, *this* was why he had come. Tom and the press were just convenient excuses.

This was his salvation, his purifying baptismal fire. This was where he lost himself, purged himself of all the images from the last week that haunted him whenever he closed his eyes. It didn't matter whose body he lost himself in, whose lips he was kissing. It meant nothing. It was simply a means to an end.

A way of remembering the joy of being alive, the pleasures of the flesh.

A way of forgetting.

Lily pulled away, taking a deep, gasping breath of air, trying to steady herself against the swelling tide of pure desire that threatened to sweep her away. The light was fading quickly now; the sky beyond the arched windows was the soft, lush purple of clematis petals and the walls of the tower room had melted into it, making it feel as if they'd been cut adrift from reality and were floating far out at sea. Tristan's hands rested on her shoulders, his thumbs beneath her jaw, stopping her from dropping her head, ducking away from meeting his gaze. In a world of smudged inky shades of blue and mauve his eyes were as deep and dark as a tropical ocean.

'I have to warn you,' he said roughly, 'this is just tonight. One night. No strings, no commitment, no happy ever after. Is that what you want?'

His honesty made her breath catch. No promises, no lies. Somewhere, distantly, she was aware of pain, of disappointment, but it was numbed by the dizzying lust that circulated through her body like a drug. In the morning she was leaving for Africa—a different world, a new direction in her life. Tonight stood alone; a bridge between the old and the new. There were no rules, only the imperatives of the moment. Of forgetting about tomorrow, and giving herself something to remember when it came.

'Yes,' she whispered, lifting her hands to the neck of his shirt, sliding them beneath the open collar. 'Just tonight.'

Outside another explosion ripped the sky apart with a shower of pink stars and she felt him flinch slightly. Carefully she began to undo the buttons of his shirt. There was nothing hurried about her movements, though her hands shook a little with the effort of keeping them steady, of reining back the powerful need that was building within her. He stood completely still as caressingly she trailed the backs of her fingers down the strip of lean, well-muscled flesh that was revealed by his unbuttoned shirt, and the only evidence of his desire was the quickening thud of his heart.

Her hand moved downwards, skimming over the buckle of his belt.

Not the only evidence... She felt his whole body tense as her palm brushed the hardness of his arousal beneath his clothes. For a second his head tipped back, as if he was in pain, but then he seemed to gather himself, and as his hands gripped her shoulders Lily couldn't tell whether he was taking control or abandoning it.

The bed was as pale and cool as a lunar landscape in the mystical blue twilight. Tristan's hands slipped down her arms, making her shiver, and then he was taking her hands in his and drawing her towards it. She wasn't aware of the ground beneath her feet any more. Stars, brighter even than the ones lighting up the washed out sky outside, filled her head, gold and glittering as, very gently, he pushed one strap of her dress down over her shoulder and stroked a circle of bliss over the skin he had exposed.

Lily bit her lip to stop herself crying out into the thick silence. With maddening, excruciating slowness Tristan turned his attention to the other shoulder. In the fading light his face bore an expression of detached intensity, which made tongues of fire leap along her nerves, burning pathways into the hungry, molten core of her. With a care that was almost abstracted he took the pleated silk between his fingers, holding it for a second before sliding it off her shoulder.

The dress slithered to the floor like a curtain coming down, and Lily stood before him, naked apart from a pair of tiny silk knickers.

She was almost too beautiful, Tristan thought with an edge of despair. Too perfect.

As she stood there, the muted evening folding around her like veils of blue voile, softening the planes and angles of her impossibly slender body and silvering the coronet of leaves in her hair, she looked like some remote and untouchable figure from ancient mythology. With careful restraint he reached out and took her waist between his hands, stroking his thumbs upwards to the small, exquisite breasts.

'Selene…' he murmured, and her head jerked back, her eyes filled with shock and hurt, but he felt the convulsive tremor that shook her as his palms brushed her hardened nipples and she didn't try to move away.

'No!' she said harshly, raggedly. 'That's not my name. I'm Lily…'

Tristan laughed softly. Her misplaced insecurity touched him. As if anyone would forget her name. 'I know that.' He bent his head, pressing his lips to the pale skin below her collarbone, unhurriedly moving downwards. 'Earlier I thought you were a golden Demeter, but now you look like Selene, the goddess of the moon.'

She closed her eyes and buried her shy smile in the silk of his hair. 'Tell me about her.'

'She fell in love with a mortal—a handsome shepherd boy called Endymion—and she couldn't bear the thought of ever being separated from him.' Tristan's mouth hovered for a second over the tight bud of her nipple, the warmth of his breath caressing the quivering, darkened flesh until he felt his own desire pounding at the barriers of his self-control. 'So she asked Zeus to grant him eternal sleep, so that he would never die and never grow older. Every night she used to go and lie with him.'

He straightened up and looked at her. Her eyes were incandescent with unconcealed need but laughter gleamed in their depths as she raised herself up onto her tiptoes to kiss him again.

'You seem to be on first name terms with all the A-list goddesses,' she said softly against his mouth. 'Either you have friends in very high places or a degree in Classics.'

He pulled away sharply, dipping his head downwards so she couldn't see his face. 'Neither,' he said tonelessly. 'I have *half* a degree in Classics.'

'You gave it up?'

'Yes. I dropped out.' His voice was soft, but he couldn't quite keep the bitterness from it as he pressed his mouth against her scented skin and pushed away the thoughts of the life he should have had. He heard her gasp as he ran the tip of his tongue around the rosy halo of her nipple and he felt her whole body momentarily convulse against him as he took her deeper into his mouth, sucking, kissing, losing himself in her.

Her arms tightened around his neck, her breath in his ear was a soft siren song of want. The familiar room, his refuge, his private sanctuary, blurred and blackened as the blood pounded in his head, a primitive, insistent rhythm, drowning out everything else but the miracle of her cool, creamy flesh on his tongue.

Sense left him. His brain—exhausted, jaded, cynical—crashed, and the jagged pattern of his constant, tormented thoughts levelled out into a flat line of submission while his body and his senses took over. Her hands were on his belt, working swiftly, deftly at the buckle, then pushing his trousers downwards, his underwear too, and together they sank down onto the bed, their mouths not leaving each other, their hands not pausing in their urgent, hungry exploration. Dimly Tristan was aware that his shirt still hung loose and unbuttoned from his shoulders, but he was too far gone to stop and take it off.

He was too far gone for anything. The awfulness of the last few days, the constant, grinding stress, the relentless horror that pushed at the steel barriers he placed around his mind had suddenly gone, sucked into the vortex of physical need, of blissful annihilation. It was as if some inbuilt survival mechanism had clicked into place inside him, finally shutting off the maddening need to think and plan and stay rigidly in control…

Did she sense this as she pushed him gently back onto the moonlit bed, and rose above him? Her flawless skin was bleached to ghostly whiteness, intensifying the dark glitter of her eyes and the crimson of her kiss-bruised mouth as she dipped her head and slid down his thighs, parting her glistening lips and…

The outside world slipped from focus. Even the machine-gun snap of the fireworks faded to a dull crackle. There was nothing beyond the sensation of her soft mouth on his burning, swollen flesh, the feathery caress of her hair brushing his skin as she bent over him. Opening his eyes, looking down, he could see the pale arc of her back. In his dazzled head her shoulder blades looked like angel's wings.

Dios… Dios mio…

He was on the edge, on the brink of oblivion, holding on by his fingernails, but he wouldn't allow himself to let go and hurtle through the secret darkness to his own bliss. Sitting up, he caught hold of her and, sliding his hands into her hair, pulled her head up.

'My turn now.'

Meeting his eyes through the blue gloom Lily was instantly flooded with slippery heat. Though his face was tense and set, they were black and liquid with arousal. Wordlessly she let him pull her towards him, so that they were facing each other on the moon-drenched bed. One hand was in her hair, his strong fingers slowly massaging her scalp, sending shivering electrical impulses down through her entire body. The other remained at his side as he looked at her.

He simply *looked…*

Lily Alexander was used to being looked at. It was her job. Her life. It made her feel many things…resentful, jaded, uncomfortable, contemptuous… Never like this before. Never as if she were burning from the inside, as if fire were spreading from the cradle of her pelvis through the centre of her, while torrents of honeyed desire soaked her. Her body was a tool of a job she'd never wanted, and over the years she had learned to regard it with dispassionate acceptance, as if it were something impersonal. But now this man was bringing it to life. Transforming it from an aesthetically successful arrangement of bones, muscles, limbs into a finely tuned network of tingling nerves, heat, pounding blood. By making it his, he was giving it back to her.

His fingers circled her navel, making the taut skin of her midriff quiver as shock waves of screaming anticipation zigzagged downwards, and then in a gesture that was more intimate than anything that had happened before he gently laid his flattened hand against her stomach.

For a few heartbeats they were both very still. Lily wondered distantly if he could feel her stomach contract and tighten with clenching desire beneath his palm. Warmth radiated into her from his touch, and she was aware that beneath the storm of need and arousal she also felt strangely still, as if the clamour that had raged inside her for so long was finally hushed.

She felt cherished.

And then the moment was gone, and another crashing wave of need hit her as he slid one finger beneath the silken top of her pants, slipping them down over her hips. She could feel her pelvis tilting upwards in brazen invitation, her head tipping backwards so that he was supporting it in his cupped hand, as the fingers of his other hand splayed downwards, towards the swollen heart of her desire. She felt herself opening for him as his clever, unhurried fingers stroked and caressed, moving inexorably closer, until she could bear the waiting no longer, twisting and writhing her hips in a wordless plea for release.

With a whisper-light touch of a fingertip he brushed the tight bud of her longing, holding her tightly as a shuddering gasp tore through her in response.

'Please, Tristan…' she begged. 'I can't wait any more…'

Her hands were on his shoulders, gripping him tightly as if to anchor herself. She felt as if she were breaking up, slipping away, as if she needed him to hold her and keep her together. Almost imperceptibly he shook his head.

'We can't.'

His voice was hard, jagged, and as he spoke his grip on her tightened as if he had anticipated the rip tide of shock and disappointment that tore through her at his words.

Her head whipped up and she gave a sharp, indrawn hiss. '*Why?* Why not?'

'Contraception. I have nothing.'

The tension left her in a rush. 'But th-that's OK, it's fine,' she stammered, inarticulate with relief, leaning in towards him again and murmuring into his neck as she trailed a line of kisses along the line of his jaw. 'I'm on the pill…and I'm clean… It's quite safe.'

He gave a harsh laugh. 'But you don't know about me.'

His words stopped her in her tracks and she pulled away to look into his face. In the half-light his deep-set eyes were shadowed, making it impossible to read the expression in them. Her gaze travelled slowly over his face. The moonlight turned his skin to marble, and accentuated the sculpted perfection of his cheekbones, the deep cleft in his chin.

She shook her head, momentarily struck dumb by his beauty, trying to find the words.

'No,' she said eventually, reaching out and stroking her hand down his face in a mixture of tenderness and reverence. 'But I trust you. I'll do what you say. If we have to stop this here…'

Her hand was on his chest now. Lily was aware of the steady, strong beat of his heart beneath her palm.

'No.' He barely moved his lips as he said the word. 'There's no need to stop. It's safe.'

Exhilaration leapt inside her, instantly detonating tiny explosions of desire along the winding pathways of her central nervous system. A low gasp of relief and longing was torn from her lips in the moment before Tristan took possession of them, and then her head was filled with nothing but the musky scent of his skin, the champagne taste of his mouth. His hands gripped her pelvis, pulling her onto him, while her fingers tore at his muscular shoulders.

He entered her with a powerful thrust that made her want to scream out with joy. She was taut and trembling with ecstasy, so stupefied with desire that she was unable to think, only to feel. Bliss flooded every cell of her body, making her pliant and helpless, but Tristan's arms were tight around her. Gently he laid her down in the cool sheets, kissing her breast, her throat, finally coming back to her parted, panting lips as the rhythm of their bodies gathered pace and her legs twined helplessly around his hips.

Lily's final, triumphant cry of release shattered the still blue evening at exactly the same time as the finale of fireworks exploded beyond the lake. They lay together, their breathing fast and laboured as the sweat dried on their bodies and pink and gold stars cartwheeled through the blue infinity above.

It had rained in the night.

Getting up from the crumpled bed Lily had gone to the window and looked out onto a cool world of silver and green. The rain had fallen in sheets, turning the glassy surface of the lake misty.

As she looked out of the window of the Jeep as it rattled over the arid African plane just a little over twenty-four hours later it was almost impossible to believe that she hadn't dreamed it. Hadn't dreamed that cool lushness; hadn't dreamed turning away, crossing the floor back to the bed where Tristan lay, his arm thrown across the place where she'd been lying.

Hadn't dreamt the expression of torment on his face.

And as she'd watched him he'd cried out, a harsh, bitter shout of anger, or of pain, and without thinking Lily had slipped back beneath the sheets beside him, cradling his beautiful head against her, stroking him, murmuring soothing, meaningless, instinctive sounds into his hair until the room had reassembled itself in the grey light of dawn and she had felt the tension leave his body.

Then she had got quietly out of bed and put on her silk dress and slipped silently out the door and down the stairs. He hadn't reminded her about the Heathrow terminal, as he'd so jokingly promised. He hadn't woken up to say goodbye.

The Jeep stopped at the camp. The heat was already almost beyond endurance, the air thick with the dust thrown up by their convoy of vehicles. Getting stiffly out, Lily wondered whether she was strong enough to face what lay ahead.

She bent her head, closing her eyes for a second and running her tongue over dry lips.

But she had found the strength to walk away from the tower yesterday morning.

If she could do that, she could do anything.

CHAPTER FOUR

London, six weeks later.

'CONGRATULATIONS, Miss Alexander.'

Lily looked uncomprehendingly into the smiling face of the doctor. She had come here expecting an explanation for why she had felt so awful since picking up a stomach bug on her trip to Africa just over a month ago, but Dr Lee looked as if he was about to tell her she'd won the lottery, not contracted some nasty tropical disease.

She frowned. 'You have the test results back?'

'I have indeed. I can now confirm that you don't have malaria, yellow fever, hepatitis…' he let each sheet of flimsy yellow lab paper drift down onto the desk between them as he went through the sheaf of test results '…typhoid, rabies or diptheria.'

Lily's heart sank.

It wasn't that she wanted a nasty tropical disease, but at least if she knew what was causing the constant, bone-deep fatigue, the metallic tang in her mouth that made everything taste like iron filings, then maybe she could do something about it. Take something to make it go away, so she could start sleeping at night instead of lying awake, hot and breathless, fighting the drag of nausea in the back of her throat and trying not to think of that other night. Of Tristan Romero.

She shook her head, trying to concentrate. That was another

thing that was almost impossible these days, but with huge effort she dragged her mind back from its now-familiar refuge in a twilit tower, a moon-bleached bed...

She had to put that behind her. Forget.

'I'm sorry, I don't understand. If all the tests have come back negative, then what—?'

'Ah, not quite *all* the tests show a negative result. There was one that has come back with a resounding positive.' Dr Lee folded his hands together on the desk and beamed at her. 'You're pregnant, Miss Alexander. Congratulations.'

The walls seemed to rush towards her, blocking out the bright September sunshine outside, compacting the air in Dr Lee's very elegant consulting room so that it was too thick to breathe. Lily felt the blood fall away from her head, leaving a roaring, echoing emptiness, which was filled a few seconds later by the distant sound of Dr Lee's voice. She was aware of his hand on the back of her head.

'That's it...just keep your head down like that, there's a good girl. This sort of reaction isn't uncommon...Your hormones... Nothing to worry about. Just give it a moment and you'll soon feel right as rain...'

Rain.

The memory of the lake at Stowell in the misty pre-dawn light rose up from the darkness inside her head; the rain falling in shining, silvery sheets on a landscape of pearly greyness. She remembered the musical sound of it, a timeless, soothing lullaby as she had held Tristan, stroking the tension from his sleeping body, while all the time, unknown, unseen, this... secret miracle had been unfurling within her own flesh.

'There. Better now?'

She sat up, inhaling deeply, and nodded. 'Yes. Sorry. The shock...'

Dr Lee's face was compassionate, concerned. 'It wasn't planned?'

'N-no,' she stammered. 'I don't understand. I'm on the pill.'

'Ah. Well, the contraceptive pill is pretty good, but nothing gives a one-hundred-per-cent guarantee, I'm afraid. The sickness bug you picked up in Africa could have impaired the pill's effectiveness, if that was quite soon after…' He cleared his throat and left the sentence tactfully unfinished.

Mutely Lily nodded.

'In that case it would tell me that it's still very early days,' he said gently. 'There are many options open to you, you know.'

Lily got clumsily to her feet and held onto the back of the chair for support as the meaning of his words penetrated her numb brain.

Options.

'Think about it,' Dr Lee said with professional neutrality. 'Talk it over with your partner, and let me know what you decide.'

She shook her head. 'I don't have a partner. He's not… He wouldn't…' She stopped, her mouth open as she tried to articulate the degree of Tristan Romero's absence from her life without making herself sound like a cheap tart. *I barely know him… I don't have his number and he made it perfectly clear that he wouldn't want to hear from me again… It was meant to be sex without strings. A one-night stand.*

Oh, God, maybe she was a cheap tart. She remembered the hunger with which she'd pushed him back on the moonlit bed and taken him in her mouth; remembered the despair that had sliced through her like forked lightning when he'd said they shouldn't go any further, that he had no contraception, and the desperation with which she had assured him it was safe.

'This is nothing to do with him.' Her knuckles were white as she gripped the back of the chair. 'It's not his fault, or his responsibility.'

Dr Lee's eyebrows rose. 'Miss Alexander—'

'It's *mine.* My fault, my responsibility. My baby.' The words sounded strange and unfamiliar, but as she spoke them the same peculiar, illogical sense of peace that she had felt that night in the tower, in Tristan's arms, came back to her, shivering through her whole body like a delicate meteor shower. She lifted her chin, meeting the concerned gaze of the doctor with a determined smile. 'It's my baby. And I'm keeping it.'

'A call for you, Señor Romero.'

Tristan looked up irritably from the computer screen. 'Bianca, I told you I did not wish to be disturbed.'

'*Lo siento*, señor, but it is Señor Montague. I thought you would wish to speak to him.'

Tristan gave an abrupt nod as he reached for the phone. '*Sí. Gracias.*' He swung his chair round so that he was looking out over the Placa St Jaume and the sunlit grand façade of the City Hall opposite. The Banco Romero de Castelan was one of the oldest and most well established in Spain, and its main offices were in a grand and prestigious building in the heart of Barcelona. It was beautiful, but oppressive. The sun had moved across the square, so that the high-ceilinged rooms with their echoing marble floors were in deep shadow from lunchtime onwards, although that wasn't the only reason Tristan felt permanently chilled when he was here.

'Tom.'

'At last. You're impossible to get hold of,' Tom grumbled good-naturedly. 'Were you in the middle of ravishing some innocent from the accounts department or something? Your secretary seemed remarkably reluctant to let me speak to you.'

'You pay too much attention to the gossip columns,' said Tristan acidly. 'I'm *working*. Believe it or not, banks don't run themselves. Bianca was under strictest instructions not to let any calls or any visitors through, so I don't know how you persuaded her.'

'It's called charm, old chap. It's what those of us who can't get women into bed merely by glancing at them have to rely on. Which one is Bianca? The dark haired one with the cleavage you could get lost in?'

Tristan grinned reluctantly. 'No. Redhead, looks like Sophia Loren, although since you're soon to be a married man I hardly think it's relevant.' His smile became a little stiffer as he said, 'How is your lovely bride-to-be?'

'Oh, you know; beautiful, sexy…and suddenly totally pre-occupied with flower arrangements and bridesmaid dresses. I tell you, it's a whole new world. In my darker moments I have actually found myself thinking that your commitment to anony-mous, emotionless one night stands might not be so insane after all.'

'At last you've seen the light,' Tristan said dryly. 'It's not too late to change your mind, you know.'

Tom laughed. 'Oh, it is. Far too late. I'm at the mercy of forces way beyond my control—namely Scarlet and my mother. My mother's decided that we have to have an engage-ment party and as best man I'm afraid you have to be there. That's why I was phoning—can you manage the last Saturday in September? Scarlet thinks that a small dinner at Stowell will be the least alarming way for her family to meet mine.'

Tristan glanced at his BlackBerry. Parties in Madrid and Lisbon, a business dinner in Milan and an invitation to spend the weekend at the island retreat of some friends were already filled in.

'What if I said no?'

'Then we'll make it October.' Tom sounded completely un-concerned. Leaning back in his chair, pushing a hand through his hair, Tristan stifled a sigh, recognising that he wasn't going to be able to get out of this one easily, but not willing to examine the reason why he wanted to.

'I'll try,' he said curtly. 'But one of the projects is at a diffi-cult stage at the moment. You know what it's like. I can't promise anything.'

'No. Of course not. You never can.' Across the miles Tristan heard the quiet resignation in Tom's voice. 'You are the undis-puted world champion of not promising anything and not com-mitting yourself. But pencil it in and try to be there if nothing more important comes up.'

'I'll get back to you,' Tristan said coldly. Cutting the call, he stood up, staring for a moment at the phone in his hand as Tom's words echoed reproachfully through his head.

Every one of them was true, of course.

He swore, slamming his fist down on the polished wood of the desk from which generations of Romeros had run their banking empire, exploiting their name, consolidating their power and their fortune, regardless of who they destroyed in the process. And he was as cold and ruthless as the rest of them. He never allowed himself to forget that or to believe any different, whatever he did by way of atonement. His blue-tinged blood ran thick with the sin and corruption of his fore-fathers. Of his father. The only way in which he differed from them was that he was honest about it.

Honest.

Honest enough to admit that he was beyond redemption. Honest enough to know that he was best alone.

He gave a short, harsh exhalation of laughter. OK, so while he was being so unswervingly truthful he might as well admit to himself the real reason that he was so reluctant to go to Tom's party. Back to Stowell. Because, he thought in self-disgust, *she* would be there.

Lily Alexander.

The girl with the skin that smelled like almonds, and felt like velvet.

The girl who had caught him at a low ebb, and got past his defences in a way that had never happened before.

And wouldn't happen again, he thought, steeling himself. What did it matter if she was there or not? He would treat her in exactly the same way he treated every other woman he had slept with and discarded. With distant courtesy. And then he would walk away.

Lily's throat was tight and her fingers nervously pleated the rose-coloured silk of her dress. 'A small dinner party to celebrate your engagement,' she whispered. 'That's what you said on the phone. Scarlet, just look at all this…'

She looked anxiously around Stowell's grand hall, where a steady stream of people in evening dress were drifting in through the vast doorway and indulging in an orgy of air-kissing. 'It's like a scene from Georgette Heyer.'

Scarlet laughed and tucked her arm through Lily's, drawing her close. 'I know, I know. Ridiculous, isn't it? We were supposed to be keeping it really small, but in the end I just couldn't bear to leave anyone out, so we've ended up inviting virtually everyone we know.'

Lily felt her heart perform an agonising twist-and-plummet motion inside her chest.

'Everyone?' She slicked her tongue over lips that were suddenly dry and stinging. 'Tom's friends too?'

'Oh, yes, he's worse than me. He's invited just about everyone he ever went to school with, and his entire family.' Scarlet dropped her voice. 'My poor parents are completely out of their depth. You will look after them, won't you, Lily?'

Lily nodded, for a moment unable to speak due to the huge lump of cement that seemed to have lodged in her chest. 'Of course,' she managed at last. 'It'll be lovely to see them.'

That much was true. When Lily was growing up Scarlet's parents had provided her with everything from home-cooked meals to help with schoolwork and advice about boyfriends, and numerous other things that her own mother had been utterly ill equipped to give her. As Scarlet gave her arm a squeeze Lily found herself wondering what Mr and Mrs Thomas would make of her current predicament.

'God, I've missed you,' Scarlet was saying. 'You can't imagine how much I've missed you.' In spite of the diamonds that glittered at her throat and her very sophisticated swept-up hairstyle, she suddenly looked very uncertain, and Lily was reminded of when they were teenagers, worrying about whether anyone would ever kiss them. 'Just because I'm getting married, things between us won't change, will they? We'll still be best friends? Still tell each other everything?'

Lily hesitated, swallowing back the guilt that choked her. 'Of course.'

Sliding her arm free of Lily's, Scarlet grabbed a couple of glasses of champagne from the tray of a hovering waitress. She thrust one into Lily's hand and clinked her own against the rim. 'Here's to us…to friendship that nothing can shake.'

A hot tide of nausea instantly erupted inside Lily's stomach as her newly heightened senses picked up the sweet-sharp scent of alcohol and rebelled against it. God, why hadn't she brought a ready supply of ginger biscuits to keep the sickness at bay? She felt the sweat break out on her upper lip as her throat tightened convulsively.

'Lily? Are you all right? What's wrong?'

Mutely Lily shook her head. In front of her Scarlet's face was a blur of concern and regret sliced through her. For the first time since she was ten years old she was keeping something from her best friend and it didn't feel right. But how could she possibly break the news that she was pregnant when she hadn't even told Scarlet about what had happened that night?

So much had happened so quickly, she thought wearily. She hadn't told Scarlet about Tristan simply because she hadn't had a chance. She'd gone straight to Africa the day after the costume ball, and when she'd returned it had been to find Scarlet starry-eyed and utterly preoccupied with her engagement to Tom Montague. He'd proposed, she told Lily dreamily, at the culmination of the firework display at the party.

Somehow Lily hadn't felt it was tactful to mention what she had been doing at that precise moment…

'I didn't think you looked well,' Scarlet was saying now as she put her arm around Lily's shoulders and guided her towards the door. 'In fact, you haven't been yourself since you got back from Africa. I think it's more than just being affected by the stuff you saw there. You need to see a doctor and get some blood tests done or something.'

'I have,' Lily muttered weakly. They had reached the wide stone stairs in the entrance hall and as they slowly began to descend the cool air from the open doors to the courtyard touched her face and dispersed the suffocating feeling of nausea a little. She took a deep breath, realising that she couldn't really put off telling Scarlet any longer, but not quite knowing how to say it. Pausing to lean against the balustrade at the foot of the stairs, she turned her face towards the doorway and felt the chill September breeze lift her hair.

Scarlet shot her a worried look. 'And? What did he say?'

'Nothing. I mean, I'm not ill.' She faltered, unable to meet Scarlet's eye and looking over her shoulder as she began hesitantly, 'The thing is, I'm—'

She stopped, her mouth open. The crimson walls of the great room billowed and swayed and the vaulted ceiling seemed to rush towards her as someone came in through the huge doors from the blue evening outside. For a moment she thought it was her mind playing tricks on her, conjuring up the image of the tall, effortlessly elegant figure, the perfect, impassive face, in the same way that someone lost in the desert might imagine a verdant oasis in the distance. But then he looked up and she was plunged straight into the pools of his eyes.

This was no mirage.

Frowning, Scarlet turned her head in the direction of Lily's gaze. 'Oh, Tristan's here. Tom'll be pleased,' she said vaguely before turning her attention back to Lily. 'So, what did the doctor say it was, then? The old "too much travel, too much work" thing again? Lily?'

'It doesn't matter.' Lily's voice had dried up to a husk of a whisper. Tristan was coming towards them, one hand loosely thrust into the pocket of his trousers. Every beautiful inch of him, every relaxed, graceful movement declared his utter self-assurance and complete ease, while she felt as if her insides were slowly being fed through a paper shredder. She wondered whether she might actually be about to pass out cold. The idea of blissful oblivion was remarkably appealing.

'Congratulations, Scarlet.' Tristan spoke gravely as he bent to kiss each of Scarlet's cheeks. 'Tom is a very lucky man. You look radiant tonight.'

There had been times in the past eight weeks when Lily had managed to convince herself that her mind was exaggerating the power of Tristan Romero de Losada Montalvo's attraction. During the blank hours of those sleepless nights the memory of his cool, moonlit perfection had taken on an almost mythical quality, mingling as she slid into restless, fragmented sleep with the story he had told her about the moon goddess and Endymion, until she could no longer distinguish reality from fantasy, dreams from memories.

But she had exaggerated nothing, and the beauty of his chiselled angel's face shocked her afresh. She flattened herself back against the stone balustrade, both dreading and burning for the moment when he would turn his attention to her, certain that the secret she carried within her body was written all over her face.

'Tristan!'

Tom's triumphant shout echoed from above, and Lily felt a mixture of frustration and relief as the spell of anticipation was broken. A second later Tom was clattering down the stairs towards them, a lopsided grin on his face. 'You're hardly over the threshold and already you're kissing my fiancée. Have you no respect for the sanctity of marriage?'

Tristan raised his hands in an elegant gesture of helplessness. 'Haven't I always said that you can't hold a woman with a piece of paper?'

'Unless she wants to be held,' laughed Scarlet slightly awkwardly as Tom put his arm around her shoulders and pulled her to him. He dropped a kiss on her cheek.

'Sorry to drag her away, but there are about five hundred distant relations of mine up there demanding to meet her, so you have to release her—just for the time being.' He started to move off, pulling Scarlet back up the stairs with him. Keeping her eyes fixed on the stone-flagged floor, Lily felt panic rising like flood water up from the soles of her feet at the prospect of being left alone with Tristan. 'We'll catch up later once the hordes have been satisfied!' Tom called back from halfway up the stairs, then added with an airy wave of his hand, 'Sorry, you two have met, haven't you? At the summer ball?'

Her heart was thudding wildly. He could probably hear it. God, he could probably *see* it. Heat bloomed in her cheeks as she steeled herself to look into his face. The face of the man who was going to be the father of her child.

His expression was cool, distant, polite. And when he spoke the tone of his voice perfectly matched it.

'Have we?'

CHAPTER FIVE

THERE were people who enjoyed deliberately inflicting pain, as Tristan Romero de Losada Montalvo knew only too well.

He was not one of them.

However, when it came to women he was firmly of the belief that it was necessary to be cruel to be kind, and he had absolutely no intention of allowing Lily Alexander to think that there would be any kind of repeat of what had happened on that hot night in the summer. Or giving her any hint of how much the memory of it had troubled him afterwards.

He watched hurt cloud her slanting, silvery eyes and tensed himself against a sudden rush of unfamiliar guilt. He had expected anger, indignation, a slap in the face—all of which he deserved, and had received from many women similarly slighted in the past. Lily Alexander's quiet dignity unsettled him.

'Yes, we have,' she said softly, almost apologetically. 'I was the girl with…with the dove.'

Instantly her words transported him back to the tower in the dusk and he felt as if the air had been forced from his lungs as he recalled the gentle murmur of her voice, the compassion that shone in her eyes. *And the effect it had had on him.*

One-nil to Lily Alexander.

He nodded slowly. 'Of course.' His lips twitched into a faint, reluctant smile. 'Selene. The girl with the dove.'

Her eyes flew to meet his, and, seeing the cautious hope that flared there, he cursed himself. The golden rules of engagement were keep it emotionless, impersonal and keep it as a one-off. He had broken the first one in the tower, and the consequences of that had been difficult enough to deal with. He certainly wasn't going to break either of the others.

He looked away.

'Yes,' she whispered. 'I wonder what happened to it?'

Tristan paused. The next morning when he'd gone up to the dovecote at the top of the tower there had been no sign of the injured dove, which probably meant it had been taken by some predator in the night. But he wasn't entirely heartless.

Not *entirely.*

'It recovered and flew away, I think,' he said before taking a step backwards and half turning towards the stairs. 'Anyway, it's nice to see you again,' he said with blank courtesy, taking a step backwards and half turning towards the stairs, 'but now, if you'll excuse me, I should…'

For the brief moments that Tristan's gaze had held hers and a thousand wordless images had risen up between them, Lily was aware of the blood rushing to her face, her chest tightening and the breath catching in her throat.

It wasn't a good combination with morning sickness. As Tristan turned away she struggled to take air into her starved lungs as a swirling tide of nausea threatened to drag her under. Groping for the stone balustrade, she felt her legs buckle, and before she could grasp at anything for support the world had gone black and she was falling.

He caught her. Of course he caught her. It would have been too much to hope for that she could just faint quietly, in private, without her humiliation being witnessed by the man who had made it perfectly plain he wanted nothing to do with her. Held tightly against the strong wall of his chest, tugged by powerful currents of sickness and dizziness, she wanted to protest, but knew that the slightest movement on her part could tip her over the edge. And the thought of throwing up all over Tristan

Romero's impeccable dinner jacket was enough to make her submit quietly.

He carried her easily, as if she really had the kind of petite build that she and Scarlet used to wish for. Cool air caressed her face, filling her lungs and sending oxygen tingling back into her bloodstream, so that she dared to risk opening her eyes again.

They were outside, walking alongside the wall of the castle. Her face was inches from the hard line of Tristan's jaw, so she could clearly see the tautness in its set, the cleft in his chin, his full, finely shaped mouth. She took a deep breath in, and just the scent of his skin was enough to make her feel faint with longing again. Her body went rigid as she fought to escape his iron hold, desperate to put some distance between her treacherous, needy body and his hard, strong one.

'I'm fine now...I'm so sorry...Please, put me down.'

'Wait.'

The word was a low snarl, and instantly Lily let the fight go out of her as humiliation and despair ebbed back. She had imagined this meeting a thousand times, planned how she would be perfectly reasonable, perfectly controlled and in command of her emotions as she told him the facts and reassured him that she expected nothing from him. No demands, no histrionics, no apologies.

And definitely no fainting.

They rounded a corner and found themselves at the side of the castle that faced the gardens, which lay in a sweeping arc before them. There was a scrolled iron bench set in the shelter of the castle wall; Tristan put Lily down on it, and stood back, looming over her.

She couldn't look at him, not trusting herself to keep the truth from showing on her face. Below, the lake was a disc of black, with the tower in its centre looking dark and forbidding. She couldn't look at that either.

'Better now?'

'Yes. I'm sorry.' Suddenly she was glad that she was sitting down. Adrenaline burned through her, making her feel shaky and spacey as the moment when she would have to tell him rushed towards her with the terrifying inevitability of an express train. She bit her lip and said hesitantly, 'In a funny kind of way it's worked out rather well.'

'Meaning?'

His voice was icy. She could feel goosebumps prickling her bare arms. 'I wanted the chance to talk to you…alone.'

His face darkened, hardened, and he sighed and turned away. 'I thought I explained. I thought you understood that the night we shared—'

'I did. I do.' She cut him off, speaking with soft determination, but her heart felt as if it might burst. *Oh, God…this is it.* 'But I thought you had a right to know. I'm pregnant.'

For a moment he didn't move. Then he took a couple of steps forward, away from her, and Lily caught a fleeting glimpse of his hands, balled tightly into fists, before he thrust them into the pockets of his trousers.

It was cold. She was aware of the chilly iron scrollwork of the bench biting into her flesh through the thin silk of her dress, but she was powerless to move.

I'm sorry. The words formed on her lips, so that she could almost taste them, sweet and tempting. But she refused to speak them. She was used to saying what other people wanted to hear and the habit was hard to break, but the truth was she wasn't sorry. She was glad.

Her own parenting, by a mother who was barely out of her teens, barely able to cope, had been haphazard and inadequate, but it had only fuelled Lily's need to nurture. Her dolls had always been carefully dressed in pyjamas, lovingly tucked into their shoebox beds and read to, even when she had not. For as long as she could remember, the need to love and to nurture had been there inside her, beating alongside her heart, echoing through the empty spaces in her life and in her body. She hadn't wanted to listen to it until that moment in Dr Lee's office when he'd told her the news. The news that should have horrified her, but had actually filled her with a profound, primitive joy.

She wanted this baby. More than she'd wanted anything, ever before.

Slowly Tristan turned round. The expression on his face was like a January dawn in Siberia—dark, bleak, and utterly forbidding.

'Congratulations,' he said, very softly. 'To you, and to the father.'

'*What?*' With a gasp of incredulity she leapt to her feet. 'No! You don't understand. I—'

He turned away from her again, looking out over the garden as he cut through her heated protest. 'I have to warn you to think very carefully about what you're just about to say, Lily.'

His voice was quiet, but there was an edge to it that was like sharpened steel against her throat. Lily felt the sweat cool to ice water on the back of her neck, and clenched her teeth against their sudden chattering, dropping back down onto the bench as her knees gave way beneath her.

'You can't intimidate me.'

To her surprise Tristan laughed; a hollow, humourless laugh, tinged with despair. 'You really don't understand at all, do you? I'm not trying to *intimidate* you. I'm trying to *save* you. I'm trying to give you a *chance*. To give you the freedom to make your own choices, because—' He broke off suddenly. Dragging a hand through his hair, he sat down wearily beside her and dropped his face into his hands for a moment. When he lifted it again the dead expression in his eyes turned her insides to ice. 'Because the second that you say this child is mine, all that will be taken away from you.'

Lily clasped her hands together in her lap, twisting and kneading at her own numb fingers as panic made the words tumble from her mouth. 'I don't want anything from you, Tristan. I don't want your money, or any kind of recognition or admission of responsibility. I was on the pill, but I was ill when I was in Africa, so it's my fault, I accept that completely, but I thought you ought to know that the baby is yours.'

'Who else knows?'

'N-no one.' Despite the mildness of the evening she was shivering violently now. 'I haven't told anyone. Not even Scarlet yet, but I can't hide it for much longer.'

'You're going ahead with it?'

'Yes!' A white-hot spark of anger glowed in the dark void of her mind at the casual brutality of the question. 'Yes, I bloody well am!'

Nothing penetrated his terrible, glacial calm. 'And you intend to name me as the father? On the birth certificate?'

'Of course!' Her chattering teeth were so firmly clamped together that she spoke almost without moving her lips, her voice a low, furious rasp. 'I *won't* have my child growing up without a name. An identity.'

'No?' He leaned back on the bench, lifting his head and inhaling deeply before turning towards her. His eyes were cold and measuring. 'How much would it take to make you reconsider, Lily? I'm only going to say this once, so I advise you to think before answering.'

'You want to *pay me off*?' Lily gasped, torn between laughter and the urge to do something violent. 'You want to *bribe* me to keep you out of your own child's life? My God, Tristan, you cold, cold, bastard! Never. No way!'

His eyes narrowed, but they stayed fixed on hers. 'You're quite sure? Even if it was for your own good?'

She shook her head determinedly as strength and assurance ebbed back into her frozen body. She was on firmer ground here. 'I'm not interested in what's good for me now, Tristan. All I care about is my baby. I want it to know who it is, to have a history. An identity. Roots.'

Things that she'd never had.

In one lithe movement he stood up. The gentle evening

seemed to darken as his broad shoulders blocked out the cloud-marbled sky. Slipping her feet from their high-heeled shoes, Lily tucked them up on the bench and wrapped her arms around her knees, hugging herself for warmth and subconsciously closing herself around the tiny, tentative life inside her.

Tristan was standing with his back to her, looking out over the garden to the dark tower. 'Well, then. I hope you're prepared for the alternative.'

'The alternative?' Something about the way he spoke made the hair stand up on the back of Lily's neck. 'What do you mean?'

He turned. 'It's all or nothing, Lily. If you name me as the father, we have to get married.'

'Married?'

The tenuous thread of certainty that had anchored her a moment ago snapped, leaving her with the feeling that she was plummeting through space, and all logic, all familiarity had diminished to a tiny point in the distance.

Married. The word that, when she was growing up, had always filled her with such wistful hope now sounded cold, comfortless, businesslike.

'But why?'

'Illegitimacy isn't an option,' he said flatly. 'You have to understand that. My family bloodline stretches back, unbroken, for six hundred years. It's my duty to respect and preserve that line. I can't…' here he faltered, but only for the briefest second '…I can't knowingly let a child of mine be born and brought up outside of its heritage.'

Stiffly, shakily, Lily got to her feet and walked slowly towards him. Standing in front of him, she looked into his eyes, trying to read the emotion that darkened them. 'And yet a moment ago you wanted to pay me off?' she said quietly. 'You wanted me and this baby out of your life and your family. I don't understand, Tristan. Why would you do that?'

Their eyes met across the chasm that separated them. His

gaze was unutterably bleak, achingly cold, but in that moment she forgot to be frightened or angry and wanted only to hold him. She wanted it so much that she almost felt dizzy.

His lips quirked into a bitter, heartbreaking smile. 'You want your child to have a history?' he said in a voice of mesmerising softness. 'In my family you get six centuries of it, and roots so deep they're like anchors of concrete, holding you so tightly that you can't move. That doesn't give you an identity, it makes it almost impossible to have one. That is why I never, ever intended to have children.' He paused, passing his hand briefly over his face in a gesture of eloquent hopelessness. 'I have no choice about the family I was born into, but you can still choose something different for your baby. Cut your losses, Lily. Get out while you still can.'

Lily's heart felt as if it were being seared with a blowtorch. Slowly, deliberately, she shook her head. 'Our baby,' she said quietly. The ground was cold beneath her bare feet and she was shivering, but her voice was strong and steady. '*Our* baby. I believe in family, Tristan. I believe in marriage.'

Tentative butterfly wings of hope were beginning to flutter inside her. He was offering her the thing she'd always longed for. Marriage; a proper family for this baby—not like the inadequate, truncated version she had grown up in. Not quite a fairy tale happy ending, but a version of it. Hadn't she always vowed that she would give her own children the family life she had never had?

'This won't be that kind of marriage,' Tristan said coldly. 'This will be in name only.'

'What do you mean?' she whispered.

He made a brief, dismissive gesture. 'I have a life. A life that I have carved out for myself against all the odds. A life that I won't give up and I won't share. You'll be my wife, but you'll have no right to ask anything about where I go or what I do.'

'That's not a marriage,' she protested fiercely, feeling the emptiness beginning to steal through her again. 'That's not a proper family.'

As she spoke he shrugged off his dinner jacket and now he laid it around her trembling shoulders, tugging the lapels so that her whole body jerked forwards. 'No. But it's the best I can offer,' he said harshly. 'I can't make you happy, Lily. I can't be a proper father to this child. Find someone who can.'

The deliciously scented warmth of his body lingered in the silk lining of his jacket, and she pulled it closer around her. The unexpected thoughtfulness of the gesture he had made breathed life back into the fragile hope inside her. Looking up into Tristan Romero's dark, aristocratic face, Lily saw the pain there, and instantly she was transported back to the tower; to standing at the window as the rain fell on the lake outside and looking at the watery moonlight washing his sleeping body on the bed. She remembered exactly the muscular curve of his back, the small, shadowy indentation of his spine at its base, the ridges of his ribs. She remembered the tracery of long, pale scars that cut across his shoulders and she remembered the suffering etched into his sleeping face and the anguish in his voice as he'd cried out...

She remembered gathering him to her. Stroking him until his heartbeat steadied, until the lines beneath his brows were smoothed away and she had chased away whatever nameless horrors tormented him. For a short while then, against the odds, she had touched him. She had reached him and he had clung to her. Could she reach him again? Not for a moment, but for a lifetime, for the sake of the baby she wanted so much?

That was what fairy tales were about. About quests that were seemingly impossible, where you had to follow your heart and fight for the things you believed in.

And she believed in love. In marriage. In families and fairy tales. She always had. Raising her chin now, she met his bleak gaze steadily.

'No. If that's how it has to be...we get married.'

He flinched, very slightly, his eyelids flickering shut for a split second before the steel shutters descended again and that small glimpse of suffering and humanity was concealed.

'Right. If that's your choice.' His voice was cold, clipped, but contained a note of weary resignation. 'Just for God's sake don't tell anyone yet.'

'But what about Scarlet?' she protested. 'I can't lie, Tristan—'

'No? Then maybe we should drop this whole charade now,' he said silkily.

'She's my best friend.'

His perfect, sculpted lips stretched into a sardonic smile. 'Then I would have thought that you would be able to see that announcing your own shotgun wedding at her engagement party might not be the most tactful thing to do. You can tell people in good time. For the moment you have to behave in a way that means it won't come as a complete surprise when you do.'

'How are we going to do that?' she whispered hoarsely.

'Just follow my lead,' he said coldly, turning on his heel and walking back towards the entrance to the castle. 'You might not be able to lie, but I hope you can act.'

For a moment Lily didn't move, watching him walk away, his head bent and his shoulders held very straight.

No. She couldn't act, as the director of the perfume commercials would certainly testify. But the thing was, in this case she suspected she wouldn't have to.

'What's going on?'

Tom's tone was as light as always but Tristan knew him well enough not to be deceived. Behind Tom's affable, self-deprecating façade was a mind sharp and incisive enough to have earned him a first at Oxford. He wouldn't be easy to fool.

Leaning against the massive stone fireplace, Tristan took a thoughtful sip of his drink and let his gaze wander around the room. 'Nothing. Why?'

The speeches officially announcing the engagement and welcoming Scarlet to Tom's illustrious family were over, and the guests had stirred and reassembled themselves as fresh bottles of champagne were circulated around. Lily was standing over by the window, talking to Scarlet's parents, who were finally beginning to lose a little of the terrified look they had worn all evening. The light from the fading, flame-streaked sky outside put roses in her pale cheeks.

'That's why,' said Tom gently. 'You haven't taken your eyes off her for the last two hours.'

Tristan's hand tightened around his glass. With some effort he tore his gaze from Lily and looked at Tom levelly.

'Come on, Tom. You're engaged, not blind. She's beautiful. Any man could be forgiven for looking.'

'As long as that's all you do.' Tom softened the warning with a smile. 'Lily's sweet. She deserves a nice steady guy who'll buy her flowers and give her breakfast in bed, not a man like you who'll—'

'Buy her diamonds and give her orgasms in bed?' Tristan cut in ruthlessly. 'It doesn't sound so bad to me.'

'Ah, well, that's because you can't see that there's more to life than money and sex.'

'How little faith you have in me.' Tristan took a swig of his drink and grimaced. 'What if I told you I've decided it's time to give up the one night stands and settle down?'

Tom laughed. 'I'd ask if it was just orange juice in that glass, or whether you've diluted it with vodka like you used to do in school. And then I'd probably look out the window to check for flying pigs and ask myself if it was April the first.' Throwing an arm round Tristan, he slapped him affectionately on the back before moving away to rejoin his other guests. 'The day you get married I'll swim naked around the moat,' he added with a grin.

Tristan didn't smile.

'Deal.'

At that moment he wished very fervently that there were vodka in his glass. And no orange juice. He wanted nothing more than to have something to slow the incessant, ruthless progress of his thoughts and bring warmth back to the frozen places inside him.

A baby.

His gaze moved inexorably back to Lily. She was sitting on the window seat now, deep in conversation with Scarlet's mother. Or rather, he noticed, Scarlet's mother was deep in conversation with her. Lily's head was bent slightly as she listened, her face thoughtful. The gentle, sleepy quality he had noticed the first time he met her struck him again as he watched the graceful movement of her hand as she smoothed a strand of hair back from her forehead.

He felt as if something were crushing his chest.

But it wasn't her beauty that caught him by the throat and squeezed. It was her goodness. Tom was right. She needed a decent man, a kind husband who would love her as she deserved to be loved.

Tristan Romero de Losada Montalvo knew with a cold, bleak certainty that he could never be that man.

He was the kind of man who was effortlessly good at everything he did, she knew that. So it came as no surprise to Lily to discover that Tristan's acting ability was excellent.

It wasn't a surprise. But it was still shocking.

She was acutely aware of his presence, as if some internal satellite navigation system were constantly signalling his whereabouts to her, inexorably pulling her towards him and making it impossible not to keep looking at him. Every time she did she found he was looking back, smiling a little, his eyes dark and glittering with obvious desire.

Acting the part.

And, of course, she was acting too. Standing with Scarlet's brother Jamie, as she smiled and talked and put her glass to her lips she was acting that everything was normal. Acting as if she weren't in the grip of raging pregnancy hormones, that she hadn't just agreed to enter into a loveless marriage with a notorious playboy, and—most challenging of all—that she weren't feeling as if her husband-to-be were slowly stripping her naked with his eyes from the other side of the room.

Husband?

The word was too domestic, too tame to be applied to the man who could make her squirm with guilty longing simply by looking at her from twenty feet away in a room full of people. Married life was going to be extremely uncomfortable if this was the effect he had on her.

Oh, God, what was she doing?

Scarlet's brother Jamie was talking about the band he was in at university. Making vague, encouraging noises, Lily tentatively turned her head to where Tristan was leaning against the huge stone fireplace talking to Tom's gorgeous teenage cousin. The cousin had her back to Lily, but Lily could imagine the expression of slavish adoration on her face from the way her head was tilted up, her whole body arched towards Tristan.

At that moment he looked up, his eyes meeting hers as if she had just pulled on some invisible wire stretching between them. The look was of such smouldering sensuality that Lily felt as if he had slammed her against the silk-covered wall and were holding her by the throat.

And then he smiled.

It was like sunrise. A slow warming, a delicious golden promise of the scorching heat to come. Lily was dimly aware of the cousin looking round, following the direction of his gaze, visibly wilting as she saw that it was directed at someone else.

'Get your coat, Ms Alexander, I think you've pulled a billionaire.'

Jamie's low, amused voice brought her back down to earth. She whipped her head round to face him again, trying to hide her flaming cheeks behind the curtain of her hair, but before she could think of a suitable explanation he dropped his voice and said, 'Right, he's coming over. This is the moment when I slip away and leave you to it. Good luck!'

She wanted to reply; she wanted to tell him to stay, but suddenly her mouth was so dry that the words didn't come. As Jamie vanished into the crowd she turned away, feigning interest in a portrait of an insipid man in a powdered wig with a sour lemon expression. Regency men were supposed to be rakish and dashing, she thought vaguely, remembering the Georgette Heyer heroes that she and Scarlet used to sigh over. They had despaired of ever finding men like that in Brighton…

'This would be a good time to leave, I think. Don't you?'

Her whole body jolted as the husky Spanish voice caressed her ear. Standing behind her, he very gently picked up the lock of hair that was falling over her shoulder and smoothed it back, tucking it behind her ear.

Tongues of flame were licking downwards into Lily's pelvis, making it hard to think straight.

'But I'm staying here tonight…'

'That was Plan A, sweetheart,' he murmured softly, putting his hands on her hips and pulling her against him as his mouth brushed her neck, her jaw, her ear lobe. 'I asked for your things to be brought down to my car. I'm taking you home.'

Lily couldn't speak.

But even if she had been able to she wouldn't have had the strength to argue.

CHAPTER SIX

ALMOST as breathtaking as the skill with which he had assumed
the act was the speed with which he dropped it.

Sitting beside him in the low passenger seat, her blood still
thrumming from his touch, Lily darted a surreptitious glance
at Tristan. The moment they had left Stowell he had distanced
himself from her completely, and in the light of the dashboard
his face was emotionless. The face of a handsome stranger.
She shivered.

'Are you cold?' he asked with distant courtesy.

'No. Well, a little.'

He flicked a switch and warm air caressed her. 'I think we
should get married as soon as possible,' he said, effortlessly
guiding the sleek black sports car around a bend in the road
without seeming to slow down.

Lily clung to the edge of her seat. 'So fast...' she murmured anxiously.

'Sorry.' He slowed down sharply. 'I'm not used to having a
passenger.'

A gust of laughter escaped her. 'I wasn't referring to your
driving. I meant life.' But as the words left her lips she knew
that he wasn't used to having passengers in that either. And that
was what she had become.

He showed no sign of having heard. 'What are your work
commitments for the next few weeks?'

She shrugged. 'Not much. When I got back from Africa and I wasn't well I told my agent not to take anything else on. And when I…well, since I found out about the baby…' the words gave her a warm little glow, like a tiny candle, deep inside; gentler, sweeter than the blowtorch of feeling he unleashed in her '…I haven't gone for any jobs. I'm still under contract to the couture people, though, and we're shooting another perfume commercial in Rome in two weeks time. And then, after that I'm pretty free, until the beginning of December…'

She bit back a hysterical giggle. It was as if she were making a dentist appointment, not arranging what should have been the most important event of her life.

'Good,' he said shortly. 'Keep it that way. I'll make all the necessary legal arrangements for the marriage and you can fly straight from Rome to Barcelona for the wedding.'

Lily swung her head round to look at him. 'Barcelona?'

One corner of Tristan's mouth lifted into an ironic smile. 'You're going to be a Romero bride. You have to get married in Spain.'

Her stomach clenched and her throat felt suddenly as if it were full of sand. She folded her hands over her stomach in an automatic gesture of comfort.

Romero bride.

'Of course,' she said hoarsely. 'I didn't think. Your family—'

'Leave them to me.' He frowned, as if something had just occurred to him. 'What about your family? Do you want them to be there?'

'God, no.' Lily swept her hand over the frosted window, clearing a space and looking out into the blackness beyond the cocoon of the car. 'My mother's in some ashram in India, balancing her chakras or something.'

Susannah Alexander had been searching for spiritual enlightenment and inner peace for as long as Lily could remember, but the search had shifted to more high-budget locations since being funded by Lily's modelling income.

'And your father?'

Lily gave a soft laugh. 'I wouldn't know where to send the invitation.'

Tristan said nothing, merely flicking a glance towards the rear-view mirror as he pulled out to overtake a line of cars and accelerate away into the darkness beyond. Lily was pressed back into the soft leather upholstery. The speed ought to have been frightening, but not for a second did she doubt that he was in absolute control of the powerful car.

Of everything.

'What's happening at the beginning of December?' he asked eventually.

'I'm going back to Africa.' she said, unable to maintain her frostiness and keep the enthusiasm from her voice as the words spilled out of her. 'It's early days yet, but I've been asked to be an ambassador for a children's medical charity, and at the moment it's just a case of finding out exactly what I can do, and what issues I can best highlight. I'm just hoping they'll continue to use me because I'd love to give up modelling and do it full time. I've only been over there once so far…' she faltered '…just after we—'

'So you said.' There was a dangerously silky note in Tristan's voice as he cut her off. 'It was where you picked up the bug that put us in our current position.' He gave a short, scornful laugh. 'You can't seriously be thinking of going back?'

A small dart of alarm shot through Lily, leaving a trail of bright anger in its wake. 'And you can't seriously be thinking that I won't!' she said tersely. 'If you'd seen what I saw… Orphaned children, sick and malnourished. Babies whose mothers were too ill to feed them, or even to pick them up and cuddle them; ten-year-old boys forced to take on the role of father to their brothers and sisters, desperately trying to keep their families together—'

'Thanks, but you can spare me the humanitarian lecture.'

He sounded almost bored. The spark of anger flowered into

a blaze, fuelled by the anxiety and the frustration and uncertainty of the evening. 'And spare *me* the autocratic alpha male routine!' she hissed. 'You were very quick to tell me that you had no intention of having your life disrupted, but I assume that as *a Romero bride* I'm not to enjoy the same freedom? Well, I've gone along with you this far, Tristan, and I've tried to respect your family and your history because that's going to be the heritage of the child that I'm carrying, but just because you have wealth and privilege and titles doesn't mean you have the right to bully or control or intimidate me.'

'I thought you wanted to keep this baby.' Tristan's voice was icy cold, but in the sodium glow of the streetlights Lily could see a muscle flickering in his cheek.

She sat bolt upright, feeling the seat belt pull tight against her. It was holding her back, restraining her, just like Tristan. Angrily she yanked it away from her body.

'I do! I want that more than anything, I—'

'Then I would have thought,' he said with a lethal softness that chilled her to the bone, 'that you'd want to do what was best for it. Your desire to *help* is laudable, but do you really think that the most deprived and disease-ridden parts of Africa are the best place for a pregnant woman? You were ill last time. Who's to say you won't pick up something again?'

Lily sank back against the seat, turning away from him and closing her eyes as horror at her own stupidity hit her, along with another wave of dizzying sickness, as if the baby too were trying to remind her of its presence. Groping blindly for the controls for the window to let in some air, she mistakenly took hold of the door handle. The next moment there was a roaring sound as the door swung open and a wall of cold air hit them like an avalanche.

Tristan's reactions were like lightning. Steadying the wildly swerving vehicle with one hand, he pushed her back against the seat with the weight of his body as, with an ear-splitting screech of tyres, he hauled the steering wheel round to bring the car into the side of the road. The engine cut out, and the sudden silence was filled by the sound of their rapid breathing.

Very slowly Lily turned her head to look at him. His head was bent, his eyes closed, and his arm still lay across her body, shielding her, protecting her more surely than any seat belt.

'I'm sorry,' she whispered.

For a moment he didn't move. Then she watched as the fingers of the hand that lay on her thigh curled slowly into a tight fist before he straightened up, placing it with terrifying precision on the steering wheel.

When he turned to her the expression on his face made Lily's heart turn over.

'Understand this, Lily. I will never be a good husband or a perfect father, but I am *not* a tyrant. I will *never* bully or control you.' Just for a second his mask of control cracked and Lily caught a glimpse of the terrible bleakness and anguish that lay behind it. She felt her lungs constrict, sucking her breath inwards in a sort of hiccupping gasp, as all her instincts told her to reach out to him. But it was too late. The mask was back, more chillingly perfect than ever. 'I can't offer you love,' he said in a low voice, 'but I'll give you security. I will do everything in my power to protect you and the baby, and keep you safe. Do you understand?'

Shocked into silence, Lily nodded mutely.

Tristan pulled up outside the Primrose Hill address he'd managed to extract from Lily just before she fell asleep. He looked up at the house—a pretty Victorian town house with a late-flowering rose trailing over the stucco frontage—and then across into the sleeping face of the girl beside him. The street-light above gleamed on the flawless skin, and cast deep shadows beneath the sweep of her thick eyelashes and sharp cheekbones. It was a composition that would have made photographers and magazine editors the world over sigh with bliss.

Gripping the steering wheel tightly, he exhaled a long, slow breath and closed his eyes.

If only she weren't so beautiful.

He probably wouldn't be in this position to start with, he thought acidly. But even if he was, it would make the role he was being forced into a damned sight easier to play. A business arrangement; that was what this had to be. A simple matter of legality—of a name, and money.

Not sex, because, unless it was of the one night stand variety, sex involved emotion.

And emotion was something he didn't do.

Once, on a long distance flight, he had read a newspaper article saying that scientists had proved that if certain neurological pathways weren't opened up in the early years of life they would never be forged at all. Reading with clinical detachment he had recognised himself in every line, and as he closed the paper had smiled thinly to think that the teary accusations of many of his past lovers were actually now backed up by scientific fact.

Having never experienced love as a child, he was simply incapable of it.

The realisation had brought with it a strange kind of relief, and left him free to pursue his emotionless liaisons without guilt. He was careful, considerate, always making it clear that there was no possibility of anything long term…

How naïve that carefulness seemed now.

With a small sigh she stirred, and he watched her forehead crease into a frown in the second before her eyes flickered open.

'We're home?' she asked softly, sitting up and looking out of the window. 'Sorry, I didn't mean to fall asleep. I'm so tired I could sleep on a clothes line most of the time at the moment.' She bent to pick up her bag, then looked up at him hesitantly. 'Would you like to come in for coffee?'

He felt his eyebrows lift and couldn't keep the sardonic smile from his lips. 'Coffee?'

'Yes, coffee.' She held his gaze. 'I'm a hormonally unbalanced pregnant woman. You're quite safe.'

'I think,' he said cruelly, 'that's what you said last time. I'll pass on the coffee, but I need to get a copy of your birth certificate for the marriage licence. Do you have it?'

She nodded, not meeting his eyes.

Tristan took her overnight bag from the boot of the car while she went ahead of him up the short black and white chequered path. Opening the front door, she switched on a table lamp just inside the hallway and slipped off first one high-heeled sandal and then the other. The light from the lamp shone through the thin silk of her dress, clearly showing the outline of her endless legs.

It was a momentary snapshot, but it was of such pure, concentrated sexuality that Tristan felt the breath rush from his lungs as if he'd been punched in the stomach.

Slamming the boot of the car with unnecessary force, he followed her inside.

The interior of the flat surprised him. He had expected something modern, impersonal—a base for two career girls who spent their time either travelling or partying. What he found was a home filled with beautiful things. Interesting things that looked as if they'd been collected over time, with no regard for value or fashion.

Lily had her back to him and was looking through a drawer in a pretty rosewood desk in the corner of the sitting room. Leaning against the doorframe Tristan looked around. The faded velvet sofa was piled high with cushions in turquoise and raspberry-pink silk, and the walls were hung with a mixture of Victorian oils, modern advertising prints and photographs that demanded to be looked at more closely.

He gritted his teeth and turned his head away.

A grey cat slipped through the open front door and slunk between his feet, disappearing in the direction of the kitchen. Another two, smaller versions of the first, followed.

'How many cats do you have?' he asked, breaking the silence.

Lily turned around, a bundle of papers tied with a faded red ribbon in her hand.

'Officially, none. I'm away too much, but there are lots of strays round here and I feed them whenever I can and keep an eye on them.' She untied the ribbon and took a piece of paper from the top of the bundle. 'That little grey one was just a baby herself when she had the kittens. I feel awful—I should have taken her to be spayed.'

She crossed the room and handed him a piece of paper. Tristan took it without looking at it, then, levering himself up from the doorframe, walked back down the hall, saying with cold sarcasm, 'It's a little ironic, given our current situation, that you're worried about your failure to take responsibility for the contraception of the feline population, wouldn't you say?'

She stopped in the doorway, her eyes downcast, running the length of tattered silk ribbon through her long fingers.

'Yes, maybe.'

Her quiet acceptance sent an arrow of guilt and self-loathing shooting straight into his derelict heart, and he tensed against the acute and unfamiliar pain that flashed through him.

'I'm sorry,' he said tersely. 'That was unfair.'

'No, you're right.' She shook her head, and looked up at him. She was smiling, but her eyes shimmered silver with unshed tears and Tristan felt as if someone had taken hold of the arrow in his heart and was trying to wrench it out. And failing.

Taking the ribbon from her, he took her left hand in his, scowling blackly down at it as he tied the faded silk around her ring finger.

'What are you doing?'

'I need to know your ring size.'

For a moment both of them looked down at her hand in his— pale as milk against the dark gold of his skin, her fingers slender and delicate in his powerful grip. 'You don't have to do this, you know,' she said in a low voice.

Tristan raised his head and forced himself to look at her. 'What?'

'Marry me.'

Her eyes were as gentle as smoke from an autumn bonfire. He slid the ribbon from her finger, unable to stop a bitter laugh escaping him. 'Oh, but I do,' he said bleakly, pushing a hand through his hair. 'I do, you see, because although Romero men don't do love, or…or *fatherhood*, there is something we're very, very good at.'

'And what's that?' she whispered.

'Duty.' He said the word as if it were a curse.

Lily nodded, biting her lip. 'Is that what this is?' she asked quietly. 'Duty?'

'Yes,' he said flatly. 'Duty. That's all, and if that's not enough for you it's not too late to change your mind. But don't fool yourself, Lily. Don't think for a moment that you're getting something you're not, or that you can change me into some kind of new man who's in touch with his emotions because—'

'Ah, but I think you already are in touch with your emotions.' Her voice was thoughtful, almost apologetic. She took a step forwards, so that she was close enough for him to smell the almond sweetness of her skin. Shock juddered through him as she laid a hand on his chest, over his heart. 'And I think the emotion you're most in touch with at the moment is fear.'

It was as if someone had taken a needle of pure adrenaline and stabbed it straight into a vein. Tristan felt heat pulse through his body, closely followed by an ice-cold wave of anger. Circling her wrist with his fingers, he jerked her hand off him, bringing it viciously down to her side so that she lost her balance and fell against him. Her head snapped back, so that she was looking up at him, her face flushed and her eyes blazing with defiance.

With desire.

Tristan felt the blood rush to his groin in instant, primitive response. They were both breathing very hard

'Don't ever make the mistake of thinking you understand me, Lily,' he said harshly. 'I can assure you, you don't. There's only one…*emotion*…I'm in touch with.'

It was a singularly crass, Neanderthal thing to say, but she seemed to bring that side out in him, he thought viciously. He'd expected her to shrink away from the deliberate coarseness of his words. But she didn't. With one hand still imprisoned in his iron grip, she raised the other and gently cupped his jaw.

'I don't believe that,' she murmured.

Afterwards he couldn't have said who made the first move, but suddenly their mouths had come together and her fingers were digging into his flesh as she gripped his arm, her breasts thrusting against his chest. They kissed with a savagery that was totally at odds with her gentleness, and which shattered his memories of the dreamy, languid night in the tower.

She was all things. Anything he wanted, everything he needed at just the moment he needed it most—even when he hardly knew it himself. Her mouth was hard and hungry on his now, meeting the brutal insistence of his kiss with a passion and a fury that matched his own.

But it was he who pulled away, thrusting her backwards and pulling himself upright as he reassembled the barriers of his self-control.

'Then you're fooling yourself,' he said viciously, turning away so he didn't have to confront the bewilderment in her eyes or the broken promise of her ripe, reddened lips.

'You're confusing lust with something deep and significant. You're a beautiful, desirable woman—*hostias*, I'll make love to you a hundred times a day if you want me to, and I'll love doing it. But I won't love *you*. You have to understand that.'

She was leaning against the wall of the hallway, the back of her hand pressed against her reddened mouth. Above it her eyes were huge and luminous with emotion.

'But what if I can't live with that?' she whispered.

'Then I respect that. I won't touch you. I'm not a monster.' His tone hardened. 'But I am a man. There's only so much temptation I can stand. You have to be careful, Lily; if you play with fire, you're going to get burned. It's up to you to choose what sort of marriage this is going to be.'

'A loveless marriage, or a loveless, sexless one.' She made a sound that was halfway between a laugh and a sob. 'That's my choice?'

He sighed heavily. 'Not entirely. You can also choose to leave me out of your life and the life of your child.'

Her face was half in shadow but he caught the glimmer of a single tear as it slid silently down her cheek. Her hand moved instinctively to her midriff and slowly she shook her head.

'No. I want my baby to have a father, but I won't prostitute myself for the privilege,' she said dully.

Tristan shrugged helplessly. 'OK. Your choice.' Turning away, he began to walk back down the path to the car. 'I'll be in touch with travel details for Barcelona as soon as I have them.'

As he drove away he caught a glimpse of her, silhouetted in the light from the hallway, and felt guilt rise like acid in the back of his throat. Bracing his arms against the steering wheel, he swore tersely.

Why was she letting him do this to her?

He had offered her the only way out he could think of and she had stubbornly refused to take it. He had given her a chance to walk away, to live a normal life, and she wouldn't go.

Why?

Pulling up at a red light, he noticed the folded paper on the seat next to him, and opened it up. 'Lily Alexander,' he read. 'Birthplace—Brighton, England. Mother—Susannah Alexander. Father—unknown.'

So that was it, he thought with a despairing gust of laughter. That explained the fervour with which she'd spoken earlier. I won't have my child growing up without a name. An identity, she'd said, as if having no father were the worst thing that could happen.

He dragged a hand across his face as the lights changed to green, and he accelerated away with unnecessary force.

Her naiveté would have been almost endearing if it weren't so dangerous.

Everyone was just a victim of their own past, he thought despairingly.

He wondered how long he could go on hiding how much of a victim he was.

CHAPTER SEVEN

LILY walked down the aisle of the beautiful old church as if she were in a dream.

From behind the snowy tulle of her designer veil the world had taken on a soft-focus haze, so that she was barely aware of the anonymous smiling faces that turned towards her as she passed, the artistic posies tied onto the pew ends, the candles flickering in sconces on the pillars. She just had to concentrate on putting one expensive ivory satin-shod foot in front of the other…on suppressing the ever-present morning sickness…on making it down to the man who stood waiting at the altar with his back towards her.

As she gripped her bouquet of white roses and lily of the valley her diamond engagement ring bit into her finger, heavy and still unfamiliar. It had arrived a week ago, by courier, accompanied by a terse note giving details of her journey to Barcelona.

That was it.

No explanation, no additional words to strengthen the gossamer-fine threads that tied her to the remote, handsome stranger she was marrying. Nothing to reassure her that she was doing the right thing.

Oh, God, *was* she doing the right thing?

'Cut!'

There was a palpable release of tension in the 'congregation' as the director of the perfume commercial stepped in front of her, making slashing motions with his arms. 'Lily, darling, you're walking towards your bridegroom, the love of your life, not your executioner! Some sense of joyous serenity, darling, please! This is supposed to be your wedding! The happiest day of a girl's life!'

'Sorry, sorry…' Lily muttered, gripping her bouquet of slightly wilting roses in anguish. The director's face softened as he peered through her veil and said quietly, 'Look, are you OK under there? Perhaps you'd like to take a quick break? Grab something to eat?'

Lily shook her head. The wedding dress supplied by the couture arm of the company was already so tight it felt like some barbaric method of medieval torture, and a car was due to collect her in just a few hours to take her to the private airfield where Tristan's jet would be waiting. Her stomach swooped at the thought. 'No, really, I'm fine,' she said determinedly. 'I'm sorry, I'm ready now. Let's do it again.'

The director gave her arm a quick squeeze and nodded at the bridegroom, who was leaning against the altar rail talking on his mobile to his boyfriend in Milan. Gathering up her papery silk skirts, Lily hurried back to the church doorway while the director clapped his hands to bring the congregation of extras back to order, hushing the musical babble of Italian conversation that had risen during the hiatus.

Beneath her veil Lily felt the heat of panic rise to her cheeks and breathed deeply, steadying herself against it as she smoothed a hand over the silk that stretched across her thickening midriff. Her heart twisted with primitive love as she thought of the baby inside her. That was why she was doing it. That was why she was shortly going to be getting on a plane and flying to a strange city to marry a man she didn't know. She was giving her baby a father. A name. That had to be right, didn't it?

'OK, people, let's take that again. And remember, Lily, you're drifting on a cloud of bliss, darling. You're in love and getting married to the man of your dreams! What could be better?'

If he loved me back, thought Lily sadly as she stepped forwards once more into the bright lights.

Tristan didn't even glance at his father's secretary as he stalked through her office and pushed open the tall double doors to Juan Carlos Romero de Losada's inner sanctum. He was holding a piece of paper—a printout of the transactions made by the bank in the last week, which he'd been studying ahead of tomorrow's meeting with the chancellors of some of Europe's major banks—and as he threw it down on his father's desk the secretary appeared at the door looking worried.

'*Señor*, I am sorry—'

From behind the fortress of his enormous desk Juan Carlos held up a regal and perfectly manicured hand, the Romero signet ring glinting heavily on his little finger.

'Please, Luisa, it is not your fault. My son has yet to learn some manners.' Settling his face into a smooth smile, he turned his cold gaze on Tristan as the secretary retreated with obvious relief. 'Perhaps you would like to explain what is so important that you neglect the most basic courtesy to my staff?'

Tristan's face was set into a rigid mask of barely controlled anger. When he spoke it was through gritted teeth, his lips hardly moving.

'You authorised a further loan to the Khazakismiri army. Last week. Another four million euros. Do you know who these people are? They're *terrorists*, guerillas, who are responsible for mass genocide.'

Juan Carlos gave a minute shrug of his elegant shoulders. 'Their generals are also very likely to form a large part of the cabinet of the next Khazakismiri government. This is business, Tristan. We cannot afford to be emotional.'

The word hit Tristan like an unexpected blow, reminding him so suddenly of Lily that he felt the air being knocked from his lungs.

I think you already are in touch with your emotions, she had said. *And I think the emotion you're most in touch with at the moment is fear.*

She was wrong, he thought bitterly as he stared unflinchingly into the brutally handsome face of his father; the face that his own echoed so clearly. He knew fear. Fear was the element in which he had lived for the first eight years of his life, until boarding school had delivered him from it. Fear had coloured every day, so that he knew all its shades of blackness. Fear was being small, powerless, not in control, and he had made sure that he was as far removed from all those things as it was possible to be.

'I'm not talking about *emotion*,' he said icily. 'I'm talking about *ethics*.'

'Tristan, this is Spain's oldest and most venerated bank, not some ramshackle, politically correct charity,' Juan Carlos said silkily, and not for the first time Tristan wondered just how much his father knew about his double life. 'Khazakismir is going through a turbulent time in its history at the moment, but it is an area that is potentially rich in natural gas and oil, and when things are more settled our investment will be richly rewarded. I have a duty to provide the best return for our investors.'

Tristan swore with quiet disgust. 'And you think they would agree with that if they knew exactly what kind of atrocities their money was funding?'

'We don't have to burden them with moral dilemmas or complicated political issues. I think of myself as a father figure to our customers,' Juan Carlos continued complacently. 'I make decisions with their best interests at heart. It's not always an easy role, or a comfortable one, but it is my duty. Just as your duty is to the family.'

Just the word 'father' coming from Juan Carlos's lips made Tristan's hands bunch into fists and adrenaline pulse through him. His eyes were drawn, as they always were whenever he had any cause to penetrate Juan Carlos's private citadel, to the large silver-framed photograph that stood on the desk. To the casual observer it showed the Romero de Losada Montalvo family posing happily together on the steps of El Paraiso, but Tristan always suspected it was placed there, not so much to impress visitors, but to remind Tristan of the real nature and extent of his 'duty'.

'As if I could forget,' said Tristan tonelessly, still looking at the picture.

The casual observer probably wouldn't notice the person, standing shoulder to shoulder with Tristan, who had been cropped out of the picture. They would be far more likely to look at Nico, Juan Carlos's youngest son, standing at the front, and remark on the openness of his expression, the infectious charm of his smile.

They would, of course, never suspect what it had cost his older brother to keep it there.

'*Bueno*. Talking of which…' Juan Carlos leaned back in his chair and looked at Tristan speculatively '…I am pleased to see that there haven't been so many unfortunate photographs of you cavorting with unsuitable women in the press lately. I thought that when you gave up that pointless Oxford degree and came to work for the bank that you were ready to apply yourself to your duty as a Romero, but I have been bitterly disappointed by your conduct over the years. Perhaps at last you are beginning to take your responsibilities more seriously?'

Turning to leave, Tristan gave a short, ironic laugh. 'You could say that.'

'Not before time. You need to settle down, Tristan. I hope you're not forgetting the reception tomorrow, after our meeting tomorrow with the European finance committee. Sofia Carranzo will be there. Such a charming girl.'

'By which you mean wealthy, well-bred and Catholic,' Tristan said scathingly.

Juan Carlos's eyes narrowed. 'I hardly need remind you of your duty to make a good marriage. Provide an heir.'

Tristan paused with his hand on the door. 'No. As a matter of fact you don't,' he said quietly.

'So you'll be there?' Juan Carlos pressed. 'Good. I'll look forward to it.'

'Oh, yes, I'll be there.'

As he passed Luisa on the way out Tristan smiled. In a funny way he was quite looking forward to it too.

The light of the short autumn afternoon was fading as the car wound its way through the traffic into the centre of Barcelona. Giving up on the book she had chosen for the journey— Cervantes' *Don Quixote*—Lily sat back in her seat and stared out into the brightly lit shop fronts and cafés, trying to keep her breathing slow and even.

She had no idea where she was being taken, since the enquiries she had made in basic Spanish to the menacing-looking driver who had hauled her bags into the back of the car had been met by a stone wall of silence. Despite the gloom he wore a pair of dark glasses and from beneath these an angry scar ran down his cheek to the corner of his unsmiling mouth.

Lily shivered. There was something intimidating, hostile, in his unresponsiveness that did nothing to dispel the nervous tension that had dogged her since she'd stepped into the plush interior of Tristan's private jet in Rome. The fact that Tristan hadn't bothered to come and meet her himself added a frisson of anger to the apprehension and terrible, treacherous excitement that churned inside her at the thought of seeing him again.

Pregnancy hormones, she told herself firmly. He'd made it quite clear in London what the terms of their marriage would be and she had taken the only option that left her with a shred of dignity. She couldn't accept the alternative, but as the moment of meeting him drew closer she couldn't think how she was going to live with her choice either...

The huge black car slid through streets that grew increasingly narrow, increasingly empty, and Lily twisted the diamond ring on her finger anxiously as she craned out into the gloom, searching for landmarks to give her a clue as to where they were. No one knew she was here, she thought as fear began to prickle at the back of her neck. Maybe the car wasn't sent by Tristan at all, she thought with a thud of horror. Maybe she was being kidnapped by someone who had somehow learned that she was engaged to the heir to the Romero billions...Maybe Tristan was even now receiving a ransom note, demanding a huge sum for her safe release...

Folding her shaking hands protectively across her softly rounded stomach, Lily bit her lip, trying to stamp out the flare of panic that leapt inside her.

No matter how much the demand, the Marqués de Montesa could afford to pay it, she thought with an attempt at self-mockery. This was the man who went to parties by helicopter and sent five carat diamonds by post. *But he doesn't love me,* whispered an unpleasant, persistent little voice in her head. *That's the flaw in the kidnapper's plan. The baby and I are a problem, an inconvenience, and if I were to disappear...*

The car stopped. Lily jumped, her eyes widening with alarm as she saw that they were in a narrow street squeezed between very high, very old buildings. Beside the car there was an archway, its mouth yawning blackly in the gloom. Her pulse went into overdrive. The taciturn chauffeur got out, his foot-steps ringing on the stone flags, echoing off the tall walls around them, keeping time with the hammering of Lily's heart as she sat, bolt upright and trembling, in the back of the car. A moment later he opened the door and stood back.

Lily gave a little gasp of terror as she glimpsed a man standing in the shadows of the archway. Instinct told her to get out of the car, that she might still have a chance to run for it, and she stumbled to her feet just as he stepped forward into the dying grey afternoon. He was tall, lean, powerfully built, but even in the gloom there was no mistaking the sharp angles of his cheekbones, the sensual mouth.

'Tristan!'

The breath seemed to catch in her throat, so that the word

came out as a strangled croak, and suddenly she was in his arms, burying her face in the hardness of his chest as relief flooded her. He smelled clean and warm and she breathed in the scent, waiting for the wild crashing of her heart to steady.

It didn't.

From deep in the pit of her stomach she felt bolts of heat shoot along her nerve endings as his hands closed over her shoulders, firm and powerful.

'What an unexpectedly enthusiastic welcome,' he drawled with quiet mockery. 'Do I take it you've reconsidered your decision about the nature of our marriage?'

'No!' she exclaimed, blushing hotly as she stepped away from him, folding her cashmere wrap tightly around her and hugging herself to stop the trembling that racked her body. 'I'm just glad that it's you and not some cold-blooded kidnapper with a gun and a ransom demand.' Suddenly the fear of a moment ago felt suddenly silly and childish. 'I didn't know where we were going, and your driver wasn't very forthcoming.'

'Dimitri's Russian. He doesn't speak any English, or much Spanish.' Tristan turned to him and spoke briefly in rapid, flawless Russian, which brought a flicker of a smile to Dimitri's lugubrious features. 'He'll take care of your bags. We go on foot from here.'

Lily had to almost run to keep up with his long, rapid stride.

'Where are we going?'

'To church.'

'Church? The church where we're getting married?'

'Of course.'

A shiver rippled down her spine, excitement mixed with apprehension as the reality of what they were doing edged a little closer. They were walking along a narrow street, just a passageway between ancient buildings, and Tristan was walking slightly ahead of her, his hands thrust deep into the pockets of his black jacket, his collar turned up, demons at his back.

Just looking at him made Lily's legs feel weak.

Another stone archway blocked out the remains of the light for a moment, and then suddenly they were in an open space again, a small square hemmed in on all sides by a jumble of ancient buildings, all crammed together as if supporting each other. In the centre stood a hexagonal fountain, and trees stretched their branches up to the pewter sky.

'Oh!' Lily stopped, looking around. Apart from a couple drinking coffee at one of the tables of the bar of the hotel in one corner, the square was empty. The only sound was the gentle trickle of water from the fountain, the soft crooning of pigeons. It was like stepping through a magic doorway, into another time.

Her gaze returned to where he stood beside a huge and ornately decorated doorway set into a wall of pockmarked stone and she smiled. 'It's lovely—so perfect and romantic.'

The words were met with a mocking twist of his mouth. 'Romantic?' he repeated sardonically, pushing open a small door set into the tall, imposing entrance. 'I never really thought of it that way before.'

'Really? You do surprise me,' said Lily dryly, glancing up at him from under her lashes as she stepped through the door he held open for her. For a moment he scowled down at her, and then he gave her a reluctant smile.

'Don't push your luck, Señorita Alexander,' he murmured. 'And remember what I said. If you play with fire…'

'I haven't forgotten.'

Lily followed him into a cavernous space with a high domed ceiling. Her eye was immediately drawn past the rows of wooden pews to the dramatic edifice that rose up behind the altar, of gilded and polished marble pillars supporting a row of angels with their magnificent wings unfurled, and life-sized saints in various attitudes of dramatic supplication. Wrapping her arms around herself Lily walked slowly forward, looking around, trying to imagine what it would be like on the day of their wedding…

Now the building was dimly lit and the pews were empty, apart from an elderly man sitting in the second row, head bent over his rosary beads, fingers working silently. At the back of the church a woman was threading long-stemmed red roses and sprays of gypsophila into an extravagant display of greenery on a tall stand, while a small girl played with the flowers at her feet.

Lily watched, noticing the absorption with which the girl held the flowers, the slight frown on her small face as she walked a couple of slow, solemn steps, and realised she was playing a game. She was pretending to be a bride, holding her bunch of flowers in front of her like a bouquet. Lily smiled, feeling a lump form in the back of her throat as unconsciously her hand moved to her stomach, moving over the almost imperceptible bump of her own child.

The past weeks had been exhausting and often joyless, the constant drag of morning sickness made worse by the fact there was no one to share it with, no one to confide in. But there were moments, like this one, when she was struck by the sheer miracle of what was happening inside her body, when the astonishing privilege of having a baby of her own to love and look after almost made her gasp out loud. And she knew in those moments that she would do anything at all to protect it and to give it a safe and happy life.

'Lily.'

She turned her head, and Tristan saw her soft smile fade slightly as she came to where he was standing with the priest. She had been looking at the child, he realised with a stabbing sensation in his chest. That was what had given her eyes that luminescence. When he spoke his voice was flinty.

'If you're ready, perhaps we could get on with what we came for.'

'What we came for?' She frowned.

Aware of the priest at his side, Tristan gave her a smooth, blank smile, hoping that she was sensible enough to detect the warning it contained. 'Getting married, of course, *querida*.'

'Now?' Her eyes widened in shock and colour seeped into her pale cheeks. Grasping her firmly by the elbow, Tristan muttered a few apologetic words in Spanish to Father Angelico as he drew her to one side before she could say anything else that was likely to make the priest have second thoughts about conducting this highly unconventional wedding. It had taken considerable amounts of string-pulling and a more than generous donation to the church fund to silence Father Angelico's doubts about officiating at the secret marriage between the son of one of Spain's most important families and a socially insignificant English non-Catholic girl. Any sign of further irregularity in the circumstances might force him to reconsider.

'Yes, now,' he said, carefully keeping his tone level. 'Or have you changed your mind?'

Her eyes were the dark grey of the English sky before a storm, but whether clouded by anger or by hurt he couldn't tell. 'No, of course not. I just thought…I mean, I wanted—'

'What? A designer dress and a dozen small bridesmaids?' he mocked.

Lily looked down with a sad, self-deprecating smile. 'You make it sound so outrageous. I knew it was going to be a quiet wedding, but I thought that maybe some members of your family could be there, and Scarlet and Tom…'

Tristan wanted to laugh out loud at the idea of Juan Carlos and Allegra sitting passively by and watching him marry this English nobody, but he managed to restrain himself. Taking hold of her chin between his fingers, he tilted her face up to his and spoke very softly.

'It's a business arrangement, remember? You know that, and I know that, but as far as Father Angelico is concerned we are two people so madly in love that we can't wait to marry, so if you really do want to go ahead with this I suggest you play the part of the enthusiastic bride.' He paused, dropping his voice even further, so that it was little more than a breathy caress. 'But this is how this marriage will be, Lily. No grand romantic gestures, no epic emotions, and if you're not absolutely sure you can accept that, then you walk out of here now.'

She said nothing, but her eyes stayed locked on his, opaque with emotions he couldn't interpret, and the silence that wrapped itself around them as they stood close together in the huge, high space was filled with tension. He was aware of his heart beating hard, measuring the seconds while he waited for her to answer.

And then, very gently, she pulled away from him and took a step back.

And then another.

And another.

Tristan felt his stomach twist and the air momentarily leave his lungs as adrenalin hit his bloodstream. Lily had turned and was walking away from him, back up the aisle towards the door, and for a moment all he could think, focus on, was how beautiful she was with the lamplight glinting on her hair and making it shine like a halo of old gold in the incense-scented dimness of the church.

And then, of course, it hit him. What he was seeing. What she was doing.

Walking away.

CHAPTER EIGHT

PAIN shot through Tristan from somewhere, and dimly he realised it was his jaw—that he was tensing it with the effort of not calling out to stop her. Spinning round he looked furiously up at the imposing altarpiece, waiting for the moment when he would hear the door at the other end of the church swing shut behind her, signifying that it was over and he could resume the normal course of his life. The women and the parties. The aloneness that he so cherished.

Didn't he?

It didn't come.

Stiffly he turned round.

Lily was standing in the shadows at the back of the church talking to the woman with the flowers. As he watched she laid a gentle hand on her arm and gestured to the child. The little girl had stopped playing and was looking shyly up at Lily, her expression almost awe-struck.

The mother smiled, nodded. Then Lily dropped to her knees in front of the little girl, smoothing her hair away from her face and gathering her straggling bunch of flowers into a neat posy, showing her how to hold them. The child's small face glowed with pleasure and pride as Lily straightened up again and took her hand.

And suddenly he understood. She wasn't walking out on him. She was doing this her way, with her own peculiar blend of stubborn, determined *sweetness* that made him feel exasperated and guilty by turns.

He felt the tension leave his body, and realised his hands were shaking slightly. Not with relief, he told himself harshly. Nothing so selfless. It was vindication, that was all. Pride. No woman had ever walked out on him yet, and the feeling was unfamiliar. The child's mother, beaming with suppressed excitement, quickly extracted one of the long-stemmed roses from her arrangement and handed it to Lily. Tristan watched as she accepted it, and briefly embraced the woman before stepping forward with the little girl beside her.

She was going to be a fantastic mother.

The thought stole into his head uninvited, causing a wrenching sensation in the pit of his stomach. She had a natural instinct for love and kindness that would make up for his own emotional sterility. And, he thought, watching her walk down the aisle towards him, an inner strength that meant she stood up to him. She lifted her head and her eyes found his. Soft as cashmere, shining with her quiet determination, they held him, and although he wanted to turn away, he found he couldn't.

The priest cleared his throat, obviously eager to get the service under way, and Tristan moved slowly back towards him, his eyes not leaving Lily's. She was close enough for him to see the darkness in the centre of the silver grey iris now, close enough to smell her milk-and-honey sweetness.

Close enough to touch.

His fingers burned with sudden need, and as the priest began to speak about the sanctity of marriage, his mind filled with a taunting kaleidoscope of images and memories that were wholly inappropriate for church: Lily in the field at Stowell, golden and beautiful with her dress blowing up around her bare brown legs; Lily naked in the tower, her skin silver in the moonlight, and the satin soft feel of it against his lips...

From that, had come this.

'Señor Romero?'

They were all looking at him, he realised suddenly: the elderly priest, the little girl, and Lily. Waiting for him.

'*Lo siento*. Sorry.'

Father Angelico looked at him sternly over the top of his glasses. '*Repetid despues de mi. Yo, Tristan Leandro, te recibo a ti Lily, como esposa y me entrego a ti.*'

Almost reluctantly Tristan took Lily's hand in his. The diamond ring he had sent glittered on her finger, sending out sharp rainbows of light in the gloom, and he could suddenly see it was all wrong for her—too showy, too cold—just like the marriage she was about to submit herself to, he thought despairingly. Did she really know what she was getting into?

Of course she didn't. She didn't even understand the vows. He hesitated, and then said in English, 'I, Tristan Leandro, take you, Lily, to be my wife.'

A small smile touched her strawberry-coloured lips.

Father Angelico continued, utterly matter-of-fact, as if he were reading out a report in the financial pages. Tristan felt his throat constrict around the words he had never intended to say. Never wanted to say. As he spoke them to the girl standing before him his voice was a harsh, sardonic rasp.

'I promise to be faithful to you in prosperous times and adverse times, in healthy times and times of sickness.' He felt his mouth twist into an ironic smile. 'To love and respect you every day of my life.'

Lies, all lies. Standing beneath the imposing marble altarpiece in the sight of God and all his plaster saints as he slid the plain gold band onto Lily's slender finger, Tristan wondered savagely what punishments would be visited on him for this blasphemy.

There was always a punishment. He had learned that from a very early age.

The priest was talking to Lily now, enunciating slowly and precisely, and Tristan kept his eyes fixed on the face of a particularly stern looking angel on a gilded plinth as she began to repeat his words in slow, halting Spanish.

Her voice was soft, but it seemed to carry into the high, draughty spaces of the ancient church as she made her promises of faith and love. Empty promises, he reminded himself derisively, but glancing at the priest, and across at the woman doing the flowers, he could tell that they were listening with rapt attention, all openly affected by the tenderness in Lily's voice. Even the old man with the rosary was watching them, his lined face curiously sad.

Tristan looked away again. Staring blankly at the face of that same damned angel, his face a hard, scowling mask from behind which he was forced to act out this charade for the sake of his family name, his blood and his history.

And then she touched him.

As she spoke the words that would bind them together she raised her hand and pressed it to his cheek.

Instantly he felt heat melt the brittle carapace as his gaze was dragged back to hers. Her eyes were like moonlight, gentle and yet so bright it hurt him to look at them, and their soft luminescence seemed to reach into the darkest places inside his head. As she reached the end of her vows there was a moment's pause while the echo of her breathless, slightly hesitant voice died away in the ancient church. But the spell cast by its tenderness remained.

In that silence Tristan bent his head slowly and brought his mouth down on hers in the lightest of kisses.

It was a gesture, nothing more. Part of the act, to satisfy the romantic notions of their small audience, and yet as his lips brushed hers he felt every nerve and sinew in his body tauten as fire blazed through them. He heard the sharp gasp of indrawn breath, felt her arch towards him, parting her lips to welcome his. The rose she held fell to the floor as she slid both hands around the back of his neck so that she was cradling his head; gentle, generous, loving, and the kiss wasn't a gesture any more.

It was hot and real.

As if from a great distance Tristan heard the sound of

applause. It broke into the dark and private world to which they had retreated, pulling them back into reality. He felt Lily's smile against his lips as she gently disentangled herself from his hold, then she ducked her head and dropped to her knees, gathering up her little flower girl and hugging her. Father Angelico shook Tristan's hand, and then waited until Lily had finished hugging the girl's mother before leaning across and kissing her on both cheeks.

Everyone was damp-eyed and smiling.

Except him, of course. Everyone except him.

Darkness had fallen properly outside, and the light from the lamps on either side of the church door made puddles of gold on the wet cobblestones in the square. The crisp, cold evening was filled with the delicious scent of garlic from the hotel restaurant opposite.

Tristan let go of her hand the moment they were out of the church, and Lily felt the little flare of hope that had leapt inside her when he had kissed her fade. Her throat felt thick with the vows she'd just made, her chest tight with the enormity of what she had done. For her baby.

That was what she had to hang onto. This was a practical arrangement for the baby. The blistering heat that had turned her insides into a churning volcano of molten longing when Tristan had kissed her had nothing whatsoever to do with it.

He held out to her the rose she had dropped. She took it, unable to look up at him in case he read the shameful need in her face. 'So what happens now?'

He tucked his hands deep into the pockets of his jacket and walked over to the fountain. 'I think that wedding nights traditionally involve considerable amounts of both champagne and passion,' he said blandly. 'However, ours was hardly a traditional wedding.'

Disappointment sliced through her.

'No,' she said, unable to entirely keep the sadness from her voice as she followed him and sat on the stone rim of the fountain. 'Or a traditional marriage.'

'Second thoughts, Marquesa?

His use of the unfamiliar title made her raise her head in surprise. He was standing in front of her, looking down at her, his eyes gleaming in the lamplight. But it was his mouth that held her attention—his sculpted, sensuous mouth, which she hadn't been able to stop herself from looking at all through their brief wedding service. He had a particular way of moving his lips when he spoke that made it look as if he were caressing the words, or saying something indecently sensual even when his voice was quite cold.

'Yes,' she said fiercely.

His brows swooped downwards in a scowl, and he opened his mouth to make some stinging retort. Swiftly she reached up and put her fingers against his mouth, silencing him.

'Yes,' she repeated in a whisper. 'But not about the wedding. About what kind of marriage this is going to be.'

For a moment his face was blank with bewilderment, but then realisation dawned in his eyes, so that their blackness seemed to deepen and intensify. Slowly, wordlessly, he took her hand and pulled her to her feet.

'You're sure? It's what you want, even though—'

'I know. I thought I couldn't bear to take you into my bed...into my body...and know that you don't love me. I thought I could never do that, but now I know that I can't bear *not* to. I'm sure it's what I want.' She rose up onto her tiptoes and brushed her lips against his ear, breathing in the clean masculine scent of his hair as she mouthed, 'And I want it right now...'

'Well, then...' he said in a voice that made her spine melt with longing as he slipped his hands beneath the cashmere wrap, beneath the little top she wore under it. Lily gasped as they met her bare skin and slowly moved upwards, covering her breasts so that her nipples sprang up against his palms. 'It's just as well there's a decent hotel just over there.'

Taking hold of her hand, he began to walk quickly across the square. 'Have you booked a room?' she asked breathlessly.

'No, but I don't think that'll be a problem.'

'But it's a weekend…'

Tristan stopped, looking at her thoughtfully for a second, his beautiful face grave.

'Lily, you have a lot to learn about being a Romero. It has many, many drawbacks…' he kissed her lingeringly on the mouth '…so you just have to learn to make the most of the advantages. Believe me, they'll find us a room.'

'Great Aunt Agatha simply cannot be seated anywhere near the Duchess of Cranthorpe, any of Tom's university friends, or anyone who's ever played lacrosse for Cheltenham Ladies' College first team. I know it's awkward, but we cannot risk a scene like the one at the Talbot-Hesketh wedding last year…' Lady Montague adjusted her spectacles and peered at the vast roll of paper on the breakfast table, weighted down at one end by the silver coffee pot and by the sugar tongs at the other. 'I think if we put her on a table with…'

The names of Great Aunt Agatha's hapless dinner companions remained a mystery as a burst of electronic noise from Tom's mobile phone interrupted his mother. Apologising, he picked it up and read the text message that had just come through.

'It's from Tristan.' Tom frowned, reading out the message in a tone of deep bewilderment. '"One circuit of the moat, this morning. Naked. Photographic evidence required."'

Neither Scarlet nor Lady Montague looked up from the seating plan. 'What *is* he talking about?' said Scarlet vaguely.

'No idea…' Tom's frown deepened. 'Unless…'

At that moment Scarlet's phone let out a trill that made them all jump. But not as much as the shriek of astonishment that she gave a second later as she read the message that had just come through.

Tristan and I got married last night.
Will be in touch soon to explain all.
In the meantime, please try to be happy.
I am.
Love L x

CHAPTER NINE

'OK. So, explain.'

Leaning against the wall of the hotel room, Lily stifled both a sigh and the urge to hang up the phone. It wasn't that she didn't want to talk to Scarlet, it was just she wasn't sure where to start. How to explain.

'I'm pregnant.'

As she said the words she felt the swirling mist of confusion lift a little and certainty flow back into her. That, after all, was the reason at the heart of all that had happened. A shaft of pure sunlight in the midst of the fog.

'Oh, Lily!' Scarlet's tone was warm, but Lily could hear its edge of anxiety and reproach. 'That's wonderful. I mean, *really* wonderful…but, darling—' She stopped abruptly. 'Is Tristan there?'

'No. He went out a little while ago.' She didn't know where. Or why, or who with. He had offered no explanation and she had asked for none. Those were the terms that he had laid down at the outset and Lily understood that she had to abide by them. No matter how hard.

'Good, then we can talk properly.' Scarlet's voice became suddenly businesslike, which Lily felt was a bad sign. 'Look, I'm totally thrilled for you about the baby. Surprised,' she said slightly tartly, 'but I know how much having a family means to you. And that's exactly what's worrying me…'

She let the sentence trail off. In the little silence that followed Lily pushed back the muslin drapes at the windows and looked down at the square below. Directly opposite she could see the high doorway in the scarred stone wall through which Tristan had led her yesterday, the doorway through which she had emerged such a short time later as his wife.

'You didn't have to marry him, you know, honey.'

'I did, actually,' Lily said quietly. 'Don't you see? I of all people couldn't bring a baby up without a father or a name— I know how unfair that would be to the child.' She paused, watching a pair of pigeons bathing in the fountain in the centre of the square, scattering rainbows of shining droplets onto the worn cobbles. 'And it would have been unfair to Tristan too, because of who he is. What he is.'

'*Who he is?* He's a playboy, Lily! *What he is* is a sexy, gorgeous, charismatic Alpha male. *What he isn't* is husband material!'

'He's doing all right so far.'

The words came out without her thinking, but Lily found herself smiling as she looked out into the rain-grey square. It was empty now, silent except for the musical trickle of the fountain, but earlier she and Tristan had been woken by the sound of children's voices—their shouts and laughter—echoing off the high walls. There was a school attached to the church, Tristan had told her, his fingers sleepily tracing a circle of shivering pleasure across the gentle curve of her stomach. The children used the square as their playground. To Lily it felt like a blessing. A sign.

Scarlet gave an impatient snort. 'I'm sure,' she said huffily. 'But there's more to marriage than sex, you know.'

Lily looked at the empty bed that had been the scene of such prolonged, such passionate lovemaking last night, and felt the smile fade and an ache run through her tired, sated body.

Not to this one there wasn't, she thought sadly. Not as far as her husband was concerned, anyway.

* * *

Tristan came back in the early afternoon, bringing a blast of crisp autumn air into the warm room as well as several expensive-looking carrier bags. Dropping them by the door, he sauntered over to the bed, slipping off his jacket as he did so and throwing it onto a chair.

Dozing in bed with *Don Quixote*, Lily felt her stomach instantly melt with desire. It was as if in the short amount of time he'd been out she'd already forgotten how incredibly handsome he was.

Incredibly handsome, and incredibly…powerful. His presence filled the room, changing the atmosphere from one of peaceful languor to that peculiar kind of sinister stillness that preceded a thunderstorm.

'What are you reading?'

'*Don Quixote,*' she muttered, feigning sudden interest in page thirty seven, which she'd already attempted to read about four times that morning. Anything to avoid having to confront his raw, menacing beauty.

He gave a short, scornful laugh. 'How appropriate. The ultimate romantic idealist.'

Lily put the book down, bending her head so that he wouldn't see the hurt on her face. 'You've been gone ages,' she said lightly, simply trying to make conversation, but as soon as she'd said the words she regretted them. He turned, pacing moodily back towards the bags he had left by the door.

'It was business,' he said tersely. 'I had a meeting that I couldn't miss.' The words were innocuous enough but tension screamed from every line of his lean body as he scooped up the bags and tossed them onto the bed beside her. 'I stopped on the way home to pick these up for you.'

Hesitantly Lily reached out and pulled the first bag towards her. It was made of the sort of stiff, shiny card that would make Scarlet swoon with delight and as she glanced tentatively inside all she could see was tissue paper. It crackled like the static she could feel in the air as she pulled out the delicate parcel.

'What is it?'

He came towards her, undoing the top two buttons of his shirt with sharp, stabbing movements. Lily felt her breath stall.

'Have a look.'

She wanted to, but that meant tearing her eyes away from the strip of olive skin that was being revealed at his throat. Blindly her fingers fumbled with the paper, until they met cool, slippery satin. She looked down.

The dress was the colour of old ivory, or bone. For a moment she just gazed down at it lying against her bare legs, looking almost incongruously expensive and precious in the rumpled chaos of the bed.

'Tristan, it's beautiful…but why?'

A guilt present? Had the meeting that was so important been with one of his women…his mistresses? That would explain the dangerous tension that lay just beneath the surface, and the glitter in his eyes.

'Because you didn't get your white dress yesterday.'

Lily felt her eyes sting with the threat of sudden tears. He had done it again. Every time she just about convinced herself that she could live by his cold rules and keep her own treacherous feelings hidden he brought her resolve crashing down by doing something unexpectedly, unfairly lovely. Slowly unfolding her cramped legs, she got unsteadily to her feet, so that she was standing on the bed in her tiny vest top and knickers and holding the dress up against her. It was simple and exquisite—short and close-fitting with a low neckline that swept almost from shoulder to shoulder. She let it fall again and walked across the tangle of covers towards him and bent down to wrap her arms around his neck.

'Thank you. You didn't have to do that.'

Raised up by the height of the bed, her stomach was almost level with his face and for a second she felt him rest his head against it. Then he stiffened, pulling away and turning his back on her.

'Actually I did. You'll need something to wear tonight, and I wasn't sure you would have brought anything smart enough.'

'Smart enough for what?'

He turned back to face her, and the expression on his face made her heart stop. She wasn't sure whether it made her want to run away from him, or to take him in her arms as she had done that night in the tower.

'A black tie reception for a few European chancellors and bankers at El Paraiso.'

'El Paraiso?' she echoed, her heart sinking.

'My parents' house.'

There was something oddly flat in the way he said the words, as if he was being very careful not to let any feeling seep into them. Lily remembered him standing in the garden at Stowell the evening she'd told him about the pregnancy. *I have no choice about the family I was born into*, he'd said, and his voice had vibrated with all the emotion he was being so careful to keep in check now.

'Ah,' she said softly, stepping down from the bed and walking towards him with a demure smile. 'A black-tie reception for Europe's major financiers, and meeting your parents. Sounds like a fun evening. I can see now why the "gorgeous-dress-as-bribe" was necessary, because otherwise I might just decide I need to catch up on some of the sleep we missed out on last night and spend the evening in bed.'

She came to a standstill in front of him, looking up at him without really lifting her head. He seemed so tall, so very lean and strong and well muscled, but somehow that just seemed to emphasise the hollowness in his eyes. There was a bitter edge to his smile.

'Not a chance. Technically you're my wife now, remember?'

'Of course.' She placed her hands flat against his chest, feeling the steady beat of his heart. Her whole body ached with the longing to put her arms round him and soothe away the tension, but she already understood him well enough to know that he was too proud to lower his guard for such an obvious approach.

Wide-eyed, she looked up at him. 'And as your wife,' she said very gravely, 'I suppose it's my *duty* to accompany you?'

'Exactly.' His smile widened a little. 'You're catching on fast.'

'OK, then, let's compromise.'

His eyebrows rose. 'Meaning?'

Lily rolled her eyes in an exaggerated display of exasperation. 'Compromise?' she said emphatically as if she were talking to a small child, while all the time slowly undoing the buttons of his shirt. 'It means each of us getting a little bit of what we want. I believe it's widely held to be one of the essential ingredients in a marriage—although I'm not sure if the same principles apply to marriages of convenience. However, I think, just to be on the safe side, that we'd better assume that they do.'

'So, let me guess—you want to spend a little bit of the evening in bed?'

'Now look who's catching on fast,' Lily said huskily, grasping hold of the edges of his open shirt. 'A little bit of the evening, and most of the afternoon too…'

He was smiling broadly as he lifted her up and laid her on the bed, and the anger and the pain that shadowed his eyes had dissolved away leaving clear, gleaming pools of pure desire. Lily's tender heart blossomed and ached as she lay back against the pillows. Leaning over her, Tristan impatiently tore off his shirt while he trailed a path of kisses over her collarbone and down her arm.

The light of the pale autumn sun slanted through the window, brushing Tristan's smooth butterscotch skin with gold dust, and highlighting the faint cross-hatching of scars on his back.

Lily bit her lip, closing her eyes and sliding her hand into his hair, her whole body throbbing with love and need while simultaneously being racked with pain.

Pain that she sensed in him and longed to heal, if only he'd let her near.

But he wouldn't. She gasped as he took her hips between his big hands and brought his mouth down on her navel, kissing, sucking, moving his mouth lower...

This was the only closeness she was allowed, and while she craved it with every cell of her being she also knew that it wasn't enough. It would *never* be enough.

She wanted what she could never have.

Not just his body, but his heart.

Modelling would never have been Lily's first choice of career. She had fallen into it thanks to a combination of chance and financial necessity, shelving her dreams to go to university in order to make the most of the undreamt of riches that were suddenly within her reach.

But at times like this, she reflected hazily as she walked with Tristan across the grand entrance hall at El Paraiso, she was glad that she had. Confidence was easier to fake if you knew how to hold yourself and how to walk.

Although, given the thoroughness with which Tristan had just made love to her, that wasn't exactly easy. Especially not in four inch heels, and with Tristan, mouthwateringly handsome in black tie, so close beside her. Close enough that she could smell the clean scent of his skin from the hasty, last minute shower they had shared while Dimitri had waited for them in the car below. Close enough to sense the tension in his body, despite his outward show of utter indifference.

They were late.

Lily's heels made a rapid, staccato rhythm on the marble floor as she struggled to keep up with him. Silently she cursed the fact that she'd spent the car journey here staring into the blackness of the window while her mind mentally replayed the blissfully erotic events of the afternoon in glorious freeze-frame detail, rather than asking Tristan to fill her in on his family. Too late now, she thought in panic. From behind double doors between the symmetrical sweeping staircases that rose on either side of the hallway, she could hear the sound of voices, and her chest constricted with nerves.

'Wait,' she croaked, putting an arm on his sleeve.

Tristan stopped. He was composed to the point of complete detachment, far removed from the man who had buried his face in her neck and gasped her name just an hour earlier. 'Are you OK? You don't feel sick?'

Lily gave a half-laugh and pressed her hand to her stomach. 'Yes, but then I do all the time. It's not that, it's just…' she twisted nervously at a strand of hair that had escaped the pins that held it in a sophisticated twist on top of her head '…I'm about to meet your family and I don't know anything about them.'

'Believe me, that's a good thing,' he said acidly, his face hardening as he looked in the direction of the doors in front of them.

'Tristan, don't,' Lily said in anguish. 'I mean—for example, do you have any brothers and sisters?'

He flinched. Only slightly, but she caught the minute narrowing of his eyes, the tiny indrawn breath. 'Yes. I have…one brother. Nico. He's in Madrid, so he won't be here tonight. Now, if that answers your questions, perhaps we could go in?'

He moved to open the door, but Lily stayed where she was, fighting the nerves that were shredding her insides.

'Tristan?'

'What?' He spun round, not bothering to conceal his impatience. She was standing in the middle of the oppressively grand hallway, her chin lowered, her hands plucking nervously at her dress.

The dress he'd chosen for her earlier, sensing without knowing much about such things that the colour would bring out the pale gold of her skin, and that the low scooped neck would show off the fragile perfection of her collarbones.

It did.

Dios mio, it did…

She bit her lip, looking up at him with smoky, hesitant and unreasonably lovely eyes. 'Do I look OK?'

Tristan stiffened, straightening his shoulders, his head jerking back slightly as he forced back the almost overwhelming urge to cross the stretch of marble floor between them and take her in his arms and kiss her until her lips were bare of gloss and her hair had tumbled from its pins.

He pushed open the door. 'You look fine,' he said tonelessly. 'Now, let's get this over and done with.'

Lily had never seen a room so luxurious or so chilling.

Long, high-ceilinged and decorated entirely in shades of cream and gold, it made Stowell, with its faded silks and threadbare Persian rugs, look positively down at heel by comparison. And although Scarlet frequently joked about the drafts there, Lily felt an icy chill creep down her spine as she followed Tristan into the crowded room. It was as if the temperature had just dropped several degrees, and almost without thinking Lily felt for Tristan's hand as they made their way through the crowd towards a group of people at the far end of the room.

She couldn't be sure exactly how she knew that the tall man with his back to them was Tristan's father. Perhaps it was something to do with the breadth of his shoulders, a certain arrogance in the tilt of his head that was already familiar. He was talking to another man, gesturing eloquently, confidently with a hand that held a crystal champagne flute. Beside them two women— one about Lily's age in an impeccable but rather conservative little black dress, one older and wearing a high necked dress in midnight blue—stood mutely.

Draining her glass, the older woman looked up suddenly. She was slender, elegant and immaculately made up in a way that obscured rather than enhanced her considerable beauty. As she saw them a look—shock? fear?—flickered across her face. Before Lily had time to put her finger on what it was, it was gone; replaced by a gracious smile of welcome.

'Tristan, darling boy! You're here!'

Juan Carlos Romero de Losada turned round slowly, flicking

back the cuff of his expensively tailored jacket and checking his watch before looking at his son.

'At last,' he said with a sinister smile. 'You are precisely one hour and five minutes late.'

Tristan ignored him, leaning across to kiss both women, but Lily felt his hold on her hand tighten. 'Good evening, Mama, Sofia...' His lips twitched into the ghost of a smile. 'Sorry we're late. We rather lost track of time.'

Lily was aware of all eyes turning in her direction. Her heart was crashing against her ribs as Tristan raised her hand so that everyone could see her fingers laced through his, with the diamond glittering beside her new wedding band. Slowly he brought it to his lips, kissing it gently before saying, 'I'd like to introduce Lily Alexander. My wife, and the new Marquesa de Montesa.'

For a second it seemed that a spell had fallen on the small group. While all around them the rest of the guests talked and laughed and drank the excellent vintage cava, no one in the circle around the fireplace moved or spoke. Lily glanced at Juan Carlos and felt a sickening thud of horror as she saw the fury rising in his eyes like some dark liquid coming to the boil. Fury that in this setting, in front of his guests, he was powerless to express.

It was Tristan's mother who broke the terrible silence, stepping forward and kissing Lily on both cheeks with a blast of designer perfume and alcohol fumes.

'But, my dear, how delightful! You must forgive us for being so unmannerly, but this is such a shock. I had almost given up hoping that Tristan would settle down—and with such a beautiful girl.' She gave an awkward little laugh. 'It is almost too much to take in!'

As Lily submitted to Allegra Montalvo y Romero de Losada's gracious embrace she had the strangest feeling that she were floating amongst the painted clouds and cherubs on the ceiling, looking down on the tableau of figures below.

Sofia, whose olive skin had flushed with telltale colour when Tristan had kissed her cheek, now seemed to stiffen and shrink backwards, clearly desperate to move away. Tristan's father, the oddly compelling Juan Carlos, stepped forward to take Lily's hand in his.

For an awkward moment she stood, one hand still clasped in Tristan's, one imprisoned between Juan Carlos's soft fingers. She could almost feel the animosity between the two men crackling through her, as though she were some kind of conductor.

'Lily…Alexander?' Juan Carlos repeated quietly, with a smile that didn't quite reach his eyes. 'I think our paths have not crossed before?'

It was a clever question, Lily thought with a stab of anguish. Everyone must have been thinking the same thing—that the idea of her ever having brushed even the most outward peripheries of Juan Carlos's exclusive social circle was utterly preposterous. Sofia gave a strange snort of amusement, which she quickly suppressed with a swig of cava.

'No,' she said quietly. 'I don't think so.'

'No. Of course,' Juan Carlos continued softly, 'I would have remembered such a pretty face. You must tell us all about yourself—where you come from and what you do for a living.'

'I'm a model. I live in London.'

From the look on Juan Carlos's patrician face it was as if Lily had said she was a high class hooker. His brows rose almost into his distinguished grey-streaked hair.

'My dear, how fascinating. What surprising people my son seems to mix with. And where did you meet?'

'At Tom's,' Tristan said coldly. 'At a party in the summer.'

Allegra's exclamation of delight sounded almost genuine. 'How romantic!' she exclaimed a little too brightly. 'And how sudden. It must have been love at first sight!'

Frowning a little, Tristan tucked the stray lock of hair behind Lily's ear. 'I don't remember it being *love* at first sight. I don't think that came until we woke up the next morning.'

Lily was aware of the brittle tinkle of Allegra's laugh, but only distantly.

A shiver of helpless longing rippled across Lily's skin—skin that still tingled from the ecstasy he had awoken in her earlier. But she was aware that beside her Juan Carlos's face had taken on a bland and dangerous look. Giving an abrupt nod in the direction of the ladies, he turned to Tristan.

'A word in private, if you please.'

For a moment Tristan hesitated, as if he was going to argue, and then Allegra stepped forward and tucked her arm through Lily's.

'You men go and talk business! I'm going to show Lily around our home, and get to know her properly.'

'I assume she's pregnant?'

In the masculine enclave of Juan Carlos's wood-panelled office there was no place for such feminine refinements as champagne flutes and cava. Picking up a solid, square cut decanter from a cedarwood tray, Juan Carlos sloshed dark liquid into two glasses. He held one out to Tristan, who ignored it.

'And why would you assume that?'

Juan Carlos looked at him over the rim of his glass. 'Because,' he said with slow, unpleasant relish, 'I can't think why else you have married her. Women like that are mistresses, not wives.'

Don't react. Don't show him that he's got to you. Don't let him see that it hurt. It was the mantra that had echoed through Tristan's head countless times before when he'd stood in this room. No doubt at some point during all those years the ability to conceal his emotions successfully had gone from being an effort of will to being a habit.

With deceptive nonchalance he leaned against one corner of Juan Carlos's impressive desk and raised his eyebrows slightly. 'Women like that?'

'Women with no breeding,' Juan Carlos said dismissively, taking a mouthful of his drink and giving a grimace that

Tristan understood was not directed at the excellent brandy. 'A *model*, Tristan! Such a cliché.' He looked down into his glass, swirling the liquid around for a moment before saying quite conversationally, 'I take it you are doing this to deliberately undermine me?'

'Just like you undermined me at the meeting this morning?' Tristan said with quiet contempt. 'How did you get those men to vote with you—against me—on increasing the interest on the African loans? That money is going to come straight out of that country's healthcare budget or education, or farming subsidies, as everyone in that meeting knew. How much did you have to pay them for their votes?'

Juan Carlos moved round to the other side of the desk and sank into the huge leather chair. 'Not everything comes down to money,' he said thoughtfully, examining his manicured fingernails. 'Most things, but not all.'

'Oh, *Dios*... Sofia.' Tristan got up from the desk and took a few paces, thrusting his hand through his hair as his mind raced. 'The deal was to do with me and Sofia, wasn't it?'

'Would that be such a bad idea? Do you think I married your mother for love?'

'No.' Tristan's laugh was edged with bitterness and despair. 'No, I *never* thought that.'

Acid burned at the back of his throat and the darkness that he constantly felt crouched around him encroached a little further. It was something that he was used to—he had lived with it for as long as he could remember, without ever really wanting to look directly at it, or give it a name. Until now. Standing here, in the room that had been the scene of so much suffering, he remembered again Lily's soft voice, the warmth of her hand on his heart. *The emotion you're most in touch with at the moment is fear...*

He hadn't wanted to admit she was right. He hadn't even wanted to consider the possibility.

But suddenly he knew she had been absolutely spot on. Looking into the empty eyes of his father, so similar to the ones that looked back at him from the mirror every morning, he was afraid.

For a long time he had accepted that because of the man in front of him he wasn't able to love. Neurological fact. But for the first time he allowed himself to look right into the blackness and confront what had been lurking there all the time; the fear that where there should have been love, all the cruelty and the coldness of those crucial early years had been hardwired into his brain instead. What if it was there, waiting for an outlet, and when Lily had this child…?

Dios, oh, Dios, what had he done?

He had forced her into this out of his innate sense of family honour, but what about her? What about his duty to her and to the baby? He had promised to protect her and keep her safe, but how could he do that if the biggest danger she faced was from him? She made him feel things that scared him. Things that he knew he couldn't control.

He had told her that he wasn't a monster. But what if he was? What if he was just like his father and he didn't know it yet?

His fists were tight balls of tension, and he pressed them to his temples as Juan Carlos's quiet, eminently reasonable voice washed over him.

'It would have been a brilliant match, surely you can see that? A link between our bank and the largest privately owned bank in Greece. Sofia would have been a good wife, and you could have had your sordid little affairs with models on the side.' He paused and shook his head uncomprehendingly. 'But instead you *married* one. It's a shame, Tristan—I thought you were more in control of your emotions. I thought you were too sensible to get carried away by stupid notions of romance.'

'I didn't,' Tristan said icily. 'You were right first time. Our marriage has nothing to do with emotion or romance. Lily is pregnant, and I'm doing my duty—to her and to our ancient, rotten, noble *family*.'

From the other side of the desk he saw something gleam in his father's cold eyes, and thought it might be triumph. 'She trapped you into this deliberately,' said Juan Carlos harshly.

Walking towards the door, Tristan laughed—a sound as hollow and bleak as his own heart. 'I think she's the one who's been trapped, don't you? Trapped into a loveless, sterile, dutiful marriage.'

'Hardly,' said Juan Carlos pompously. 'You are a Romero— the Marqués de—'

Tristan opened the door. 'Exactly,' he said, with bitter resignation. 'Who in their right mind would want anything to do with that?'

'You have a lovely home,' Lily said awkwardly as she stood in the small sitting room in Allegra's private suite of rooms. It seemed that they had come a long way from the large, crowded place where the reception was being held. This room, with its thick, thick carpets, quilted sofas, acres and acres of swagged silk curtain, was in a different world entirely: still opulent, still expensive, but warm and comfortable to the point of being suffocating. Lily was beginning to feel faint.

Allegra smiled and took another mouthful of cava. 'Thank you. I hope that in time you will come to think of it as your home too. None of the children spend much time here any more, but maybe…' She faltered, and Lily glanced sharply up.

'None of them?'

'Sorry.' With a little laugh, Allegra shook her head and waved her glass in a sweeping arc. 'I mean *neither* of them. Maybe now he is married Tristan will have more time. He's always so busy, you see…'

The words faded and she looked around, as if trying to remember why they were there. Lily was wondering the same thing. Allegra Montalvo y Romero de Losada was beautiful, glamorous, generous and welcoming, but she was also extremely drunk. From the fact that this hadn't been immediately apparent at the reception, Lily realised that it was a state of affairs Allegra was obviously quite used to. She also thought that it probably explained the rather large bruise that was discernible on one of her elegant cheekbones, beneath the pancake make-up.

'I think,' said Lily carefully, 'that perhaps I'd better be getting back. Tristan will be wondering where I've got to.'

Would he?

Once again her mind wandered back to the afternoon. There had been a fervour to his lovemaking that was almost fierce in its intensity. A ripple of profound, private delight shimmered through her as she recalled it...

'Wait! You can't go until I've given you what I brought you up here for,' Allegra said, sashaying into the bedroom and disappearing into another small room leading off it. Left alone, Lily pressed her palm over the tiny roundness of her bump and silently pleaded with the baby to ease up on the sickness. The waves of nausea were getting closer together now, each one threatening to tip her right over...

'Here!' Allegra was back, holding a large, flat box out in one hand and her glass in the other. It was full again, Lily noticed with concern. She must have bottles stashed all over the place.

Allegra set the box on the low table and sat back on one of the feather sofas. 'Open it.'

Lily approached the box warily as if it were likely to contain something highly explosive, or liable to scuttle out and sting her. Lifting the tooled leather lid, she felt as if she were in one of those children's cartoons where the characters opened the treasure chest and their faces were illuminated with the glow of the gold, only now the light coming from the treasure wasn't a yellow glow, but a shimmering meteor shower of bright rainbows from the collar of ruby and diamonds that lay against the black velvet.

Allegra was watching her face. 'You're a Romero now,' she said quietly, and suddenly she sounded absolutely sober. 'A Romero bride, just as I was all those years ago. These are the Romero jewels, so it's only right that they should be passed on to you.'

Lily's hand had automatically flown to her mouth when she'd first seen the diamonds, but she dropped it now and tried to speak. 'Oh...*señora*....'

'Please, call me Allegra.'

'Allegra, I can't accept these,' she protested a little breathlessly. 'They're beautiful—more beautiful than anything I've ever seen, but so expensive...'

'Priceless.' Allegra got up, swaying very slightly as she leaned forward and picked up the necklace. 'But you already have my son, Lily, and although he might not think it he is worth so much more to me than these are. Please, let me put them on.'

The stones felt very cold against Lily's bare skin, and Allegra's long fingernails scraped at her neck as she struggled with the clasp. Lily closed her eyes, fighting back the rising nausea and the feeling that she was being strangled...suffocated...

'There.' With a triumphant flourish Allegra stood back and, taking Lily by the hand, led her over to a mirror that hung on the wall.

The collar was wide, seeming to elongate her neck, and the large diamonds glittered with a brilliance that dazzled her. In the centre a single ruby nestled exactly in the hollow at the base of her throat, and it looked like a drop of blood.

Lily jumped slightly as Allegra's face appeared beside hers in the mirror, and with a strange, dreamlike expression Allegra removed Lily's own cheap costume earrings and slipped a pair of ruby droplets in their place.

'I...I don't know what to say...' she said, truthfully. She felt a little faint, a little dizzy and it was taking all her energy just to suppress the sickness. Allegra's fingers bit into her flesh a little too hard as she held Lily in front of the mirror.

'Welcome to the family, Lily,' she said in a strange, choked voice. 'I hope that—'

She didn't get any further. At that moment the door opened, and Tristan appeared.

'There you are.'

He stopped, and although his expression didn't change much there was something about the stillness that suddenly seemed to come over him that made Lily's heart batter against her ribs. In the light of the silk-shaded lamps he looked very pale.

And terrifyingly angry.

Allegra stepped back, away from Lily. 'Tristan, we were just—' she began, falteringly and then started again. 'The Romero jewels belong to Lily now.'

Tristan didn't look at her. Not for a second did his eyes leave Lily. They glittered with a dark brilliance like the diamonds.

'Take them off,' he said in a voice of frosted steel.

'It's so kind of your mother,' Lily said breathlessly, but her throat tightened around the words and she got no further. Her heartbeat drummed in her ears, and an icy mist of horror and panic seemed to be closing around her, blurring everything that was familiar and normal and logical.

'Take. Them. Off,' he snapped. *'Now.'*

Understanding tore into her head like a cyclone. Her fingers flew to the clasp and shakily fumbled with it. Of course, she thought despairingly, of course. He was telling her she had no right to wear the priceless Romero jewels. Her chest burned with the effort of breathing and acid tears gathered behind her eyes as the clasp opened and the necklace slithered off in a shimmer of brilliance that only real diamonds gave off.

Their marriage was a sham. Paste and plastic. Not real. The Romero jewels belonged around the neck of a woman Tristan loved, a woman he had willingly taken to be his bride, not the one who had trapped him into it.

She handed them back to Allegra, opening her mouth to say something, but discovering that she didn't know what to say. Thank you?

Sorry?

In the end she settled instead for a frozen little smile before following Tristan from the room.

'Well, that went well, then.'

It was a pretty feeble attempt at humour, Lily knew that. She couldn't blame Tristan for completely ignoring it and keeping his stony face turned towards the blank, dark window of the car. But still it left the problem of the gaping chasm that had opened up between them. The closeness they had shared this afternoon now seemed about a million years ago. Miserably she tried again.

'Tristan, I'm sorry. I didn't know that she was going to do that, and I wasn't going to—'

'Forget it.' His voice stung her like the lash of a whip. He took a deep breath, regaining his formidable self-control again before saying, 'It's not your fault.'

There was a terrible finality in his voice and he kept his face turned away. His profile looked as if it had been carved in ice.

Not her fault. Of course not. She couldn't help what she was, or, more importantly, what she wasn't—aristocratic, well-connected, with a string of surnames that would never fit in the strip on the back of a credit card, and a Christmas-card list that included all the crowned heads of Europe.

And that was what all this was about.

She had failed to pull it off, this business of being the Romero bride. Her face might have graced some of the most prestigious magazine covers in the world, but it had failed to fit in the Romeros' exclusive circle. Juan Carlos hadn't bothered to pretend, and although any fool could see that Tristan had issues with his family, it was also obvious that on some deep and primitive level he was also deeply bonded to them. *In my family you get…roots so deep they're like anchors of concrete, holding you so tightly that you can't move.*

That was how it was. How he was, and there was nothing anyone could do to change it. The question was, could they somehow find a way to live with it? As the car made its way through the narrow streets of the Barri Gotic she very tentatively reached out and covered his hand with hers.

'Tristan, I know I was wrong to—'

Very gently he moved his hand away and turned his head to face her. The streetlights shone on the rain-wet, night-black window, lining his face with watery shadows.

'No,' he said flatly. 'You weren't wrong. *I* was. I was wrong to think this could be more than just a business arrangement, Lily. I was wrong to let you think it was ever going to work.'

Lily felt the blood drain from her face as his shocking, hurtful words sank in. 'But what about this afternoon?

'A mistake.'

'No…' she whimpered. 'Tristan, no.'

'Yes.' His voice was low and forceful. 'I'm thinking of you, Lily; I'm trying to do what's best for you. We have to keep up this charade in front of everyone else, but I can't do it all the time in private as well.' He sighed. 'From now on, it's as we discussed at the start. A business arrangement. A marriage in name only.'

Lily was too shocked to cry. She had gambled, and she had lost. Everything, including her dignity and her heart. All she had left was her baby.

That night Lily lay on her side of the wide bed that had been the scene of such rapturous lovemaking earlier. She felt as if she were balanced on the edge of some dark and fathomless abyss.

The next morning Tristan went to the office and Dimitri collected her from the hotel and took her to Tristan's apartment in the Eixample. Left by herself, she walked slowly around her new home, admiring the pale blond wooden floors, the sleekly efficient kitchen with its stainless steel surfaces and gleaming run of fitted units, the big windows that looked out over the city to the sea in the distance, and thought wistfully of the cluttered house in Primrose Hill.

She felt very alone. And very certain that, not only had her brief honeymoon ended, but so, effectively, had her marriage.

CHAPTER TEN

'LILY, my darling!'

The nicotine-soaked rasp of Lily's agent in London reached down the telephone line into the quiet of the Barcelona apartment like an echo from another planet.

'Now, don't hang up, angel—I'm not ringing to pressure you about work, I just want to know how you are. And of course make sure that you're eating properly and getting plenty of sleep, darling. I'm worried about you.'

'Just like the old days, Maggie,' said Lily with a smile as she sank down into one of Tristan's squat, modern sofas and slid a cushion into the small of her back. When Lily and Scarlet had arrived in London as green seventeen-year-olds Maggie Mason had clucked over them like a mother hen, although her motives were largely financial.

'Ah, the old days, when I had to beg clients to cast you because you always looked so shy and serious until you got in front of a camera. That *does* seem a long time ago. Now you're all grown up and married to the most eligible man in Europe! How's it going, darling?'

'Fine.' Lily heard the slight stiffness in her voice and forced herself to smile. 'I'm doing everything by the book. Tristan has registered me with the top obstetrician here, so I'm being well looked after.'

'That's good! Fantastic!' There was a pause, and Lily could

vividly picture Maggie briskly tapping the ash from her ciga-
rette into an ashtray placed precariously on the landslide of
paper and magazines on her desk. 'Well, in that case, darling,
how's everything else? You're keeping busy? Only you would
not believe how inundated I am with requests for you to work.
Simply swamped with demands from just about every luxury
brand imaginable, all wanting the new Marquesa de Montesa
to represent them. Of course I tell them all that it's impossible—
that you're absolutely off the circuit and far too busy with your
gorgeous husband and your glamorous life to *work*, for
heaven's sake... Am I right?'

Lily hesitated for a fraction of a second, before saying
brightly, 'Yes, yes, that's right, very busy,' but the lie seemed to
echo around the emptiness of Tristan's stark and beautiful apartment. She tried to soften it a little. 'It's the baby, really. I mean,
I'm sure if you could see me now the only work you'd be offering
me would be the back end of a cow in a butter commercial.'

Unconsciously while she'd been talking she found that she'd
pushed up the cashmere jumper of Tristan's that she was wearing
and was gently rubbing the flat of her hand over the neat mound
of her bump. At almost six months pregnant she already felt huge,
and although she was deeply relieved that the stage of morning
sickness had passed she found it constantly surprising how the
simplest tasks suddenly seemed overwhelmingly challenging.

Maggie was not to be deflected. 'Come, come now, darling.
I saw that picture in *Hello!* of you and Tristan at some function
last week. Pregnancy suits you—although,' she teased, 'I'm not
sure it can be entirely responsible for the luminous glow in your
cheeks...'

Lily felt her face grow warm. The reception had been held at
one of the impossibly grand function rooms at the Banco Romero
and had been a stilted affair with endless formal photographs, for
which Lily had been expected to take her place at Tristan's side.

That was the reason for the glow in her cheeks, she thought
miserably. Because for a few moments her husband had circled

his arm around her waist and held her against him. Because just the feel of his body against hers in a room full of strangers was enough to turn her knees to water. Who, looking at those photographs of the Marqués de Montesa so close to his pregnant wife, would have guessed that that was the first time he had touched or held her in weeks?

Ten weeks, to be precise. Since the night that she had worn the Romero jewels.

'No, really,' Lily stammered now, 'I love being pregnant. I know it sounds mad, but I really do.' Her voice softened, and her hand stilled on the bump as a wave of primitive love washed through her. Tristan's coldness and distance were so much more bearable because she had the constant comfort of the child inside her, making its gentle, rippling, fishlike movements. 'It's like being under some astonishing enchantment. My body has taken on this amazing life of its own.'

'Oh, rats,' drawled Maggie. 'I was hoping I'd find you bored to tears and desperate to get back to work. You're still doing the next instalment of the perfume ad, I suppose—but that's not until after the baby's due, which is ages away.' Maggie paused, and Lily heard her take a deep drag of nicotine before she continued thoughtfully. 'I don't suppose you'd consider a lifestyle feature, just to keep the masses happy would you? Something along the lines of "my fairy-tale marriage to the gorgeous blue-blooded Spanish billionaire"?'

Lily suddenly felt very cold. 'No. No, I don't think that would be a good idea.'

'Darling, why not? You're so buried in domestic bliss that you're perhaps not aware that your fabulously romantic marriage has made you absolutely the hottest ticket in town. I've heard rumours about paparazzi photographers remortgaging their houses to pay for tip-offs about your antenatal appointments, and which parties you and Tristan will be appearing at. You can't buy this kind of publicity, so when it comes along, by God, you have to make the most of it…'

Lily's knuckles were white as she gripped the phone. 'No, Maggie, and—oh, gosh—talking of antenatal appointments reminds me, I'm going to be late for one if I don't get a move on. Thanks so much for ringing. It's gorgeous to talk, and I'll phone you if I change my mind about work or anything.'

A little later as she sat behind the silent Dimitri on the way to her appointment at Dr Alvarez's office Lily thought back over the conversation. *My fairy-tale marriage to the gorgeous blue-blooded Spanish billionaire indeed.*

What a joke.

What would Maggie say if she knew that at this moment Lily didn't even know where the gorgeous blue-blooded Spanish billionaire was, or who he was with? He had left two days ago on one of his frequent 'business trips', as usual giving no clue as to when he would be back. And although in many ways his physical absence was easier to bear than the great yawning distance that he so carefully put between them when he was home, it still hurt.

How, she thought bleakly, had she ended up deceiving all the people she cared about most?

She was saved from coming up with the answer to that question by Dimitri's guttural voice with its impenetrable Russian accent.

'Nearly there, Marquesa. I park at front?'

'Yes, please, Dimitri.' She smiled ruefully. It made no difference how many times she told him to call her Lily. 'How is Irina?'

He didn't reply, but once the car had come to a standstill in front of Dr Alvarez's building he reached into his pocket for a creased piece of paper and handed it to her with a little grunt. It showed the grainy amphibian outline of his sister's unborn twins.

'Oh, Dimitri, look! They're adorable! And getting so big… When are they due?'

He had come round to open the car door for her. 'Six weeks. But maybe they come sooner.'

Lily gathered up her bag and prepared to ease her bulk out

of the car and Dimitri put a steady hand beneath her elbow. It made her smile to think that she'd mistaken the gentle giant for a gangster the night she'd arrived in Barcelona. It seemed so ridiculously naïve now. But then so did a lot of the things she'd thought back then.

'How is she?' Lily asked gently. Dimitri had told her that Irina had lost her husband and both of their families in a terrible bombing raid on their village. Dimitri had been trying to persuade her to come to Barcelona before the babies were born, but she was unwilling to leave the place that was her last link with her husband.

'Always tired. Her blood has not enough…' he frowned '…metal?'

'Iron,' said Lily. 'Are they looking after her all right?'

Dimitri nodded, implacable behind his dark glasses. 'Señor Romero make sure. He pay for best doctors. He look after her.'

How typical of Tristan, thought Lily as she made her way slowly up the steps to Dr Alvarez's consulting rooms. Dutiful to the last—even to the unknown sister of his driver, thousands of miles away in Russia. She hated the mean little part of her that resented the idea of Tristan looking after anyone else. But she had so little of him, so very, very little, that it hurt to know that she shared those dry crumbs with anyone else.

Sighing, Lily paused at the top of the steps and took the mobile phone from her bag and dialled his number. Waiting for him to answer, she pictured him sprawled across the bed in some lavish hotel, a sultry beauty lying with her head on her chest, her dark hair spilling over the rumpled sheets. As the ringing continued she imagined him reluctantly disentangling himself from the long, tanned limbs of the beautiful woman and cursing quietly as he searched through the pile of hastily discarded clothes on the floor for his mobile…

'Hello?'

Lily's heart rocketed as his voice reached her ear; dark, rich, husky. She felt the heat flood her face. Her face, and her body.

'Tristan, it's me. Lily.'

'I know.'

'Oh, yes. Yes, of course.' She closed her eyes, willing the surge of stupefying need that just hearing his voice had aroused to subside again. 'Look, I've just arrived at Dr Alvarez's office for my scan. He has this high-tech equipment that means that you can see it on the Internet…' She felt her throat tighten. 'I just thought…if you're anywhere near a computer…'

There was a long pause.

'Tristan? Are you still there?'

'Yes.' She thought she heard him sigh, but it could have been static on the line. 'I'll connect my laptop now.'

It sounded so easy, Tristan thought as he switched on the computer and waited to see if there was any chance that the wireless connection was going to play ball today. The things that people took so much for granted in the modern world, like electricity or phone signals, were erratic and unreliable in Khazakismir, which was almost more difficult to deal with than if they hadn't been available at all.

The health centre's small office was currently doubling up as a storeroom to house the massive influx of basic medicinal supplies that Tristan had demanded on the day of the village raid all those months ago, meaning the desk was pushed right up against the window in the corner. Since that time things had been quieter here, and the rhythm of day-to-day life—never smooth or easy—had gradually been restored, giving them a chance to finish off the building and recruit and train some more staff from the local population. The health centre was still full, still struggling to cope, but the cases they were dealing with were the effects of the harsh winter and poor nutrition; influenza, pneumonia, sheer exhaustion from the grinding stress of living in poverty, rather than the bloody aftermath of deliberate violence. Today the cries that echoed through the corridors were not those of the maimed and bereaved, but of a woman giving birth.

Things were running fairly smoothly now, and the staff Tristan employed via the charitable trust had proved to be competent and courageous beyond anything he could have hoped. He didn't need to be here at all.

And yet he kept coming back.

Kept running away.

Swearing softly, he stared at the screen of the small computer, until the little hourglass danced in front of his eyes. He remembered Lily telling him about the scan a while ago, and about the latest technology that enabled absent fathers to view their babies over an Internet connection, but he had pushed the information to the back of his mind.

Or maybe he hadn't.

Maybe that was why he had flown out here two days ago, on the private mental pretext of dealing with a missing consignment of supplies, which, if he was honest, was never likely to be recovered. Maybe it was because all the red tape and tightrope negotiations with volatile local government officials was easier than being at his wife's side and getting a first glimpse at his unborn child.

Straightening up he slammed his fist down on the desk, making the laptop bounce alarmingly. A second later the screen changed, signalling that the elusive Internet connection had finally been established.

From down the hallway the woman in labour gave a low cry, like an animal in pain. Tristan's mobile phone rang.

'Señor Romero? It's Dr Alvarez's secretary. Are you ready to be put through to the scan room?'

For a moment there was nothing to be seen but a grainy moonscape of grey, broken by a paler crescent of white. Tristan straightened up and exhaled, realising only then that he had been holding his breath, mentally bracing himself against whatever he might see. But this he could deal with. The screen in front of him showed a picture like television static, a tiny white arrow racing across meaningless ghostly shapes in the snowstorm, clicking and measuring.

Measuring what? His chest lurched as he wondered if, whatever they were, the measurements were OK.

And then suddenly the screen split, and on the right hand side another window opened up onto a sepia-toned underwater world. For a moment Tristan wasn't sure what he was looking at as the sonogram moved around and the image swirled and billowed, but then the screen stilled and the picture resolved itself, and he was looking at his baby's face.

It was astonishingly clear, astonishingly *real*. The baby was in half profile, its eyes closed, a tiny, perfect hand pressed against one rounded cheek. As he watched a frown flickered across its face and the hand moved, the delicate fingers stretching and uncurling like fronds of coral as the baby opened its rosebud mouth wide and gave a restless movement of its head, as if it were looking for something. And then a second later it stilled again as the thumb of the small, flailing hand found its place in the tiny mouth.

Tristan was dimly aware of the ache in his back, but it was only when the screen flickered and went blank that he realised he had half risen to his feet and was leaning forward, gripping the edge of the desk, every muscle taut as wire. He straightened up, blinking fast, balling his hands into fists as the blood returned to his fingers and the drumming in his ears subsided.

He felt dizzy, as if the weight of the responsibility he had been keeping so distant had suddenly come crashing down on him, crushing him. The walls of the small, cluttered office seemed to inch inwards, closing in on him and he looked around wildly at the stacks of boxes and files of paperwork and the whiteboards on the walls filled with scrawled updates about roadside patrols and rebel movements.

None of it made sense.

He had thrown himself into this project, ploughing money, time, energy into it under some ridiculous illusion that he was being completely altruistic. His way of putting back some of the wealth his family had taken from those who needed it most over the years. His way of making amends, living with himself, sleeping at night. He had taken on despotic dictators, violent warlords, disease and hunger simply to avoid having to confront the real things in his life. The things that *really* scared him.

That he might not be a good father. That if he got close he would pass on the legacy of his father to his child. But as he snatched up the laptop and shrugged into his coat Tristan knew that it wasn't the weight of responsibility he could feel pressing the air from his lungs, or fear that was making his heart pound.

How stupid of him not to have realised earlier that it was love.

'The heartbeat is just a little accelerated, but it's nothing to worry about. Probably the *bambino's* excitement at being on camera. Go home and take it easy. Get an early night, and, above all, don't worry.'

That was easier said than done, Lily thought as she lay down her book with a sigh. She had followed the rest of Dr Alvarez's advice to the letter, and being in bed at just after nine o'clock was a record even for her, but the not worrying had proved impossible. Rearranging the bank of pillows behind her, she sighed and turned out the light.

Dr Alvarez's words seemed to echo a little more loudly, a little more ominously in the darkness of the silent apartment. *The heartbeat is just a little accelerated...* He had looked worried when he'd said that, hadn't he?

She switched the light back on and sat up.

'I'm being silly,' she said aloud, her voice cracking slightly from not having spoken to anyone since she'd left the surgery all those hours ago. 'Auntie Scarlet would say I need to get out more.'

She hadn't spoken to anyone *visible*, she amended with a rueful smile as she wearily got out of bed and padded into the kitchen to make a cup of chamomile tea. Talking to the baby was something she did automatically; naturally. Sometimes

she wondered if it was normal. Mostly she didn't care. She had
to talk to someone.

Anyway, who was to say what was normal any more?

In the kitchen she poured boiling water onto a teabag to
produce something that looked and smelled like pondwater. She
felt a tug of pain, deep inside her. Normal would be having a
husband here to bring her tea in bed, rub her back, tell her she
was worrying about nothing. Normal would be being able to
phone him, just to hear his voice, just to share her concerns and
have him reassure her…

She got back into bed and looked wistfully at the phone for
a second, her fingers tingling with the overwhelming urge to
pick it up and dial his number. She wanted to talk to him, to
ask him if he'd been able to see the scan pictures. What had he
thought? Had he been as blown away by them as she had?

The ache inside her intensified as the unwelcome answer to
that question presented itself in her head. Turning out the light,
she curled up, pulling her knees up tight against her and feeling
the baby press against her thighs.

She sighed.

'Goodnight, little one,' she said sadly. 'I love you.'

She was woken by a tearing pain that seemed to grip her whole
body, making it feel as if huge, cruel hands were grasping at
her flesh, twisting it without mercy. For a mute, horror-struck
moment she didn't move as doors in her mind seemed to clang
shut, trying to close out the terrible, nightmarish truth.

But it was like trying to hold back the sea. It burst in,
smashing the light from her world.

'No, no, no…' She was saying it out loud, her voice rising
in a crescendo of screaming panic as she struggled from the bed
and tried to stand up.

Her legs buckled beneath her and she fell to the floor, still
clutching at the duvet. It slithered off the bed to show sheets
that were red with blood.

CHAPTER ELEVEN

THE light filtering through the slats of the blind was thin and grey, but to Lily it felt as if someone were shining a spotlight on the inside of her skull. Squeezing her eyes tightly shut, she tried to turn over to face the other way, to shut it out for ever.

Ten thousand red-hot razor blades of pain bit into her, brutally dragging her back into consciousness, and jagged terror snagged in her brain.

Blood.

Blood everywhere. She remembered sticky warmth running down her legs…remembered putting her hand down to touch it, and the terrible jewel-bright redness on her fingers. Clumsily now she tried to lift her hand to see if she had dreamed it, but the movement sent a guillotine of pain slicing through her arm.

'Shh…Lie still.'

Tristan's face swam in front of her, grave and perfectly still, as if it had been carved in granite. Lily felt the pain recede a little as he brushed the hair back from her forehead and stroked his fingers down her cheek. He was here, and the sheer strength of his presence soothed her. Whatever had happened, Tristan could make it all right again.

With his hand still warm against her cheek, Lily let herself be pulled back down into blissful oblivion.

* * *

So this was his punishment.

Tristan felt the ache of exhaustion bite into his bones and scream along the muscles and nerves of his arm. Lily was asleep again now, her exquisite face as pale as milk from all the blood she had lost, but still he forced himself to go on stroking her hair, her cheek. As a gesture of comfort it was so pitifully small, so very inadequate, but it was all he could do.

All he could bloody well do.

He had promised to protect her, to keep her safe and he'd failed. Spectacularly. He had offered her *security*, and thought that that was nothing more than a luxurious home. A *name*.

And in the end that name had counted for nothing. A title and a bloodline and all the Romero riches hadn't kept their baby safe, because the only thing that could have done that was Tristan himself.

And he wasn't there.

A baby girl, the doctor had told him. His jaw set like steel and he kept his eyes fixed unblinkingly ahead, refusing to look down at the fragile figure in the bed. Her peacefulness was like a deliberate reproach, because he knew that soon he would have to shatter it when he tried to explain to her just what she had lost. Outside a watery winter dawn was breaking over Barcelona, filtering into the room through the slats of the blind. They seemed to Tristan like bars of a prison.

A prison of guilt, in which he would serve a life sentence.

'You're here.'

Her voice was a whisper—barely more than a breath—but it made Tristan jump just as if she'd shouted. He forced himself to look down at her, but suddenly found that his throat had closed around and he couldn't speak. *Yes, I'm here. Where I should have been all along.*

He nodded.

'I thought I'd dreamed it earlier,' she said softly.

'No. You didn't dream it. I'm here.'

'That's good, but…' Her eyelashes fluttered down over her cheeks for a moment and her brows drew together in a frown. When she looked back up at him her eyes were clouded with anxiety. 'But that means I didn't dream the rest either, doesn't it?'

'Yes. I'm afraid so.'

Her face was ashen and she spoke through bloodless lips. 'What happened?'

Tristan stood up abruptly, turning his back on her and going over to the window. It was early afternoon, and a pale winter sun had broken through the leaden clouds and was now making the wet city streets gleam like polished silver. Finding the words, speaking them without breaking down, was going to be the hardest thing he had ever done, but he had to be strong for her.

He had done so little else, after all.

'It was something called a…' He stopped, ruthlessly slashing back the emotion that threatened to crack his voice. '…a placental abruption. That's what caused the bleeding. By the time I found you, you had lost a lot of blood, and the baby…'

He squeezed his eyes very tightly shut for a second, as if that could dispel the image of what he had found when he'd finally let himself into the apartment late last night. But there was a part of him that knew already that it would always be there in his head, a lifelong reminder of his culpability. Savagely he thrust his clenched fists into his pockets and turned around. *Dios*, he had to at least look at her when he said this.

'The baby had died already.'

The only movement she made was to close her eyes. Apart from two small lines between her fine brows her paper-white face was completely composed, so that for a moment he thought she might have slipped back into her morphine-induced slumber. And then he saw that tears were running down her cheeks and into her hair in a steady, glistening river.

He stood, stony and utterly helpless in the face of her silent, dignified suffering. Slowly he approached the bed and sat down beside her again, picking up her hand from the sheet. It felt cold, and his chest contracted painfully as he looked down and saw how very pale and fragile her fingers looked against his.

'I'm sorry.' His voice was a low, hoarse rasp.

Almost imperceptibly she nodded, but her eyes stayed closed, shutting him out of her private grief. It was hardly surprising, he thought bitterly. It was his fault. How on earth could he expect her to forgive him when he would never be able to forgive himself?

Especially when she eventually found out the rest, and understood the devastating extent of her loss: that by the time he had found her she had lost too much blood, and they hadn't been able to stop it coming and had had to operate to remove her womb...

That she had not only lost this baby, but any chance she might have had of having any more.

Because he hadn't been there.

After a few more minutes he got up and very quietly left the room. She didn't open her eyes, so she never saw the tears that were running down his face.

Steadily the room filled up with flowers, exotic fleshy blooms sent by Scarlet and Tom and Maggie and the cosmetics company and all the crew from the perfume advertisement shoot, which made the air turn heavy with their intoxicating hot-house scent. Nurses came and went, some silent and compassionate, some brisk and matter-of-fact. Lily was indifferent to them all.

She felt hollowed out and as insubstantial as air. All the feelings that had nagged at her before that fateful night at Stowell—of emptiness and futility—came back now; swollen to huge and grotesque proportions, ballooning inside her until there was no space for anything else.

Which was good, she thought distantly, watching a nurse change the bag of fluid that had been dripping into her arm, because at least it stopped her from thinking about Tristan. Longing for him.

She wondered where he was; if he had gone back to

wherever he had been once he had broken the news about the baby. The image of his set, emotionless face as he told her what had happened kept coming back to her, and the carefully controlled way he'd said, 'I'm sorry.'

It must have been hard for him, she recognised that. So hard for him to keep his relief from showing, but typical of him to try so dutifully.

The nurse smiled kindly, folding back the heavy hospital blankets to check the dressing covering Lily's scar. 'Your husband rang, *señora*,' she said in her cheerful, sing-song Catalan. 'To ask how you are and to see if he might come back to see you this afternoon?'

Lily turned her head away, biting her lip as several explanations for Tristan's desire to see her flashed into her brain; none of them good.

'I… I'm not sure…I…'

She looked down. The nurse had peeled back the gauze dressing to show the livid scar that cut across her pitifully flat stomach. Lily felt her insides turn cold with horror, everything in her recoiling from the square of torn and deflated flesh and what it meant.

The nurse seemed pleased.

'Healing nicely,' she said with a complacent smile, dabbing iodine onto Lily's skin as if she were glazing pastry. 'You will be able to go home in no time.'

Lily moistened her cracked lips with her tongue. 'But will it happen again? Next time?'

The nurse seemed to freeze for a moment, and then several different expressions crossed her face in quick succession: shock, pity, fear—and finally, as the doctor appeared in the doorway, relief.

'The doctor will explain everything.' She patted Lily's hand, hastily gathered up her tray of equipment and bustled towards the door.

When she went back later, she found Lily curled up into a

foetal position, her face turned to the wall. Thinking she was asleep, the nurse was just about to tiptoe out again when Lily said, 'I'd like you to telephone Señor Romero and tell him not to come. Today, or any day.'

'Ah, *bambino*…' The nurse crossed to the bed in a rustle of starch and compassion and touched Lily's shoulder. 'Do not say that… A husband and wife must stick together in such terrible times. That is what marriage is for; for love and support…'

Slowly Lily turned over, and the expression on her face shocked the cheerful nurse into silence. Later she described it to her colleague on the ward as like an animal who knew it was dying and wanted to be left alone to do it.

'Not my marriage,' she said dully. 'My marriage is over now. There is nothing between us any more. Please tell him.'

There was a primal, ferocious glitter in her eyes as she spoke. Nodding mutely, the nurse bolted from the room.

CHAPTER TWELVE

Stowell, England. August.

'DEARLY beloved, we are gathered here in the sight of God to witness the marriage of Scarlet to Tom...'

Lily stared fixedly down at her ringless hands, clasped so tightly together on her knee that the knuckles gleamed, opal-white against the flowered silk of her dress.

'God and the world's media,' muttered Scarlet's brother Jamie beside her as the drone of helicopters circling the cloudless blue sky outside threatened to drown out the thin voice of the vicar. Lily managed a smile. The small church at Stowell was packed to the gills, and, while she would much rather have slipped anonymously into a back pew, Scarlet had other ideas.

'I completely understand that you don't want to be a brides-maid, honey,' she had said gently as the hairdresser had teased and smoothed her dark hair around the stunning Montague diamond tiara, 'but you're the closest thing I have to a sister and I want you there, right next to Mum and Dad and Jamie. They need all the support they can get against the full force of Tom's crowd, believe me.'

But both of them had known that it was Scarlet's family who would be doing the supporting. The day that Scarlet had been waiting and planning for for a whole year was going to test every ounce of the strength and fragile sense of acceptance that

Lily had built up over the six difficult months since she left Barcelona. The fact that Scarlet and Tom had picked the anniversary of their engagement at the Stowell summer ball to get married was just one more blow for Lily to absorb on flesh that was already bruised and bleeding.

The organ swelled for the first hymn and the congregation got to their feet. Lily opened her hymn book, relieved to have something to look at. The words to the hymn were familiar enough that she didn't need to read them, but at least staring down at them offered a temporary respite from the effort of not looking at Tristan.

He was standing just a few feet away at the front of the church beside Tom, the two of them tall and romantic in their morning suits. Lily had allowed herself a brief glance at him when she had first taken her place in the pew the moment before Scarlet had begun her stately progress down the aisle, but just the sight of his broad shoulders, the tanned hand he laid on Tom's arm in a brief gesture of support, had impaled her on a shaft of pure, intense pain.

"'Love divine, all loves excelling,'" sang the congregation. The printed words danced in front of Lily's eyes and her empty body wrenched with loneliness and misery. With massive effort she averted her thoughts, focusing instead on the enormous arrangement of tumbling flowers just in front of her. In the last six months she had become pretty expert in the art of refocusing, of training her mind to steer away from the danger areas, and she was proud of the progress she'd made. After the first terrible month when she'd returned to London and shut herself into the house in Primrose Hill and cried herself dry, gradually she had felt herself coming back to life.

Not the life she wanted and not the life she had had before. A new life.

"'Visit us with thy salvation. Enter every trembling heart…'"

Maggie had continued to try to tempt her with offers of work, but Lily knew that her modelling days were behind her.

Externally her scars had healed—the exhausted emergency doctor who had received her from the ambulance in the small hours of the morning had done a great job—and to the outside world she looked almost the same. But inside she had changed.

She felt blank. Scoured out. Sterile. A clean slate waiting for a new start.

The hymn ended and the congregation sat down gratefully, fanning themselves with service sheets in the August heat. At the altar, Scarlet and Tom stood shoulder to shoulder preparing to bind their lives together as the sun poured through the magnificent stained glass window above them, raining jewelled drops onto Scarlet's shimmering satin train. One of the many tiny bridesmaids recruited from the ranks of Tom's millions of cousins was steadily picking flowers out of her tightly bound bouquet and dropping them on the floor, and Lily closed her eyes as an image of the unknown little girl who had acted as her impromptu bridesmaid in the church in Barcelona came back to her.

She felt a smile steal across her lips, remembering how cross she'd been at the time at the hurried and unceremonious wedding Tristan had arranged. Now, looking back, all she could think of was how perfect it was. No pageantry, no theatre, just the beautiful church, empty and dark in the autumn evening, a few strangers whose lives had touched hers for a brief, significant moment, the sparse service, stripped back to its simplest form...

Tom's 'I will' was drowned out by a sudden wail as the small bridesmaid's bouquet disintegrated entirely, scattering flowers everywhere. Then an audible sigh of pleasure went up from the female members of the congregation as the strikingly handsome best man stepped forward and took her by the hand, bending to scoop up her fallen roses and giving them back to her.

Lily felt as if nails were being driven into her heart.

He looked thinner, she thought in anguish, the hollows beneath his cheekbones more pronounced. His brows were pulled down severely, which somehow made the tenderness of his actions all the more affecting.

It was no use, she thought despairingly. No matter how much she tried to avert her thoughts and her eyes, no matter how much she filled her days with activity or her head with new ideas, the truth was stamped on every cell of her body and in every beat of her heart. She lifted her head and looked to the front of the church, where everything she had ever wanted was symbolised before her.

Tristan, holding the hand of a little girl.

It should have been *her* husband, *her* child. The empty spaces inside her head seemed to stretch and darken as the grief that still stalked her crept a little closer again, but she gritted her teeth and pushed it back. She had something to hold onto now…a plan to focus on that had come to feel like a sort of lifeline over the past few weeks.

She just had to hope that he would help her.

The child's hand in his felt very small and soft, but her grip was surprisingly strong. Tristan loosened his own fingers in the hope that she would let go. Instead she seemed to hold on even more tightly.

Typical female, he thought with a sardonic twitch of his lips. He had stepped forward and taken hold of her hand completely instinctively, thinking only of heading off the storm of weeping that he could see had been just about to disrupt the whole service. Now he was beginning to regret the impulse. It appeared to be programmed into all women's DNA to cling on more tightly when they sensed you wanted to distance yourself from them.

No. Not all women…

A great weariness descended on him as the persistent whisper in his head tauntingly reminded him of the woman who had proved to be the exception to that and every other rule. Lily had never clung to him, in any way. Not throughout the brief weeks of their doomed marriage, when she had conducted herself with nothing but dignity in the face of his appalling coldness. Not at any stage of her pregnancy, when she had been tired or sick or worried, and not even at the end, when he had so badly wanted her to.

Dios, she hadn't even bothered with goodbye—not personally anyway, although he expected the one he had got via the kindly nurse was a lot more gentle and sympathetic than hers would have been.

'To have and to hold from this day forward…'

From across the aisle he was aware of Tatiana, one of Scarlet's modelling friends who was filling Lily's role of chief bridesmaid, eyeing him seductively from under her coronet of flowers. Deliberately he looked away, focusing his attention on the bride and groom. Tom was holding Scarlet's hand, looking straight into her eyes as he made his vows. His voice cracked with emotion, and Tristan gave a twisted smile. Tom had always been way too sensitive and sentimental—which had been why Tristan was constantly having to stop people beating him up at school.

'For better, for worse…in sickness and in health…'

The smile vanished and he couldn't stop the memory of another church, another wedding from stealing into the back of his mind. Another bride, in jeans and boots, her face bare of make-up and her hair tumbling down about her shoulders like a veil of spun gold.

The little bridesmaid's small hand felt as if it were burning his, and suddenly he wanted to walk away from it all—from the palpable love between the man and woman standing in front of him, from the child holding his hand, from the mass of people grouped behind him, amongst which was Lily…

Tom said that since she'd come back to London she was doing OK. She was coping, beginning to pick up the pieces and move on. He had also added with uncharacteristic vehemence that if Tristan did or said *anything* to upset her today he would never forgive him. Scarlet had suggested he just stayed well out of her way.

'As long as we both shall live.'

She was probably right. Wouldn't anything he could say just sound insultingly inadequate? Grinding his teeth together, Tristan stared straight ahead, concentrating on a memorial stone set into the wall right in front of him. *Edmund Montague, fourth Earl of Cotebrook,* he read quickly, as if by filling his brain with facts he could hold back the tide of emotion that he could sense rising all around him, threatening to breach the defences of a lifetime, *Officer in the King's Regiment…Loving husband and devoted father…*

And as Tom drew back the veil from his bride's face and kissed her lingeringly, and the congregation—mainly on Scarlet's side—burst into a round of spontaneous applause, Tristan extricated himself from the warm grasp of the small girl beside him and stood alone.

Alone with his failings.

In all of its seven-hundred-year history, surely Stowell Castle had never looked lovelier than it did that afternoon, reclining gently in its rolling fields of yellow and green, the flags flying from the turrets almost motionless against a sky of flawless blue.

Jamie appeared at Lily's side with two glasses of champagne. 'It's far too hot for this ridiculous get-up,' he complained, looking at Lily's bare arms with envy. 'How soon can I take off my jacket and this tie thing, do you think?'

Lily gave him a sympathetic look. 'I think etiquette would say not until Tom does.'

Jamie groaned, and gave his cravat a vicious tug. 'Do you think blue blood is a bit colder than normal blood? Like reptiles?'

Lily had just leaned forward to straighten Jamie's tie when a shadow fell across them and the bright afternoon seemed to darken. She looked up and felt the breath stop in her throat. This was the moment she'd been dreading, the moment she'd been hoping and wishing and waiting for for the last three months. Her fingers froze, clutching the silk of Jamie's cravat, and her heart hammered crazily against her ribs as she looked up into Tristan's face.

It was like an Arctic wind in the heat of the soft English afternoon.

'I think you could be right.' She stepped back, dropping her gaze. 'Jamie, have you met Tom's best man, Tristan Romero? Tristan, this is Jamie Thomas.'

Jamie looked at Tristan and then back at Lily, his mouth opening as realisation dawned.

'Tom's…Oh. Right,' said Jamie awkwardly, clearly wondering whether he should bow in deference to Tristan's title, apologise for the reptile comment, or punch him for walking out on his sister's best friend. 'Well, I was just going to get another drink, so…'

Jamie melted away. And as far as Lily was concerned so did the other guests, the rose-garlanded marquee, the waiters with their trays of vintage champagne, the castle, the lake, the rest of the world. As she stood a few feet away from Tristan, looking into his eyes, nothing else existed but themselves and the history that no one else understood. For a moment, a wonderful, terrible, wrenching moment, Lily thought she saw the pain she carried around secretly inside herself reflected in the intense blue of his eyes.

And then he looked away and the moment was gone.

'How are you, Lily?' he said. Courteous, civilised, *dutiful*. Of course.

'I'm fine.'

A lie, but an excusable one. One told with the best of intentions—to save him awkwardness, to protect herself, to make him more likely to consider the question she needed to ask him. And besides, in a relationship built on half-truths and evasions, what difference did one more small deceit make?

'Good. I'm glad. You're looking…' he paused, a frown flickering over his face as his gaze swept over her '…as beautiful as ever.'

So he was clearly not averse to lying either. Lily gave a small, painful smile. The connection she thought she had felt a moment ago had completely vanished now and a bleak, frozen continent of unspoken misery lay between them.

'Thank you,' she said ruefully. 'I appreciate your dishonesty. I wish my agent was as good at lying as you are.'

With narrowed eyes Tristan looked out into the distance, away from her. His voice was distant too. Polite.

'You're not working?'

She shook her head, holding onto her champagne glass with both hands to keep it steady. 'Not since the last perfume commercial.' She laughed. 'And after that disaster I probably won't work again.'

'What happened?'

'It was the follow up to the wedding one we shot in…in Rome that day.' *Our wedding day.* 'It was the next instalment in the story.'

'Let me guess,' he said gruffly. 'A baby?'

She nodded. 'I don't think the director or the crew were terribly impressed with my lack of professionalism.'

'*Dios*, Lily—'

'It doesn't matter,' she said quickly, desperately trying to withstand the annihilating wave of longing that smashed through her as she heard the slight rasp of emotion behind his words. She took a swift mouthful of champagne. 'I never wanted to be a model anyway. It was something I fell into and I kept on doing it because there was no reason not to. But in the last year everything has changed.'

They both found themselves looking down towards the lake. Tristan felt as if he were tied to a railway track and the train were getting closer. He nodded.

'Dimitri's sister,' she said quietly. 'I often think about her. Did she have her twins?'

'Yes. A boy and a girl. Emilia and Andrei.'

She exhaled slowly; a mixture of joy and anguish. 'Ah. How lovely…'

Tristan's head jerked round. 'Lily…'

'No, really, it's fine. I'm thrilled for her. I have to get over what happened…move on,' she said more wistfully. 'I want to move out of London, try to do something useful. The original charity who asked me to be an ambassador in Africa aren't keen to proceed at the moment because…because of what happened. They don't feel I could cope with seeing children suffering just yet, and they're probably right, but I'm looking into other ways I can be useful to them, and—'

She stopped, aware that she was talking faster and faster in her desperation to get to the point, and finding that now she had she didn't know what to say. Her head throbbed with dread and hope.

'Tristan, there's something else. Something I need your help with.'

He turned back, looking at her blankly. 'Money? If you're not working, I'd be happy to help out. We are still married, after all.'

'No. It's not that.' She took a deep breath. 'Not the money anyway, although the being married part is relevant, I suppose. You see, I want to try to adopt a child. I know it's very soon after…we lost our daughter…but I feel, deep down, that it's something I profoundly want to do. I just can't imagine…the rest of my life…without…'

She was breathing hard, unevenly, trying to hold the tears back. Trying to ignore the voice in her head that whispered, *You. I can't imagine the rest of my life without children and you…*

He stood very still, his inscrutable face giving nothing away. 'How can I help?' he said tonelessly. 'Can you do this privately? Can I pay?'

She shook her head. 'Unfortunately even the Romero billions can't buy what I want,' she said ruefully. 'There's a process—a long, difficult process to go through with social workers and being vetted for suitability, and approval is by no means certain. I don't want to get turned down. This is my last, my only chance. I want to make sure this happens for me, Tristan.'

A muscle ticced in his cheek. 'What do you want of me?'

'I want us to apply together. I think the chances of success will be greater if I'm part of a couple than if I apply by myself—an ex-model from a single parent family with a broken marriage behind her doesn't look good. I know our marriage was something you never wanted, and neither did I, but I did it for you. And now I'm asking you to do this for me.'

'Do what exactly?'

'Continue the pretence that we're a normal married couple…' there was a hard, cold edge to her voice now '…very much in love. It won't be easy, but of course privately we can go on as before. You can live your life, have your freedom and I won't ask any questions. And then at the end of it we go our separate ways.'

Very slowly he shook his head. 'It's impossible.'

'Tristan, don't say that—'

'Lily, you must know that it is,' he said despairingly. 'We tried it before and it nearly destroyed us both. Living a lie like that, pretending out of some sense of obligation or duty—I can't do it again.'

A sheet of ice formed itself instantly over Lily's heart. She felt the blood leave her face. *It wasn't a lie for me,* she wanted to shout. *I wasn't pretending to love you.* Light-headed, cold with horror, she began to back away as Tristan's face blurred behind a veil of humiliating tears.

'OK. I understand…' she gasped, holding up her hands in front of her as he opened his mouth to protest.

'Lily, wait!' he growled. 'Just listen—'

But at that moment an arm slid round her shoulders and she looked up to see Jamie had appeared beside her. He was looking at Tristan with unconcealed dislike.

'They're waiting for you to start the receiving line,' he said coldly. 'Although I think that Lily can be excused that ordeal.' He turned his attention to her, his face softening with concern. 'Are you all right?'

She nodded, closing her eyes against the tears.

When she opened them again Tristan was gone.

CHAPTER THIRTEEN

HELL, thy name is wedding reception.

Sitting at the top table in the sweltering afternoon heat, Tristan gritted his teeth and looked at his still-full champagne glass. He felt as if he were the victim of some sadistic, protracted torture technique designed to test his strength and endurance and will power in every way possible.

The wedding breakfast was over, and as the guests dozed over coffee Scarlet's father turned over yet another page of his speech. Beside Tristan, Tatiana's slim thigh, encased in duck-egg blue silk, pressed against his.

There had been a time when his automatic response to any kind of emotion would have been to obliterate it with some hot, meaningless, commitment-free sex, and back in those days the sultry looks coming his way from the chief bridesmaid would have been extremely good news.

He moved away slightly.

Unfortunately for Tatiana it had been a long time since he had dealt with things that way. A year, to be precise. And as a strategy for emotional avoidance it had to be said that particular night had backfired spectacularly.

Automatically his hand moved across the table and his fingers closed around the stem of his glass, twisting it round while he resisted the temptation to pick it up and drain it. He badly wanted something to take the edge off the torment, and in the absence of a revolver and a single bullet alcohol seemed to offer his best chance, but unfortunately he had to stand up and make a speech in a minute.

Or perhaps that was being optimistic, he thought sourly. If Scarlet's father continued at his present rate Tristan would have plenty of time to down a bottle and sober up again before it was his turn.

If he leaned forward he could just see Lily's profile, half hidden by Jamie Thomas's lean frame. The razor wire wrapped around Tristan's heart tightened a little and his chest burned with the effort of not getting up, vaulting across the table and snatching her up into his arms.

Dios. Dios mio... Why hadn't she given him a chance to finish?

Finally Mr Thomas brought his speech to a close and everyone rose to their feet and toasted the bride and groom with enthusiastic relief. Tristan's hand was like a vice around his glass as he put it to his lips, wondering whether to take this chance to grab Lily and slip out. His head buzzed with the need to talk to her.

Too late. Tom was already getting to his feet as everyone else settled down into their seats once again. Tristan, caged and crucified by his own moral code of courtesy and duty, sat down too, clenching his hands together and resting his forehead on them as Tom started to speak.

'Ladies and gentlemen...I'll make this brief.'

Not bloody brief enough, thought Tristan dully, his heart jerking violently against his ribs as he looked at Lily. Not brief enough.

Tom was as good as his word. His speech was short and typically full of wry, self-deprecating humour and as the guests rose to their feet again to toast the bridesmaids they were still smiling.

The vintage champagne burned Lily's throat like acid as she choked back sudden tears and stared out of the marquee into the melting, strawberry-sorbet sunset. It was nearly over now, she told herself desperately. She only had to hold it together for a little bit longer before she could slip away quietly and howl out her sorrow and frustration and emptiness into the goose-down pillows of her room.

Tristan's refusal earlier had felt like another loss. Not of a real child this time, but of hope. Of another little bit of her future. She wasn't sure how much more loss she could take.

It would be so much easier if she could hate him, she thought bleakly, absent-mindedly twirling a sugar flower from the top of the wedding cake between her fingers. She *should* hate him: this was the man who had delivered the news of their baby's death in flat, emotionless tones, and then left her alone in the hospital. The same man who had just crushed her fragile dream with a single word.

But then she would remember the pain she sometimes glimpsed beneath the layer of ice in his eyes, the mask of honour and duty she suspected he wore to cover up the loneliness of his upbringing. She remembered the torment on his face sometimes when sleep had stripped away that mask, and she knew that it was hopeless. He touched her in places she couldn't help responding to, regardless of how sensible that response was, or how healthy. She hadn't chosen to fall in love with him, just as she hadn't chosen anything else that had happened to her in the last year, but now it had happened she had to live with it. Minimise the damage.

Around her she felt a frisson of interest stir the syrupy afternoon air. The girls on her table—a mixture of heiresses and models—were all sitting up a little straighter, fluffing up hair that had been flattened earlier beneath extravagant hats. Looking up, Lily immediately saw why.

At the top table Tristan had got to his feet.

Lily had the sensation of being in a lift as it plunged quickly downwards. He was so golden and gorgeous, but as she looked up at him she recognised a new severity in his features that she hadn't seen before. The intense blue eyes were the same, and the perfect cheekbones and the square chin with its deeply carved cleft, but, indefinably, gone was any trace of that louche, wicked playboy who had stepped out of the helicopter last summer and kissed her so audaciously. Looking away quickly, she saw that the sugar flower had crumbled to dust in her fingers.

'As a Spaniard this role of 'best man' is not one I'm very familiar with…' Tristan began, and a little sigh of female appreciation went round the marquee as that deep, husky Spanish voice filled the evening. Gazing out across the lawns, Lily felt it shiver across her skin, spreading goosebumps of longing as her poor, ravaged body stirred with feelings she had suppressed for a long time and her head was filled with a picture of a dark church, a handful of people.

'And when Tom asked me to do it I initially refused on the grounds that he's clearly a far better man than I am,' Tristan went on. A ripple of laughter greeted this. He had them all in the palm of his hand, thought Lily painfully. It was completely impossible to remain immune to that combination of grave intelligence and those killer good looks.

'However, when he sent me a copy of a book called *The Complete Guide to Being a Best Man* I discovered that it was not so much a competitive event as a series of clearly defined duties.'

More laughter.

Duties. Lily closed her eyes for a second against the pain.

'There are quite a lot of them,' he went on huskily, holding the book up and bending it back so that the pages flickered out like a fan, 'but I have learned recently that to do something out of *duty* is not always the best approach…'

Every word was another turn of the screw. Wasn't it enough that he had shattered her last hope, she thought numbly, without making her suffer so publicly too?

Tristan gave Tom a lopsided smile and put the book down on the table. 'Thanks for the thought, Tom, but I'm going to do this my way.'

Outside beyond the silken drapes of the marquee, the blush-pink sun was dipping down behind the trees around the lake, staining the sky the same colour as the roses in Scarlet's bouquet. In the centre of the lake the tower stood, dark and forbidding, its windows reflecting the sinking crimson sun and making it look as if it were on fire. Tristan's voice, deep and grave, went on, talking about the perfection of the day. Lily's head was filled with a sort of roaring, as if she were standing on the top of a mountain in a high wind.

Wishful thinking.

'...everything a wedding should be...' Tristan's voice reached her as if from a great distance '...champagne and roses; beautiful dresses and beautiful bridesmaids...'

Back in the real world, all around her, people smiled fondly. But then they couldn't know that the perfect, proper wedding that the best man was describing was the opposite in every way of his own hasty, hole-in-the-corner one to a woman he didn't love.

'It's about friends and families and laughing and dancing and fun.'

He stopped, looking down for a moment, frowning as if he was wondering how to go on. Everyone waited. The dying sun cast everything in a soft, rosy glow, adding to the sense of enchantment.

'That's a wedding. A *marriage* is a different thing entirely.' His voice was soft now, and filled with a kind of weary resignation. 'A marriage is about sharing, talking, compromising. It's about being honest. Being *there*.'

Enough.

Lily's throat burned and her eyes felt as if they were full of splinters as she got up and slipped quietly out from her place at the table. She walked quickly away from the marquee across the grass. The dew was falling and it was damp underfoot, making her heels sink into the soft ground so she paused for a second to kick them off and gather them up before stumbling onwards, blinded by tears. Tristan's voice followed her, filling her head and seeming to wrap itself around her in the velvety air, in a ceaseless, caressing taunt.

'Lily…'

She jerked to a standstill for a second as she realised that he was behind her, that what he was saying was her name. Then she carried on, faster than before, almost running down the sloping lawn towards the lake.

'Leave me alone, Tristan. Go back to your rapturous audience. I think I've heard enough.'

'Have you? I don't think so.'

She did stop then, whirling round to face him, her face blazing with anger that she no longer had the strength or the inclination to hide. 'How could you?' she croaked, and the rawness in her voice was shocking in the perfect, rose-pink evening. 'How could you stand up there in front of all those people and say that stuff about sharing and talking and…and *compromise*, for God's sake? How could you say it in front of *me*?'

Her voice was rising to a shout and there were tears running down her face. Taking a step towards him, she raised her hands, clenching her fists and pounding them against his chest as the anger and the grief, sealed in for so long, came spilling out.

'I never asked anything of you, Tristan! I didn't ask to be your wife, I didn't ask to be taken to a country where I knew no one and left alone there for days on end while you went away…' She gave a wild laugh. 'God, I didn't even ask where you went to! I asked for *nothing* and that's *exactly* what I got!'

Still her fists flailed at him, raining blows on his chest and his arms that he had absorbed without flinching, but now he caught hold of her wrists and held them tightly. 'What do you want?' His voice was a low rasp, edged with despair. 'What do you want, Lily?'

She went suddenly still. Their faces were inches apart and she could smell the citrus scent of his skin. It brought back a rush of memories that sent heat flooding downwards through her stomach. Heat and wetness and need.

I want everything we nearly had and didn't.

I want the impossible.
I want you.

'I just want some…consideration,' she said hoarsely, ruthlessly stamping out the need and the longing, fighting to hang onto the anger of a moment ago. 'I want to not have to listen to you standing up there theorising about what makes a successful marriage, when ours was nothing but misery and loneliness.' Her voice cracked and she tried to hide it with an ironic, self-mocking laugh. 'Stupid as it sounds now, I wanted all that stuff that you mentioned—the sharing and the talking, but most of all I wanted…our baby. I wanted our baby so much.'

The sob that escaped her was muffled by his mouth coming down on hers as he gathered her into his arms and pulled her into his body. Her tears ran over his fingers as he held her face in a kiss that went on and on, fuelled by despair and rage and sadness and guilt.

Guilt that after all that had happened, after the enormity of what she had lost, Lily found herself wanting to forget, just for a moment. To be the person she had been—full of love, instead of empty and angry and hollowed out by grief. Her hands tangled into his hair, gripping tightly, and their teeth clashed as she kissed him back with the ferocity of her anger. And then he was lifting her up, sweeping her into his arms and carrying her across the lawn, his breath coming in harsh, shaky gasps, his chest rising and falling as he held her against it.

She didn't look up, didn't tear her mouth from his for a moment, but she knew where they were going. Even before she felt his footsteps slow, or heard the clatter of his feet against the wooden boards of the walkway, she knew where he was taking her.

Her tattered heart cried out in the emptiness inside her as he carried her back to the place where it had all started.

Back to the tower.

* * *

It was as if time had caught, taken a wrong turning, looped back on itself.

Everything was as she remembered, exactly the same. The dying light coming through the arched windows, the apricot glow behind the trees, the sparse room with the bed at its centre, like a stage. Everything.

Except…

Themselves.

The slow, dreamy languor with which they had touched each other last year was gone now, replaced by a desperation that made their movements swift and clumsy. Tristan didn't take her straight to the bed. Kicking the door shut, he let her slide from his arms and she slammed herself back against it, pulling him into her with a savagery that made him gasp.

'Lily…'

She didn't want gentle.

She couldn't do tender.

Gentleness had died in her along with her baby. Tenderness had been ripped out of her by the surgeons afterwards. Now she wanted oblivion.

'No,' she said harshly, grasping handfuls of his shirt and bunching it into her fists. 'No words. You don't have to worry, Tristan, I don't want love or tenderness or a happy ever after any more. Just make me forget, all right?'

Her voice was as jagged and cruel as broken glass, her movements swift and vicious. Her hips arched up towards his, grinding against the hardness of his arousal as her hands grappled with the buttons of his shirt until impatience got the better of her and she tore it open, exposing his bare chest to her fingernails, raking the flesh as he pushed up her skirt and tugged at her knickers, tearing the silk before entering her with a single powerful thrust that made her cry out in fierce triumph.

He drove into her with a relentlessness that made her dried and shrivelled heart sing, and with every hard push she felt the twin demons of anger and grief receding. Heat was spreading inside her, sending out bright tongues of flame to the furthest extremities of her body and building to a core of white brightness at a point in the cradle of her pelvis.

She closed her eyes, focusing on the light, and the movements of the muscles under his skin as she held onto his shoulders. He was carrying her, holding her and she was going to shatter…

She let go, crying out and throwing her head back so that it banged against the door, opening her eyes and looking at him through the fiery haze of sensation that claimed her.

And then she felt herself crashing down, spiralling back to earth.

Her heart stuttered and stopped and she felt the heat in her veins turn to ice. With a final shuddering thrust Tristan bent his head and hid his face in her hair, but not before she'd seen the expression of extreme suffering it bore.

They stood, motionless, still locked together as their breathing steadied. Staring into the melting remains of the day, Lily's eyes stung with tears she couldn't shed. Tristan's head was heavy on her shoulder. Then he seemed to gather himself, straightening up as if it hurt him. Wordlessly he picked her up and carried her to the bed.

Ecstasy and despair, balanced on a knife edge, she thought numbly. After the pleasure, the pain.

Except for him there had been no pleasure.

Duty.

That was all.

Always Duty.

The moment he placed her down on the bed, Lily rolled away, lying with her back to him and tucking her knees up against her body. Tristan felt the ever-present guilt harden inside him, mixing uneasily with self-loathing.

How could he have been so crass?

He had wanted her so badly, but that was no excuse for behaving like an animal, taking her standing up against a wall, for God's sake. When he had brought her here he had intended it to be like closing the circle. A new beginning. Instead he had only ended up hurting her even more.

Dios.

'Lily, I'm sorry.'

She didn't move. Only the barest nod of her head, rustling her hair against the pillow, showed that she had heard him. He sighed and raised himself up to sit on the edge of the bed, his back to her.

'I didn't mean for that to happen. I came after you to tell you that…' He paused, remembering with a cold, sickening feeling what she'd said. *I don't want love or tenderness or a happy ever after any more…* 'I just came to tell you that the answer is yes. I'll help you with the…the adoption.'

'You don't have to. I shouldn't have asked.' There was a note of resignation in her voice that turned him inside out.

He got up stiffly. 'No. You should. It's fine.' He looked down at her for a moment, feeling the knife in his gut twist. 'We'll work out some way of…being together.'

For a long moment their eyes held and a fathomless sea of unspoken words swelled between them.

'OK,' Lily said very quietly. 'Thank you.'

'It's the least I can do.'

He went over to the chair that stood against the wall and sat down.

'What are you doing?' she said in a small voice.

'I'll sleep here tonight.'

He hadn't expected her to argue, but it still hurt that she didn't. She lay down with a soft sigh and turned her back towards him, reminding him unbearably of the time in the hospital. In the soft grey light he watched her, until the delicate ridge of her spine, her creamy shoulder, the pale undersides of her narrow feet had faded into the gathering darkness.

CHAPTER FOURTEEN

'So, Mrs Romero… It's all right if I call you Mrs Romero, is it? Only I don't think your full name, or—er—your *title* would fit on the forms.'

'No, no, of course. That's fine.' Lily caught the sharp, critical edge in Miss Squires's voice, but forced herself to ignore it. She could call Lily whatever she damn well liked as long as it brought her closer to getting a child at the end of all this.

They were sitting in the Primrose Hill garden in the shade of the cherry tree. Laying the little French café table with a polka dotted cloth earlier Lily had hoped that Miss Squires would be won round by the rectangle of lawn that would be perfect for kicking a ball around, and the cherry tree that was crying out for a pram beneath it. But that was before she'd met Miss Squires. She looked as if it would take a lot more to win her round—a lifetime subscription to an ecological group and a fondness for knitting, for a start. Lily watched as she busily ticked boxes on the paper in front of her, trying not to let her heart sink.

'Please forgive me for asking,' said Miss Squires with a little laugh. 'We don't have a huge number of marquesas applying for adoption. Your husband would say the same about the title, would he—*if* he were here?'

'Absolutely. My husband never uses his title. It's really an irrelevance.'

Miss Squires's thin brows shot up beyond the rim of her glasses and she quickly wrote something on the paper. 'So, where exactly is he, Mrs Romero? It is usual for us to see both partners at a home assessment meeting, you know.'

'I know,' Lily said quickly, 'and he sends his most sincere apologies. He got held up at work, but he'll be here any moment now.' Tristan had telephoned half an hour ago to say that he'd just landed the helicopter at London City Airport and was on his way. The bit about apologising sincerely was a slight overstatement.

'And where does he work?'

'Barcelona.'

'I see.' Miss Squires' tone suggested she'd been to Barcelona and not enjoyed the experience.

'In a bank,' Lily added desperately, as if that made it better somehow. She suppressed a sigh of sheer frustration and sprang to her feet. 'Let me just get some more biscuits,' she said, picking up the empty plate and going towards the house. Anything to buy a few moments of breathing space. She had understood that the process would be difficult, but already she felt as if she were taking part in some kind of examination where the questions were in code.

The kitchen was quiet in the buttery late morning sunlight. A salmon she was marinading in the hope that it might make it look as if she and Tristan often shared cosy dinners at home lay on a dish on the side. As Lily arranged the last of the biscuits—home-made that morning; was that good or did it show she had too much time on her hands?—on the plate she had the feeling its glassy eye was looking at her critically.

Get a grip, she told herself shortly. After all, if she, with her commitment to the programme, couldn't cope, how the hell could she expect Tristan to?

Miss Squires looked up as she came back outside into the sunlight. 'I can see from my notes that you haven't been married very long, Mrs Romero. Just a year. That's a very short time compared to other couples on our waiting list. I think I remember reading about your marriage in the newspapers. It was rather sudden, wasn't it?'

Lily's heart plummeted as she set the biscuits down on the table. *Oh, God. Our adoption process is being handled by someone who reads the tabloids.* For a split second it crossed her mind that Miss Squires was not actually a local authority social worker but an undercover journalist out to get to the definitive story on the Romero marriage. The press interest in this subject had been intense over the past few weeks, and Tristan had an unfailing instinct for courting it to perfection, with the result that a rash of pictures had appeared in papers of them walking hand in hand on Primrose Hill, or kissing outside the house.

Seeing these pictures always cut Lily to the core.

Forcing her mind back to the question, she attempted what she hoped was a confident smile.

'Not really' she said, resisting the urge to cross her fingers. 'I'm afraid the papers don't always know the full story.'

Miss Squires looked a little piqued at this, and Lily realised she'd scored a hollow victory. 'I see. Would you say that press attention is a major issue for you and your husband?'

'Yes—I mean, no.' Lily felt the heat rise to her cheeks. There was no point in trying to hide the truth over this—the woman would have had to have been an illiterate Martian not to have been aware of the paparazzi interest in their marriage and Tristan's reputation as a reformed playboy, but she sensed it would not go down well to be too honest. 'Obviously we both have a reasonably high profile, so it's something we have to live with, but we're planning to move out of London in the near future, which will give us a lot more privacy.'

'I see. And where are you planning on moving to?'

'We've found a house in Cornwall, by the sea. It's deep in the countryside, miles from anywhere really, which should keep the paparazzi away.' Lily couldn't stop the smile from spreading across her face as she spoke. Dolphin House was perfect—closer to her childhood dream than she had ever dared to hope, with a yard at the back for chickens and a little sunny paddock where they could keep a pony. It also came with a mile of private beach. Miss Squires didn't have to know that what it didn't come with was Tristan, on any long-term basis anyway.

Lily dragged her mind away from the edge of that particularly lethal chasm, back to what the social worker was saying.

'…very isolated. We find our children thrive in communities where there is access to support groups and social workers and other families coping with similar issues. You might like to reconsider a move away from London at this stage. We recommend that change is kept to a minimum during the adoption process, since it inevitably disrupts things. For that reason we also insist that, whatever fertility problems you may have had, you resume using contraception. What method would be best for you?'

Lily couldn't stop a bitterly ironic laugh from escaping her. 'I can assure you there's no need for any method at all,' she said in a low voice. Tristan hadn't touched her since the night in the tower at Scarlet's wedding.

'Mrs Romero? Experience shows that even in couples who have experienced years of fertility difficulties, pregnancy can still occur, and for obvious reasons this would instantly eliminate you from the adoption procedure. Unless you're telling me that you and your husband have no sex life at all…'

She gave a little conspiratorial laugh at this, indicating that the idea of being in a sexless marriage with a man as gorgeous and famously sexy as Tristan Romero was utterly preposterous. Lily felt her nails digging into the palm of her hand.

She was right.

It was preposterous.

'I'm telling you that after I lost my baby the doctors had to operate to stop the bleeding,' Lily replied tonelessly. 'I had a hysterectomy. So you see, pregnancy would be a physical impossibility.'

'I see. And was Mr Romero supportive during that difficult time?'

Lily dropped her gaze to where her hands twisted the flower-sprigged cotton of her designed-to-look-wholesome skirt. From inside the house came a noise, like a door slamming.

'Yes,' Lily said quietly. Any minute now God was going to strike her down for all these lies, but in this case the truth wasn't really an option.

The older woman's face softened a little. 'What was it that first attracted you to him?'

Lily looked her straight in the eye. 'His strength. I don't mean physically, but he has this sort of aura about him that tells you you're safe. That he'll look after you, and somehow, no matter what, everything will be all right because he'll make it all right—'

'Why, thank you, *querida*.'

The dry, husky voice behind her made Lily jump. Whirling round in her seat, she saw Tristan standing in the kitchen doorway. He was dressed for the office, but his tie was loose and his collar unbuttoned and he held his jacket over one shoulder. For a moment their eyes met, and Lily felt the usual shyness that assaulted her afresh every time she saw him. Then, remembering the presence of Miss Squires and its purpose, she got awkwardly to her feet.

Perhaps Tristan remembered at the same time, because as she went towards him he came down the steps to meet her, one arm outstretched to take her into an easy, loving embrace. He kissed her on the mouth, firmly, lingering just long enough to look like a husband who had been away and missed his wife.

Lily's heart turned over with gratitude.

And love, of course. But she was trying to wean herself off that particularly destructive habit.

'Darling, come and meet Miss Squires. She's going to be our case officer now we're starting the process properly. I'll make a fresh pot of tea.'

Tristan leaned over and took Miss Squires's rather limp hand in his own strong one, and before she turned to go into the kitchen Lily saw the older woman colour slightly. As he sat down Miss Squires rearranged her papers busily and quite unnecessarily. 'So Mr Romero, I'm glad you could join us,' she said briskly. 'I've already had the chance to talk a bit to your wife, so now it's time to find out about you. Why don't you start by telling me about your parents?'

'What would you like to know?'

It was like being trapped in some private nightmare. An individually tailored version of his own personal hell, with every element hand-selected by sadists who knew his every weakness and wanted to expose his darkest fears.

And this particular sadist was disguised in a deceptively harmless-looking hand-knitted jumper and called herself a social worker. Tristan looked up at the leafy branches of the tree and made a conscious effort to relax, and not to show the tension that had suddenly turned his shoulders to granite. Lily's garden was lovely and usually he found the house in Primrose Hill oddly soothing after a high-pressure week in Barcelona or at one of the charitable projects, which he had now set up in two African countries as well as Khazakismir. Not today though. Right now even Tom's wedding reception seemed like a day at the seaside…

The voice of the social worker cut through his thoughts. She was looking at him steadily. 'What sort of childhood did you have?'

Tristan gave her a bland smile. 'Very privileged. I grew up in a big house with servants and a swimming pool. We were very lucky.'

'We? Who's we, Mr Romero? You and your brothers and sisters?'

Tristan felt the smile die on his lips, but kept it there with some effort. 'Me and my…brother.'

'Just one?'

Lily came out of the house carrying a tray. She was wearing

a simple white blouse with little cap sleeves and a short cotton skirt strewn with daisies that made her look fresh and pure and sweet. Tristan felt his heart lurch.

He had to do this for her.

'Yes,' he said, tersely. 'Just one. Nico. He's ten years younger than me. He works in a charity based in Madrid.'

Miss Squires was writing everything down, and Tristan was glad that her eyes were directed at the paper in front of her rather than at him.

'Not in the bank?'

'No.' Tristan had made sure of that. He'd sacrificed finishing his degree and doing something he wanted in life to make sure of that.

'What about your parents?' Miss Squires said, clearly deciding that Nico was of little interest. 'Are you close to them?'

Across the table Lily's eyes met his. They were soft and sunlight dappled, and they reached out to him. Looking into them, holding on, he said tonelessly, 'I see them quite often. I work alongside my father.'

Miss Squires looked up. 'That's not really what I'm asking.'

Gently Lily placed a pale blue pottery mug of tea in front of him. Tristan rubbed his fingers wearily across his eyes. 'Why do you want to know this?

'This is the next part of the process, Mr Romero,' said Miss Squires slightly archly. 'I think you've done the basic induction days, where you've heard a bit about some of the issues faced by the children in the adoption system?'

Tristan tried to keep the grimace from his face as he remembered the three grim Saturdays spent in a community centre in North London being told about the physical effects on babies born to mothers addicted to drugs or alcohol, the mental effects of neglect, violence or abuse.

Areas he was pretty much expert in already. At times he had felt like getting up and giving the talk himself.

'Well,' the social worker continued, with a small shake of

her head at Lily's offer of sugar, 'this is the time when we find out more about you. About what kind of person you are, which will help us match you to a child. We feel that the experiences people had when they were children play a crucial role in defining what kind of parents they'll end up becoming.'

No kidding.

'It's important to be as honest as you can—things have a habit of coming out further down the line anyway. Were you close to your mother, would you say?'

This must be how it feels to stand on the gallows, thought Tristan bleakly. *This realisation that there's no longer any possibility of running or hiding.* 'Not really,' he said stiffly. 'My mother's only close relationship is with alcohol, and I was sent to boarding school in England when I was eight.'

Behind her glasses the social worker blinked. 'How did you feel about that?'

'Absolutely delighted.'

Miss Squires looked deeply shocked, as if he'd just admitted to a fondness for torturing kittens. 'Really? So you're in favour of sending children away to be educated in impersonal institutions, away from the family?'

He met her eyes steadily. 'Yes, if the family is like mine was.'

Beneath the table Lily found his hand and took it in hers. The sunlight filtering through the cherry tree made her hair shimmer and turned her skin to honeyed gold. For a moment there was no sound apart from birdsong and the distant drone of an aeroplane in the cornflower-blue sky above.

'Could you explain that a bit more?'

Dios, was she never going to give up? Panic was beginning to close in on him, like a cloth coming down over his face, making it difficult to breathe, difficult to think. The tranquil garden with the cherry tree and the sound of birds seemed suddenly unreal, insubstantial and all he could see was the darkness inside himself.

Lily's hand was the only thing anchoring him to reality. He felt her fingers tighten around his as the darkness sucked him down.

He laughed, and even to his own ears it was a horrible, harsh sound. 'My father is the eleventh Duke of Tarraco, and a direct descendent of one of the first *familiares*—collaborators of the Spanish Inquisition. That should tell you something. My family rose to prominence and gained wealth and favour from the royal court thanks to their fondness for the rack and the thumb-screw. Cruelty is a family trait.'

'Are you saying that your father was *cruel* to you, Mr Romero?' Miss Squires persisted.

'Of course not,' Tristan replied with deep, drawling irony. 'It wasn't *cruelty*. No—every blow, every lash of the belt, every stroke of the whip was for our own good. He wasn't being cruel to us, he was simply doing his *duty*, forging us into proper Romero men, making sure he passed on the legacy of violence and brutality to us, just as his father had passed it on to him.'

Lily's hand. Holding his. Keeping him from the edge. A part of his mind stayed fixed on that while he continued, almost conversationally, 'The Banco Romero was initially founded to process the money confiscated from victims of the Inquisition. In fact,' he drawled coldly, 'my family now own a set of price-less jewels that once belonged to someone that one of our distinguished ancestors had executed for heresy.'

Lily's face was pale, stricken, reflecting all the suffering he had taught himself not to show.

'The Romero jewels,' she whispered.

Tristan's smile was glacial. 'Exactly. A symbol of our corruption and guilt.'

'That's why you didn't want me to have them?'

Adrenaline was coursing through him and the chasm gaped before him, dark and deep and full of horror. He had to stay strong to stop himself slipping down into it. Pulling his hand from hers he shrugged. 'Yes. And because I can't look at them without remembering the night when my father ripped the earrings out of my mother's ears for some comment that she'd made over dinner that he considered disrespectful. So you see, it wasn't only me and my brothers who bore the brunt of it…'

His throat constricted suddenly, cutting off the terrible litany of memories, and Tristan brought his fist up to his forehead in a jerky, helpless movement. Lily had shifted forwards to the edge of her seat so that she was facing him, both her hands folded around his.

'*Brothers?*' Miss Squires enquired. Tristan felt his blood turn to ice as she glanced down at the paper she'd been writing on. 'I thought you only had one?'

He had to hand it to her, Tristan thought dully, dropping his head into his hands for a moment. She'd said that the truth had a habit of coming out. He lifted his head and looked straight at the social worker with a bitter smile.

'I do now. But once there were three of us. My older brother, Emilio was the true Romero heir. It should have been he who inherited the title and the position in the company.'

'What happened to him?' Lily asked in a whisper.

'He killed himself the day before his twenty-first birthday.'

CHAPTER FIFTEEN

'HE COULDN'T take it any more, you see. The pressure of being the Romero heir and the position in the bank, so he—'

Tristan's voice sounded as if he had swallowed broken glass. Numb with horror, Lily stumbled to her feet so that her chair fell backwards. 'Tristan, stop!' she said in a low wail of anguish, going to stand behind him and sliding her arms around his shoulders, trying to hold all of him. 'Please, stop now…you don't have to say any more.'

Across the table Miss Squires averted her eyes and wrote more notes.

In her arms Tristan's body felt utterly rigid, utterly unyielding, as if she were holding a block of stone. And then very slowly he unpeeled her arms from around him and got stiffly to his feet. Standing behind him, Lily couldn't see his face, but his voice was like black ice.

'Sorry.'

The tense little silence that followed was broken by the ring of a mobile phone, which made them all start. Tristan stooped to take it from the pocket of his jacket that hung on the back of the chair. 'Sorry,' he said again, but this time all trace of emotion had left his voice and the word was perfectly bland. 'I have to take this.' Slipping out from the table, he walked away into the house.

Miss Squires was gathering together her sheets of paper and tucking them into a folder. 'Well, I think we'll leave it there for today,' she said, tucking the folder back in her recycled hessian bag and carefully not meeting Lily's eye. For a moment Lily almost hated her for making Tristan talk about those things. But she hated herself more. She had made him do this.

They got up and went through the kitchen and into the hallway. It was cool in here, and, after the sunlit garden, very dim. Tristan's voice drifted down the stairs, strong, staccato, decisive. At the door Miss Squires turned to Lily with a rather forced smile. 'Thank you for the tea, Mrs Romero, and I'll be in touch about our next meeting.' She paused. 'If you and your husband decide to proceed, that is.'

Outside Lily gathered up the mugs and the plate of biscuits she had laid out with such high hopes and such meticulous care. How foolish it seemed now that she had thought that biscuits and the kind of skirt she wore were important when all the time she hadn't known anything about what really mattered. She carried the tray into the kitchen and set it down beside the salmon. The carefully chosen, stage managed salmon that had played its part to perfection, and which Miss Squires hadn't even seemed to notice. She looked up as Tristan appeared in the doorway.

'I have to go.'

She froze, and the apology she had been about to deliver died on her lips. There was something terrifyingly bleak about the way he spoke. Something final that invited no further discussion. His face had a waxen quality about it and his lips were white.

'Tristan, what is it? What's happened?'

He shook his head quickly, backing away from her with his hands held in front of him, as if he wanted to hold her off him.

'An emergency. Dimitri is waiting outside. I'm sorry, I have to leave immediately.' He turned, running a hand through his hair distractedly as he looked around before moving into the hallway. 'It's probably for the best, anyway.'

'What do you mean?'

He shrugged, terrifying in his bleakness. 'I've ruined it for you.'

'No,' Lily said fiercely. 'I should never have asked you to do this. It was stupid and selfish.' She bit her lip, struggling to keep the anguish and the pain from her voice. 'You even tried to say no, and then I made you change your mind.'

He gave a harsh laugh. One hand was on the open door, the knuckles gleaming like pearls. 'After…the baby, how could I not? How could I not help?'

Duty. That was what had made him do this for her.

Of course.

She remembered the look on his face just after they'd made love, just before he'd agreed to do it. The look of a man who was enduring torment.

People said that when you were stabbed you didn't feel the pain at first. That there was a strange numb sensation of tingling heat before the pain kicked in. Lily knew that she had to speak while she still could. Before the pain started and she couldn't do anything. On the street beyond the gate his long black car crouched menacingly, Dimitri's expressionless face just visible through the glass. Fixing her eyes on it, Lily said hoarsely, 'You'd better go.'

'Yes.'

He hesitated, head bent, looking as if there was something else he wanted to say. Lily waited, her breath burning in her chest, her torn heart still as he lifted his head and gave her a twisted, heartbreaking smile.

'I'm sorry,' he said, and walked away.

He didn't look back, didn't turn his head as the car pulled away. Because if he had he might have told Dimitri to stop and he would have got out and gone back to her. He imagined running back up the path towards her and snatching her up in his arms and kissing her hard enough to tell her what he didn't have the words to say.

No, it wasn't that he didn't have the words. He knew exactly what words he wanted to say, but the Romero curse of duty and honour made it impossible to say them because he knew that telling Lily Alexander that he loved her would be a singularly selfish act. What could he offer her? Tainted wealth and a heart so damaged and twisted it was barely recognisable as human. Nothing that she wanted or needed. He thought of what Tom had said all those months ago at Stowell, about her needing someone nice and steady. Someone who could help her fulfil her dream of becoming a mother, not stand in the way of it.

Feeling infinitely weary, he kept his eyes fixed straight ahead until they had left the narrow network of streets around Lily's house, the restaurant where he'd once kissed her for the benefit of a photographer he'd spotted lurking in a car parked further up the street, the stretch of open ground on Primrose Hill where they'd walked sometimes, holding hands. He smiled ruefully to himself. In these last few months he'd really learned to love the paparazzi.

When they reached the wide, impersonal road around Regent's Park he turned to Dimitri, making a huge effort to turn outwards from his own tragedy to the wider suffering.

'So how bad is it?'

Behind his glasses Dimitri's face was grey. 'Earthquake was six point eight on Richter Scale. Epicentre about thirty kilometers to the north of the village.'

Tristan's mind raced. Below seven on the Richter scale. That was encouraging. He turned his head and gazed unseeingly out of the window where it was business as usual in London. People were going about life oblivious to the disaster on the other side of the world, the smaller one a few miles away in Primrose Hill.

'The health centre?'

'Some damage, but still standing.'

He nodded, briefly. Khazakismir lay a little to the north of the East Anatolian fault, and Tristan had ensured that the health centre was built to the latest earthquake construction standards. Unlike most of the other buildings in the village.

'Irina?'

'I do not know…' Dimitri's voice cracked. 'The house is gone. They have not found her yet. Or the twins. We just have to hope.'

'Yes. There's always hope,' lied Tristan.

The bright morning had faded into a dull afternoon and a wind had sprung up. It whipped the polka-dotted cloth off the table in the garden and hurled it across the lawn.

Lily was cold. So cold that she couldn't remember what it had felt like to be warm. In the hours since Tristan had left she had been pacing around the house, numbly going about the business of sorting, ordering, tidying away, almost as if she were getting ready to leave. Going upstairs to get a jumper, she saw the ivory satin dress that Tristan had bought her hanging in the wardrobe, and she finally gave way to tears.

It was over. The last infinitely fine silken thread that had tied her to Tristan had been severed and he had gone, leaving her in the ruins of a life with which she felt no connection. All the things she'd wanted, all the dreams she had spent so many years building in her head had crumbled into ashes and dust the moment she had tried to grasp hold of them.

As the clouds gathered and blackened outside she moved through the house like a sleepwalker, shivering, picking things up and putting them back in different places, tears falling erratically and unheeded as she tidied up the loose ends from which she had hoped to make a life. She found the estate agent's brochure on Dolphin House, with its glossy photographs of the huge sun-filled kitchen, the master bedroom, the view from the beautiful landing window over the garden to the sea, and remembered how she had imagined living there, with the children she was going to make hers. She had told Miss Squires over the phone that she would be open to taking any child, no matter what its background or problems, because she had believed there was no damage that couldn't be overcome with love.

But she had been wrong.

She had loved Tristan, and she hadn't been able to reach him at all. She had never managed to break through the shell of duty and obligation and touch the damaged heart beneath. Instead she had just become another one of the people for whom he felt responsible.

Duty, not love. That was what had bound him to her. He had told her that he was incapable of love, incapable of any emotion, but on some level she had thought she could change that.

Fix him.

She wiped her sleeve impatiently across one wet cheek. How was it possible to be so arrogant and at the same time so naïve? She hadn't even tried to find out what had made him like that in the first place—into the kind of man who didn't show a flicker of emotion when his own child died.

In the kitchen the salmon fixed her with its baleful, accusing eye. *What difference would it have made if you knew?* it seemed to say. *He just didn't love you and he didn't want the baby. Nothing could have changed that.*

'Shut up,' she said out loud, and, opening the back door in a gust of wind, she picked it up and put it outside for the little grey cat.

The house seemed terrifyingly quiet. Pulling the sleeves of her jumper down over her hands, she wandered through to the sitting room and switched on the television, finally stopping her pacing and sinking down into the embrace of the old velvet sofa and drawing her knees up to her chest. The screen in front of her was filled with the images of some distant disaster, of people sifting through the rubble of what had been houses with bare hands, grey with dust. The noise, condensed and filtered through the speakers of the television, was that of collective pain, and Lily recognised that the people she was watching were engaged in what she, in her own way, had spent the time doing since Tristan left. Trying to make order out of chaos. Hoping for some sign that it was worth carrying on.

An earthquake, read the rolling titles at the bottom of the screen. In the remote northern territories of Khazakismir.

Hundreds feared dead. The authoritative voice of the newsreader painted colour into the bare details of lunchtime in the middle of an ordinary day when an act of God had brought destruction of a more thorough and impersonal kind to people used to bombs and machine guns. An aid organisation already had an established base in the region, he said, and was working on the ground, doing what it could until an international effort could be launched.

Numbly Lily watched, her own grief not diminished by the suffering she saw in front of her, but somehow put into context by larger sorrow. Life was painful. All you could do was find someone to hold onto.

And hope that you didn't lose them.

When the mobile phone rang beside her she leapt up and seized it immediately, irrationally hoping that it might be Tristan, but the voice on the other end of the line was female. Disappointment hit her like a blow to the stomach, doubling her up as she sank back onto the sofa again, barely focusing on what the woman on the other end of the line was saying. Distractedly she turned the television to mute.

'Señor Romero?'

'No, I'm sorry. He's not here.'

'But that is his phone, is it not? I am trying to contact him on a matter of urgency.'

With a thud of surprise Lily realised that the phone in her hand was Tristan's, and that he must have accidentally put it down after he took the call earlier.

'Yes, this is his phone, but I'm afraid he left—' she looked at the clock above the fireplace '—maybe five or six hours ago.' Was that all? It felt like days ago that they had sat in the garden in the sunshine with the social worker. 'I don't expect him to come back,' Lily added bleakly.

'Do you know where he was going?'

She was Spanish, Lily registered. She sounded young and self-possessed and sexy. Not like the kind of person to spend an afternoon huddled on a sofa in the half-darkness, mesmer-ised by misery.

'He left because there was some crisis at work. You could try him at the bank,' she said without thinking, and then regret-ted it. Why was she helping this woman to get in touch with *her* husband?

'No,' said the voice impatiently. 'I am calling from the bank. I am Bianca, his secretary. He is not here, and there was no crisis at work until a moment ago. Señora, I need to find him urgently. It is his father—he has had a heart attack and is in hospital. Señora? Are you still there?'

Lily heard her.

She heard, but at that moment she was unable to respond. Letting the phone slide down until she was clutching it to her chest, she stood up in the sad early evening darkness and stared, dumbstruck, at the bright screen in front of her.

A news reporter stood amid the devastation of what was once a village, his face grave, his mouth opening and closing as he spoke to camera, while behind him workers moved rubble with their bare hands.

Tristan.

One of them was Tristan.

CHAPTER SIXTEEN

LILY's first thought was that it was someone else. Someone tall and dark, with the same high cheekbones and square jaw, but as she watched he straightened up, raising his arm and issuing directions, sweeping his hand across his face as he glanced into the camera for a moment.

And then he turned away, and the camera cut back to the London studio and Lily realised she had walked over to the television and sunk down to her knees in front of the screen.

She blinked, her eyes stinging, and suddenly remembered that she was still holding the phone.

'Bianca? Sorry, I'm still here. What did you say?'

'His father is very ill, señora. They do not know at this stage whether he will survive. I need to inform Señor Romero, but I don't know where to find him.'

'It's all right,' Lily said faintly. 'I do.' She paused. 'Bianca— I don't suppose… I mean, would you possibly know how to go about organising some kind of private flight?'

'Of course.' Bianca sounded slightly condescending. 'I do it all the time.'

'Good. Then get me a flight from London to Khazakismir. I want to leave tonight.'

Too late Tristan spotted the film crew.

He had arrived in the village a little over an hour ago, having spent the flight with the satellite phone continuously jammed up against his ear as he organised for manpower to be deflected from projects in other parts of the world and flown out to Khazakismir, along with medical teams and the first wave of supplies. The most important thing in the immediate aftermath of a disaster was organisation, and Tristan's utter lack of faith in the Khazakismiri government and army meant it was vital that someone was there to make sure the immediate relief effort was co-ordinated and efficient.

That was what he had been thinking of as he stood in the centre of the village. That, and the fact that Dimitri had just been told by a neighbour of Irina's that his sister's lifeless body had been pulled from the chaos that used to be her kitchen a few hours ago. He hadn't been thinking of the journalists that had miraculously managed to appear on the scene when Nico and countless other of his aid workers were still battling through red tape to get there. But as soon as he looked up into the dark eye of the camera he knew he had slipped up.

Turning away, he wiped the dust from his face and looked around for Dimitri. He knew, in some distant part of his brain, that in the sophisticated game of bluff and counter bluff that he had been playing with the newspapers and the paparazzi for years he had just made a very grave tactical error. One that could just spell his defeat.

The thing was he didn't care.

Lily barely had time to pack a few things into a bag before Bianca rang back. A plane was ready to leave immediately from London City Airport, she said. Lily was about to protest that it would take her some time to get there when from down below she heard the sound of the doorbell. *'Bueno,'* Bianca said crisply from Barcelona. 'There is your car. I have arranged for someone to meet you at the airport in Khazakismir. Have a good flight, and please ask Señor Romero to contact me as soon as possible.'

So this was Tristan's world, thought Lily numbly as the

small, luxurious Citation jet launched itself upwards into the
dark night. A world where you could go wherever you wanted
to go at a moment's notice, where there were rafts of people to
make the arrangements for you and pick you up and drop you
off. But no one for you to talk to. No one you could confide in.

Below her London lay in a glittering sprawl, and Lily felt
as if a band were tightening around her chest as the lights grew
smaller and fainter in the spreading pool of blackness. She was
leaving behind everything that was familiar and hurtling out
into the unknown. She hadn't really had time to think about
what she was doing and had acted purely on instinct. Looking
down, she noticed with a thud of dismay that she was still
wearing the flower-sprigged skirt and thin shirt that seemed to
belong to another lifetime.

The smiling steward appeared beside her and reeled off a
long list of the drinks and snacks on offer, as if Lily were flying
off on some indulgent holiday. It had been a long time since
the tea and biscuits with Miss Squires, and she wasn't sure
when she would get the chance to eat again, so she asked for
coffee and a club sandwich that she really didn't want and
picked up the evening paper that had been left on the table.

The front page was dominated by pictures of the earthquake.
Buildings leant at drunken angles next to those that had completely collapsed, leaving only wires and steel joists sticking
up into the dusty air like fractured bones. Lily's sandwich went
untouched as her eyes skimmed the columns of print.

Tristan's name leapt out at her, almost as if it had been
printed in foot high letters and highlighted in neon rather than
mentioned in a narrow sidebar under a small heading. 'Playboy
shows his serious side. Full story pages 6-7.'

Lily's hands were shaking so much she could hardly turn the
pages.

It was a double page spread. The headline that stretched
across both pages was THE PARTY'S OVER FOR EUROPE'S BAD-
BOY BILLIONAIRE and beneath it was a row of photographs

showing Tristan with his arm around a variety of beauties at parties and in nightclubs. 'Never the same girl twice!' said the caption underneath. The photo in the centre was bigger, and showed him sitting alone in the back of a car.

Lily's heart stopped.

The picture had clearly been taken with a long-lens camera through a blacked out window. Tristan's head was tipped back against the headrest, his eyes were closed, but the flash of the camera had clearly picked up the tears glistening on his cheeks. The caption beneath read: *'Suffering: A clearly devastated Tristan Romero de Losada Montalvo leaves the hospital where his wife was taken after miscarrying their child earlier this year.'*

The smiling steward appeared at her side. 'Is there anything you'd like, Mrs Romero?'

Oh, God, thought Lily. Where to start to answer that question? How about *my husband's forgiveness*?

Tristan sat on a hard wooden pew in the village church, his head tipped back against the wall.

His eyes were closed but he wasn't asleep. He wouldn't let himself sleep because, although every muscle and every cell in his body screamed with exhaustion, he knew he had to stay awake and keep holding onto the baby in his arms. Behind his closed eyelids the events of the night before replayed themselves in a constant, tightening loop, so that repeatedly he relived the moment when he had heard the baby crying, then the frantic, adrenaline-fuelled desperation to try to reach it and the feeling of suffocation when he'd finally crawled into the tiny gap between the collapsed roof joist and the rubble of bricks and plaster that had once been the walls to Irina's house.

And that was the part where the film kept stalling, like a tape getting stuck and then jerking backwards. He could see the baby—see her small foot in its dirty pink sleepsuit, kicking and flexing, but as he reached out his hand, ramming his shoulder into the narrow space between the roof beam and a slab of wall, it seemed always to slip through his fingers…

He came to with a cry, his arms tightening reflexively around the bundle in his arms, his eyes flying open and widening in horror as he looked down at the empty blanket clutched to his chest…

'It's OK. Tristan, it's all right. She's safe, look—she's here.' Lily.

It was Lily, standing over him and cradling the sleeping baby in her arms.

Tristan dropped his head into his hands, rubbing his fingers hard into eyes that still felt as if they were full of grit. He wasn't sure any more if he was asleep or awake. Was this just another scene in his disjointed series of dreams?

He heard the quiet whisper of her skirt as she sat down beside him. The skirt she had been wearing in the garden when the social worker came, he thought randomly; was it a day or a month or a lifetime ago? And then he caught a breath of her clean milk and almonds fragrance and he knew that she was really there.

Slowly he lifted his head and straightened up, feeling his muscles protest at every movement. Lily said nothing, but she took his hand in her free one, and they just sat like that for a while, his rough, grit-encrusted fingers entwined with her cool, pale, clean ones, her head leaning very lightly against his shoulder, listening to the sound of the baby's breathing.

'Why did you come?' he said at last. His voice was rusty and his throat ached from shouting last night. Shouting instructions to Nico, and Dimitri and hundreds of others who were engaged in the same race against time to free those trapped in the rubble.

She sighed softly and shifted just a little on the pew, so that she was facing him more, her grey eyes serious. 'Bianca called. Your father had a heart attack yesterday. A serious one. They don't think he'll survive.'

Tristan exhaled heavily, tipping his head back again as

despair came down like the night. Not for Juan Carlos, but because he had thought, for a moment, that Lily had come because she wanted him. Because she loved him.

'You came all the way here to tell me that?'

'I thought you might want to see him, before he died,' she said quietly. She was rocking the baby very gently, almost imperceptibly, in an instinctive maternal rhythm as old as time. 'I wanted you to have that chance, before it's too late.'

'I'm afraid it's been a wasted journey,' he snapped. 'Juan Carlos can go to the corner of hell he reserved for himself years ago without any kind of goodbye from me.' He looked up, frowning as a thought suddenly struck him. 'How did you know where to find me?'

'Oh, you know, the usual way wives know where their husbands are,' she said with gentle irony. 'There was a report about the earthquake on the news and I saw you in the background.'

He gave a ragged laugh. 'That's it, then. Game over. The press will no doubt pick it up and then—'

'They're onto it already. Does it matter?'

'Yes,' he said very wearily. 'I don't know; probably.'

She had been looking down at the child in her arms, but now she lifted her head and looked at him, and the intensity in her beautiful eyes made his sore throat close. 'Why?' she said fiercely. 'Because now everyone will know that Tristan Romero has a heart? That behind the cold façade of the womanising billionaire businessman there's actually a man who cares about people?'

He leaned back in the hard pew, trying to ease the ache in his back and his arms and his shoulders and his heart. 'Is there?' he said cynically. 'Or is that just a new image, a fresh angle that they'll use to sell papers?'

'I think you care,' she said huskily.

'OK,' he admitted, on a heavy outward breath, 'I care. *Dios*, Lily, I *care* so much…but what's the point when I can't help the people I care about? I let you down yesterday, by saying too much. I ruined it for you. My toxic past just keeps coming back to poison your life, doesn't it?'

She got to her feet while he was speaking and stood in front of him, shifting the baby easily up onto her shoulder, cupping the downy hair that was still matted with grit and dust in her hand. Her face was creased with anguish. 'Tristan, that doesn't matter,' she said and her voice was low and urgent. 'None of that matters. I should never, never have put you through that, but at least it made me realise that the most important thing—'

Just then the door at the back of the church burst open and the tranquillity was momentarily disturbed by the sound of heavy feet hurrying across the tiled floor. People sitting quietly in the pews praying or huddled in little groups giving comfort to each other looked round.

'Señor Romero!'

Quickly Lily slipped out of the pew and went towards Dimitri, taking his hand. His face was wet with tears.

'Dimitri, what is it?'

'Oh, Marquesa,' he sobbed, 'they have found Andrei!'

Tristan had got to his feet and was standing perfectly still, his face white and tense beneath the streaks of dirt. Agony shot through Lily as an image of him standing by the window in the hospital suddenly flashed into her head, and she recognised the same desperate attempt to maintain emotional control. How could she have been stupid enough to think he didn't care?

'Is he alive?' Tristan said tersely.

'Yes. Dehydrated. He is on drip in health centre, but he will be all right soon.' Dimitri's expression of tentative joy wavered again as he glanced at the baby against Lily's chest. 'How is Emilia?'

'She's fine,' Lily soothed. 'Sleeping peacefully. She's so beautiful, Dimitri.'

Dimitri looked down at the floor and shuffled his feet in helpless misery. 'Yes. Just like Irina when she was small.' His voice broke. 'They have no one now.'

'Dimitri, they have you,' Lily said softly, and she held out the sleeping baby to him. Clumsily he took her into his arms and held her awkwardly, but his hands just seemed too big to manage the fragile bundle and the expression on his fleshy, implacable face was one of pained bewilderment.

'I cannot care for them,' he said hopelessly. 'Khazakismiri men not brought up to look after babies. I not know how to start now, after so many years without a wife and family. If I was younger perhaps…' He thrust the baby back to Lily almost imploringly. 'But you could care for them, Marquesa. You and Señor Romero—'

'It's out of the question.'

Tristan leapt to his feet and he pushed past Lily, walking a little distance away before swinging round to face them both. Beneath the grime his face was pale and taut with fury. 'There are legal procedures. It's not simple.'

'Sorry, Señor.' Dimitri looked stricken. 'Sorry. I should not have asked. It is a miracle that they are safe, but now I worry about what will happen to them…'

Lily laid a hand on Dimitri's arm. 'It's perfectly natural that you're worried, but try not to think about that now. It's too early to make any plans for the twins' future yet, but of course I'll take care of them for the time being, for as long as it takes to sort something out.' Dimitri's face broke into a relieved smile. 'On one condition,' she added.

'Marquesa…?'

'That you go and get something to eat and some rest.'

After Dimitri had gone, Lily carefully laid Emilia down in the makeshift bed someone had provided for her and went to where Tristan was standing, leaning with his back against a wall by the altar, his eyes closed. The old stone church had withstood the earthquake, but the stained glass window above his head was broken, and coloured shards of glass crunched beneath Lily's feet as she went towards him. Her heart was hammering, a sickening drumbeat of quiet dread.

'It seems so obvious, doesn't it?' he said bitterly, without opening his eyes. 'And I know that it's what you want more than anything, but I can't do it, Lily.'

She was aware of pain crouching in the corners of her mind, inching forwards, waiting to strike when he said the words that would spell the end, once and for all. She stopped a few feet away from him, clasping her hands together and pressing them to her lips.

'No. It's OK. I understand.'

Still his eyes stayed shut, his long lashes dark against his white cheeks. His brow was creased as if he was in pain. 'Do you?'

'Yes.' It was barely more than a whisper. 'You never wanted to get married. You never wanted children. You said all along you'd never love me. So, yes, I understand why you can't do it.'

His eyes flew open and he pushed himself violently away from the wall, taking her by the shoulders and staring down into her face with an expression of intense suffering that tore into her, filling her with anguish but also a peculiar kind of hope.

'No! I love you more than I thought it was possible to love anyone…anything.' He spoke slowly, clearly, his voice raw with terrible emotion. 'God, Lily—I love you so much it's killing me, because I can't give you the one thing that you want and because loving you means that I *have* to do what's best for you, and that's leave you alone.'

She shook her head, vehemently in denial. *'No—'*

'Yes.' Still holding her by the shoulders, he shook her slightly, his eyes searing into hers. 'Because I can't risk it. What if I turn out to be like him?'

'Your father?

'Yes. Him and all the other Romero men before him.' He let her go abruptly, stepping back and raising his clenched fists to his temples. 'You were right when you said I was afraid, though it took me a long time to admit it to myself. But I'm absolutely bloody terrified, Lily. I'm scared witless that somewhere that behaviour has been branded into me, hardwired into my brain, and that whether I mean to or not I'll just end up repeating the cycle.'

Hope flickered, a tiny flame in the darkness. She smiled steadily into the deep blue anguish of his eyes. 'You won't.'

'You don't know that,' he said fiercely. 'Look at you—you're a natural. It's who you are. You look after things—from injured birds to stray cats. It's instinctive. Intuitive. Whereas I'm—'

'Like that too.'

'No!' He took an angry step forward, thrusting his hands into his pockets, almost as if he was afraid he might hurt her. 'My instinct is to run away from anything remotely emotional,' he said in a voice that dripped with self-disgust. 'I'm the man who tried to buy you off, remember? I'm the man who tried to pay to have nothing to do with my own child. I'm the man who left you on your own when you were pregnant, and wasn't there when—'

Lily didn't move, didn't flinch. 'No,' she said quietly. 'You're not that man. That wasn't instinct. That was desperation. Your instinct was to be the man who holds a little girl's hand in church when she drops her flowers. Your instinct was to put your younger brother before yourself. That was why you dropped out of university, wasn't it?'

He nodded, almost imperceptibly, his eyes fixed on hers. Lily didn't miss a beat, continuing in the same gentle, hypnotic voice. 'Your instinct was to look after a pregnant woman on the other side of the world, and provide for whole communities and bring hope to people whose lives have been torn apart. Your instinct was to risk your own life to rescue a child. Tristan, I watched you when you were asleep…' for the first time her voice caught, and she moved towards him '…and you were holding the blanket as if you were still cradling her in your arms. Even then, even when you were half dead with exhaustion, your instinct was to protect her.'

'Do you think so?'

The expression on his face was one of exquisite torment, and it took all Lily's powers of self restraint not to throw herself into his arms and kiss away the hurt. But she couldn't do that. Not yet. She stood a few inches away from him trembling with longing and hope.

'I *know* so. I *know* that as well as being the man I want to be married to for the rest of my life, you'd also make the most fantastic, incredible father.' She took a deep breath as her eyes blurred with hot, stinging tears. 'But that doesn't mean that we have to do this, Tristan. You were wrong when you said that this is the one thing I want. It's not. I'd be lying if I said I didn't still want children, but only with you. Only if we're doing it together, and if it's not what you want then just having you will be enough for me because…'

Here she faltered, and bowed her head as the tears ran down her face and splashed on the dusty floor. For a moment neither of them moved, and then she felt Tristan very gently take her chin between his fingers and lift her face to his. His blue eyes burned with passion and pain.

'Because what?' he said hoarsely.

'Because I love you so much.'

He scowled down at her, trying to take it in. 'So much that you'd give up your dream for me?'

'You are my dream,' she said simply. 'It all begins and ends with you. And if some day, somehow, we had a family then that would be…amazing, but if we didn't, then I'd still have more than I had any right to wish for.' She paused, her eyelids flickering closed for a second, almost as if she were praying. '*If* I had you.'

Tristan gave a moan of helpless longing. 'You have me. Oh, *Dios*, Lily, you have me, for all of eternity…'

As he bent his head to kiss her Lily saw a tear fall, leaving a clean trail through the grime on his cheek, and as his lips met hers she felt them tremble. He kissed her with slow and tender passion that felt almost like reverence, his hands cupping her face, his heart beating against hers. And then when both of them were gasping for breath and his fingers were wet with her tears he folded her into his body and wrapped his arms tightly around her, and just held her.

After a long time Lily raised her head and looked up at him.

'Is it wrong to be happy in the midst of all this devastation?' she whispered.

Tristan shook his head slowly. 'No. It's the only thing that's right. The only thing that makes sense. The only thing that makes it possible to go on from this. And we will, I promise you we will.'

Strength and certainty blazed in the depths of the blue eyes Lily loved so much. She closed her eyes and leaned her head against him.

'Tristan, please…' she said quietly, 'hold me again. Don't let go.'

'I won't,' he whispered fiercely into her hair. 'I'll never let go.

EPILOGUE

LILY paused, a little blue birthday candle held between her fingers as she stood at the window of the big sunny kitchen.

Outside the garden swooned in the syrupy heat of the summer afternoon and the sea sparkled in the distance. At the far side of the lawn a table stood, half in the shade of the huge cedar tree whose branches were hung with brightly striped bunting, and Emilia's squeals of delighted laughter drifted across the drowsy air and in through the open door.

Lily's face broke into a smile of pure adoration as she watched her, delicious in the pink tutu and fairy wings Scarlet and Tom had given her, sitting on the bit of Scarlet's knee that wasn't taken up with the bulk of advanced pregnancy and giggling infectiously as Scarlet tickled her plump little arms with the feather-trimmed fairy wand.

At the other end of the table Andrei sat in his highchair carefully scrutinising the wooden fire engine that Dimitri had given him. Lily's heart clenched with helpless love. He was quieter, more timid and reserved than his easy-going sister, his small face was solemn, setting him slightly apart from the celebration going on around him.

It was a double celebration: for the twins' first birthday and also to toast their permanent acceptance into Lily and Tristan's lives. The interim care order that had allowed them to bring them home to Cornwall had at last been approved as a formal adoption, in no small part thanks to the efforts of Miss Squires who had turned out to be a staunch ally. Her report had stated that Tristan's own difficult past, and the strength and courage with which he had dealt with it, made him ideally placed to care for the twins.

Tristan joked that she had supported them solely so that she had an excuse to keep coming down to Dolphin House and seeing Dimitri, who sat beside her now with his arm thrown protectively round the back of her chair, his careworn face serene. Next to him Nico leaned back in his chair and laughed at something Tom had said, and his laid-back, charismatic charm reminded Lily with sudden piercing poignancy of the beautiful stranger who had jumped down from the helicopter and pulled her straight into his arms a lifetime ago.

She gasped as those same strong arms slid around her from behind, and the same lips that had flamed ecstasy into her body and changed her life for ever brushed the nape of her neck. Their touch was gentle and loving now, but still powerful enough to make the earth tilt on its axis.

'All right *cariño mio*?' Tristan murmured against her skin, his warm breath sending shivers of delicate joy down her spine.

'Mmm…' she sighed, closing her eyes. 'Although if you carry on like that I might just have to keep everyone waiting for the cake.'

Tristan pulled her close, wrapping his arms around her. 'That would be a shame.' His mouth was close to her ear and she could hear the smile in his voice. 'It is, after all, the most fantastic cake ever.'

Together they looked at the fairy tale castle Lily had painstakingly constructed from sponge and chocolate buttercream, and she smiled as she placed the pink candle alongside the blue one in the top of the turret, next to the tiny sugar-icing dove. Then, kissing the side of her neck, Tristan let her go and went to the fridge to take out a bottle of champagne. Sucking chocolate buttercream from her fingers, Lily dreamily watched him open the bottle.

'Shouldn't you wait and open that outside?'

Suddenly serious, Tristan shook his head as he poured pale golden fizz into two glasses. 'Today is for Andrei and Emilia, but this is a private toast to us.' He handed one to her. 'To *you*—for loving me when I didn't deserve to be loved and giving me more than I ever dared to hope for.' He kissed her lingeringly on the mouth and glanced out of the window to the table beneath the tree. 'Today feels a bit like the wedding we never had.'

Lovingly, Lily's fingers traced the outline of his lips, the indentation in his chin. 'We never had the wedding,' she murmured, kissing the corner of his mouth, 'but we have the marriage, which is what matters.'

She felt his lips curve into a rueful, sexy smile. 'Come on. If we stay in here much longer I won't be responsible for my actions, and if Miss Squires finds me making love to you on the kitchen floor she might just change her mind about my suitability as a parent.'

He picked up the open bottle and took another one from the fridge while Lily lit the candles on the cake. Holding aloft her fragile cargo, Lily followed her husband out into the sunlit garden.

The air was scented with summer and the sea. As they crossed the lawn Tom saw them coming and got to his feet, leading everyone in a joyful, if slightly tuneless, rendition of 'Happy Birthday'.

Perched precariously on Scarlet's knee, Emilia bounced up and down in excitement, ecstatic at being the centre of attention. Imperiously ignoring the singing, she held up her arms squealing, 'Dada!' as her sloe-dark gaze fixed adoringly on Tristan.

He handed the open bottle to Nico, putting the other one down on the table so he could scoop his daughter up into his arms where she crowed in delight and pointed at the cake. Across the table Andrei fastened huge, worried eyes on the candle and for a moment it looked as if he might cry. But then Tristan picked him up in his other arm, kissing his dark silky head and murmuring reassurance, and the little face relaxed into a cautious smile.

Scarlet got to her feet with difficulty and came round to stand beside Lily as the singing reached its enthusiastic climax. Nico was circulating with the champagne, pausing beside Dimitri and squeezing his arm as he filled his glass. Holding the two babies in his arms, Tristan knelt down so they were at eye level with the cake. The candles cast a halo of soft golden light on their three faces, making stars dance in their eyes.

Closing her eyes in comical bliss, Emilia pursed her plump rosebud mouth and blew extravagantly. Scarlet clapped her hands with delight, blinking back tears. 'Don't forget to make a wish!' she cried.

Across the table Tristan looked up, and his gaze met Lily's. The candles guttered and died, but his eyes still shone with love.

'I don't need to,' he said with quiet, ironic emphasis. 'It's already come true.'

Spanish Magnate, Red-Hot Revenge

LYNN RAYE HARRIS

Lynn Raye Harris read her first Mills & Boon® romance when her grandmother carted home a box from a yard sale. She didn't know she wanted to be a writer then, but she definitely knew she wanted to marry a sheikh or a prince and live the glamorous life she read about in the pages. Instead, she married a military man and moved around the world. These days she makes her home in North Alabama, with her handsome husband and two crazy cats. Writing for Mills & Boon is a dream come true. You can visit her at www.lynnrayeharris.com.

To my husband, Mike, who bought me my first computer and who always believed. Thanks for putting up with take-out, frozen dinners, and no dinners. You are my hero.

CHAPTER ONE

"This can't be happening," Rebecca Layton murmured.

She lifted her stunned gaze to the floor-to-ceiling picture window fronting her Waikiki suite. Of all the times to be away from New York. Palms swayed in the tropical trade winds, danced rhythmically against white-capped turquoise waves. So beautiful and peaceful. A stark contrast to the turmoil raging inside her.

She'd just gotten off the phone with Layton International's chief financial officer. The news wasn't good. If she didn't get back to New York and take control of the situation she could lose everything. Her cell phone rang again and she automatically picked it up. Very few people had her private number, and even fewer would dare disturb her when she was on a business trip.

Unless it was important. And right now Layton International's vulnerability was nothing short of cataclysmic.

"Yes?" she said as she reached for her planner. She could at least make a few calls while her executive assistant booked their return flight. She would *not* lose this company her family had built, in spite of the problems her father had left her with when he had died unexpectedly. He'd trusted her to take care of things. She would not fail him.

"Hello, Rebecca."

Rebecca's breath sliced into her lungs as her head whipped up. The planner slid from her lap. "Alejandro?"

"You did not expect to hear from me again, *no*?"

Rebecca closed her eyes, her gut clenching with a mixture of need and sorrow. Five long years since she'd heard that voice speak her name. Once he'd meant everything to her. Now?

Now she couldn't even begin to sort out how speaking to him made her feel. Sweat moistened her palms. "This is a bad time, Alejandro. I really can't talk."

His laugh, so cool and controlled, brought an image back to her. Alejandro Arroyo Rivera de Ramirez, the sexiest man she'd ever seen, naked to the waist, water streaming from his muscular chest in rivulets as he'd lifted himself from the pool. His sexy laugh as he'd scooped her up and hauled her into the bedroom. He hadn't even dried off. The second she'd said yes he'd come for her. And then he'd spent the night showing her how amazing he truly was.

"You need only listen, *querida*."

Something in his tone silenced her automatic protest.

Her heart kicked into double time. She reached for her forgotten wineglass, took a steadying sip.

"I expect you in Madrid in twenty-four hours. Spend the flight thinking how you will convince me to keep you on Layton International's board of directors."

Shock rocketed her to her feet. Her heart threatened to pound right out of her chest. "*You're* the one trying to steal my company?"

"You have made poor decisions, Rebecca. Do not continue to do so." His voice dripped ice.

Rebecca speared a hand through her hair as cold sweat spread over her skin. *Oh, God.* She wasn't the one who'd made poor decisions—but what did it matter now? Her father had thought he'd been doing the right thing.

They'd tumbled far in the five years since she'd last seen

Alejandro. Then, she'd been the one with the knowledge about the hotel business, the one with the might of a multi-million-dollar company behind her. He'd been the new kid on the block, the one with everything to learn.

How had everything changed so drastically?

There was still time. Not much, but a little. She could turn it around, could stop him. She *would* stop him, or she wasn't a Layton through and through. She forced herself to sound calm, controlled—though she was anything but. "It's not over yet. You're counting chickens."

"Counting chickens?" His laugh jarred her with its sudden warmth. "Ah, one of your Americanisms." She heard him speaking to someone in Spanish. "It is a done deal, Rebecca. Layton International belongs to Ramirez Enterprises."

She felt the chill of his words as if someone had picked her up and thrust her into the arctic. It was an odd sensation, totally at odds with her memory of the heat he'd once incited. She swallowed the knot in her throat. "I don't believe you."

"Then stay in Hawaii while I hire a new CEO. Or come advise the board on how to handle my new acquisition. Your choice."

He knew she was in Hawaii? Did he also know about the deal she'd just closed to acquire a chain of resorts in the islands?

The deal that would have saved everything in just a few short months. Rebecca sank onto a rattan chair as her legs refused to hold her up any longer. The certainty in his voice was undeniable.

She knew from personal experience how determined Alejandro could be when he wanted something. He didn't rest until he'd won, until he'd imposed his will and gotten exactly what he wanted. If he was calling her now, he was very certain he had control.

Lock, stock and barrel, as her dad would have said. Jackson Layton was probably spinning in his grave right this instant.

He'd never liked Alejandro, would be shattered to know the company he'd built had fallen into his enemy's hands. And all because his daughter hadn't seen it coming.

"I think I hate you," she said softly.

"Then we are even." The line went dead.

Rebecca leaned numbly against the soft leather seat of the Mercedes that had picked her up at the Madrid Barajas International Airport. She stared bleary-eyed at the scenery as the car carried her down the Gran Via.

He'd said he hated her. It shouldn't surprise her, but somehow it did.

Five long years. She hadn't seen him—other than glimpses on television or in the pages of a magazine—in all that time. For one month he'd been everything to her. He'd been there when she woke, when she fell asleep, when she swam or shopped or ate. He'd laughed and made love to her and made her think she was the most special woman in the world.

Now? She pinched the bridge of her nose. God only knew what happened now. He was ruthless, and he'd gained control of Layton International. He owned every last share. She'd confirmed it during her endless hours of travel.

She had nothing left. If he fired her, she could only limp away in shame. Without her company she was stone-cold broke. She could pay her mortgage for the next three months, and she could eat. If she hadn't found a job by then she'd lose her apartment and all her belongings.

Somehow the loss didn't compare to the loss of self-respect, the knowledge that she'd failed to protect her family legacy. She didn't know how to do anything except run a chain of hotels. It was what she'd been brought up to do—however reluctantly on her father's behalf—what she'd spent her life training for and trying to excel at. What would her father say if he could see her now? He'd wanted a son to leave the business to, but she was all he'd had. Would he now believe his concern about leaving a woman in charge was justified? She couldn't bear to think of his disappointment.

The car wound through the busy streets, nearing the ornate gray facade of the Villa de Musica, the Ramirez crown jewel in the heart of Madrid. Her heart hurt with the memories seeing it again brought. She'd been staying in the newly reno-vated hotel when she had first met Alejandro.

Rebecca shoved away thoughts of the sexy Spaniard who had ruined her life. She'd see him soon enough, and though her stomach twisted, she reminded herself—firmly—that she was here for business. She would not be intimidated. His mere presence wouldn't turn her to mush like it once had.

She was only mildly surprised when the car continued past the hotel. She hadn't really expected to be shown to a room, allowed to freshen up, maybe sleep a little, before being dragged into Alejandro's presence. Since she had no idea where they were going, she tried to close her eyes and get a few minutes' sleep—but rest eluded her.

Finally, after what seemed like hours in traffic, the limo pulled into a private drive somewhere in the hills of Madrid. She wasn't sure where they were, but she vaguely remem-bered passing the Palacio Real, the official residence of the King and Queen of Spain. A uniformed man helped her from the vehicle while another retrieved her bags. Within moments she was whisked through a stunning marble atrium and into a masculine office overlooking a terrace with a pool. How far Alejandro had come in five years.

Rebecca drifted over to the window and clasped her hands together. Oddly, they were shaking. But she'd been traveling for almost twenty-four hours straight. Her wrinkled suit clung to her body like an old rag, her curls had lost their bounce hours ago and she desperately needed a hot shower. Clearly

Alejandro would give her no quarter before he gloated over his triumph.

Well, fine. She'd endure it, and she'd refuse to react to his insults.

When the door behind her opened again, she put on her battle face and turned to meet him head-on.

And, oh heavens, he was still the most amazingly handsome man she'd ever met. Her knees threatened to buckle at the sight of him. She had an inexplicable urge to rush into his embrace, the way she used to do, but she crossed her arms and stood her ground. It took every ounce of reserve she had not to give in to the desire to touch him.

Why?

She didn't know if she was questioning her reaction or if the word was meant for him.

Why, Alejandro? Why did you deceive me when I loved you? Why have you done this to me now?

As if she'd spoken aloud, he halted, his gaze locking with hers. What lay behind those silver-gray eyes was anyone's guess, but she didn't think they held any warmth for her. And it hurt. Surprisingly, it hurt. She felt like she should do or say something, but she simply stood and drank him in.

If he'd changed at all, she couldn't see it. He was tall, six-three or six-four, and as muscular as ever. The years had not been unkind to him. He still looked every inch the hardened ex-bullfighter. She'd once teased him that he was a warrior clad in Armani.

Had she really spent hours exploring his tanned skin? It seemed so long ago that it must surely be her imagination. But she remembered with every last nerve-ending in her body how extraordinary it had felt when he slid his hard length inside her. Over and over and over, until she'd shuddered from the exquisite pleasure.

Rebecca pushed a hand against the stucco window casing

to steady herself. Alejandro didn't seem to notice. He was completely unaffected by the current whipping through the room. It was all she could do to keep from being sucked into the vortex, while he pressed on as if nothing had changed.

For him, it probably hadn't.

"I have a schedule for you," he said, walking to the desk and pulling out a folder. "You will read through these papers and be prepared to meet with the board first thing in the morning. We will discuss your duties then."

Rebecca stepped forward and clutched the folder, glad to have a new focus. Something hot and thick lurched to life in her sluggish veins. "That's it? No *Hi, how have you been?* No explanation?"

Ice-gray eyes regarded her dispassionately. "I owe you no explanation, Rebecca. I owe you nothing, in fact. Be grateful you're getting this much."

"I've been doing okay, thanks for asking, Alejandro," she said, ignoring him. "Or I was until yesterday. And you? How are you? Did you marry the woman you conveniently forgot to tell me about?"

"I did," he said coolly.

She blinked back tears. Ridiculous to still be hurt over such a thing, or to expect an explanation so many years after the fact. He was Alejandro Arroyo Rivera de Ramirez, international playboy, billionaire financier.

Women had always fallen over him. Always would.

And she'd been no different, had she? He hadn't been a billionaire back then, merely a famous man in his own country, making his way in a new business. *She'd* been the one with a privileged background, the one from hotel royalty. But she'd fallen hard for him; his betrayal still stung even now. She should have known better.

"You will be pleased to know we are divorced," he continued. "Alas, arranged marriages never work as planned."

"Good for her, for wising up."

"Like you did?"

A bitter laugh burst from her throat before she could stop it. "There was never a choice for me, Alejandro. You were already engaged."

"Promised, not engaged."

Rebecca scoffed, hoping he wouldn't see how the subject still affected her. "What is that? Spanish hair-splitting? The truth is you were to marry another woman when you so conveniently seduced me."

"You did not mind being seduced, as I recall."

Heat blossomed in her belly. Flooded her senses. Gathered between her thighs. "I was stupid—and blind to your true nature."

His square jaw flexed. He hitched a leg onto the corner of the desk, his custom-made trousers stretching tight against one hard thigh. "And just what is my true nature, *querida*?"

Danger saturated his voice, but she was too angry and hurt to heed the warning. No, what she itched to do was slap his sculpted profile. How dare he steal her company and then stand there and defend his actions of five years ago like he'd been the one wronged?

"You're a liar and a cheat."

She stood her ground as he stalked her. One arm snaked around her waist, yanked her against every last inch of his muscled body. The other hand gripped her jaw, forcing her to accept his kiss. Fire exploded in her veins when his lips pressed to hers.

Shock reverberated through her system. It was too much, too soon. She was still processing what it meant to see him again, to be flooded with conflicting emotions. She didn't want this, didn't need it.

Couldn't resist it for much longer.

Her hands went to his chest of their own volition, whether

to push away or touch him she wasn't sure. She marshaled what was left of her willpower and pressed her palms against a granite wall. He simply upped the ante, his tongue sliding along the seam of her lips, teasing her with remembered bliss.

She gave one last push. But he smelled good, felt good, and—

There would be time for recriminations later. Besides, nothing was ever as good as the memory. Surely one kiss would inoculate her to Alejandro's masculine charm. It was just what she needed to prove to herself he no longer meant a thing to her.

Her mouth parted and his tongue slipped inside. *Big mistake.*

But it was too late. She shuddered as she met him stroke for stroke. Was she out of her mind? She had to stop—but she didn't want to. Not yet. For a moment she was flooded with memories—his mouth on hers, his naked skin beneath her fingers, their bodies moving together in perfect rhythm. Ecstasy unlike any she'd ever known. Happiness and love and a feeling of rightness.

One of her hands threaded into his hair, luxuriated in its obsidian crispness. His fingers slid beneath her blouse, teased her nipple through the lace of her bra. It budded under his touch, sensitive and painful and neglected.

She held on to his shoulders, all sense of time and place leaching away as she lost herself in the hot need he called up. She very much feared that if he pressed her to the floor right now, ripped off her clothes and impaled her with his hard maleness, she'd wrap her legs around him and hold on for the ride. Just to feel that perfect rightness once more, even if it was only an illusion.

But, no, it *was* an illusion. She had to stop this. Now—

He broke the kiss first. "You're still sizzling, Rebecca," he said, his breath hot against her moist lips. "And you are still a slut."

Her hand connected with his cheek before he could block the blow. He moved away from her, laughing. She thanked God for the fury coursing through her right now, because without it shame would have eaten her alive. How had she managed to lose every last shred of dignity she possessed the instant he kissed her?

"Then I guess we know where we stand," she said, her breath razoring in and out. She would *not* hyperventilate. Not now. Stupid to let down her guard like that, to feel any softness at all toward this man. "And now I'd like to go to the hotel and get some rest—if you're finished trying to humiliate me."

"Your room is upstairs."

She gaped at him. "I'm staying here? In your villa? Is that wise?" she added, on what she hoped was a cool note.

"I cannot possibly refuse paying guests simply to house an employee. You will stay here."

An *employee*. The word grated like nothing else ever had. Worse, it stung that he could kiss her so hotly and then act as though it was nothing more than a joke. "Fine. But don't you ever touch me again."

His mouth twitched. "Are you sure about that? You were not so chilly a moment ago. Were you not remembering what it was like between us?"

She lifted her chin. No sense lying, because he'd see right through it. "You're a fine lover, Alejandro, but you aren't the only man who knows his way around a woman's body. Men like you are easy to find if a woman knows where to look."

"And where would that be?" His look was half amused, half curious.

"I believe they like to hang out at resorts and fleece rich women out of their money."

His brows drew together. "You are calling me a gigolo?"

"Keep it in mind if the hotel thing doesn't work out."

He threw back his head and laughed. Rebecca had to bite her lip to keep from grinning at the sound. She'd always loved his laugh. But the last thing she needed was to share a light moment with this man. He'd just stolen her company and ruined her career. The thought was enough to harden her resolve.

He reached for the phone on his desk, touched a button. "Señora Flores will show you to your room." She was almost to the door when his voice stopped her. "And do not worry, Rebecca. I have no intention of ever again accepting what you offer each time you look at me."

Rebecca's spine snapped ramrod-straight. "What's that? Sudden death? Because if you see anything else, you *are* a deluded man."

"Do not make me prove you wrong again."

She gave him her best glare, the one she'd perfected as a woman working hard to succeed in a man's business. "Try me when I'm no longer jet-lagged, Alejandro. I promise you the response will be much different."

Alejandro returned to the villa late, having spent several hours at his sleek downtown office. He tossed his jacket across a chair in the master suite, loosened his tie and tugged it from his collar. He started to pour a drink from the bar in his room, but changed his mind and pulled on a pair of swim trunks instead. Right now he needed the release heavy exercise could bring.

He hadn't expected Rebecca Layton to get under his skin ever again. It was purely physical now, and yet it annoyed him nonetheless. He'd spent one month with her five years ago. One incredibly hot month that he couldn't seem to forget, no matter how he tried. He'd enjoyed her company like none other. Enjoyed the way she'd looked at him, the way she'd smelled like wildflowers, and her funny way of saying things that meant something entirely different in American than they did in the British English he'd learned.

He'd cared for her; he'd planned to marry her in spite of what his father expected. No matter what he told her now, he hadn't been promised at all; it had been his brother who was to marry Caridad Mendoza, not him. Until Roberto had died of a drug overdose in a Middle Eastern hellhole.

Still, Alejandro had no intention of taking his brother's place in the arrangement. He'd spent years fighting in the ring, making himself into something. His future had been bright and he'd choose his own wife. Rebecca Layton, daughter of a successful American hotel magnate, had been exactly the type of woman he needed to marry.

Until she'd betrayed him. An ex-bullfighter and fledgling entrepreneur wasn't good enough for the pampered heiress, apparently. The dirt, sweat and blood of the ring would never wash completely away for someone like her. She'd accepted him as her lover, sworn she loved him, and then tried to steal his future from under his nose.

Her betrayal had cost him more than he could ever make her pay. Taking Layton International was only the beginning. He'd set it up carefully, made sure he would own her completely when it was done. It had taken years of planning and months of careful execution, but the culmination was here. Rebecca Layton would regret the day she'd crossed paths with him.

Alejandro pushed open the French doors and padded out to the pool. Lights flooded the water from below, illuminating the terracotta and turquoise tiles. He dove into the coolness, hoping it would drive the heat of kissing her from his memory.

Why had he succumbed to the urge? That one kiss had brought every bittersweet memory flooding back—especially when she'd clung to him, her soft moans coiling at the base of his spine, poisoning him with the urge to strip her naked and take her right there on the floor of his office.

"What in heaven's name do you think you're doing?"

Alejandro reached the wall, did a flip turn and propelled himself back toward the voice.

"Swimming." The water came up to his abdomen as he stood and looked at her.

"Not that," she said. "This." Rebecca thrust a handful of papers at him.

He ignored it and let his gaze wander over her sleek form. A red headband held her curls back from her face and matched the muted Hawaiian-print dress she wore. Slim legs tapered down to bare feet, but it was the circle of tiny white shells around one ankle that caught his attention. They caressed her ankle with every tap of her foot, kissed her bare skin like a lover.

Like he'd once done.

His gaze snapped to her face. "Those would be my plans to sell off a few of Layton's less lucrative holdings."

She took a step toward the pool. "The New York location? *New York?* Are you crazy?"

"Not at all. That hotel is small, outdated. It costs more in upkeep each year than it makes in profit."

The papers crinkled in her fist. "Why do you hate me so much?" she said, in a smaller voice than he would have expected.

She seemed almost bewildered. But it was a ploy. She would use anything to distract him, including sex. How well he knew that about her.

Her *poor little me* act angered him. "You know why. You used me to get information. You slept with me, then stole what you learned about the London deal to grab it for yourself. That move nearly destroyed Ramirez Enterprises."

Ramirez Enterprises had been little more than bravado and a dream back then. But losing the Cahill Group's financing had destroyed far more precious things than his fledgling enterprise. He wasn't about to tell her what she'd really cost him—what she'd forced him into to save everything.

She tilted her head to one side. "I didn't…"

"Didn't what?" he said, when she stopped speaking and stood there gazing off into space.

"You're lying." She crossed her arms and glared down at him. "You couldn't possibly be wiped out by one deal gone bad."

Of course she didn't realize how he'd struggled. She'd never struggled for anything a day in her life. From her first moments everything had been handed to her on a silver platter. He very much enjoyed being the one to take it all away.

Alejandro pressed his hands on the pool deck and levered himself out of the water. She took a step backward as he suddenly towered over her. He wanted to grab her, wanted to yank her into his arms and plunder her sweet mouth again. He turned away before his body betrayed his reaction to her. "Things were less certain then."

"So you bought a controlling interest in my company and now you plan to sell off my hotels one by one?"

Grabbing a towel from the lounge chair, he wiped his face dry before giving her a dangerous smile. "Only the unprofitable ones, *querida*."

"La Belle Amelie was the first hotel my father opened after he married," she said. "He named it for my mother."

Alejandro finished drying off and tossed the towel aside. She looked at him like he'd kicked her puppy. He hated it, hated the way she made him feel. But she was oh so good at manipulating him, wasn't she?

Never again.

"It goes."

Her laugh was bitter. "To think I once believed—" She shook her head, inched her chin higher. Met his gaze firmly. "I'll buy it from you. Give me a couple of weeks to put together the financing and I'll—"

"You once believed what?"

"Make you a good offer."

"Believed what, Rebecca?"

"Did you hear what I said? I want to buy La Belle Amelie. What I believed is of no consequence."

"Did you think I would marry you after a month together? Is that why you left?"

"God, no!"

She took another step back and he realized he'd been stalking her. He moved casually toward the edge of the pool, gave her space. The restless energy in him still demanded release, pounded through his body in waves. The hum was almost sexual, primal. Not much different from the way he'd felt whenever he'd faced a bull in the ring. He wanted to conquer, subdue, triumph.

"I left because you were engaged, Alejandro." Her chin fell as she studied the tiles at her feet. "I thought you were an honorable man. That's what I once believed."

If he'd been gored by a bull he'd have felt less pain. Less anger.

The unbelievable nerve of this woman.

"You dare to question my honor when it was you who left—*you* who went to London and talked the Cahill Group into backing you instead of me? I spent *months* putting that deal together and you yanked the rug from under me. No, I will never sell La Belle Amelie to you!"

Alejandro dragged in a breath, willed calm to replace the seething fury roiling inside him. "I'll have it demolished first, Rebecca. You can pick through the rubble and see what you can salvage then."

She remained unnaturally silent, her slender form shaking. He'd expected fury. Tears maybe. Pleading if she thought it would work. Sex as a last resort.

But the last thing he ever expected was for her to tackle him.

CHAPTER TWO

EVERYTHING went wrong the instant Rebecca lunged. Fury ate at her gut like battery acid. She'd planned to shove his arrogant carcass into the pool and go back to her room. And then she was going to call financier Roger Cahill. What Alejandro accused her of couldn't possibly be true.

Except the momentum required to throw Alejandro off balance tipped her too far forward. Her arms windmilled like crazy before she lost the fight and splashed down, landing on fifteen stone worth of angry Spanish male.

Something collided hard with the top of her head, and then she was sinking beneath the surface. She sucked in a breath, gulped chlorine. She needed to fight her way back up, needed to kick hard and breach the liquid barrier above her. But she couldn't seem to do it. Her limbs wouldn't cooperate.

How ironic to die in Alejandro's pool. The last thought rattling through her brain was that if there were any justice in the world, he'd get blamed for her death.

A second later, air burst into her lungs. She coughed sharply, spitting up water. Her head lolled against something hard and warm.

Alejandro.

"*Querida*, speak to me," he urged in a harsh voice.

Her back pressed down on a hard surface and she realized he'd laid her on the tile beside the pool. A moment later he hovered over her, his hands bracketing her head, water dripping from his skin onto hers.

She coughed again, her throat raw and burning. A sob welled up from somewhere inside, but she refused to give in to it. She gulped it back and stuffed it down deep. The last thing she would ever do was show weakness in front of this man.

"Rebecca, *amor*, say something. Call me a name if it pleases you."

"Arrogant idiot," she sputtered, though it came out as little more than a whisper. "Foolish Spaniard."

He grinned down at her. "I said one name, did I not?"

Her heart lurched. Not a good thing. "It makes me happy, calling you names."

It also made her happy to see him smile at her, but that was a piece of information she had no intention of sharing. One tear slipped from the corner of her eye and blazed a hot trail down her temple. She'd only been here a few hours and already a part of her longed for what used to be. *Get over it, Becca. He's not the right man for you, never was. He used you, same as Parker Gaines did.*

"What happened?" she asked, dashing the tear away with her fingers.

"I was trying to move out of the way when you fell on top of me. Your head connected with my elbow."

"Oh."

His fingers spanned her skull, probing softly. He was so close his breath whispered over her skin, sent a shiver skimming. "No bumps. I think you will live."

"Sell me the hotel, Alejandro," she urged, her eyes searching his. "It means nothing to you."

"And everything to you."

"Yes." She pulled a deep breath into her lungs, savoring

the sweet night air, forcing herself to go on though her throat was raw. "They built it together. He knew she missed Paris, and he gave it a French theme. There are family antiques in the hotel even now."

"You may have them." His eyes were flat, the concession seeming to cost him a great deal to say. "I won't prevent you from taking what is sentimental to you."

"The *hotel* is sentimental to me. I—" she swallowed "—I was born there. I beg you to reconsider."

His gaze slid down her body, over the wet dress clinging to every curve. One dark hand settled on her thigh, traced the outline of her leg, moving slowly up to her hip. His touch burned her, even through the layer of wet material between them. Mercy, what those fingers had done to her the last time they'd been together.

Rebecca bit her lip.

"To what lengths are you willing to go, *bella*, to secure your hotel?" His look was intense, as if a word or a nod from her would set in motion a seismic event that could not be stopped until they sprawled together in bed sated, replete— utterly ruined.

Her heart tapped hard inside her chest. His head descended in slow motion to her throat, his tongue pressing against an erratic pulse-point. "You want this," he murmured. His fingers spread over the wet material on her thigh. Her skin was cold from the pool and the night air, but his hand sizzled where it touched, branding her.

Once she would have welcomed his touch. Would have opened herself to him and reveled in the way he made her feel. Part of her still wanted to.

But she couldn't. It would cost her too much.

"No," she said softly. And again, stronger, "No."

His head lifted. His eyes searched hers, almost as if he couldn't believe what she'd said. Oddly, it gave her courage.

She pushed him away, satisfied when he rocked back, breaking all contact between them.

She lifted herself onto her elbows, and then to a sitting position when her head no longer spun. "I will buy it from you, Alejandro. I won't sleep with you for it."

"My, how you've changed." Sarcasm thickened his voice. "You weren't so principled five years ago."

"It's funny that you talk about principles when you were the one with a secret fiancée. Or was I the secret mistress?"

He unfolded from the tile deck, rose to his full height. "The only secrets were the ones you kept while you lied to me about your true reasons for being at the Villa de Musica."

Rebecca shook her head softly, stopped when a wave of nausea threatened. "You're unbelievable, Alejandro. You say I lied to you and stole your deal, but *you* were the one using me to learn how to expand your reach beyond Spain—"

"What?" He looked incredulous, his voice snapping into the night like a whip.

Rebecca shoved herself to her feet. The movement was too quick, and she almost sank to the ground, but Alejandro reached out and steadied her.

"I'm fine," she said, shrugging away from his touch. "We talked all the time, Alejandro. You asked me about every detail of the business, and I told you all I knew. You used *me*."

His hand dropped away. "I did not need *you* to succeed, Rebecca," he said coldly. "That I now own Layton International is proof of that, do you not think?"

She wrapped her arms around her wet body, her teeth beginning to chatter though she was burning up with fury on the inside. No, he hadn't needed her at all. Not in the way she'd wanted anyway. "You got lucky."

"Lucky? I make my own luck, *querida*. I don't wait for chance."

One temple throbbed with the beginnings of a headache.

He'd gotten lucky because her father had made mistakes, taken risks. If making his own luck meant watching Layton International like a panther and pouncing when they were crippled beneath the weight of obligations, then fine. He hadn't left anything to chance.

The exhaustion of the day sat like a lead weight on her shoulders. She just wanted to go to her room and pretend she was anywhere but here. With her ex-lover. Her ex-*love*.

"If you give me a few days, I'll put together a fair offer for La Belle Amelie."

He snapped his towel from the chaise, where he'd dropped it the first time. "You may have the family antiques, Rebecca, but the hotel is not negotiable."

"You just offered to let me buy it if I'd sleep with you."

He laughed. "No, I asked to what lengths you would go for the hotel. I did not say I would accept the offer."

Rebecca grabbed the papers she'd tossed onto one of the chaises. Then she spun to face him again, the documents crumpling in her chilled fist. "You can't deny you were aroused, Alejandro. If I'd said yes, we'd be in bed right now."

He looked bored. "I'm a man. A woman pressed against my body causes a reaction, *sí*. This is true of many men, I believe."

"Some more than others, apparently. I should have believed the stories I read about you. When you weren't fighting bulls you were bedding every woman in sight. I could have saved myself a lot of trouble."

The look he gave her was sharp. "The press enjoys telling tales. If I'd bedded half the women they accused me of, I'd have been too tired to fight and the bulls would have won."

"Well, it certainly didn't stop you from sleeping with me and a fiancée at the same time. Were there others too?" She flung the words at him, surprised at the vehemence knotting her throat. For years she'd thought of the face-to-face confrontation they'd never had. Would he have denied it if she'd given him the chance? Would he have apologized? He'd tried to convince her over the phone that he was not engaged. But his denials had fallen short because the truth was irrefutable.

"There was no one but you."

"You were engaged," she said, forcing the words past the wedge of pain in her throat. "I think that counts as someone else."

"I was *not* engaged."

"But you married her anyway. How convenient."

He took a step toward her, menace rolling from him in waves. "I married her because of you—because you stole from me and left me no choice."

This time she stood her ground. "I didn't steal anything, Alejandro. That's a lie."

"Of course you would say that. But it does not change the truth. When the Cahill Group informed me of their decision, they said they were investing in Layton International instead. Do you intend to tell me Roger Cahill lied?"

Rebecca tried to remember exactly what had happened then. She'd left Spain and gone to London to meet with Roger, at her father's direction, about a financing deal. They had not discussed Ramirez Enterprises. She would have remembered since the pain of Alejandro's betrayal had still been so raw.

"We were working with Roger on a South American deal. What he and his investors decided about you had nothing to do with us."

Alejandro snorted. "You expect me to believe that? Layton International wanted to shut out the competition. You tried to ruin me, or at least contain me to Spain."

"No," she said softly. "There was no reason. You weren't important enough."

He stiffened as if she'd dealt him a body-blow. "Or good enough, *si*?"

"That's not what I meant." Ramirez Enterprises hadn't

been big enough to be a threat, but he didn't give her a chance to explain.

"I know what you meant, *querida*. How difficult it must have been for you to endure my touch. To sacrifice your body for the sake of your precious Layton International." He stalked closer until he towered over her—so close she could feel the heat of his skin, could smell the mixture of chlorine and male that threatened to overwhelm her senses. "You did a fine job of playing the whore, Rebecca. You were quite natural at it. But do not worry that you will ever need to lie beneath this dirty *torero* again. There are plenty of women who find it no chore to do so."

His words stung. "I slept with you because I wanted to. No other reason."

"Yes, tell yourself that if it makes you feel better."

Rebecca took a step away from him, her belly churning with hurt and anger. How dare he question her feelings, her integrity. He suggested she'd thought he was beneath her, unworthy of her because of what he'd been. God, it was untenable! "I *loved* you, Alejandro," she whispered fiercely. "You—"

"*Silencio!* I will not listen to your lies." He wrapped the towel around his waist and stood with fists on lean hips. Moonlight limned the hard contours of his chest, glistened on the water that still dripped from his head and left a trail of silver down his skin.

"Nothing you say will change the past, Rebecca, nor the fact I own Layton International. Spend your time worrying about your job, and cease trying to convince me you ever cared for me. We both know the truth."

Señora Flores coolly informed Rebecca that breakfast was usually served on the terrace in summer. There would be no coffee or pastries delivered to her room, no matter how sweetly she asked. But the last thing she thought she could do right now was sit across from Alejandro and share a meal. In fact, if she managed to avoid him altogether that would make her day nearly perfect. He'd accused her of so much ugliness. Of sleeping with him for information, of stealing from him and of lying about being in love with him.

Oddly, it was the last thing that bothered her most. She'd been so naive. She'd fallen fast and hard, and then she'd let the words fall from her lips often and easily. And, though he'd never repeated them, she'd believed he had cared for her. Believed what they had was special.

Until his fiancée sent a wedding coordinator to his hotel suite. *A wedding coordinator.* The woman had invitation samples, possible menus and fabric samples for his tuxedo. And he'd still denied he was engaged.

She was the one who'd been wronged, damn him! The one who'd had her heart broken and the pieces pulverized beneath his boot heels. Previous experience should have taught her he was only using her for the information she could give him, for her status as Jackson Layton's daughter, but she'd denied the truth and carried on blissfully with the affair. And he accused *her* of betraying *him*? Was the man insane?

She'd wanted to call Roger Cahill last night, see if she could find out what really happened, but it had been too late when she'd returned to her room. Today, however, she would make that call. There must have been a reason the Cahill Group had pulled their backing. A reason that had nothing to do with her or Layton International. Alejandro might never believe it, but at least she would know the truth.

Until then, how could she go out on that terrace and face him like nothing had ever happened between them? Eating with him was too intimate, too much like the past. And after last night her nerves were scraped raw.

She briefly considered refusing to join him, but she was too hungry—and she definitely needed the caffeine. Rebecca ran a comb through her honeyed curls one last time, before twisting them into a knot and securing it with a clip. Then she smoothed a stray wrinkle from her cream pantsuit and grabbed her briefcase, before shoving on a pair of matching sunglasses and heading for the terrace. She didn't want Alejandro to see the dark circles beneath her eyes. He'd only gloat at her distress, and she was in no mood for it.

She passed through a large great room, with soaring ceilings and pale stucco walls. Dark Spanish timbers spanned the ceiling at regular intervals. Cool cream furniture and inlaid Syrian wood tables clustered on silk Oriental carpets near a giant fireplace. Priceless art graced the walls—a Bellini madonna, a Picasso etching and a Velázquez oil among them. Even at his best, her father could only have afforded one or two of those paintings. Alejandro must be very rich indeed to have such a collection.

She went through large double doors propped open onto the terrace. Alejandro sat in profile to her. His white shirt hung open casually, the paleness of the fabric in contrast to his sun-warmed skin. A gray suit jacket was draped across a chair, the expensive fabric gleaming richly in the dappled sunlight falling through the arbor. He spoke a rapid stream of Castilian into the phone wedged to his ear. He didn't look up as she approached.

A uniformed man held out a chair. Rebecca gave him a smile as she sank onto it.

"Coffee, *señorita*?"

"Please."

He poured a steaming cup for her while she helped herself to a slice of toast, spread it with jam and took a bite. She could eat a side of beef, she was so hungry, but the typical Spanish breakfast was toast and jam, or *churros* with a pot of chocolate. After polishing off the first slice, she fixed another, biting into it as she let her gaze roam the courtyard.

"You wish for eggs and bacon?"

The sudden English startled her, whipped her concentration from the hot-pink bougainvillea vines overflowing the arbor. Alejandro's attention was on her now, the phone resting on the table beside his plate.

"This is fine."

"You do not want something more American?"

"Toast is American." She avoided meeting his eyes.

Alejandro shrugged. "It is not a problem. If you wish for something more, you have only to say so."

She continued to eat her toast. In light of all they'd said to each other last night, she didn't want to be thankful to him for anything. Knowing she owed him for dragging her out of the pool before she drowned was bad enough. Though if he hadn't made her so angry she wouldn't have been in the pool in the first place.

"You slept well?"

"Well enough," she said, spreading a third slice with jam. Praying he wouldn't guess she'd done anything but. That her heart was doing double time and her nerve-endings sizzled simply from being near him.

Before she knew what he was doing, he was standing beside her. He removed the clip holding her hair back and dropped it on the table as he tunneled his fingers into the loosened strands.

"Alejandro—"

"Shh." His touch was gentle, sure—and as startling as ever. He was so close his scent invaded her senses. No chlorine this time. Just expensive soap and man. Her eyes drifted closed as warmth spread through her.

"Ouch!" Her eyes snapped open again.

"It's a small bump," he said, his fingers exploring the swelling on her head. "Nothing serious."

Rebecca marshaled her resolve as awareness followed hard

on the heels of the warmth permeating her body. "Stop touching me," she said, batting at his hand.

"I have experience of these things, *bella*. You wouldn't want it to be serious, would you?"

"It's not. Leave me alone."

A second later, he whipped off her sunglasses. She tried to pull away, but he gripped her chin firmly, his eyes searching hers. "You did not sleep well."

Rebecca managed to jerk away. She snatched the shades from his hand and replaced them, praying he wouldn't see how she suddenly trembled with his nearness. How her skin sizzled and her blood hummed from the contact. "No thanks to you."

He returned to his chair and picked up his coffee cup. "It was you who pushed me into the pool, not the other way around."

"I wasn't talking about the pool. I'm talking about jet lag. I was in Hawaii yesterday, New York the day before. You could have given me more time to get here."

Hardly the full truth of why she hadn't been able to sleep, but that was all he was getting out of her.

He shrugged. "It's business. I do not have time to wait while you make your way leisurely around the world."

"No, I imagine stealing works best when done quickly."

His eyes glittered. "Careful, Rebecca."

"Or what? You'll drown me in your pool?" She knew she went too far, but she couldn't help it. Her bitterness from his accusations of last night boiled beneath the surface.

He set the cup down and stood, tossing his napkin onto the table. "We leave for the office in ten minutes. Be in the car if you wish to salvage anything of Layton International."

"Is that even possible? Or do you plan to sell it off piece by piece just to hurt me?"

He grabbed his jacket from the chair. "You will have to wait and find out. There is no other option, *sí*?"

Rebecca set the toast down, no longer hungry. "You really like being the one in control. You're enjoying this very much, aren't you?"

Alejandro's smile sent a chill skimming down her spine. "You have no idea, Señorita Layton."

Ramirez Enterprises was housed in a sleek glass-and-steel building in Madrid's financial district. The ride took over an hour in the thick traffic congesting the city's heart. The limo crawled like a beetle, inching forward until an opening appeared, then shooting between narrow gaps that had Rebecca cringing each time, expecting the scrape of steel on steel. By the time the car pulled into the drive in front of the building and a doorman appeared, Rebecca was exhausted.

When Alejandro exited the car, Rebecca on his heels, a cadre of men and women with cameras rushed forward. Flashes snapped, and Rebecca instinctively pasted on her public persona. Growing up with a wealthy father and a social butterfly mother had at least given her unfailing poise when the media appeared. It didn't happen to her much anymore, but of course Alejandro was a famous man in his own country. They'd been photographed often when she was last here. In fact, he'd gotten more attention than a pop star. She'd have thought it would have lessened now that he'd been away from bullfighting for so long, but apparently not.

"Señor Ramirez," the reporters called in unison. "Señor Ramirez."

Alejandro stopped, smiling broadly. He said a few words in Spanish, which caused several of the reporters to laugh.

"Can you tell us about the accusations of impropriety with construction permits in Dubai?" a man said in German-accented English.

"We are working with the Dubai authorities to get to the

bottom of the matter," Alejandro said smoothly. "I expect to begin construction very soon."

"You've been accused of bribing officials and short-circuiting the process. How do you answer that charge?"

His smile never wavered. "I deny it, of course. If you will excuse me, my business awaits. Miss Layton?" he said, turning to where she stood near the car.

"Rebecca Layton?" someone said. "Of Layton International?"

Alejandro faced the cameras again. "I have recently acquired Layton International, as you will have seen if you read the business section. Miss Layton is here to ensure the smooth transfer of her former company's holdings."

Former company. Rebecca's smile ached at the corners.

"How do you feel about the takeover, Miss Layton?"

Alejandro's smile didn't waver, but he shot her a warning glance. *To hell with him.*

Rebecca stepped forward. "I'm not happy about it, you may be assured. Layton International has been in the luxury hotel business for over a half century. We had hoped to continue, and were pursuing projects guaranteed to bring the Layton brand of luxury to new markets. This takeover is not the outcome we'd hoped for."

The reporters buzzed. One question rose above the others. "Do you suspect any impropriety in the acquisition process?"

Rebecca clasped her hands together in front of her. She knew it made her look innocent and somewhat vulnerable. "No—that's not possible, is it? The laws of our nations are very specific in regards to company stock and corporate mergers. Though Señor Ramirez might have wished to act immorally, I'm sure he did not do so."

The questions rose to a fever-pitch. Rebecca strained to hear a single one over the din, but Alejandro appeared at her side, his hand on her elbow.

"That's all for now," he said, ushering her toward the sleek glass doors of the building.

She resisted the urge to smile when the doors closed behind them, leaving them in the quiet of a polished lobby. A pretty receptionist greeted them warmly. Alejandro nodded his head to the young woman and propelled Rebecca toward an elevator. Her shoes clicked across black marble inlaid with shiny gold squares. She briefly wondered if they were real gold—if Alejandro would dare to display his wealth so garishly. A uniformed man greeted them as they passed inside a private elevator, then pressed a button and exited, leaving them alone as the gleaming doors slid closed.

"What the hell do you think you're doing?"

Rebecca leaned back against the brass rail and tried not to look like the cat that ate the canary. "What do you mean? I told them you did everything legally." Legally, but not morally. She had no doubt he'd understood what she'd said out there.

His gray eyes flashed. "You know very well you are jeopardizing our stock value with comments such as those."

"I'm sure you'll recover from the dip."

"Yes, but will I need to shed a few assets to keep earnings on projection?"

Her heart thumped at the threat, but she remained coolly unaffected on the outside. "*Did* you pay bribes in Dubai?"

"Do you think I would admit it to you if I had?"

She spoke before she could talk herself out of it. "You've grown fast over the years. I've wondered how you did it, but perhaps the secret to your success has little to do with business acumen and everything to do with your willingness to play dirty."

His gaze sharpened. "You'd like to think so, no doubt. But I assure you everything I've gained has been earned through hard work. Unlike yourself, no?"

His reaction was not as harsh as she'd expected, but it sliced deep. It was a charge that stung, but not one she could deny. At least not in any way he would understand. She'd had to work hard to prove herself to her father, to prove that a daughter would be every bit as good as a son when it came to captaining the family business. Harder than anyone would ever know.

She would not, however, share those struggles with Alejandro—or indeed with anyone. The memories of what she'd endured were too painful.

His look was telling. "How it must anger you to know your fate is in my hands. Perhaps you should be nicer to me? Encourage me to be gracious? How is it you say in America? That you must use honey to get the flies, not vinegar?"

She stiffened. "Don't you dare insult me by pretending I have a chance. You've already made up your mind, so why not just tell me what you want and be done with it? It's clear you have a plan, regardless of what I say or do. Save us both the hassle."

His gray gaze bored into hers. "What makes you think this is a—what was the word?—*hassle* for me?"

She speared her hair away from her face, having left the clip on the breakfast table. "I mean that since you already know what you want from me, let's just get right to it and skip this other stuff."

She sounded brave, though she was anything but. He could fire her here and now, put her on a plane and send her back to New York with nothing more than a bad case of jet lag and a rapidly dwindling bank account. She probably shouldn't have baited him with her statement to the reporters, but she was tired of being at his mercy. She wanted this nightmare over, wanted her company back and her life free of this man.

"Get right to it?" he said softly. "Skip the foreplay? Sometimes this is a good idea."

Rebecca's breath caught at the sensual undertone of his

voice. Was she imagining the heat in his gaze? The elevator seemed suddenly too small to contain the two of them.

"But not always," he said, his voice caressing the words. "You may plead your case in front of my board."

"They will vote as you want. What's the point?" she said, her voice far huskier than she would have liked.

"Maybe." He reached into his jacket and pulled out his PDA, frowning at the screen. The sexual tension emanating from him died as if he'd flipped a switch. He clicked the wheel, scrolling through the information there, shutting her out.

Rebecca gripped the railing, stunned both at the immediacy of her reaction and at his ability to turn off his own response. Because he *had* wanted her. She'd seen it. Hadn't she? Or was this simply another part of his game?

Unbidden, images of him flashed into her head. The jagged scar of a bull's horn slicing across his rib cage, the taut ripple and glide of muscle when he moved, the impressive jut of his erection. The ecstasy on his face when she straddled him and drove them both out of their minds with her slow thrusts.

He'd accused her of enduring his touch for the sake of her family business, of seeing him as nothing more than a bull-fighter dirty from the ring. If only he believed that she'd truly loved him, how sexy she'd found him in spite of the barbarity of his former profession.

Standing in this elevator in his custom-fit suit, he was as far from the glittering garb of a matador as any man could be—and yet she still saw the bullfighter beneath the polish. The raw, hungry, intense man who could stand in a ring with one ton of angry bull barreling toward him and never, not even once, flinch. This was a man who could stare death in the face and not blink.

After their affair had ended, she'd actually gone through a torturous phase of tracking down and watching his recorded fights. Holding her breath while the bull charged, while the cape swept down, then whirled away as Alejandro went up high on his toes and plunged his sword home. She'd thought it barbaric, and yet Alejandro had once explained, when she'd been tracing his scar in the aftermath of their lovemaking, how honorable the fight was for both man and bull. It wasn't her kind of thing—and yet there was a beauty in it.

A beauty in him.

She closed her eyes, remembered the heat of him, of the two of them twined together in his sheets. It had all gone so wrong, so horribly wrong. And she wasn't the same person she'd been back then—the same starry-eyed girl with dreams of love and a life with the most magnetic man she'd ever met. The world had certainly taught her the folly of those beliefs, hadn't it?

The elevator glided to a halt, the doors whispering open to let them into a spacious private office. Overstuffed chairs and a sleek sofa sat beneath a wall of books. A chrome and glass desk was positioned in front of floor-to-ceiling windows that ran the length of one wall. Alejandro went behind the desk and sat down without looking at her.

In the distance, the twin glass and steel structures of the Puerta de Europa leaned toward each other across the busy Paseo de Castellana. Much closer, the giant Estadio Santiago Bernabéu, where Madrilenians flocked to watch their soccer team, squatted against a bright blue sky.

"The board meeting will be in an hour. I suggest you prepare." He picked up the phone and spoke to someone. A second later, a pretty woman opened the door.

"Please escort Señorita Layton to a desk, Maria."

Rebecca followed the woman without another word, smiling and giving her thanks when Maria deposited her in a small, windowless office. Though she needed to prepare for the meeting, she first placed a call to the Cahill Group's offices in London. Roger was out of town until tomorrow, so she hung up and clicked open her briefcase. A glance at the clock told her she had fifty minutes left.

She didn't know what she'd encounter in that boardroom, but she wasn't going down without a fight.

When she was finally called to the meeting, more than an hour after she'd been told she would be, she was ready. She'd spent the last two hours completing her projections, dragging her finance people out of bed to give her numbers, and making sure her arguments were sound. Layton International would be out of the red in six months if she were allowed to continue on the path she'd chosen.

And though it burned her up to have to humble herself to these people, to explain her plans and defend her actions, she had no choice. She had to keep her company intact until she could somehow manage to get it back.

But the board meeting went exactly as she'd predicted. What Alejandro wanted, the board would do. If he decided to dissect her company limb from limb, he was within his rights to do so.

Rebecca shoved papers into her briefcase as the board filed out. She was on dangerous ground here. She was only technically still CEO until Alejandro decided otherwise.

A wave of apprehension rolled through her. And he *would* decide otherwise. She had no doubt. He was simply dragging this out to torture her.

How could she be the one who lost the company started by her grandfather? No matter that her father had taken out astronomical loans and pledged every last share of stock as collateral, she was still the one in control when the axe fell. She should have stopped it.

How? a little voice asked.

It didn't matter how. She should have simply *known* what to do. Her father would have.

Rebecca pinched the bridge of her nose, breathed deeply.

No—no one could have gotten them out of this mess. She simply had to deal with the situation as it was. She had to protect Layton International and the people who depended on her for their jobs.

"Why did you make me go through with that?" Rebecca demanded, frustration and anger churning together.

Alejandro shrugged a shoulder, his lazy stare infuriating. "If you do not like your new position, you can always quit."

Rebecca snapped her briefcase closed, then stood and stared down at him as coolly as she could muster, given the erratic beating of her heart. "I'm returning to New York to do my job."

"You forget who is in charge here, Señorita Layton." Alejandro leaned back in his chair, legs sprawled out in front of him as he toyed with a pen on the table. He looked nothing like a billionaire and everything like a mischievous Greek god who'd deigned to dabble with the mortals again. "You work at my pleasure and you leave when I say so."

"You don't own me." Her voice was little more than a whisper.

"Oh, but I do."

He meant it. She could see that. And he intended to make her suffer for it.

"What did I ever see in you?" she forced out past the knot in her throat.

For some reason that got his attention. He climbed slowly to his feet, his eyes glittering. The look on his face was pure danger. For reasons she preferred not to explore, a tiny thrill shot through her.

She straightened her spine, refused to back down as he moved closer. "What are you going to do? Kiss me again?" Her voice was huskier than she would have liked. The thought of him kissing her, pressing his body against her, wasn't nearly as repugnant as she wanted it to be.

Was she crazy? She didn't want to remember what it was

like between them, how much she'd once loved him. To feel anything at all for him, besides hate, was to betray everything her family had ever done for her.

"Would you like that, *querida*?" he said, moving toward her with lethal grace. "My mouth against yours?"

"No!" She resisted the urge to slink away. Where would she go? Against a wall? No, she'd stand here, take whatever he dished out. Give as good as she got. He might own her company—own *her*, in fact—but he would not control her. If he kissed her, she would remain cold and unresponsive.

She *would*.

"Your body says otherwise." He practically purred as his finger grazed her cheek. She was proud when she didn't betray herself with even the hint of a shiver. She stood stone-still and endured his touch. His fingers left fire in their wake as they ghosted over her skin.

"You are flushed, Rebecca." His fingers fell away, his hot gaze dropping to caress her body inch by inch. He no longer touched her, but she felt like his hands were everywhere at once.

His eyes caught and held hers. He took a step closer, still not touching her, but invading her space with his overwhelming physicality. "Your nipples bud for me. Feel how they want my touch. Should I kiss them?"

"You're mistaken," she said, forcing herself not to glance down, not to see the proof of his words.

A sensual grin creased his handsome features. "I am never mistaken about such things. Your heart pounds for me. I can see it. It is like a frightened rabbit."

"You're standing too close. I don't like it."

He stepped in again, until the hard length of his body hemmed her against the conference table. He placed his arms on either side of her, trapping her. "I think you do. I think, in fact, that you want me desperately."

"You're wrong, Alejandro," she said, lifting her head to

look him in the eye and deliver what she prayed was a stern look. "I hate you. I *don't* want you."

And yet her skin sizzled from his nearness. Her brain threatened to disengage completely. Her body trembled in spite of her resolve; an ache bloomed in the feminine core of her, spread outward on currents of liquid heat.

Alejandro's smile was too knowing, too masculine. "*Sí*, I feel your hatred. It is very strong. Very frightening for me."

His head dipped toward her. Her eyes drifted closed and he chuckled low in his throat, a sound of male triumph. Any second he would kiss her. Any second she would allow it. In spite of all she'd said. She was too weak, too lonely and needy—

No.

She found the strength to lift her palms, to push against his chest. At the same instant a buzzer sliced through the room. Alejandro stepped away, Spanish curses—or so she assumed—falling from his lips as he reached for the phone.

"*Sí?*" he barked.

Rebecca snatched up her briefcase and purse. She had to get away from here. She had to get home, back to New York, before Alejandro stripped her of far more than her company.

Her hand was on the door when his fingers closed over her shoulder. She gasped as he spun her around, pressed her against the door, his hard thigh wedged between her legs. He gripped her chin, pushed her head back until she was staring him in the eye.

"You will not leave me again, Rebecca. I call the shots—*comprende*?" His voice was low, intense. She had the feeling his words were more than a statement of fact.

They were a vow.

In spite of the heat between them, a chill slid over her. "I'm going to the airport, Alejandro. There's nothing for me here."

His eyes were colder than frost as he let her go and took a step back. "Walk out that door and I will destroy Layton

International. Your employees will be without jobs, your hotels sold or demolished, your assets carved up and absorbed into Ramirez Enterprises. I will make sure you never work in this industry again. No one will *ever* hire you, Rebecca. Walk out and it's over."

The depth of his fury stunned her. She wished she had the strength to do it, to walk out and not give a damn. But she couldn't let him take away the livelihood of the people who depended on her. At this moment she didn't care about herself—being anywhere but here, with him, would be less painful to her—but she couldn't desert them.

"What do you want from me?"

He glared at her without speaking for so long that she wondered if he'd heard her. Just when she started to repeat the question, he turned away.

"All in good time." He flicked a hand as if shooing away a bothersome fly. "You may go now."

CHAPTER THREE

WHAT did he want from her, she'd asked. Alejandro stared at the blinking skyline of Madrid at night. His problems in Dubai should take precedence—he had a hotel to build and permits to straighten out before he could do so—yet he couldn't seem to get the problem of Rebecca Layton out of his mind while he worked late.

He reached for the sherry he'd poured over twenty minutes ago, took a sip.

Damn her and her lies.

It was her fault he'd married Caridad. He would never have agreed to it had Rebecca not left him. Had she not *stolen* from him.

It wasn't just that she'd yanked the safety net out from under him. While it would have taken him far longer to take Ramirez Enterprises global without the Cahill Group's backing, he still could have done it without Caridad's family contributing to his coffers.

No, what Rebecca's betrayal had confirmed was the folly of allowing emotion to rule his head. He'd cared for her, had sometimes even envisioned the children they would have if he'd married her. He'd grown up with parents whose daily emotional drama should have inured him to any hint of sentiment, but Rebecca's smokescreen of naive charm had pulled him into her web.

What a bloody idiot.

And then he'd returned to his suite one afternoon and found a severe-looking woman waiting for him and no sign of Rebecca. The woman had fanned open a thick folder and nattered at him about planning a wedding.

It had taken him several more minutes to realize that Rebecca's suitcases were gone. The woman had simply shrugged. "*Sí*," she'd said. "There was a pretty young woman. She wished you a happy marriage to Señorita Mendoza."

That was when it dawned on him. His father, the old fool, had been urging him to marry Caridad since Roberto's death. Arranged marriages were no longer commonplace, but they did happen from time to time. His father had seen it as a measure of his own importance to find a bride for his eldest son. Roberto hadn't had the guts to object, which Juan Ramirez had known full well. He'd never have tried it with Alejandro. But then Roberto died. Señor Mendoza had loaned his father a lot of money, and Juan intended to deliver his famous son as payment if it was the last thing he did.

Alejandro had steadfastly refused. Apparently Juan had decided to step up the campaign. The timing could not have been worse.

Alejandro's first thought had been to go after Rebecca. But she'd had a head start and he'd had no idea where she'd gone. His calls to her mobile phone had gone unanswered. Two days later she'd finally picked up. From London. She'd been cool and aloof, and he'd lost his temper. How dared she expect an explanation? All she'd needed was to accept that what he told her was the truth: he was not engaged.

Not surprisingly, she hadn't believed him. He'd realized later that his alleged engagement was merely a convenient excuse for her to do what she'd always intended to do. The next day Roger Cahill had told him they were backing Layton International instead.

Rebecca had said she loved him, but she'd lied. He wasn't good enough for her and never would be in her eyes.

You weren't important enough.

It had pricked his pride, sliced a wound in his soul, the knowledge that this woman he'd cared about had used him. He'd vowed never again to believe protestations of love from any female. So he'd agreed to marry Caridad. Why not? Her breeding and social standing were impeccable. She would be the perfect hostess, the perfect tycoon's wife, the perfect mother to his children.

He'd certainly been mistaken on that point. He could not have chosen a colder, more unfeeling woman for his wife if he'd tried.

Alejandro swallowed a mouthful of alcohol, welcomed the burn as it slid down his throat. Who could have guessed how much pain he would have to endure before his marriage was over? He'd never known such despair, such aching emptiness. Everything that had happened to him, everything that had sliced his soul to shreds and left him hollow inside, could be traced to that moment when Rebecca Layton had left him. If not for her, it would have turned out so differently.

He'd vowed long ago that every ounce of pain she'd ever dealt him would be returned to her before he was through. That was what he wanted from her.

Rebecca had no real destination as she wandered through Alejandro's darkened house. It was after ten, and everything was quiet. A small lamp burned on the desk in the home office she'd first seen him in yesterday. She went inside, thinking to find a book to read since she wasn't sleeping so well.

She studied the titles lining the bookshelves with interest.

What did Alejandro like to read? It surprised her to realize she hadn't known before. Hadn't known much about him, in fact, if she thought about it. He'd come far indeed in the five years since she'd last seen him.

But his fury and hatred stunned her. Clearly he believed she had ruined his deal with the Cahill Group. But even if it were true, which it was not, why would that be enough to make him hate her so much? The business world was often unfair. *Life* was unfair. Sometimes it was downright cruel. Plenty of times in the last few months she'd wanted to bury her head in her hands and scream at the unfairness that had left her in charge of Layton International so soon. The monstrous bad luck that had her father climbing on a tiny plane in Thailand so he could tour the resorts he'd just acquired.

But she hadn't. She'd picked herself up and dusted herself off and got back to work. There had been no other choice.

Most of the books were in Spanish. *Don Quixote*, naturally. *The Count of Monte Cristo* in English. Interesting. She started to reach for Dumas's tale of wrongful imprisonment and revenge, but another book caught her eye. This one had the word "Photos" emblazoned on the spine.

What sort of photos would a man like Alejandro find important enough to paste into an album? Bullfighting ones, no doubt. Curious, she pulled the book from the shelf and placed it on the desk in front of her.

She opened the cover and sank into Alejandro's chair, her knees no longer strong enough to hold her upright. A little girl smiled back at her. A beautiful black-haired child, with gray eyes and a smile so familiar it hurt to see it.

But to see it in a toddler?

His child. Without a doubt this girl was Alejandro's child. She had his smile, his eyes, the stubborn tilt of his chin. When he appeared in a picture with her, the resemblance was unmistakable. Tears sprang to Rebecca's eyes. Why? She wiped at them furiously, flipping pages until she came to a photo that made her heart stop. Alejandro holding the little girl on a beach. He was healthy and tanned, his smile glowing as he gazed at his daughter. The girl stared at whoever took the photo, a finger in her mouth, her eyes wide.

Rebecca chewed absently on a knuckle. He'd had a child after she'd gone back to America. He'd married the woman and had a beautiful little girl with her. Jealousy speared Rebecca like a poisoned barb. *You have no right*, she told herself. *You left.*

But she'd had to go. He'd been engaged.

He said he wasn't, a voice whispered. *You gave him no chance to prove it to you.*

She shook her head. If he hadn't been engaged, why had he gone through with it? You didn't marry someone and have a child with her if you weren't committed somehow.

Rebecca forced herself to flip more pages. It was mostly the little girl, though her mother appeared in a couple. Never smiling, that woman. Never looking anything other than irritated.

A nanny, perhaps?

But, no, the little girl had her mother's bone structure. Rebecca turned the pages faster. She could almost be glad that Alejandro had had a sour-faced wife if not for the little girl who was probably tugged between divorced parents even now. No child deserved to have parents who disliked each other.

At least her own parents had been in love, even if her father had never been home long enough to pay any attention to a disappointing girl-child who'd craved his affection and approval. Her mother, who'd been addicted to shopping and socializing, had often left Rebecca in the care of a nanny. She'd been a lonely, lonely child.

Who'd grown into a lonely adult. She swiped a hand beneath her nose, sniffed back her tears. *Get over it.*

On the last page of the album was an official-looking document, but it was in Spanish and she couldn't read it. *Certificado de defunción.* What did that mean?

"What are you doing in here?"

Rebecca's head whipped up at the angry demand. She'd been so focused she hadn't heard him come in. She slapped the album closed a little too hard—a guilty reaction at being caught going through his personal things.

Alejandro strode into the room and snatched the album from the desk. "You are never to touch this again, *comprende*?" He spun from her and disappeared through the door.

She sat in stunned silence. Whatever she'd expected, that hadn't been it. Why was he so upset with her? It didn't matter; she had to get out and get back to her room before he returned—before he confronted her with whatever nastiness was on his mind.

But she waited too long to move. Before she reached the door, Alejandro was back, looming in the entry, anger rolling off him in waves.

"You dare to go through my things? After what you did the last time?"

"I'm sorry," she said. Because she had, in fact, violated his privacy. She hadn't meant to, but when she'd seen the album she'd simply been too curious to stop. "Your daughter is very pretty, Alejandro. I'm sorry if I upset you by looking at her photos."

He passed a hand over his face, swore under his breath while shaking his head. It made no sense to her, but when his hand dropped away what she saw on his face twisted her heart. Pain like nothing she'd ever experienced. Longing and regret.

Loneliness.

He pulled in a ragged breath. "*Sí*, Anya was very pretty. She was the best thing I have ever done."

Was? Rebecca's heart squeezed, hard. Oh, dear God. The official document at the end was a death certificate. *Defunción*—death. How had she blundered so badly?

She swallowed the knot clogging her throat. "I'm sorry," she said again.

"Get out of my sight." The words fell like empty bullets onto the floor. Hollow, dull. He sounded suddenly very tired, very worn. Very unlike the vibrant man she knew.

She came out from behind the desk and walked to the door. He flinched when she put her hand on his arm. The movement saddened her. Once he would have welcomed her touch. No longer. "I'm sorry for your loss, Alejandro."

She truly, truly was. No one should have to endure such a thing. The experience had changed him. She could see that. It had made him harder, colder, less sympathetic than he'd once been. It explained so much and made her ache for him.

His hand closed over hers before she could pull it away, held it there as his pain-filled eyes raked her.

"You think I am like the lion with the thorn in his paw, yes? You think if you pull it out I will be forever in your debt?" As much as he tried, the malice was missing.

"I didn't say that."

"You didn't have to."

She swallowed. "No one should lose a child. I can't know your pain; but I'm sorry for it." She knew what it was like to lose a parent unexpectedly, but her father had at least had a life first. Alejandro's little girl never got the chance.

His fingers tightened. "You would offer to comfort me, perhaps? Take me to bed and make me forget?"

Rebecca couldn't speak. She watched him, her breath tight in her chest, her eyes filling with unshed tears. A part of her was ready to hold him, to let him take whatever he wanted from her. Another part—the angry, betrayed part—wanted to hold on to her fury at him. She was paralyzed by opposite urges.

Alejandro was not. "You can keep your pity and comfort to yourself, Rebecca Layton. I do not need it."

He let go of her hand.

"I'm sorry," she said again. Because there was nothing else to say.

"Go."

For once, she obeyed without question.

By the time Rebecca stood at the pool's edge and considered taking off her robe and underwear and going for a swim, it was nearly three in the morning. She'd tried to sleep. She'd turned on the television and watched a Spanish movie—not that she'd understood a word—and hoped it would bore her enough.

It hadn't. But was it jet lag or Alejandro that kept her awake?

She swirled a toe in the water and thought of the look on his face when he'd told her his child was gone forever. A hand drifted over her abdomen almost without conscious thought. Once she'd thought *she* would be the mother of Alejandro's children.

Her heart swelled with sorrow. His poor, poor wife. Rebecca had never spared any good will for the woman who'd crushed her dreams with her mere existence, but she hurt for the former Señora Ramirez now. Had their child's death torn their marriage apart?

Alejandro had been so angry earlier, so defeated. Not at all the man she knew. She'd had no idea what to say to him, no words to breach the barrier of anger and mistrust between them. She'd been so focused on her own problems since arriving; the shock of realizing he was very much as human and vulnerable as anyone else was hard to reconcile with the brutal tycoon who wanted to destroy her life.

His loneliness had reached out to her and she'd been almost powerless to resist it. In spite of the hurt, in spite of all he'd done to humiliate and control her, she'd felt in that instant like they shared a connection. A very, *very* dangerous feeling.

Rebecca blew out a breath. The night air was warm, the pool inviting. She hadn't come out here with the intention of swimming—if she had, she'd have worn her swimsuit—but the temptation to do so was strong. Or maybe she'd just slip her clothes off and sit on the terraced stone steps beneath the waterline.

What had happened to little Anya? She'd been such a beautiful child, so sweet-looking. Then again, weren't all babies sweet-looking? She didn't know much about babies, really. Tears threatened, lodging in her throat, a ball of pain she couldn't swallow. *Damn it, she had to stop thinking about this, about him.*

Rebecca slipped her robe off and tossed it onto a chaise. A second later her camisole and panties followed, and she hurried down the steps before she could change her mind. Goose bumps rose on her skin the lower she sank into the water. Though the air was warm, the pool was slightly cooler than she'd expected after dipping her toe in. She almost turned around and went back, but she forged on until she could sink onto the lowest step, the water right below her naked breasts.

Water lapped at her nipples and she sucked in her breath as they budded tight. It had been so long since anyone had touched them. She was tormented with sadness and hurt, yet she threaded one hand up her torso, her heart thudding, and softly pinched one of the peaks between her thumb and forefinger. Was it wrong to want to feel good again, even if only for a moment?

A sound from the direction of the arbor lodged her heart into her throat. She craned her head to try and see, her heart shooting into overdrive. Did Madrid have wild animals inside the city limits? Did burglars dare to rob someone as wealthy and powerful as Alejandro?

Maybe she should run into the house—but her feet refused

to move. What if it was nothing? She strained to hear any odd noises against the backdrop of ordinary night sounds, but the blood was so loud in her ears she couldn't separate any one sound from the others.

Until something scraped.

"Who's there?" she said, and immediately felt ridiculous. An animal wouldn't answer, and neither would an intruder.

She stared hard at the arbor, her heart skipping a beat as a shape unfolded itself from the darkness, growing bigger as the light caressed its shadow. A lifetime later, it resolved into the shape of a man.

A tall man, with dark hair and the body of a god, dressed in jeans and a dark T-shirt. Her heart went out to him.

"You are enjoying yourself, *no*?"

Rebecca pulled her knees to her chin to hide her nakedness, her skin flushing. "You scared me half to death, Alejandro. How long have you been there?"

"Long enough."

She nibbled her lip between her teeth, wanting to ask him if he was all right and yet sensing he would not welcome the question. "You could have announced yourself," she said instead.

And saved her the embarrassment sizzling through her now. It didn't matter that he'd seen her naked in the past, that he'd probably kissed every inch of her skin and shown her things no man ever had. To think he'd watched her the whole time—even when she'd let her hand trail up her body...

"I'd like you to go," she said, with as much dignity as she could muster. *Please, please go.*

His smirk told her he would do nothing of the sort. He settled into a chair, crossing one leg casually. An arm draped over the side, fingers rubbing back and forth against the chair's edge. "Why would I want to leave, Señorita Layton? It is my house, is it not? And I was here first."

"Then I'll leave. Would you hand me my robe, please?"

"No."

Frustration hummed beneath the surface. "Alejandro, please. What is the point in this?"

His eyes narrowed. "Are you uncomfortable?"

"I think you know the answer."

"Then perhaps that is the point."

Rebecca swallowed. "I'm sorry I looked at the photos. I didn't know it would upset you."

He made a rough noise. "You may apologize, but this does not explain why you thought it acceptable to go through my things in the first place. Looking for information you could use against me, Rebecca? Something you could sell to the press, perhaps? I assure you that you will not find anything."

"What? No!" She hugged herself tighter. It was disconcerting to argue with him while she sat here without a stitch of clothing. He lounged in the chair so casually, like there weren't oceans of pain between them. She had a sudden urge to be completely truthful with him, to try and bridge the gap somehow. "I want a chance to redeem Layton International, yes. If you would let me repurchase the stock, I'd be grateful. I'm not trying to hurt your business. I only want my company back."

He didn't say anything for a long moment. "How grateful?"

She couldn't tell by his tone how he meant the question. Was he baiting her? Making fun of her? Heat prickled her nerve endings. "Um, well, I think we could work out some profit-sharing. Perhaps even a partnership or two?"

He didn't answer. Instead, he got to his feet, tugged at the waist of his T-shirt with one hand. A moment later it fell to the tile deck. Rebecca's pulse skipped. "What are you doing?"

"Considering your proposal." He unsnapped his jeans, shrugged them down his lean hips in a graceful movement that had her blood pounding in her ears. When he stood at the edge of the pool in nothing but his briefs, Rebecca had to remind herself to breathe. She'd dreamt of that body for five years. Dear heaven, she remembered at the most inopportune moments what his flesh felt like pressed to hers, moving inside her. She'd even called her ex-boyfriend Alejandro once during sex. No wonder she'd been alone for the past year and a half.

Her mouth went dry at the sight of all that hard muscle and tan skin. "Wh-what proposal? What are you talking about?" And why did her head feel as if it were stuffed with cotton wool?

"How grateful would you be, *querida*?"

She cast her mind back over the conversation, tried to piece together what exactly he meant. And then her brain shut down and her jaw slipped open as the last of Alejandro's clothing fell away.

A second later he was in the water.

CHAPTER FOUR

ALEJANDRO swam toward her, idly wondering if she would shoot up the steps and into the house. If she did, then perhaps she wasn't as calculating as he thought. Perhaps she really hadn't known he was beneath the arbor, watching her.

He half hoped she would run. It would be nice to think she wasn't trying to use him this once, especially when his memories were so raw. After she'd left him in his office he'd gone for a walk in the grounds. Then he'd sat under the arbor and hoped his mind would quiet. It hadn't.

When she'd appeared, stealing through the night like a wraith, he'd watched her curiously. And then she'd dropped her clothes, like the calculating slut she was.

And, like it or not, her striptease had made him harder than the stone this pool was built out of. Which had no doubt been her intention. She'd played at asking him to leave, but he hadn't bought her act. The truth had emerged, of course, when she'd said she'd be grateful if he would sell her Layton International.

She didn't move as he stopped in front of her. He was both disappointed and pleased. He hadn't intended to touch her ever again, but that had been before he'd watched her strip down and caress herself.

Madre de Dios, he wanted to bury himself inside her right

this moment. Would she be as hot and tight as he remembered?

But, no, he would not give in to his body's demands. He would, however, prove to them both that she was a mercenary bitch who would do anything to get what she wanted.

"What are you doing?" she asked, still clasping her knees, her eyes wide. He didn't miss how her gaze dropped, shot back to his face. *Little Miss Innocent.*

The water caressed his hip bones, the evidence of her effect on him hidden beneath the surface of the pool. If she stood, however, she would see he was more than ready for her.

"I am giving you a chance to show your gratitude."

"You haven't given me anything to be grateful for," she shot back, her facade cracking.

"What would you like, Rebecca? La Belle Amelie?"

Her head dipped as she turned her gaze from him. Calculating, no doubt. "I won't sleep with you for a hotel."

"What if that is my price?" He knew she would break. She was simply trying to get more out of him first.

Blue eyes gleamed as she met his cool stare. "You're saying you will *give* me my hotel if I let you make love to me?"

Alejandro chuckled. So predictable. "What I wish to do to you right now has nothing to do with love."

She blinked. "How do I know you mean it, Alejandro? How do I know this isn't part of your game?"

"So you will accept if I am serious?"

She looked away again. "I didn't say that."

He reached for her hand. The contact of skin on skin sizzled into his brain, made his manhood leap in anticipation. She did not resist when he twined his fingers with hers and pulled her toward him.

Of course she didn't.

He took her into deeper water without looking back at her.

When he stopped and turned, the crests of her nipples were just below the surface.

She chewed her bottom lip, watched him warily.

"I will give you your hotel, Rebecca. You need only give me your body. Surely this is a fair trade?"

A moment later, her chin tilted up. Ah, so the imperious heiress had arrived.

"I want it all. I want a chance to buy back my stock."

Anger simmered deep inside though he smiled to cover it. He'd known she was playing him, hadn't he?

"I will consider it."

She took a deep breath. He had her now. She would not pass up the opportunity. If he'd told her yes, she would know he was lying. But if he offered to consider it, she would believe he could still be persuaded. And she would turn all her considerable charms toward convincing him.

He waited almost eagerly for her next move.

"I'm leaving," she said, turning away from him and stroking toward the closest ladder.

Not at all what he'd expected, but that only made the game more fun.

Rebecca swam for the ladder. What was she thinking, telling him she wanted everything if she gave in to his demands? She had absolutely no intention of making love to him for a hotel, or company stock, or anything else. She would not be brought down to his level. He believed her to be mercenary. Though a rebellious part of her wanted very much to be in his arms again, she would not give in to the temptation. Every nasty thing he'd ever thought about her would be justified in his mind if she did.

She reached for the ladder, put her foot on the first rung. Strong arms twined around her torso and pulled her against his body.

Oh, dear heaven, his *aroused* body.

The hard length of him was hot against her backside. In fact, every last inch of his skin seared her as he held her close. His fingers snaked across her belly; his other hand slid up to cup her breast, tested the weight of it in his palm.

She shivered with longing.

"I will give you the hotel, Rebecca. I will consider the rest, though perhaps we will need a repeat performance or two to persuade me."

His breath was hot in her ear, teasing her, tempting her with remembered bliss. It wasn't fair to want this man so much in spite of all he'd done, to turn to mush the instant he touched her.

She knew he only wanted her because she was here, because she was female, and because he knew she was vulnerable to him. She'd proven that when she'd let him lead her into the pool. If she'd truly wanted to get away she would have gone into the house the instant he entered the water.

She was an idiot, a lonely needy girl who still wanted to be loved by *someone* in her life. Was it asking too much to want what so many other people had?

What Alejandro had had with his wife and baby girl?

But, no, it was an illusion. Everything with him was an illusion, and she wouldn't allow herself to believe it ever again.

But he's hurting. He lost a precious child and he's so very different because of it. He needs you.

She gritted her teeth against the onslaught. *No.*

"I can't do it," she said, as much to convince herself as him. "I don't want to."

It was a lie, though she prayed he would not figure out the truth.

Alejandro turned her in his arms, pressed her against the side of the pool. The water was over her head here, so she had no choice but to cling to him. His dark head dipped down, his lips ghosting over her cheek, touching the shell of her ear.

"You want me, *querida*. You cannot deny this."

"I don't," she said desperately.

"Not even for your precious hotel?"

She started to shake her head, realized her mistake when her mouth grazed his jaw and he turned his head, his lips capturing hers. She moaned—but was it protest or acquiescence?—as her head fell back and her mouth opened beneath his. Whatever the reason, he took advantage of the lapse to tangle his tongue with hers. Wild, hot, sucking—their mouths devoured each other. Flame licked up her belly, blossomed between her thighs.

How could she possibly want this man after all he'd done? His loneliness called out to her, connected with her own inner feelings of isolation, tempted her in spite of her best intentions.

His hands slid down her buttocks, over her thighs, lifted them until she wrapped her legs around his waist, the hard length of him pressing against her center. Her body remembered all too well how wonderful it had been between them. He'd left his impression on every nerve, every cell. Five years had not been enough to erase it.

Even as she shuddered, part of her brain remained lucid, sent the message to drop her legs, to end this before it went too far. He lifted them again, urging her to open to him. He gave her no chance to refuse as his thumb glided between her thighs, found the hot, wet center of her.

Rebecca gasped. It had been so long…

Alejandro pulled back, gazed down at her with an expression that contained both surprise and confusion, as if he too were a little rattled by how quickly the situation was spiraling out of control.

"You are so hot for me. Like a flash fire."

Something inside her was breaking—breaking all her control and shattering her best intentions. She had to find her balance, had to resist the siren pull of him on her soul and her body before it was too late.

Panic set in, demanded she slow this thing between them before she was completely lost, before she gave in and did exactly what she knew she shouldn't do. Before she lost herself.

She blurted the first thing that came to mind. "La Belle Amelie."

Alejandro's expression froze. A second later, his smile turned cold. "Yes, of course. Ask me about your hotel."

He didn't stop touching her, didn't give her a chance to react before he slipped a finger inside her, stroked her hot flesh. Sensation spun her higher, rocketed her toward the peak.

But Alejandro's heart was no longer in it. She could see the disconnect in his expression. Icy anger had been replaced by cool neutrality. He was completely unaffected while she was close to meltdown.

Why had she mentioned the hotel? Stupid, stupid, stupid.

"Stop," she said, fighting her body's reaction, fighting him.

"Are you certain?" His thumb moved faster against her sensitive flesh, sent pleasure spiking.

"Yes, stop," she gasped.

Too late. A wave of sensation crashed over her long-neglected senses, hurtling her into forgotten pleasure. Her body left her brain behind as she quivered and moaned in his arms.

Alejandro didn't stop touching her, kept the pleasure spiking and cresting. His mouth touched hers. Softly, sweetly, completely at odds with the look he'd given her when she mentioned the hotel.

What was she thinking to have said such a thing?

"Alejandro," she gasped when he nuzzled her ear, whispering something in Spanish. She had to explain, had to make him understand. "About the hotel—"

She felt him stiffen.

"*Sí*, the hotel," he said, pushing away from her suddenly. Water dripped from his tanned skin, glistened over the molded perfection of his lips. Every line of his face was set in a hard angle as he glared at her. "Would you care to ask me for something else before you allow me into your body? Name your price, Rebecca, for surely I am desperate for you now and will give you anything you wish."

Ice dripped from his words, freezing the languid warmth swimming in her veins.

"That's not what I meant—"

"No, of course not. You meant to ask for more. How often have you lain on your back to get what you want from a man, I wonder?"

Rebecca shoved at his chest, forcing him to let her go. She gripped the ladder to keep from sliding beneath the surface. Her body still tingled from his touch, and yet she'd never felt more cold and alone in her life.

"How can you be so cruel?" she asked. "I'm not a cheap whore—"

"No, you are actually quite expensive—"

"Stop interrupting me!" she shouted, uncaring who might hear or come running to see what was going on. "You push and push, Alejandro, and you have *no* idea what you're talking about." She sucked in a breath to stop her angry tears before rushing on. "You're a cruel, bitter man that no woman could *ever* love for very long! It's no wonder your wife left you after Anya died—" Rebecca slapped a hand over her mouth.

A muscle ticked in his jaw as he glared at her. And yet something in his hard stare had changed. There had been a moment, when she'd said it, that she would have sworn he flinched. That defeated look crossed his features again, but only for a second.

"Oh, God, I'm sorry. I didn't mean to say that."

"*Sí*, you said exactly what you wanted to say." He crowded

her against the ladder so suddenly she gasped. "And now I say to you that you are a whore who will sleep with anyone, tell any lies, in order to win. You and I are much alike in our willingness to do whatever it takes, *no?*"

Her chest rose and fell, her emotions on the edge of a precipice. "I am *nothing* like you."

"You only lie to yourself, Rebecca, because I know the truth." He leaned down until his breath was hot on her cheek. "Remember when you think to fool me again that I am twice as ruthless as you. I will *always* win."

Sadness gripped her as she looked at his proud, cold, hard features. He'd changed so much in five years. The life and spark of him was extinguished, leaving nothing but a shell. "How can you call it winning, Alejandro, if it makes you so miserable?"

Alejandro sat in the plush leather club chair and buckled his seat belt as the pilot announced they were next in line for take-off. Moments later the Ramirez jet lifted off, banking to the right to give him a spectacular view of the financial district and, far beyond, the residential section where his villa lay. Where Rebecca still slept.

Was it only three hours ago he'd held her in his arms and watched the ecstasy on her face when she'd shattered? *Dios*, in that moment he'd strongly considered forsaking his vow not to bed her. She was so vibrant, so alive and warm—she pulsed with life in his arms.

And he'd wanted to feel it with her. After his divorce, he'd tried to lose himself in a string of women, to forget what he'd lost when he'd lost his child. Every encounter had been empty, cold. He'd thought he would feel relief when it was over, but he'd felt nothing. *Nothing.*

His heart was frozen. He'd felt nothing since Anya died. Until Rebecca had walked into his house and glared at him with all the hurt and loneliness she'd ever felt shining in her eyes.

He wanted to ruin her. And he wanted to possess her. It made no sense, though he usually prided himself on making decisions based on sound judgment.

It was simply a physical need. He'd almost forgotten she had an ulterior motive until she made the mistake of mentioning the hotel. Another moment, another hot kiss, and he'd have been so deep inside her he'd still be entangled in bed with her now, instead of flying to Dubai to meet with the government officials holding up his construction.

The bell dinged to signal the jet had reached ten thousand feet, but he made no move to turn his phone back on or to power up his laptop. She'd asked why he was miserable. It had shocked him. He'd wanted to deny it, but he hadn't. He'd wanted to tell her she was terminated, to go back to New York and her life there. But the words hadn't come. And she hadn't moved, had merely clung to the ladder and stared at him with a pitying expression on her face.

Madre de Dios. He hadn't felt so exposed since Anya's doctors had stared at him with that same pitying expression.

He would not allow Rebecca to get inside his head. It shouldn't even be a possibility! No, what he had to do was becoming clear. He had to take her into his bed, had to dominate her as completely personally as he had professionally.

It was simply another layer to his revenge. He would bed her, let her think she had him exactly where she wanted him, that she could manipulate him into giving her back her company, and then he would destroy her utterly.

Alejandro accepted a mineral water from a flight attendant as he opened his laptop. Decision made, he already felt a world better. Rebecca Layton would never defeat him. Never again.

Rebecca was quite relieved she didn't have to face Alejandro over a breakfast table, though she was somewhat surprised to learn he'd flown to Dubai. But now—oh, thankfully—*now* she didn't have to look at him and know he'd touched her so intimately, made her want to do things with him that in her right mind she'd never do again. She knew she couldn't allow her sympathy for his loss, for the pain and anger she saw in his eyes, to divert her from her goals. She *had* to keep Layton International safe and whole, and she had to find a way to get it back. It was all that mattered.

He'd left her no instructions while he was gone, had not revealed a single element to his plan for her company. So until the man fired her, or she convinced him to let her buy back her stock, she had a business to run.

Rebecca frowned at her reflection. After last night she had no illusions Alejandro would ever allow her to buy back her stock. The only way to retrieve Layton International would be if Alejandro suddenly found himself in trouble and needed to sell some assets. And, according to all her contacts, that wasn't happening. Ramirez Enterprises was a juggernaut. Not only that, but Alejandro would sell her company piece by piece if forced. He would never allow it to be bought whole, and certainly not by her.

Yet she couldn't simply give up and cower like a whipped puppy.

After a quick shower and something to eat, she phoned Roger Cahill again. She still needed to know what had happened five years ago, if there was even the smallest chance she could prove to Alejandro that she hadn't stolen his deal.

"Becca," Roger said when his secretary put her through. "I was just thinking about you. It's been a long time."

"Yes. Thank you for the flowers you sent to Dad's funeral."

He cleared his throat. "Jackson was a good man. I'm sorry I won't get to play a round of golf with him at St. Andrews this year."

"I know he would have enjoyed it."

"You mustn't blame yourself for losing Layton International," he said, launching straight into the heart of the matter. "When Jackson came to me, I told him it was a bad idea to stake so much on those Thailand resorts."

Rebecca's mouth twisted. If only the bank that had loaned him the money had felt the same. The bank they'd usually dealt with had refused, but her father found a bank that had been willing to take the risk. Too late now. "Yes, well, he loved to take on new projects, and he was certain he had a winner."

Roger cleared his throat again. "So, what can I help you with, love?"

Though everyone had told her Ramirez Enterprises was invulnerable, she asked Roger if he knew of any weaknesses in Alejandro's company.

"I understand there may be some trouble in Dubai," Roger said. "Rumor has it they could lose the property they've sunk so much into. I have another client interested in property there, and they've heard rumblings."

Rebecca tapped her chin with a fingernail. "There *is* an accusation of impropriety in the permits process, right? Do you know anything about that?"

Roger sighed. "There's no evidence to support the charge thus far, but I know the man himself took the corporate jet over this morning. It must be something to get Ramirez to fly in."

He told her a few other things, about permits and engineers, architects, the Emir and a relative of some sort. Nothing specific, but things that could add up to trouble for a hotel chain trying to build a new resort. She'd fielded similar problems in the past, so understood both the import of the issues and the hassle of bureaucratic red tape.

"You'll let me know if you hear anything?" he finished.

"I'll keep my ears open." After what Alejandro had done to her, she refused to feel guilty about it. If there was even a remote chance she could wrest Layton International from him, she had to take it. Her father would have demanded no less.

An image of Alejandro talking about his daughter in the past tense sprang to mind. *No.* No room for weakness. This was business, not personal.

"I'd appreciate that," he replied. "We're digging, looking for an Achilles' heel, but so far there's nothing to report."

"Roger," Rebecca said, when they were wrapping up the conversation. "I wanted to ask you something else before you go."

"Shoot, love."

"Why'd you pull out of the Ramirez deal five years ago?"

He hesitated a moment before speaking. "We decided it wasn't a good investment after all."

"But you financed *our* South American acquisitions."

"The stake was less than Ramirez required."

Rebecca's temples throbbed. "But you didn't pull out of Ramirez because of us, right?"

He sighed. "Your father thought it was a bad bet, love, and he didn't want to do business with us if we took the risk. Ramirez had a reputation as a risk-taker, you see. He was unorthodox, and several of our investors were already wary. Your father's opinion simply helped put the nail in the coffin."

Rebecca's heart pinched. Yes, her father had been at the top of his game then. He'd had a lot of influence in the industry and would have been listened to with the reverence of an Oracle. She drew a breath into her painfully tight chest. "All right, thanks."

"Ring me if you hear anything about Dubai."

"I will."

They said their goodbyes, and Rebecca laid her cell phone on the desk before leaning back in her chair. Icy dread dripped down her spine. It just might be her fault that Alejandro had lost his backing after all.

Oh, God.

In a moment of weakness she'd called her mother when she'd been sitting in the Madrid airport five years ago, her eyes puffy and red, her throat sore. She'd had no one else to talk to. She'd been stunned, hurt, humiliated. She could still see the severe-looking wedding coordinator, with her folder and her samples, asking for the groom and saying, *"Gracias,* I will wait for him to return. His fiancée is anxious to begin the plans, yes?"

Ridiculously, she'd hoped for a mother-daughter connection, some sage advice. How she'd forgotten for those few moments that her mother was as shallow as a puddle, she'd never know. Amelie Layton had made sympathetic noises, but she'd spent more time talking to her dog than she had offering advice.

Later, Rebecca had realized she'd just needed to say it aloud to someone. Once she'd confessed, she'd had the good sense to regret it. She'd made her mother promise not to say anything to her father—a "just us girls" pact. After the incident with Parker Gaines—hired by her father to prove that she was a weak, vulnerable female—she didn't want to give him any further evidence of her "feminine weakness". She had to be strong, had to prove she could run Layton International someday.

Since it wasn't like her father to keep quiet about her personal life—especially something negative—she'd breathed a sigh of relief when he'd never said anything. Her mother, bless her, had kept the secret. Indeed, thinking back on it, her father's dislike of Alejandro seemed to have come later. Rebecca thought the explanation was simple rivalry; Ramirez Enterprises' influence and reach had grown while the Layton star was sinking. It'd been hard for her father to accept as the years went by and their positions were reversed.

Fury boiled over. She wanted the truth, no matter how difficult. She stabbed the number of her mother's cell phone.

"Did you tell Dad about Alejandro Ramirez?" she demanded, when Amelie Layton answered.

"Is that any way to talk to your mother, *ma belle*?" Amelie's voice trailed off as she shushed her dogs. "I may have. I can't remember."

CHAPTER FIVE

SEVERAL days of fighting with government officials had put Alejandro in a foul mood, especially since nothing was solved yet. Worse, his parents' anniversary party was tonight at the Villa de Musica. As much as he'd like to stay home and sit on the terrace with a glass of sherry, he had to put in an appearance.

The plane had landed half an hour ago. How his chauffeur had got them through the mess that was Madrid traffic and to his villa in that little amount of time was nothing short of a miracle. One of these days he would put in that helicopter pad he kept thinking about. As his business spread, so did the necessity for trips abroad.

He usually kept a tuxedo on the jet, along with several suits and other things he might need, but his personal assistant had somehow sent everything to the cleaners without first rotating in a fresh supply. He had barely an hour to change and be on his way to the hotel.

Alejandro ripped at his tie and tossed it on the bed. Señora Flores had laid out a fresh shirt for him, and his tux was hanging nearby, ready to go. Why must he suffer through these damnable parties every year? On the outside, Carmen and Juan Ramirez seemed the happy couple. They played it up quite well, in fact, except for a few public incidents Alejandro didn't like to recall in detail.

But Alejandro knew the truth. So did his sister, Valencia—which was why she always found an excuse to stay in Paris with her husband—and Roberto before he had died.

Juan enjoyed his various mistresses *du jour*, and Carmen enjoyed her society committees as well as a little too much wine. Still, it mostly worked for them, even if there were moments of drama. Carmen forcing a mistress out of Juan's city apartment naked, for instance. Juan cutting off Carmen's credit line the moment she went abroad on a shopping trip.

It was always something. As if Alejandro needed more confirmation that being chained to another person for life was bad. He'd tried it once—albeit without the drama and emotion—and that was enough. Emotionless or not, marriage wasn't for him. Sometimes he thought it might be nice to have more children, but his sister's children would inherit the business when it was time. He did not need to risk the heartbreak that marrying and having a child could bring ever again.

He finished inserting the studs into his shirt and sleeves and went to work on the tie. After three attempts he was ready to ring for Señora Flores—except this was her night off and she wasn't here.

Swearing, he grabbed his jacket and headed for the limo. The doors to the terrace were open as he passed through the Great Room. A female voice drifted to his ears and he changed direction. Something kicked him low in the gut when he emerged onto the terrace and saw her. It should surprise him, the physical jolt, but it didn't. Not any longer, and not since he'd decided to do something about it.

Rebecca sat at the broad table under the arbor, the last rays of sunlight turning her hair to molten gold. She had her computer open, a pen in her mouth, and a cell phone to her ear. She did not hear him approach, so he took time to study her profile. Her golden hair was unadorned, falling to a point just below her shoulders in soft waves. She'd tucked it behind her ear, and a small diamond winked in her lobe. Her legs were crossed at the ankles as she leaned forward, concentrating on her screen and on the person on the other end of the phone. She wore a short tropical-print skirt. He let his gaze caress the length of those long legs before traveling up her body, over the white tank top molding her breasts, coming to rest on her face.

He was going to enjoy taking her to bed. His groin tightened in anticipation, his body remembering how it'd been with her all those years ago.

Dios, in spite of everything she fired his blood, made him burn to possess her.

"Do you have those projections?" she said to the person on the other end, and a jolt of awareness shot through him. He'd once had a liaison with an accountant, but his usual companions were actresses or models or idle heiresses. Rebecca, for all her pampering, knew her way around the business world. He liked that about her.

Oh, yes, he'd made the right decision. He was going to thoroughly enjoy her before his revenge was complete.

She glanced sideways, her eyes widening when she saw him.

"Yes, thanks, John. Get me those numbers as soon as you can. I'll talk to you later." She set the phone down and offered him a wary smile. "How was your trip?"

"Tiring," he said. He held the tie up. "Can you fix this?"

He thought vaguely that he ought to hate asking her, that he was merely confirming her opinion he was more suited to a bullring than a boardroom, but he was too irritated at the prospect of the party to care.

If he'd expected a superior look from the spoiled woman sitting in his courtyard, he didn't get it.

"I can try," she said, standing, biting her lip between her teeth as she took the tie and slipped it around his neck. Her fingers were cool where they brushed his skin, and yet a spark of awareness lingered where she'd touched. Her sweet scent stole into his nostrils. He couldn't understand why, of all the women in the world, he currently wanted this one. But he intended to have her. Now that he'd decided bedding her fit into his plans, there was no need to wait. Tonight, one way or the other, she would be his.

Awareness of her crept through him, made him hard. What would she think if she realized he was on the edge of burying himself inside her?

Her gaze never wavered from his throat as she worked, almost as if she feared what she might see if she looked up at him. *Sí, be afraid of me, amor. I intend to possess you, to ruin you. You are finished and don't even know it.*

"Did you miss me?" he teased, his sensual tone at odds with his dark thoughts.

Her brows shot up, her expression a strange mixture of disbelief and—was it guilt? Interesting. He filed it away for future contemplation.

"You're kidding, right?" Her voice broke at the last. She refocused on his tie, twisting and tugging.

Alejandro pressed his advantage. "Perhaps I am not. Did you not enjoy our time together in the pool, *bella*?"

She yanked the tie too tight, nearly choking him, then jerked it loose and swore before trying again. "I've forgotten all about it," she said. "It didn't mean a thing."

Her red face and clumsy fingers told him differently.

"I wanted to taste you," he said, just to see what she would do. "To lay you back and dip my tongue into your sweetness. Are you still sweet, Rebecca?"

Her chest heaved, once. She bent her head lower, her lip undergoing punishment from her teeth as she concentrated. He wanted to suck that lip between his own, make love to it until she was pliant, begging him to move on to another delicious part of her.

How could he want this woman he hated? He didn't know,

but *maldito sea*, since he'd freed himself to do so he could think of almost nothing else.

She tugged the tie and stepped back with a triumphant expression. "There—all done."

He touched the knot, tested it for tightness. *"Gracias."* Then he closed the distance between them, giving her no quarter. It was not in his nature to prevaricate once he'd decided he wanted something. "Would you like that, *querida*? Would you like me to taste you?"

She made a choked sound, slipped past him and fiddled with the briefcase she'd left open on the table. "Stop, I don't want to hear it."

"Are you certain? Imagine it…imagine the ecstasy."

Her eyes closed. "No."

"Do you remember the first time?"

He thought she wouldn't respond, but she nodded—just a quick dip of her chin.

"It could be like that again." *Dios*, he wanted it. Right now, this second, he wanted it to be that way just once more. To forget why he had to hate her, why he had to destroy her. To just feel the good things again.

She snapped her laptop closed and stuffed it into her briefcase before glaring at him with fiery blue eyes. "That's impossible, Alejandro. The first time we were together, I stupidly thought I was the only woman in your life. You let me find out in the most humiliating way possible that I wasn't the only one—or even the primary one."

He recognized that she needed to cloak herself in her mantle of righteous anger so she wouldn't feel the pull of desire between them. But he did not intend to allow her that comfort. "Anyone can hire a wedding planner, Rebecca. That particular one was hired by my father, with the express purpose of chasing you away and pushing me into a marriage I had not agreed to."

She looked a bit shocked—and very doubtful. "Why should I believe you? And why, if that's the case, didn't you tell me five years ago?"

His laugh was bitter. He snapped it off in midstream and pinned her with a hard stare. "Because you were a coward. You ran away like a petulant child. What was I to do? Chase you back to New York and force you to listen to me?"

Rebecca's heart skipped a beat. This was not what she'd expected tonight. She'd been working with her chief financial officer on some projections for the Kai Lani chain of resorts, and fielding calls from her human resources director about Ramirez's plans and how it would affect jobs. Except she didn't yet know what Alejandro had in mind, so she'd had to put the woman off with vague platitudes about the future. Which had angered and frustrated her. And reminded her how precarious her position was.

She hadn't expected Alejandro to return in the midst of it all, and she certainly hadn't expected *this*. A discussion of their painful past was the last thing she'd have thought was possible tonight. Yet here he was, telling her it was his father who'd sent the wedding planner and that it had been deliberate.

She could hardly wrap her mind around it. Worse, she feared he was right in at least one respect: she'd run away because she couldn't take it, because she'd already shown poor judgment once before. She hadn't trusted herself to make a sound decision. She'd needed distance, time, space to think.

She'd got her time, and plenty of it, hadn't she? "You should have made me understand," she forced from her dry throat. Could it possibly be true that his family had wanted to manipulate him into the wedding? That his father would have done such a thing?

Why not? Her own father had gone to extraordinary

lengths, hiring Parker to insinuate himself into her life, hadn't he? And all to prove a point to her. A painful point about her own vulnerability and neediness. Rebecca shivered as she stared at Alejandro. He was fully capable of lying to her in order to make her feel worse than she already did about what had happened between them.

He stood before her, devilishly dark and deliciously handsome in his custom-fit tuxedo. His skin had darkened beneath the hot Arabian sun over the last few days, setting off the lightning-silver of his eyes. Eyes that speared her with scorn.

"Perhaps you should have *trusted* me," he bit out. A second later, he raked a hand through his dark hair, swore in Spanish. "As if it would have mattered. No, your plan was always to ruin me, to take what you could and destroy Ramirez Enterprises in the process. You nearly succeeded."

Her throat ached with denials. But what was the point? Though her mother couldn't say definitively whether or not she'd told Rebecca's father about the aborted affair, it was still Jackson Layton's threat to take his business elsewhere that had cost Alejandro the deal he'd worked so hard to procure. Like it or not, the Laytons *were* responsible.

But she could defend *her* motives without hesitation. "You haven't proved anything to me, Alejandro. My only plan when I came to the Villa de Musica was to see the restoration. I didn't plan to meet you, and I certainly didn't plan to fall in love with you. It would have been so much easier if I'd never met you."

Wasn't that the truth? Five long years, and she'd never really succeeded in forgetting him. Before he'd summoned her to Madrid she'd still been blissfully able to deceive herself that the years had done their work. But she hadn't forgotten after all, and every day she spent with him only made the memories more painful.

"Yes, it is hard to look a man in the eye before you cut him down," he said, more to himself than to her, glancing at his watch. "I have no time for this now, but be assured I have no need to lie. It matters not whether you believe me."

"Then why did you say it?" she said, her throat tight. What if he was telling her the truth? What if she'd been as mistaken about his engagement as he had about her motives?

He shrugged. "Because I am tired of your self-righteousness."

Rebecca blinked. "Self-righteousness?" Who was he kidding? He was the most self-righteous man on the planet. She snatched up the folder she'd been working on. She couldn't deal with this right now. "I'm going inside now. Have a nice time."

Alejandro caught her arm as she turned away. "You're coming with me."

"What? Where?" she stammered. He was wearing a tuxedo, not a casual pair of trousers and a shirt. Wherever he was going, she couldn't show up in a tank top and wispy skirt. "I have work to do. I can't go with you."

"This is not a request, Rebecca. You will come. Now."

"I don't have anything suitable to wear," she said, thrusting her chin up and stating the obvious. Or the not so obvious if the way he looked at her was any indication.

"There is a boutique in the hotel. You will buy a dress. Now, come—we are out of time."

"But, Alejandro, really—"

"Need I remind you I am the one in control here?" he ground out, slamming the door on her protest. "You have no choice, Rebecca."

She gripped her briefcase, her knuckles whitening. She had an urge to close her eyes and count to a hundred before speaking, the way her mother had used to make her do when she was upset and crying over something. It had worked to calm her down when she was ten, though it had also made her feel unimportant and unloved.

Ah, but you are unloved. This man does not love you, never did. Never could and never will.

She concentrated on his cold, handsome features. Not that she wanted him to love her now. No, that desire was in the past. This man was nothing like the Alejandro she'd once loved.

But he's still inside there.

No.

She closed the door firmly on such thoughts. "Very well," she said, as coolly as she could manage given the erratic beating of her heart. "If you will allow me to drop these things in my room?"

His nod was brief. Arrogant and sure. She itched to smack him. Instead, she put her things away and returned to join him beside the limousine waiting out front. He held the door open for her, then followed her inside. A moment later they were being whisked through the darkening streets of Madrid.

"We're going where?" Rebecca's heart climbed into her throat, thrumming in panic. His parents' anniversary party? But *why*? She closed her eyes, swallowed. *Oh, God.* She'd never met his parents—had, in fact, no idea what his relationship with them was like. He'd spoken of a brother and sister, she remembered that much. His brother had died tragically only a few months before she'd met Alejandro. He'd never talked of it, and she hadn't asked because their relationship had been so new.

But would his parents know who *she* was? That she was the woman he'd been sleeping with while he was engaged to someone else? How could she possibly show up at their special party tonight and hold her head up?

Alejandro glanced up from his PDA, his expression showing he hadn't missed the note of alarm threading through her voice. "The party is a grand affair, Rebecca. No one will notice another guest. Besides, I am the one paying for it."

It was true she'd envisioned some sort of small, lavish dinner party instead of a "grand affair", but the idea of several hundred people at this event did nothing to quell her uneasiness. His parents would still be there, and if she were with Alejandro she'd still have to meet them. Perhaps that was his plan: *Mom, Dad, meet Rebecca Layton—the slut who stole my deal and tried to ruin me five years ago.*

But that wasn't the source of her deepest anxiety. No, if she were brutally honest with herself, most of her unease was brought on by the proximity of the man sitting across from her, his legs sprawled casually to either side of hers. Long lashes shadowed his eyes as he concentrated on the screen of his PDA. Tanned fingers manipulated the keys deftly, sending and receiving information at the touch of a few buttons.

He'd talked of tasting her. She'd thought of almost nothing else since.

Memories of long ago crashed into her mind with alarming regularity. Sexual memories. Of Alejandro's skin against hers, of his hot tongue slicking a path down her body, finding her—

Rebecca pressed two fingers to her temples, willing the erotic images out of her head. She had to focus, had to prepare herself for whatever she would find at this party. Maybe no one would notice her—or maybe it really was another facet of Alejandro's plan to humiliate her in front of as many people as possible. Why else had he ordered her to come with him?

He couldn't know how tormented she was, simply looking at him, how part of her wanted to reach out and find the man he used to be beneath the hard exterior. How she ached to touch his smooth skin, to trace her fingers along the seam of his lips, to breathe in the warm scent of him the way she'd once done. To see him actually smile at her with warmth.

Stop, just stop. He hates you.

When the limousine pulled into the circular drive of the

Villa de Musica, Rebecca wanted to melt into the plush leather seat. A horde of photographers clustered together near the entrance, snapping away as people emerged from the cars that crawled in a steady stream through the driveway.

She wiped clammy palms down her skirt, tried to straighten it out as best as possible. What would she look like beside Alejandro in the papers, dressed like a beach bum?

Alejandro slipped his phone into his pocket and frowned at her. "There is nothing to be afraid of," he said.

She tilted her chin up, reached down deep for her inner socialite. Her mother would expect nothing less than total poise, regardless of the situation. "I'm not afraid. I'm just not prepared. You gave me no warning."

"Sometimes the best things in life are spontaneous, yes?"

She wasn't sure if he was joking or needling her. The car ahead of them disgorged its passengers. A woman stopped and posed, tossing long dark hair over her shoulders and tilting her hips from side to side. Flashes burst into life, lighting the entry as if it had been pitch-black before.

Alejandro swore. He stabbed the intercom button and snapped out an order in Spanish. The limo didn't stop when their turn came but continued through the drive and out to the street.

"I forgot about the paparazzi. We'll use the back entrance."

"Won't a few of them be stationed back there for just that purpose?"

He shrugged. "*Sí*, but my security is very thorough."

Rebecca let out her breath. "Thank you," she said.

"It is not for you," he said curtly. "I have no wish to answer questions tonight."

She crossed her arms and willed away the stab of hurt. Of course he hadn't ordered the car to go around to the back in order to spare her any embarrassment. Was she an idiot? No, the more pain he could cause her, the better. Worse, she actually understood it. If her father hadn't pressured Roger into backing out of the deal, what else might Alejandro have accomplished?

Rebecca studied the hotel as they snaked around behind it. The Villa de Musica was one of the grander buildings in Madrid. It had once belonged to a famous opera singer. It had been sold over the years, falling into a state of shabby decline before being rescued by Alejandro and restored to its glory days. She hadn't been inside since she'd left his suite five years ago.

How would she feel walking inside, remembering? She would soon find out.

The limo slipped behind a security barrier. Moments later someone popped open the door and they rushed into a small service entrance at the rear of the hotel.

The hall was narrow, and she had no choice but to follow Alejandro as he worked his way through the labyrinth. He ushered her into an elevator. A minute later the doors slid open and they were hurrying down another hall. Alejandro stopped and keyed in a code on a pad beside a door. So he'd gone high-tech in the last five years. Interesting.

Rebecca stumbled to a halt behind him as the door swung open. *The* suite. The one he'd lived in five years ago, because he'd sunk everything he had into the hotel. It wasn't the first place they had made love, but it was the location where she'd felt like she'd shared a home with him. She'd been staying in the luxurious private suite on the top floor, with its own pool and rooftop terrace, but this suite was smaller, more private, and they'd retreated here often. Eventually she had checked out of her room and moved into his.

"I'll have one of the saleswomen bring up some things," Alejandro said, pulling out his phone. "You can get dressed and come downstairs when you're ready."

She dragged her gaze from the door to the bedroom, forced

herself to focus on what he was saying. To breathe normally. *In. Out. In. Out.*

"Fine," she said evenly, determined not to let him see how affected she was by being back in this room with him. She managed to stroll over to the couch, sink down on it and cross her legs casually.

He finished calling the boutique, then turned to her. His mouth snapped shut, whatever he was about to say forgotten. He usually moved with the easy grace of a panther, but now he took a halting step forward. Stopped. Shook his head and scrubbed a hand through his dark hair.

She started to ask him what was wrong, but a memory hurtled into her brain and her mouth went slack. This couch. Him. The two of them. Nothing between them but sweat, passionate words, breathy moans.

The heat in his gaze told her he was remembering it too. It shocked her, the raw primal urge she saw in his face, and it compelled her. She wanted him. Oh, God, how she wanted him. The only time she'd ever felt truly cherished was with him. It was everything she could do not to rise, go to him, pull his head down to hers. Try to recapture that feeling.

She closed her eyes, swallowed. Willed the memory away: the scents, tastes and sounds of it. It was too real, too painful.

The door clicked quietly and her eyes shot open. But there was no saleswoman arriving with dresses. The room was empty and she was alone.

CHAPTER SIX

WHAT was wrong with him? Why had he fled the suite like a bull was shadowing his heels, running him to ground? He'd stayed there dozens of times since she'd left. Hundreds of times. He'd even taken other women to bed there, in an effort to erase her from his memory. He'd been positive he'd done it too—until he'd turned around and seen her on the couch.

He should have left her in the villa and ignored the dark demon urging him to bring her along tonight. It would have been easier. And made more sense.

Alejandro stalked into the hotel offices and went over some paperwork the manager had been asking him to approve. But he kept seeing Rebecca, her arms crossed beneath her breasts, her legs so long and bare in her little skirt. Superimposed over the picture of her sitting there tonight was a picture of her on the same couch, beneath him, naked and writhing and *begging*.

Madre de Dios, how much could a man take?

"Alejandro, please, I love you. Please, before I die. Please, please, please, I need you…"

He'd obliged her, of course, but not before making them both crazy with need. What would have happened had he done what he wanted tonight? Had he walked over there and stripped her naked? Would he be lost in her right now?

Sí, without a doubt.

He shouldn't have brought her up here. It hadn't been his plan. Until the flashbulbs had gone off and he had registered the alarm on Rebecca's face. He didn't know why he'd felt compelled to order the driver to the back, but he'd done it before thinking about it. He should have let her face the cameras in her casual clothes, let her feel the embarrassment. Except it was his doing she was here tonight, and he'd felt obligated to protect her.

He grabbed a pen and signed off on the paperwork. After he left the office, it took him nearly three quarters of an hour to get to the ballroom because he kept running into people who needed his time or attention. A cabinet minister, a senior-ranking diplomat, a wealthy diamond merchant, an actress he'd once bedded—the last was particularly difficult to extract himself from. She was beautiful, sleek and expensive, in a sheer designer gown that left no doubt about the assets underneath the material—and she left him completely cold.

He needed to find Rebecca. He was starting to feel just a little bit guilty he'd stayed away so long. She would have had to enter the packed room alone, not knowing anyone and not speaking the language. Of course nearly everyone also spoke English these days, so she would not find it difficult to converse. But he should have been with her nevertheless. Easing her into this situation didn't mean he was going soft, or that he was giving up his plans for her. On the contrary, the more relaxed he made her, the more devastating it would be when he threw her out with nothing.

He accepted a glass of champagne from a tray and idly surveyed the crowd. His mother stood near the bar, surrounded by women. He went over to give her a kiss.

"Alejandro, my love! I feared you would not make it back in time."

"I would never miss your party, *Madre*."

Carmen Ramirez pursed her lips. "Unlike Valencia. She canceled yet again—can you believe it?"

"Where is Father?" Alejandro asked, unwilling to indulge a mini-tantrum against his sister for even a second. He understood why Valencia canceled each year. His presence would have to be enough for them both. Thankfully, Valencia had finally given up apologizing to him for making him bear the burden alone.

Carmen waved a bejeweled hand as she took a sip of champagne. "He has found a woman to dance with, I believe."

At that moment the crowd parted, clearing a path to the floor. Juan Ramirez embraced a sleek woman in a shimmering midnight-blue gown, staring down at her with such intent that Alejandro decided to intervene before the evening digressed into a very public Ramirez family drama.

He excused himself from his mother, who had already turned back to her friends, and threaded his way through the guests. Juan swayed back and forth, his attention solely on the woman in his arms.

Her back was to Alejandro, but he had to acknowledge that if her front was as enticing as her back he couldn't blame Juan for his interest. Blonde hair was swept into a pile on her head, revealing a slender neck, bare shoulders and a plunging dress that stopped just short of the curve of her buttocks. Long legs seemed to go on forever, accentuated by four-inch heels.

Interest stirred, surprising him. And relieving him. So he *could* feel desire for a woman other than Rebecca Layton. *Gracias, Dios.* When he tired of her, it would be simple to move on to someone else.

But right now it was his father's interest that most concerned him. Juan's hand rested on the smooth flesh of the woman's back, its darkness in contrast to the pearlescent sheen of her skin.

Ten more minutes and Alejandro would have been too late. Juan would have whisked her away to somewhere more private, party and wife be damned. His father looked up, frowning when he caught sight of Alejandro. He bent to say something in the delicate shell of the woman's ear. She stopped moving to the music, turned as if startled.

Alejandro stumbled to a halt as her blue eyes collided with his. Shock, fury and lust blazed to life all at once, roaring up inside him like an inferno. One word echoed through his brain: *mine*.

He closed the distance between them and yanked her from his father's lecherous fingers. He barely registered the gasps around them as she stumbled into him. He caught her around the waist, steadying her. His fingertips brushed the warm silky skin of her exposed back. Inexplicable fury coursed though him and he aimed it at the easiest target.

"Attempting to buy another hotel with your body, Rebecca?" he grated, as much to mask the force of his desire as to hurt her for making him want her like this. Without *reason*, without *sense*.

She jerked away from him, her expression caving. "You bastard!" she whispered fiercely.

"Alejandro, you will apologize to the lady," his father said, disapproval drawing his brows together in sharp slashes. "Your mother would be ashamed."

Before he could speak, Rebecca turned to his father and smiled. The corners of her mouth wavered. "Thank you, Señor Ramirez, but it's not necessary. Your son and I are old enemies, I'm afraid. We hurl words like daggers."

"But this is no way to treat one's guest," Juan insisted. "My son was not raised this way, *señorita*. I apologize for his rudeness."

She refused to look at him as she spoke to his father. "I'm afraid I bring out the worst in him."

His father looked aghast. "Alejandro, how is this possible? This lady is so charming, so lovely—"

"As are all ladies to you, Father." *Maldito sea*, the old reprobate was unbelievable. "I think Mother is near the bar. Since it is your anniversary, perhaps you should ask *her* for a dance."

Juan looked as if he would argue, but he finally nodded. "*Sí*, you are correct. Dear lady," he continued, taking Rebecca's hand and kissing it, "I hope you will enjoy yourself at our party tonight. We shall see you at our table for the toast, yes?"

"*Gracias,*" Rebecca said. "I would be honored."

The band began to play a new song as Juan walked away. Before Rebecca could escape, Alejandro pulled her into his arms. The people who'd stopped to listen began to mingle again.

"Don't touch me," she said. "Just let me go and I'll leave."

"You won't," he said, drawing her in close, fitting her against his body. She felt so good against him. Smelled good. He concentrated on tempering his body's reaction to her. *Later.* "The night is far from over."

Her palms rested on his chest, but she refused to meet his eyes. Instead, she studied his shirtfront. "I get it, Alejandro. You wanted to humiliate me by bringing me here tonight. Now that you've succeeded just let me go. I've had enough."

He hadn't brought her for that reason, but there was no sense in denying it. She would not believe him. And what could he tell her anyway? That he'd brought her with him because he'd had an impulse to do so? "How did you end up dancing with my father?"

Her lashes lifted, and he was momentarily stunned by the sheen of moisture in her eyes. She blinked and looked away again. "He looks like you. I introduced myself and asked where I could find you. He said he would take me to you, but we ended up here."

Yes, he didn't doubt it for a moment. His father could not resist a beautiful woman.

"But then, of course," she continued with a half-choked laugh, "I realized that I could implement my diabolical plan to sleep my way to another hotel. I was just about to claim my victim when you intervened. I'm sure I could have gotten several hotels out of him, assuming he owns a single one."

Alejandro blew out a breath. For once he had been wrong about her. But just this once. "I should not have said that."

She didn't look at him. "You shouldn't have, but you'd do it again in a heartbeat. You insist on believing the worst about me."

It was true. Part of him always wanted to stomp on her spirit. He wanted to grind her beneath his heels, make her feel every moment of every day how wrong she'd been to steal from him. She'd forced him into a choice he should have never made, *would* never have made if she hadn't left and ripped away whatever happiness he'd felt with her.

And yet he was drawn to her. Could still feel sympathy for her. It was a paradox he didn't understand. "We will not talk about this tonight," he declared. He didn't want to think too deeply about his feelings for this woman right now. He wanted to savor her body, that was all. No feelings, no past. Just heat and passion and the sweetness of release.

Her laugh was bitter. "No, of course not. God forbid that you might actually be forced to rethink your opinion of me. I wasn't seducing your father, but naturally the same can't be said of how far I will go with you, right? And you'll allow nothing to contradict that opinion, so we won't even discuss it."

"What could you possibly say to change my mind?" he bit out. "There is nothing you can say, no proof you can offer, that changes what you did to me."

Her throat moved as she swallowed. "No, I can't prove my innocence," she said softly, her voice heavy with emotion.

People began to clap politely. It took a moment before

Alejandro realized the music had stopped. But he and Rebecca were still locked tightly together, their gazes tangled. Hers was sad, beseeching—disappointed?

He stepped back as if she were a live wire, forced his hands to his sides. "You cannot prove it because you are guilty, Rebecca. Cease trying to make me doubt what I know to be true. It will not work. We can never go back to those days before you betrayed me."

Rebecca sipped champagne and chatted with a woman who was the wife of a Spanish television star. But her attention wasn't on the woman as much as it was on the man across from her. Alejandro was so achingly handsome it hurt. And so remote it chilled her.

From the moment they'd left the dance floor and come to the head table he'd been closed off and cold. Of course he would never believe she hadn't been the one to betray him. She knew that. But being here now, in the place where she'd shared so much with him, her emotions were skewed and raw.

From the moment he'd left her in the suite she'd been on edge. She felt like an exposed nerve, reacting to every stimulus, aching with pain, wanting to escape. She'd actually hoped to see approval in his eyes when he'd first seen her at the party. The dress she'd chosen from the few the salesgirl had brought fit like it was custom-designed for her. The shoes were exquisite. A quick visit from one of the salon's stylists, and her hair and makeup were perfect. Looking at herself in the mirror, she'd never have believed that a half hour before she'd been more suited for an evening by the beach rather than a formal gathering at a posh hotel.

She'd swallowed her trepidation and gone downstairs, but Alejandro had been nowhere to be found. Seeing Juan Ramirez had been a relief. The man was a carbon copy of his son—just older and more distinguished-looking. He'd shown no signs of recognizing her name when she had introduced herself. She'd believed he would whisk her to Alejandro. It was only after he'd pulled her into his arms and started swaying that she realized she'd been deceived, that Juan was a bit of a Casanova. Rather than be impolite, she'd danced. And of course Alejandro had chosen that moment to appear. The universe had a bizarre sense of humor.

Now Alejandro sat beside his mother, listening politely while she talked about something Rebecca couldn't understand. *Complained* about something, more likely, judging from the expression on her face and the speed with which she spoke. Her champagne sloshed over the rim of the glass she clutched; she didn't seem to notice. Alejandro calmly took it and put it down, away from her. A moment later she flagged down a waiter and snagged a fresh glass.

Rebecca didn't miss the frown Alejandro gave his mother as she quaffed most of the liquid in one go. Juan Ramirez chose that moment to appear, and Carmen shot up out of her seat. She would have fallen down again had Alejandro not bolted up and steadied her.

The table grew quiet as Carmen railed at her husband. Rebecca might not understand Spanish, but she could tell the conversation wasn't a pleasant one. Juan refused to look at her. A second later she lunged. Alejandro stopped her, caught her close as she began to sob. Juan pushed his son out of the way and put his arms around his wife. Oddly enough, Carmen didn't shove him away. She clutched his lapels and buried her face against his chest, her shoulders shaking as she cried.

Alejandro sank into his chair, a stony expression on his face.

The woman beside Rebecca whispered, "My husband tells me that Señor Ramirez has been seeing Isabella Ayala. She is a young actress, very promising."

Rebecca blinked at the woman, her heart slowing to a crawl in her chest.

"No, no." She patted Rebecca's hand. "Juan—not Alejandro, darling. It is clear that Alejandro is smitten with you, though it is too bad about his parents." She tsked. "This one is far more serious than usual, though. He may even leave her for this woman. Or so my husband says. I am not so sure, however."

A few moments later Rebecca murmured an excuse and rose from her chair. Alejandro's face was frozen in a blank mask as he watched his parents. He glanced over at her and she offered him a sympathetic smile. His expression didn't change.

She hurried to the ladies' room, needing to be alone for a minute or two. She just wanted to sit and breathe and be surrounded by muted noise rather than this discordant mix of voices, clanging dishes and music. She wanted to think without watching Alejandro and wondering at every turn what he was feeling inside.

Rebecca sank onto one of the plush benches and gazed at her reflection. Her table companion, whose name she'd forgotten almost as soon as they were introduced, had been wrong, or was just being nice, about Alejandro being smitten with her. But her heart ached at the look of helplessness on his face while he dealt with his parents. Oh, he masked it well, but she saw the pain and anger he tried to hide.

She didn't *want* to feel sympathy for him. She simply couldn't afford it. She had to be hard, cold, ruthless—just like him. Layton International depended on it.

Rebecca touched up her lipstick, smoothed her dress, and returned to the party. Alejandro's parents were gone now, but Alejandro stood with a strikingly beautiful woman, his hand on her arm, his head bent close to hers as he talked. Her face seemed a little tight as she took a step away and disappeared into the crowd. Not a romantic moment, then. Rebecca didn't want to analyze the relief that washed through her at the realization.

Alejandro whirled, catching sight of her. He came and took her arm, tucked it into his. "We're going now," he said in clipped tones.

"Fine with me," she replied, her pulse thumping. She didn't like seeing him this way, didn't like the way his emotions played over his face in the rare moments when he struggled for control. It forced her to see him as human and vulnerable, reminded her that she'd once loved him with every last breath in her body.

They left the hotel by the front entrance this time. The paparazzi snapped photos and called out to him, but he ignored them. Soon they were in the car, moving down the drive and out into the *paseo*. The silence crushed down on her until she had to speak.

"The hotel is even better than I remembered," she said.

"Gracias."

"The service is impeccable."

"Sí."

Rebecca sighed. There was only one thing she could say. "I'm sorry, Alejandro."

He turned his head. She was looking out the window, her arms folded beneath her breasts, the material of her dress softly shimmering in the light leaking into the car. The fabric skimmed her curves like a lover, clung to all the peaks and hollows he wanted to explore.

"What are you sorry for, Rebecca?"

Her eyes met his, huge blue pools in her beautiful face. Her throat moved as she swallowed. "What happened. Your parents."

He was too weary to try and put a positive spin on it. "They do what they do," he said. "It has always been so."

"Is it true?" she said. "About the actress, I mean."

"It was," he replied. "But no longer."

"That was her you were talking to, wasn't it?"

He sighed. "*Sí*. But she will not get what she wants. I will ruin her first." He'd warned Isabella Ayala what he would do if he ever heard of her with his father again. Juan would find another mistress—he always did—and Carmen would accept it readily enough. But Isabella was angling for a ring, for wealth and position. He'd set her straight. Without him, his parents had no money of their own. And he would not hesitate to cut his father off without a euro should Isabella succeed in her quest.

"Do you ever get tired, Alejandro?"

"*¿Qué?*" He came back to himself with a start, focused on the woman across from him.

She leaned across the seat and put her hands on his knees. The warmth of her palms through the fabric of his trousers stunned him. The drumbeat of desire flared to life in his blood. *Dios*, he couldn't even remember the question she'd asked him. If she were to run those palms up to his groin, he'd be a very happy man.

Her soft voice brought him back to the moment. "It must be very tiring, seeing the world in black and white, ruining people right and left. It's okay to see shades of gray, you know, to not always need to control everything. The world will still go around. You don't have to make it move."

Something knifed into his heart. She pushed herself back, breaking that electric contact, and he found himself staring at her. Since he was a boy, he'd always needed to be in control, to order his world as best he could. Control was his security blanket.

"You know nothing of it," he snapped. "I have always had to be responsible, to take care of myself and my family. Control is everything."

She looked sad. "It's not the only thing."

He sliced a hand through the air, dismissing her. "*Sí*, it is everything. My parents have never understood the need for control either. Did you not notice this tonight?"

She bowed her head. "I understand you might have been embarrassed, but—"

"Embarrassed?" He laughed harshly. "*Dios*, if only it were that simple. No, those two have always subjected me—and Roberto and Valencia—to their tantrums, their rages, their personal dramas. If I hadn't found the control they lacked within myself, I would not be who I am today."

He pinched the bridge of his nose. "Roberto died because he had no strength. He was just like my parents in his own way, and he paid the price. Valencia married her Parisian and rarely returns to Spain."

"I didn't know," she said softly.

She watched him with those sympathetic eyes, and he found himself teetering on the edge. How had she seen so deeply into him? Or was it simply a coincidence?

A sudden need to lash out at her, to inflict pain, overtook him.

He spoke with scorn. "We cannot all have a privileged life like yours, Rebecca. Some of us have to work very hard to succeed."

She choked out a laugh. "Oh, God, you think you know everything, don't you?" Her blue gaze flashed. "Well, you *don't*. So don't presume to tell me how I've lived my life."

"I know that you had a fortune handed to you on a silver platter. And that you and your father mismanaged everything so badly you leveraged your company to the hilt. If you hadn't been quite so greedy we would not be sitting here now."

She glared at him. "You're a fine one to talk of greed. With all you have at your fingertips, you still couldn't resist taking my company away, could you? Don't be hypocritical with *me*, Alejandro."

Finally, this was territory he understood. He almost laughed in relief. How easy it was to shift the conversation onto things he knew, things that didn't strip him bare and threaten to expose his soul to her gaze. "It's business, Rebecca."

"And it's personal," she shot back. "You came after us and didn't stop until you found a weakness."

For a moment he thought she was talking about what he'd done to put Layton International into jeopardy, but he realized she didn't know. If she did, she'd probably launch herself at him the way his mother had tried to attack his father tonight.

He almost told her. Almost explained that he owned the bank that had made the loans when no one else would, how he'd dangled the Thailand properties in front of their noses and waited for them to take the leap into debt in the first place. But something stopped him. Now wasn't the time. He wanted to savor his revenge first, wanted to take her down even farther than he already had.

Wanted her to need him, to beg for his touch the way she once had. She might have been lying about her love for him, but some of that physical need was real. He knew it now, knew it the second he'd turned and seen her on that couch. She'd remembered, the same as he had. Her jaw had gone slack, her eyes had glazed, and he'd known what she saw because he saw it too. It was why he'd had to get out.

"It was business first," he said coolly. "Layton International was no longer relevant. You need me to keep you viable in today's marketplace."

"You?" She shifted forward on the seat, her eyes glittering with sudden anger. "What do you know about relevancy, Alejandro? Until a few years ago you were *no one* in this industry! What you know about this business could fill a thimble compared to what my father knew, what he taught me—"

"Oh, yes," he ground out. "Your precious father, who sent *you* to do his dirty work instead of facing me like a man. Spare me your analysis, Rebecca. I'm still the one in control of Layton International."

He thought she would say something else, would let her true colors show now that she'd pointed out his inferior past, but she drew in a shaky breath and fixed her gaze on a point outside the window. The car had been crawling forward for some time. Now, it drew to a halt in the Puerta del Sol. Alejandro swore. Women with placards marched and shouted, blocking the square that was the heart of Old Madrid. Protests were common here, and there was nothing to do but wait as the *policía* directed cars down the side streets.

"I have a life. I'd like to get back to it," Rebecca said after they'd sat in silence for nearly ten minutes. "So if you plan to fire me, why don't you just get it over with and put us both out of our misery."

"Layton International *is* your life," he said.

She bristled. "I have an apartment, friends. I can't stay here forever, wondering what your plans are."

He was in no mood to be delicate with her. "You don't even have a pet fish, Rebecca. You have nothing in your life but work."

Her mouth dropped open as she looked at him. She snapped it shut. "How do you know I don't have a cat or a dog? A boyfriend?"

"I know that you eat Chinese takeout from a restaurant called Tai Pan on Friday nights when you are in town, that you buy flowers from a place called Robertson's, and that you have a grocery store across the street from your apartment but rarely visit it."

His investigators had been very thorough, though they hadn't been able to tell him everything. Like when she'd last spent the night with a man. He wanted to know, but he'd steadfastly refused to ask for that kind of information. It would show a level of interest in her life he no longer had.

All he really needed to know was that she had no long-term entanglements.

He watched as shock and hurt chased each other across her face. Now, why did the hurt pierce his conscience?

"You had me watched?"

He shrugged. "I am very thorough when taking over a company."

It was several moments before she spoke. "Oh, God, I can't believe…" She clasped her arms around her waist, her chest rising and falling faster and faster. "You…spied…on me. You—"

She bent double, air whistling in and out of her body as she took deep breaths.

Alarm snaked across his nerve endings, prickled the hair on his arms and neck. Of all the things he'd expected her to say or do, this hadn't crossed his mind as a possibility. "*Querida*, what is wrong?"

She didn't answer, just kept breathing hard. She was on the verge of hyperventilating and they were stuck in the Puerta del Sol. *Dios*, he felt so helpless. Like the night Anya—

No. He had to do something, *now*.

"Rebecca, hold on," he said, reaching for the door. "Just hold on." He had to get help—had to get one of the *policía* to radio for an ambulance. He could call, but the police would be faster.

"I have to get out of here," she wheezed. "Have to…go."

Before he could stop her, she reached for the opposite door and slipped out into the churning crowd.

CHAPTER SEVEN

ALREADY she could breathe again. Rebecca hugged herself tighter and forged through the crowd. She'd forgotten her wrap, but she wasn't going back. He'd had her *watched*. Investigated. Her privacy invaded. What else did he know? That she hadn't had sex in a year and a half? That she'd kept on taking birth control pills in the pitiful belief she might someday find a man she could love the way she'd once loved him?

It was pathetic. *She* was pathetic. She swiped at her cheeks, ignored the catcalls and whistles of the men she passed. She was vaguely familiar with the Puerta del Sol, but not enough to understand where it was in relation to anything else. She knew there was a department store on one side, El Corte Inglés, but that was in the direction of the protestors, who now congregated around the statue of a Spanish king on a horse. To one end of the square was a red neon Tío Pepe sign. Ahead, there was nothing but a steady trail of people who seemed uninvolved in the protest. That was the direction she'd first headed, and the one she kept going in.

She didn't know where she was going or what she would do when she got there, but right now she couldn't sit in that car with him and know he'd spied on her. An image of Parker Gaines—his smooth lies, the voice recorders he'd used to capture their conversations, the humiliating meeting with her father—flashed into her mind, and she thrust it out again with a growl.

The cobblestone walk sloped upward, toward an archway in the medieval buildings. She kept walking, hoping it was similar to the place Alejandro had taken her years ago. If so, there were cafés, restaurants, places she could disappear and sit for a while, until she felt like returning to Alejandro's villa.

And she would have to return, wouldn't she? All her things were there. Even her purse, with her driver's license and credit cards. *Oh, for the love of God.* She ground to a stop while the foot traffic flowed around her. She had no money. She didn't even have a cell phone.

A hand settled on her shoulder and she whirled around, a little scream escaping as she stumbled backward.

Alejandro caught her to his big warm body, squeezed her before setting her away carefully. He loomed over her, so handsome and imposing in his tuxedo. She thought he looked concerned, but she must have imagined it because the next second his face was set in a harsh mask.

"Madre de Dios," he swore, shrugging out of his tuxedo jacket and placing it around her shoulders. "What were you thinking, taking off like that? I thought you were ill!"

"I'm not," she said. "Or I won't be if you leave me alone."

The jacket was still warm from his body. His scent surrounded her. She wanted to shrug the garment off, but she realized she was shivering. From adrenaline or cold she wasn't certain, but she clasped the jacket around her and held it tight like a shield.

"We will return to the car," he said.

Rebecca shook her head like a recalcitrant child, but she didn't care. "No, I'm not getting back in that car with you. You *spied* on me, Alejandro. I hate you for that."

One eyebrow quirked. "More than you hate me for taking Layton International away?"

She ground her teeth together and turned her head. "It's different."

"Tell me why."

Rebecca pulled in a deep breath, tilted her head up to look at him. His expression didn't mock her like she'd expected. He looked truly curious, as if he didn't understand why she would be so upset about him prying into her life. Why would he? Why would anyone?

"It's not the first time it's happened," she said, unwilling to share more than that. "I don't like it. It makes me feel... violated."

"It was an investigation, not a robbery. This is common enough in business, yes?"

Too common in *her* life. He couldn't understand. No one could. "It doesn't make it right."

"It was business."

"Everything with you is business. But I don't believe it, Alejandro. You brought me here because you wanted to hurt me, pay me back for what you think I did to you. Well, you've succeeded. Are you happy now? Can I go back to New York and forget I ever met you?"

"You would give up so easily? Leave Layton International?"

"Do I have a choice?" Why was she pushing him? This wasn't part of her plan. She needed to stay, needed to keep involved in the day-to-day operations, or she would lose the insider track to all that happened with her company and would never get it back.

"Perhaps you do," he said softly.

She sucked in a shaky breath. "What's that supposed to mean?"

"Come back to the car," he said. "We will go home."

Home? How could one word evoke so many feelings? But

it was his home, not hers. She had no home. Her apartment was a place to sleep and store clothes. The family home had been sold when her father had died. Her mother had moved back to Paris. The only place that felt like home was La Belle Amelie, and that was because of her connection to the place, the fact she'd been born there when her mother's water had broken a month early.

Where was home now? She honestly didn't know.

"I'm not getting back into that car right now," she said. "If you try to force me, I'll scream."

Alejandro's expression went from sober to amused. "Did you not see the protest, *amor*? The *policía* are very busy at the moment. I could drag you back by your hair, like a good caveman should, and no one would notice."

She turned her head toward the archway, ignoring him. Why was it when he gave her that little half-smile she melted into a puddle? Though she was angry with him, his humor threatened her heart in a way nothing else could. She had to focus on something else, something other than the man in front of her. "Is that like the place you took me?"

"*Sí*. It is the same—the Plaza Mayor. There are several entryways."

She loved the way his voice caressed the sound: Plaza MAY-orr. She remembered a beautiful square, similar to Venice's Piazza San Marco, though much more colorful and uniquely Spanish. There were restaurants, *tapas* bars, and shops beneath the portico that ran around the perimeter.

It was also the place where Alejandro had first kissed her. Sitting at a sidewalk café, sipping sherry, he'd leaned over and kissed her sweetly on the lips that first time. It had been everything she could do to accept the chaste kiss, not to curl her hand around his neck and demand more of him. He'd set her on fire with one touch of his lips.

In truth, she should want to run screaming from a memory

such as that. But the prospect of getting back into the car with him right now was even more frightening. "I want to go see it."

He studied her for a long moment. Was he remembering the kiss too? Or, more likely, wondering if she planned to bolt again. "Explain to me what happened in the car."

She fiddled with the edge of his jacket. "It was a panic attack, Alejandro. Nothing more. I'm not sick. But if I get back in the car right now I might be. I just need space."

Space without him in it—without him invading her senses and making her question everything she thought and said.

He rubbed a hand over his face as if he were about to make a choice he didn't want. "*Sí*, fine—we will go."

"We?" She wanted to be alone, not shadowed by this hulking shell of a man, not reminded at every turn that he'd betrayed her trust more than once.

His mouth twisted. "You think I will allow you to go alone? No, this is not possible. What if you were to have another attack?"

"I won't."

"How can you be sure?"

"Because it rarely happens. I can't even remember the last time." A lie. She remembered very well the last time she'd had an attack so bad she couldn't breathe: the moment she'd climbed into the taxi after leaving his suite five years ago. She had mild attacks from time to time, but it took exceptionally powerful emotion to make it difficult for her to breathe. "I just want some time to myself, out in the open, without you stalking after me."

"This is not an option, Rebecca. We go together, or we return to the car."

She pinched the bridge of her nose. "Fine." She sighed. "Let's go."

He tipped his head toward the jacket. "If you will permit me to get my phone? I must tell Garcia where to pick us up."

Rebecca nodded, and he parted the material. His fingers

brushed the swell of her breast as he reached into an inner pocket and she shivered involuntarily.

When he'd finished, they walked in silence to the archway and passed beneath, emerging into a huge square lined on all four sides by a portico. Painted figures adorned the portion of the facade stretching between two clock towers. All around the square, tables and chairs were set out from the restaurants. At this hour patrons were eating dinner. It always struck her as odd that Spaniards ate so late. At least there were *tapas* for people like her.

"Which café did we drink sherry at?" she asked.

Alejandro pointed to one of the arched openings leading into and out of the square. "There, near the Arco de Cuchilleros. Do you want to go?"

"No." She almost said yes, but decided it would be too much to revisit the memory in the exact spot. She was already tempting fate simply by walking through this *plaza* with him. She moved out into the square and turned slowly around, gazing at the buildings and balconies. Anything to take her mind off the man before her.

Alejandro stood casually, his hands in his pockets. His white shirt stood out against the darkened square. He was still wearing his bow tie, which she found immensely sexy for some reason.

"There are two hundred and thirty-seven balconies and nine entrances," he said.

"It's very beautiful." *He* was beautiful, damn him. Beautiful and lethal.

He shrugged. "The Inquisition once put heretics to death here."

"Yes, well, we have nothing like it in New York. Central Park, maybe—but that's a park and not a town square."

Violin music began to drift from the portico. It was soft, haunting. A street musician playing for tips, most likely.

Rebecca closed her eyes, blocking out Alejandro, and swayed to the music. So pretty, so peaceful. Inevitably she remembered making love with him beneath a moon-drenched sky while violin music drifted from the radio in the rooftop suite. Did he remember it too?

"I know what you are thinking," he said, his voice soft and sensual—and closer than she'd expected.

Her eyes popped open to find him hovering over her. She stopped swaying and gazed up at him. How could any one man be so attractive? He was like a fallen angel with his dark hair and mesmerizing stare.

"No, you don't," she replied, her heart thrumming in her breast.

He slipped an arm around her, hauled her closer. "Oh, *sí*, I do. I am thinking of it too."

Her brain sent the signal to back away, but too late. His other hand grasped one of hers, placed it on the hard muscle of his bicep. Another pull and she was flush against his body.

Breast to belly to hip. His arousal came as a surprise and her breath broke on a gasp.

"Yes, I want you," he said.

"But you hate me."

His easy grin had the power to light the dark corners of her soul. He was so much like the old Alejandro in that moment that it made her ache.

"And you hate me. This does not stop our bodies from desiring one another, *sí*?"

She realized he was swaying them in time to the music, guiding her in a slow and sensual dance. And she suddenly didn't want to be anywhere else. Her body recognized his, answered with the sweet ache of desire. Her feminine core grew damp and her breasts felt heavy, needy.

She closed her eyes, gave in to the temptation to press her cheek to his chest. His heart beat loud and strong beneath her touch. Quick, but not racing like hers. Whatever this was, he was affected too.

They moved slowly, silently. His hand slid down her back, over her buttock, and she shivered, her senses on full alert. She was like a finely tuned instrument awaiting the right hands. His hands. It had been so, so long.

"*Madre de Dios,*" he said a moment later, pulling away from her. He didn't stop the dance, didn't break the contact, but he put space between them.

"What's wrong?"

He gave her a meaningful look. "Nothing…if we were alone." His fingers skimmed her jaw, her throat, the material at her collarbone. Sparks of sensation trailed in their wake, shivered across her heated skin.

She was frozen as he tilted her chin up, dipped his head toward hers. His lips brushed across her mouth so lightly, like the touch of a butterfly wing. She wanted more, parted her lips in anticipation, but he pulled back. His breath whispered over her moistened lips.

"I want to strip you slowly, kiss every centimeter of your skin and make love to you for the rest of the night."

Rebecca gulped. Oh, God, she wanted it too.

But she couldn't. She couldn't lose her head over this man. Not ever again. And after tonight—the pain in his eyes as he had held his sobbing mother, the raw wound of losing his baby, her realization that his desperate need for control stemmed from tragedy and heartbreak, and that her own family had contributed to his losses—how could she keep her heart hardened to him?

Desperately, she seized on the bad things she knew: he'd stolen her company, he'd had her watched, he thought the worst of her. He didn't respect her as a person, didn't think she was good or honorable. He was acting on pure male instinct, animal attraction. He wanted her body, nothing more.

"I—I can't," she said, casting her eyes down, away from

his burning gaze. She slipped out of his embrace and spun blindly toward the portico. They could never go back to where they'd been before. It had been foolish of her to come here, to dance with him, to remember another, more innocent time. To open herself to the vortex of emotion that he caused inside her.

Life did not go backward. It ground forward relentlessly. If she'd endured the car, they might still be in the Puerta del Sol, but at least her heart would be intact.

Her fault. She'd allowed this to happen. What had she been thinking when she'd wanted to come here?

She was almost under the portico when he caught her, spun her around and pulled her into the shaded area of an archway. His body was hard against her, his hands framing her face. His warmth seared her skin. Her back hit a column and she realized he'd trapped her between him and the stone.

"You're mine, Rebecca," he said vehemently. "For as long and as often as I want you. I have bought and paid for you many times over. You will not deny me."

Then his mouth crushed down on hers. It was the wildest, hottest, most devastating kiss she'd ever experienced. And when it was over, when he let her go and stepped back, breathing hard in an effort to regain his icy control, all she wanted was to wrap her arms around him and make him do it again.

They didn't speak on the ride back to the villa. Rebecca huddled against the door and watched the night lights of Madrid slide by. She had no idea what Alejandro was thinking. And she didn't want to ask. *That* kiss. God in heaven, she'd have done anything he asked at that moment. Thankfully, he hadn't repeated it. He liked toying with her. She realized that now. He liked to get her teetering on the edge of her emotions before he flung her off the cliff and onto the rocks below. He had no intention of seducing her, only of proving to her again and again how vulnerable she was to him.

It was after midnight when they entered the darkened interior of the house. There was no sign of Señora Flores, or any of the other servants. A light burned softly in the Great Room, spilling out into the hall, but nothing stirred.

Though every instinct told her to flee, Rebecca paused in the foyer. Alejandro stood with hands in pockets, watching her closely.

Say goodnight—get away. "Thanks for…um…understanding when I didn't want to get back into the car right away."

"You said it wasn't the first time someone had you investigated. Who did so before?"

Rebecca removed his jacket from her shoulders, folded it over her arm and held it out. "You better take this now, before I forget."

He tossed the jacket aside, caught her wrist and held her still when she would have fled. "Rebecca?"

Irrational tears clogged her throat. "Goodnight, Alejandro." She didn't want to talk about this, most especially not with him. To share her humiliation with the one man who'd ever meant anything to her? Who'd rejected her so brutally? Impossible.

His grip tightened as she tried to pull away, preventing her from moving even a fraction. It was like playing tug-of-war with a tank.

"You don't have to tell me," he said. "It's not at all necessary for what happens now."

She stopped trying to extract herself from his grip and stared up at him, her pulse beginning to hum erratically. "I want to go to bed."

His smile was predatory. "*Sí*, as do I."

"Alone, Alejandro."

His arms encircled her, his fingers stroking down the

exposed skin of her back, trailing fire in their wake. "This is not possible, *querida*. I have told you what I intend."

Her palms came up to press against his crisp shirtfront. "You can't mean it. You can't want to make me do this."

One brow lifted. "*Make* you do this?" His fingers skimmed her spine, up and down, up and down, eliciting shivers along her nerve endings. "I think I will not need to make you do anything. You want me, Rebecca. You have wanted me since the moment you arrived."

Damn him for throwing the truth in her face. Yes, she wanted him, but she also wanted chocolate after every meal. She didn't indulge because it was bad for her. *He* was bad for her.

"No," she said firmly. "You are mistaken."

"I'm not," he replied, his lips a fraction above hers now. "And it doesn't matter anyway. You are mine."

This time when he slanted his mouth over hers she held herself firm, refused to break. He ran his tongue along the seam of her lips, slid his hands down to grasp her buttocks and pull her into the cradle of his hips.

And, oh, my, he was blessedly, hugely, gloriously hard. *For her.*

But she would not break. Her sanity depended on it, on holding part of herself separate from him. She knew more about him now than she ever had before, and that knowledge threatened to enslave her heart in spite of everything he'd done to her.

Why did she feel this pull, this intense storm of emotion, over *this* man? Why not David, her long-suffering and incredibly patient boyfriend, who'd finally left her over a year ago because she couldn't ever love him the way he'd wanted her to?

It wasn't *fair*.

"*Dios,*" Alejandro said against her tightly closed mouth.

"You are determined to fight me." His lips moved along her jawline, down her throat. Before she realized what he was doing, he slid his fingers beneath the shoulders of her dress and jerked it forward, down her arms, trapping her with her naked breasts exposed to his gaze.

"Alejandro, let me go—someone could see!"

"I thought you could not be wearing a bra beneath this," he said, almost to himself, his eyes hot as they moved over her. "I have wondered about it for hours."

The way he looked at her made her breath shorten. *Like he wanted to worship her.* She could almost forget she was standing in his foyer, bare to the waist, her nipples peaking beneath his scorching gaze.

"What else aren't you wearing, Rebecca?" he asked, his voice a sensual purr.

She couldn't speak as his hand slipped into the back of her dress. Soon enough he would know. His groan told her even before his hand settled on her bare bottom that he'd realized she wasn't wearing any panties.

"The material is too clingy," she babbled. "There would've been a line…"

"This comes off," he said. "Now."

"No, Alejandro—wait. What if someone sees me?" she said as he started to tug the material down.

"They won't." He skimmed the expensive jersey from her body until she stood in nothing but high heels and a puddle of fabric. Then he took a step back, perusing her thoroughly. "You are exquisite, Rebecca. I have waited too long for this."

Her brain kicked into gear as her skin prickled from the cool air of the foyer. The man had servants, and he'd undressed her in a public area of his house. And she just stood there like a museum exhibit while he ogled her! Anyone could come along at any minute.

She reached for her dress, but Alejandro was there first, scooping her into his arms.

"No," he growled. "I want you in my bed. You will not need any clothing for many hours yet."

CHAPTER EIGHT

A DIFFERENT kind of panic was starting to grip her by the throat as Alejandro carried her into his bedroom and kicked the door shut. She was naked in his arms, he'd brought her to his room, yet she still believed he somehow meant to shame her beyond her wildest imagination.

This was a ruse, she was certain of it, and she began to kick her legs back and forth, trying to force him to put her down.

"Be still," he said. A moment later she was on the bed and he was hovering over her, his fully clothed body pressing down on top of her. "Tell me," he said, his lips on her jaw, her throat, her collarbone. "Tell me you do not want this, Rebecca, that your body does not ache for mine…"

His mouth fastened over one aching nipple and she arched her back, cried out. He gave her absolutely no time to adjust to the feelings assailing her body. His fingers slid between her thighs, parted her, found the sensitive heart of her.

"Alejandro," she gasped.

"Tell me you don't want me," he said, his breath hot against her body as he moved to her other nipple, sucked it between his lips.

She shuddered, her body alive with more sensation than she'd felt in a very long time. Even the other night in the pool she hadn't quivered like this, hadn't thought she would die with every slick pulse of his fingers against her, inside her.

She was on the edge so quickly it shocked her, ready to tumble into an orgasm just from the feel of his tongue on her nipples and his fingers inside her. But he stopped, said heated words in Spanish, while he sat up and ripped at the studs on his shirt. She looked up at him, her heart tumbling over in her chest, breaking for the millionth time because of him.

But she couldn't stop herself from reaching for him, from raising herself until she could touch his jaw, press her hand to his skin, her fingertips sliding down to his lips, over them.

Those beautiful lips had given her more pleasure than she could ever have imagined. He'd been the first man to make love to her with his mouth. She'd never told him that.

Now he'd gone completely still as she touched him, his gaze hot and intense as he watched her.

She slipped a finger into his mouth, over the front of his teeth, across the tip of his tongue. When she would have retreated, he gripped her hand gently, sucked her finger in and out, his heated stare never leaving hers.

"Alejandro," she whispered, her blood pounding in her veins, her heart ready to burst from so much feeling. She hated him, she loved him, she hated him. Her heart ached and ached and ached until she thought she might die from it. What was this feeling really? Why couldn't she work it out?

"Sí, mi amor?" He kissed her palm, her wrist, the tip of each finger.

She'd said his name because of the maelstrom inside her, but he responded as if he expected a question.

She could think of only one. "Did—?" She swallowed the knot clogging her throat. She had to ask, had to know. "Did you love her?"

Until that moment when she'd learned he was engaged, or

supposedly engaged, her life had seemed so right with him. She wanted to understand how it had gone wrong. Why.

He lowered her hand to his chest, pressed it to the hot skin he'd exposed when he tore his shirt open. She could feel his heart, fast and strong, and her fingers trembled.

His eyes, hot as they were, somehow managed to be flat when he answered. "I have never loved any woman. I never will."

She didn't feel any relief to know he hadn't loved his wife. And though she'd known he hadn't loved *her*, it still hurt to hear it so starkly stated. "Poor Alejandro," she said softly. "You must get so lonely."

The shock on his face might have been comical if she hadn't known what he'd suffered. He would never admit it, but there had to be times when he would be relieved to share the burden of so much sorrow. To have someone understand. To love him.

"No more talking, Rebecca," he said. "No more questions." He pushed the shirt from his shoulders, stripped off his trousers and kicked them free, then stretched out over her. "Just feel—feel what you do to me, what we do to each other. *This* is what's real."

His mouth captured hers, and this time she opened to him, tangling her tongue with his as he stoked the fires in her body once more. Part of her was terrified of what was happening, and part of her wanted it more than her next breath. She knew she should go—should shove him away and leave this bed before she lost more than her pride.

But she couldn't do it. Her body sang beneath his, wanted his, seemed made especially for his. She wrapped her legs around him, opened herself to him. He rose above her on his palms, gazed down at her with a look she couldn't decipher.

She felt him pushing at her entrance, sliding forward just enough to make her pant, then withdrawing again.

"Alejandro, please. *Please, I need you.*"

He growled low in his throat, then surged forward in one

long, gliding stroke. She cried out with pleasure and shock as he filled her. He was bigger than she remembered, and his possession was intense.

He didn't move, though she could feel the pulse beat of him deep inside her.

He looked uncertain. "Did I hurt you?"

"No, no—it's okay. It's been a long time."

His eyes glazed as she moved her hips, learned how to accommodate him again.

Finally he spoke, seemed to drag his thoughts from somewhere. "A long time? You have not—?"

She rolled her head back and forth on the pillow.

He looked surprised. Fierce and possessive. "You should have told me. I would have been gentler."

"Ohhh," she gasped, as he pulled out and glided back in. "Noooo, you wouldn't have believed me."

"Rebecca," he groaned, dropping his head. She didn't know if he meant to say more, if it was agreement or denial, but he flexed his hips and she no longer cared.

He moved slowly at first, each thrust measured and sure. Trying not to hurt her. But he was so careful she wanted to scream. She ran her hands feverishly down his body, over his biceps, the scar on his side.

"Alejandro, I won't break. Make love to me. *Please.*"

His mouth crushed down on hers, their tongues mating while their bodies merged harder and faster. He lost whatever control he might have had, his movements quickening until he was pounding into her with all the passion of a man long denied. She kept a tight control on herself, thought she might hold out forever, but he slipped his hand between them, stroked her where their bodies joined.

Her orgasm didn't just slam into her; it stole her breath and brought her up off the bed as she arched into him, sobbing her pleasure. A second later Alejandro lost the hold he'd had on himself, his hips pumping into her harder as he groaned her name brokenly.

He collapsed on top of her, breathing hard. She ran her palms down his back, over his buttocks, sighed heavily. It was a glorious, earth-shattering mistake to make love with this man. She knew it, but she tried to hold the regret and pain at bay as long as possible.

He'd won, hadn't he? He'd stolen her company, dragged her halfway around the world and stripped her bare—both literally and figuratively. She had nothing left, not even her dignity. Soon he would get up from the bed, look at her with disdain and order her out of his sight.

When he lifted himself on his elbows he was still breathing hard. The look in his eyes was not what she'd expected, and it ripped her heart in two. Confusion, anger and passion collided in that one smoldering gaze.

He kissed her softly, almost sweetly. Her heart, she feared, was lost forever.

Moonlight drifted through the windows and arced across the bed, waking him. Alejandro lifted his head, momentarily disoriented. Why hadn't he closed the blinds before lying down?

It came back to him quickly, crashing into his mind in a series of images and sensations.

Dios. He turned his head slightly, gazed at the woman sleeping beside him. She'd curled up in a ball at the edge of the bed, as far away from him as she could get. Perversely, it angered him. She'd tried to get away from him when they were awake and had not succeeded. In sleep she won the battle.

He slipped the covers off and padded to the window naked. His body was satiated in a way it had not been in months. In spite of his feelings for his self-absorbed ex-wife, he'd stayed faithful to their marriage vows until the day the divorce had become final. In the months since, he'd slaked his thirst with many women. Anonymous, uncaring sex had been a balm to his ravaged soul.

Or so he'd thought.

Until tonight, when he'd lost himself in the gorgeous and willing body of the woman he hated most in this world. For those few hours he'd forgotten.

But he did hate her. He pressed a knuckle to his temple.

It was all according to plan. Bed her, make her care, ruin her. He owed it to Anya. He would do this for Anya. Anya, who should have lived. Who should have been his and Rebecca's child.

He clenched his fist, pressed it to the glass. He had done nothing wrong. He had not miscalculated. Never mind that she'd been untouched for so long, or that she'd seemed to see into his soul in the limo tonight. She was shallow, calculating. She slept with him now to try and gain an advantage. And how did he know he was really her first lover in a long time? She could be lying, faking. But if it were a ruse wouldn't she have told him earlier, tried to elicit his sympathy?

He took a deep breath, let it out. Sometimes his mind raced between so many possibilities that he couldn't keep up.

"Alejandro?"

He turned and went to the bed. Moonlight limned her features, her very messy golden-blonde hair, her kiss-swollen lips. Desire lifted its slumberous head inside him.

"I am here," he replied.

She clutched the sheet to her. The scent of sex clung to her. To him.

A new thought prickled at the back of his mind. Something he should have thought of long before now. *Sweet God in heaven, he'd forgotten to use protection.*

"I should return to my room," she said, unaware of the stark fear snaking down his spine.

"No," he said coldly.

She seemed to shrink in on herself.

"Are you protected?" he demanded.

Her head quirked to one side. "Wha—? Oh, yes. Yes," she said more firmly. "I'm on the pill. I thought you knew that."

"How would I know this?" he asked, stupefied that she would think so.

Her chin lifted. "I thought your private investigators would have told you."

"It was not that kind of investigation," he defended. Still, relief threatened to liquefy his knees. *Madre de Dios, gracias.* This was the first time he'd ever forgotten to take precautions. It was not at all like him, but he chalked it up to the mental exhaustion of dealing with so much angst and drama tonight.

On the heels of relief came a surge of lust so strong he felt it from his scalp to his toes. A second later he peeled the sheet from her grasp and laid her back on the mattress, his hands skimming up the insides of her thighs, pushing them apart.

"I've been dying to taste you," he said.

He loved her soft cries and moans, the slick sweet taste of her, the way she arched off the bed and screamed his name when she came. He didn't let her stop at one climax; he spread her wide and laved her with his tongue until she was panting and moaning again, until a fine sheen of moisture glistened on her skin, until his name was a hoarse cry on her lips.

And then he was inside her, losing himself as he thrust hard, again and again, unable this time to be gentle. He had no control, no finesse with this woman. He came in a hot hard rush, groaning and gasping like he'd run a marathon, then rolled to the side and gathered her against him.

They lay on top of the sheets. Her body twitched every now and then—aftereffects of the powerful orgasms he'd given her. It made him feel possessive, proprietary. His fingers trailed up and down her arm almost absently.

"Who had you watched, Rebecca?"

She jerked in his arms. She must have been nearly asleep, but now she grew rigid, her body vibrating with a different kind of tension.

"It doesn't matter."

"I want to know."

She pushed away from him, rose up on one elbow beside him. Her nipple brushed his arm and he felt the jolt to his groin.

"I don't want to talk about it. You don't really care. All you'll do is be smug." She traced a finger around one of his nipples, followed with her tongue. A ploy to distract him.

But her words pricked him. He didn't care that she'd been hurt by someone, it was true, but he wanted to know anyway. It fed his need for control.

"Was it a lover?" He spat the word.

She lifted her head. "No."

"A rival?"

She laughed bitterly. "Yes—you."

Who else would possibly want to investigate her? Not a lover or a rival. Unless she was lying. It had to be a business rival. Who else? Why else?

A tendril of intuition niggled at him. Who could hurt her so badly by spying on her? "Family?"

She stiffened, and he knew he had his answer.

He twined his fingers in her hair, drew her down to him. Kissed her deeply. "You can tell me, *querida*. I want to know."

She sighed, her shoulders slumping before she fell back on the bed and put an arm over her face. "Fine," she said. "What's it matter anymore?"

But she didn't say anything for so long he thought she must have fallen asleep. He bent to kiss the soft skin of her breast. She let out a little sigh and he rolled her nipple between his lips, suckled it into a sharp peak.

"I can't think when you do that," she said, on a soft susurration of breath.

He propped himself beside her, fingers stroking little circles on her skin. "Was it your father?" Truly, he couldn't see anyone *but* Jackson Layton hiring a private investigator to follow his own daughter around. And he didn't entirely disagree with it. He could imagine doing the same thing if Anya had lived. Anything to keep her safe.

"Yes." One word, nothing more.

"You will not tell me more?"

She shook her head, her eyes tightly closed, and he felt the sting of disappointment. She'd told him nothing at all. Once she would have told him anything he asked.

That time was gone forever. It was just as well. He did not need to feel pity for her.

The next morning Alejandro's business necessitated his return to Dubai. There was a break in the standoff over permits, but he needed to be there personally in order to ensure a smooth resolution to the problem.

The last thing Rebecca had expected was to be ordered to accompany him. In truth, she hadn't known what to expect after their night together.

Alejandro knew. "You are my mistress," he said, when she asked why he wanted her to go.

She'd nearly choked on the word. "Mistress? Until a few days ago, I was the president of a major international hotel chain."

His smile wasn't at all friendly. "*Sí*, until a few days ago." He tossed something into his briefcase, then speared her with a silver glare. "And not so major, *no*?"

"Does this mean you're considering selling me some of the stock?" she asked, knowing it was the wrong thing to say, yet angry enough to hurl at him what he'd said to her in the pool anyway.

Her amazing lover of the night before was gone; in his place was the ruthless businessman who'd stolen her company. In the stark light of day she had to wonder how she'd managed to forget all the hurt and betrayal long enough to fall into bed with him.

His expression was so cold she had to suppress a shiver. "It means you are my mistress. Nothing more."

When they landed in Dubai that afternoon, a black Mercedes limousine met them at the airport and ferried them to the resort Alejandro had recently bought on the Jumeirah coast. It wasn't as grand as some of the other hotels, but his plans to expand it would make it one of the top destinations in Dubai. If the permit situation was resolved.

A man in a tuxedo hurried forward to greet them when the car doors opened, snapping his fingers at a bellhop who leaped into action to collect their luggage from the trunk.

"Señor Ramirez," the man said as Alejandro stepped from the car. "We are so pleased you are back with us again. Your suite is prepared. Shall I make reservations for dinner, or will you be dining in?"

"In the suite, I think, Ali."

"Very well, sir."

The suite was truly a gorgeous place. Situated on the top floor, its view of the Persian Gulf was spectacular. Rebecca went onto the balcony, gazed out at the sparkling blue water, the ship traffic and the glorious sail-like structure of the Burj Al Arab hotel silhouetted against the hazy sky in the distance.

Palm trees swayed in a gentle breeze near the beach. Directly below her was the pool. Guests dotted the chairs while waiters moved back and forth between them. Behind her, she could hear Alejandro on the phone. He didn't sound happy.

It was strange, almost exhilarating in some respects, to be here and not be the one working. Not that she *wasn't* working. She had her phone and her laptop, and she was still—so far—

in charge of day-to-day operations at Layton International. But not to be the person fielding frantic phone calls about permits and construction issues—it was bliss. She could see, off to the left, the area where construction cranes sat silent. No trucks moved, no workers—nothing happened in the fenced-off site. Every day was money. He could afford a lot, she was sure, but at a certain point he would need to cut his losses.

She went back inside. A bank of windows ran along the front of the suite. Automatic blinds closed with the press of a button, though they were open now, to allow the afternoon light inside. A plush living area contained a couch and chairs, a bar and an entertainment system with a flat-screen television. There was a dining area near one window. The bedroom had a giant king-size bed piled high with pillows, but it was the sunken tub in the bathroom that caught her eye. The floors were marble, and marble columns surrounded the tub on four sides, making it look like a Roman bath. A peek inside told her there were jets. Heavenly. Maybe she could have a nice long bath while Alejandro went to meet with government officials.

He came into the bedroom as she was leaving the master bathroom. He wore a dark polo shirt and khakis, and his hair was mussed. He'd been raking his hands through his hair again—no doubt the result of his phone call. Perversely, she wanted to smooth it back into place.

"It meets with your approval?" he asked, nodding toward the bathroom.

"It's nice."

"Merely nice?" He seemed a little irritated.

"No, it's very nice."

His face darkened. "It is spectacular—far better than many of your own hotels. Which I will rectify, I assure you."

She stamped down on the hot anger rising to the surface. He was baiting her. He'd had bad or frustrating news and he was taking it out on her. Amazingly, the realization only made her calmer. "Of course, Alejandro."

He stalked closer. "You are making fun of me?"

She shook her head. "No."

He reached out, trailed tanned fingers down the vee of her blouse, toyed with the top button. "Take this off."

Her breath shortened. The anger she'd stamped down deep was beginning to bubble again. "I'd rather not," she forced out.

"And I say you have no choice."

She drew herself up and leveled him with her best glare. "There is always a choice, Alejandro. I choose *not* to be ordered around like a paid-by-the-hour hooker. If you need to sell a hotel or two, or dismantle Layton International and scatter it to the wind to punish me, then indulge yourself. You can't control every single minute of my life with your threats. Save them for the big stuff."

His face was dark, unreadable. And then one corner of his mouth lifted in a grin. It was like sunshine breaking through after a violent storm—and completely *not* what she'd expected. "You amuse me at the oddest moments, *bella.*"

He caught her around the waist, tugged her against his body. "My meeting has been moved to tomorrow morning, and I find I have many long, empty hours to fill." He dipped his head, touched his lips to her nose, her cheeks. "Help me fill them, yes? I want to spend the afternoon in bed with you…"

"I'm not your employee when we're alone like this," she insisted, still angry—though her blood was humming for an altogether different reason now. "You can't order me around in the bedroom like it's a boardroom."

He kissed her hard, broke away. "You would not obey me in the boardroom either," he whispered. "Not without a fight."

"If you would ask instead of order," she said, gasping as his fingers slipped inside her shirt, her bra. He softly pinched her nipple into an aching point. "You get more flies with honey, Alejandro…"

"Please, Rebecca," he said with a predatory gleam. "*Let* me taste you."

Rebecca didn't see Alejandro very often over the next couple of days. He was up at daybreak, meeting with government officials, touring the construction site, trying to get to the bottom of the permit situation. But when she did see him—

Oh, my—it took her breath away to think about it. The man was insatiable, and he worshipped her body with a thoroughness bordering on obsession. She found it impossible to say no.

Rebecca sighed and stretched her naked—and very satisfied—body. She was still sprawled on top of the covers, where he'd left her when he went into the shower. He'd tried to get her to join him, but she couldn't move. She'd been surprised to see him back so early, but he'd burst into the suite and announced he'd had a breakthrough. A few phone calls later—half of them conducted in English—she partially understood what was going on. Alejandro had a corporate spy, who'd been working with another company to hold up the construction process.

He'd been almost gleeful. She liked seeing him happy. He used to be happy all the time when she'd known him before. Marriage and tragedy had changed that.

"What are you thinking about so intently, *amor*?"

Rebecca looked up to find him watching her. He stood beside the bed, the towel slung low on his hips, every delicious inch of his rock-hard chest displayed for her delight. Her heart jumped, the way it always did when he was near. She hadn't heard him come back.

"Will you tell me what happened to Anya?" She wasn't sure where the question came from, but she realized she'd been thinking of his little girl a lot lately. About how such a tragic loss had changed him from the man she'd once known.

There were still glimpses of that man, but he was buried under the weight of tragedy, under the hardened husk of what he'd become.

She wanted to know, wanted to understand.

His eyes closed, snapped open again. She thought he would walk away. His jaw hardened.

"She was born with a congenital heart defect," he said. "It should not have been fatal, had it been diagnosed when she was an infant. But she was one of the rare ones."

Rebecca sat up, reached for him. He'd been in a good mood, and she'd managed to destroy it. He moved away before she could touch him. She clasped her arms around her knees. "I'm so very sorry. For both you and your wife."

The pain in his features was evident—the drawn mouth, the tight jaw, the flared nostrils. "Three-year-olds should not have heart attacks."

"No." Her throat ached. She wanted to get up and wrap her arms around him, press his head to her breast and hold him.

Alejandro's skin had paled beneath his tan. She'd have never believed it had she not been staring right at him.

"I shouldn't have asked. I'm sorry."

"No, she is gone now, and people always ask. I must become accustomed to it."

How did you ever get accustomed to such a thing? A vile, sorrowful, evil thing that was the death of a child?

She didn't know what else to say. She simply wanted to hold him.

But he started to shrug into his clothes, his back to her. "I have work to do. If you wish to go shopping or sightseeing, please inform Ali. He will arrange for anything you need."

Without a backward glance, he was gone.

Alejandro was restless, keyed-up, jumpy as a caged bull before a fight. He drummed his fingers against the center armrest in the limo, thought about the woman he'd left in his bed. Why had he told her about Anya? She'd surprised him with the question, but he'd surprised himself even more by answering it.

He did not want to share such things with her. Anya was none of her business. He should have choked on the words before spilling his guts to a woman like her.

A woman like what?

A woman who melted beneath him, who made him crazy with her little sighs and moans, who fought him when he pushed and who insisted on being treated with respect and dignity in spite of his plans for her?

He was going soft. Just because his body craved hers, just because he showed no signs of tiring of her—indeed, each time he made love to her he seemed to only want her more—it was no reason to lose sight of what he meant to do. He had to ruin her. He'd planned it for so long, lived for it through the darkest days. He couldn't cease now.

It was time to start knocking the foundation out from beneath her, if only to prove he could do it. He would start tonight.

CHAPTER NINE

A TEAM of waiters arrived to serve dinner in their suite. Rebecca had been surprised when Alejandro returned in time for the meal. Usually she ate alone, working on her computer since it was still only mid-afternoon in the States. She accomplished a lot in the hours Alejandro was away, even if part of her anticipated his return with growing excitement as the day waned.

She'd worked through the afternoon, but she'd been preoccupied with their conversation earlier. She couldn't imagine losing a child so cruelly. It was senseless, surreal. The grief he must have experienced was unimaginable.

And yet he'd endured it. He'd changed because of it, but she understood why now. Looking at him across the table, her heart filled to bursting with everything she was feeling toward him, she knew without a doubt that she was falling for him again.

Or perhaps she had already fallen, but she wasn't quite prepared to admit it to herself just yet. No, far better to look at him in his cream silk shirt, with his dark hair and skin such a startlingly beautiful contrast, and imagine that she had time to prevent the disaster she was hurtling herself into. He'd barely spoken since returning. She wondered what dinner would be like—how she could draw him out if he didn't speak.

Maybe she should apologize for asking him about his daughter. But she wasn't sorry he'd told her. It helped her understand. Helped her forgive him just a tiny bit for how he'd treated her since he'd ordered her to Madrid.

The sommelier uncorked a bottle of wine and poured a taste for Alejandro's approval. After the wine was decanted and the food served, all but one of the waiters left. The man stationed himself near the buffet where they'd set the dishes, and prepared to serve as needed.

"I have decided to move Layton International's offices to Madrid," Alejandro announced.

Rebecca nearly dropped her fork. The spicy rice and eggplant dish she'd just taken a bite of turned to paste in her mouth.

"You seem surprised," he said, his dark gaze giving nothing away.

She reached for her wineglass, took a fortifying sip. Her heart was beginning to flutter at breakneck speed. "I am. You haven't told me your plans for my company, and now this. What about my employees? There are over one hundred people in the New York office."

He shrugged. "Upper management will be offered jobs in Madrid. Others will be given generous severance packages and assistance in finding new employment."

"Is this because I asked you about Anya?"

His eyes flashed. "No. It's business."

She set her fork down and leaned back against her chair, no longer hungry. "Oh, really? Somehow I don't think so. I know you're angry with me, but it's unfair to take it out on my people."

He tapped long fingers on the tablecloth as he studied her. She would not think about what those fingers did to her each night. She kept her gaze firmly on his face.

"I do what's best for Ramirez Enterprises. It has nothing to do with you. They are *my* people now, not yours."

She didn't believe he did this for the good of Ramirez. Clearly he was punishing her—especially when he pointed out that she wasn't responsible for her employees any longer.

"I owe them, Alejandro. My family owes them. I can't sit by and do nothing."

"You do not have a choice. When you chose to pledge your stock as collateral for those loans, you took the risk that someone else would gain control of your company. You no longer have a say in what happens at Layton International."

That was the bitter truth, wasn't it? No matter how much it hurt, how much she disagreed, she had no legal ground to stand on.

"What about me?" she asked. "Am I fired now?"

He took a sip of wine, watched her over the top of his glass. Several seconds went by before he spoke. "Not yet."

Her relief was palpable. And yet it was suddenly too much. Everything—the way he'd manipulated her into doing what he wanted, his threats, the juxtaposition of cold businessman with white-hot lover—she couldn't take it a moment longer.

"I'm not sure I can continue this way," she said softly. Her appetite was gone, so she set her napkin over the plate.

Alejandro glanced at the waiter. A signal must have passed between them, because the man bowed and disappeared.

"Continue how, Rebecca?"

"I want to know what your plans are for me. I'm tired of wondering."

The sudden heat in his eyes wasn't what she expected. "My plans involve the bed, the shower, and maybe even this table."

A current of awareness snapped between them. But she couldn't simply fold like a house of cards. "I was talking about business, Alejandro."

"So was I. This is the business of being my mistress."

He looked amused rather than annoyed. It irritated her. Did

she have the strength to walk away from his seduction? From him? She pushed her chair back and stood. Alejandro's gaze sharpened. He looked like a great cat scenting prey.

"Where do you think you're going?" he asked.

"To the front desk to ask for my own room." She went to retrieve her purse and briefcase, her pulse tripping along in her ears like a racing piston.

"Yes, run away, Rebecca. It is what you do when things are difficult, *sí*? Better to run than face the problem."

She whirled around and marched back to the table. Her entire body shook as she stared him down. "You aren't a god, Alejandro. You can sit in your ivory tower and order people around, you can destroy companies and lives, but nothing will bring back your child. *Nothing*."

It was so obvious, and yet he was blind to it. He was consumed by rage and grief, and reacting every day to those forces in his life because he hadn't yet learned how to deal with them.

He shot to his feet. But she didn't stop. She couldn't. She tumbled on. "You accuse *me* of running away? What in the hell do you think *you're* doing? You've been running since the minute she died and you don't even know it!"

"Get out," he growled.

Rebecca refused to cry. "Yes, that's exactly what I thought you'd say. Far better to order me away than to face what you're feeling. But you won't always be able to run, Alejandro. One of these days it's going to catch up with you."

"You need to leave," he said gravely. "Now, before I—"

"Before you what? Make me regret the day I was born?" She drew herself up, laughed. But inside she was dying. "For once you're too late."

The trip back to Madrid was accomplished in silence. Alejandro watched Rebecca from beneath lowered eyelids.

She concentrated on her laptop screen, never looking at him. She'd spent last night in her own room, several floors away from his. He hadn't gone after her, much as he'd wanted to.

Madre de Dios, the things she'd said to him. He'd spent the rest of the night tossing and turning, thinking about it. Was she right? Was he running from Anya's death?

He shoved the thought aside angrily. What did she know? She'd never experienced such a loss, never sat in a waiting room alone and waited for news, never spent hours trying to locate a woman who was attending fashion week in Milan and couldn't be bothered to turn on her cell phone.

She had no idea what she was talking about!

He needed to end this. He didn't need her chipping away at him like she could break the ice surrounding his heart. It was painful, uncomfortable. She made him feel like he was on the brink of losing control, like the balls he kept spinning in the air could crash down on his head any minute.

When they landed in Madrid, he needed to tell her she was done. Tell her in the airport so she could catch a flight out. Say goodbye forever.

He leaned back against the headrest, closed his eyes. No, he had to be more deliberate about it. He'd planned it for so long. He couldn't tell her in a public place like an airport.

And he couldn't tell her now because he didn't want to deal with the dramatics for the rest of the flight. He would tell her tonight. *Sí*, this was best.

He would seduce her one final time, use her luscious body for his pleasure. And then he would ruin her life the way she'd ruined his.

After they landed, Alejandro sent Rebecca back to the villa while he went into the office. He had things to do, and he needed time to think. He'd waited so long for this day. He wanted to do it right—wanted to enjoy the full measure of her despair.

Except he looked on it with dread more than anticipation. Why? Perhaps it was the prospect of drama, of her tears and pleading. He'd once thought that would be gratifying, but now he realized he just wanted the whole mess over cleanly and quickly.

But maybe he was wrong to move so fast. It had only been a couple of weeks since he'd taken over Layton International. He needed to enjoy the full measure of his triumph, needed to watch her squirm for a while in his employ. She would think she had a chance of regaining her company and he would know it wasn't possible. In the meantime, he would enjoy her in his bed.

Yes, a much better plan. In fact, he would take her to the opera at the Teatro Real tonight. He would make nice and be solicitous. She would fall into his arms willingly when they returned home.

Señora Flores was in the entry when he came through the door a couple of hours later. She frowned at him, spun on her heel and marched away. Rebecca's suitcases were stacked off to one side.

"You're back."

His head snapped up, his gaze landing on Rebecca. She stood in the door to the office. She was dressed in a tailored gray pantsuit and carried her briefcase.

"You are going somewhere?" He'd warned her what he would do if she left. Did she think to manipulate him by threatening to walk out?

"Yes." Her chin tilted up as he moved toward her. She looked as if she wanted to flee, but she stood her ground. He took in her defiant stare, her red eyes, the puffiness—

"You have been crying, *querida*? What has happened?" Had something happened to her mother, perhaps? He would order his plane to be made ready—would take her anywhere she needed to go.

He moved to embrace her, but she shrank away so quickly he thought she might fall. "No," she gasped. "Don't touch me."

His arms fell to his sides. *Madre de Dios.* Why was his chest suddenly tight?

"Tell me," he commanded, retreating to ground he understood. He would force her to do his bidding, to tell him what was wrong.

In answer, her hand snaked out, connected with his cheek. He didn't even flinch. Their gazes clashed and held. A disconnected part of him idly wondered how this would end. But the warrior in him knew what was in store. He could see the violence shaking her in its grip.

A moment later she rushed at him, her hands balling into fists. He grabbed her wrists, held her away from him as she struggled.

"Rebecca, for God's sake—tell me what is wrong." As if he didn't have an idea.

She sucked in a breath, wrenched herself from his grasp with a strength that surprised him. Spinning away, she wrapped her arms around her body.

She faced him again, glaring. "You *own* the bank, Alejandro. You've owned it for over a year. The *only* bank that would loan my father money!" She laughed. The sound broke off into a sob. "I thought it was a mistake at first—that you'd bought it recently, along with the promissory note for Layton International's loans. But *you* financed the loan. And *you* sold the Thailand resorts to us. They belonged to you, to one of your subsidiaries. You set everything up. When you said you make your own luck, I thought you'd watched us and waited. But you *made* everything happen!"

He shrugged, tried to look casual. Unfeeling. "*Sí*, it is as you say."

She took a step forward, her fists clenching so hard her knuckles were white. "He *died* in Thailand. Touring the resorts *you* sold him in order to ruin us. My God, you *are* a bastard. How I could've thought—" She swiped at her eyes, shook her head.

"How did you learn this?" Her face was pale, her expression almost fragile. Oddly, it bothered him.

"It's too ironic, really. Roger Cahill e-mailed me the documents. He dug them up while looking for dirt on you. Funny, huh?"

"You have been in touch with Cahill?" It shouldn't surprise him, but it did. Cahill had been the financial power behind the company fighting him over the Dubai property. No doubt she'd been in close contact with him the entire time—though she'd been in no position to learn anything truly useful to report back. Strangely, the thought she would even want to stung him.

"I asked him what happened five years ago," Rebecca said, sniffling. "Perhaps you should have done the same."

"I know what happened," he snapped. How many times did he have to remember it?

"Not really," she replied, her chin thrusting out as she drew herself up. "My father killed your deal—so, yes, the Laytons tried to ruin you. I think he must have been angry because you hurt me, but I don't know that for sure. I suppose you can blame me if you want, but you need to blame yourself as well. If you hadn't had a fiancée—or whatever you want to call her—none of this would have happened."

Blame himself? What the hell was she talking about? It was *her* fault. He took a step forward—to do what, he wasn't sure.

The doorbell rang and he stopped, shook his head. Señora Flores's footsteps pattered down the hall.

"That'll be my taxi," Rebecca said. "I recommend John Barnes as the new CEO."

Surprise rooted him to the spot. This was not the way it was supposed to happen. *He* was the one in control—the one who determined when and how everything happened. She could not walk out on him again! "You are running away? What about your company?"

"What should I do? Stay and wait for you to fire me?" She shook her head. "Layton International's not mine anymore, is it? You've made sure of that. Now it's time I got on with my life."

When she shouldered past him he gripped her arm, a feeling he didn't understand seizing him in a choke hold. "This isn't over."

She shuddered in revulsion. Her gaze settled on his hand, lifted to meet his stare. "Yes, it is. Goodbye, Alejandro."

She picked his hand off her arm. The touch of her skin seared him. He had a primeval urge to grab her, haul her to the bedroom and lock her inside until she smiled at him again. Until she made love to him like he was the only man in the world.

But he didn't say anything as she turned and walked to the door. What was there to say? He'd won, hadn't he? He had Layton International. Rebecca had nothing. It was what he'd dreamed of for five years.

He didn't know how long he stood there, but when he finally looked up long shadows had crept across the tiles. It was over. Rebecca was gone.

New York in summer was predictably sweltering. Rebecca made it back to her air-conditioned apartment building before she wilted, and headed for the elevator. She didn't want to think about what she'd just bought at the drugstore, but there was no getting around it.

Fishing in her purse for her keys, she stopped in front of her door. Twenty minutes later, she stared at the test stick. Pink. She knew what that meant. How had it happened? She hadn't missed her pills at all. She'd had some breakthrough bleeding, and the doctor had said her body had grown too accustomed to the pill she was on. So he'd given her a different one about a month before she'd gone to Madrid.

She dropped the stick, her heart pounding with so many emotions. Joy, yes. Pain too. In the mirror, her face was pale. Drawn. She had dark circles beneath her eyes, and she'd lost weight. Her chest rose and fell quickly as she worked to control her rioting emotions. She would not panic.

Her baby needed her to be healthy—not this pale, sickly creature who couldn't eat or sleep properly. Her hand fluttered to her abdomen, pressed against her womb. She was pregnant. With Alejandro's baby. Already she loved this child fiercely. She wanted to run and pick up the phone, call Alejandro, tell him how wonderful and terrifying the news was. But she couldn't.

He didn't care about her. He never had. Everything with him was about control.

Rebecca shoved a trembling hand through her hair. *Oh, God.* What was she going to do? She was alone, and now she had another life to think about. How could she work and take care of her baby at the same time? Because she *had* to work. She hadn't paid herself a salary since her father had died, and her savings were nearly gone. Who would take care of them both if she didn't?

Her mother? God, no. Alejandro? She crushed down a hysterical laugh at the thought.

It had been four weeks since she'd left Madrid. Four excruciating weeks. She'd actually believed he might come after her. That he might apologize for all he'd done and beg her forgiveness. What a delusional fantasy!

She could still see his face so clearly when she'd confronted him. He hadn't denied a thing. He'd looked cold and disconnected, like he didn't care that he'd turned her world upside down.

She was still staggered by the depth of his betrayal. He

hadn't just watched Layton International from afar. He'd found her father's weakness, enticed him into the loans and the Thailand properties, and kept twisting the knife even after her father died. Twisted until he'd won the battle. She'd been devastated when Roger had sent her the proof, and she'd reacted in the only way she knew how.

Leaving her company hadn't been easy, but it had been necessary. She could no longer allow Alejandro to control her life. For her own health and sanity she'd had to go.

She'd been angry and bitter. She'd even thought for a brief time that she hated him. But her father had made his own choices in life. Alejandro might have manipulated the situation, but Jackson Layton had not been a puppet. He had wanted the Thailand property in spite of the best advice against the acquisition, and he'd single-mindedly gone after it.

His death had been unexpected, but she couldn't truly lay it at Alejandro's door. If it hadn't been Thailand, it would have been something else. Her father had been a bit of a daredevil—skydiving, rock climbing, bungee jumping, swimming with sharks—and it was a wonder he'd lived as long as he had.

Rebecca splayed a hand over her abdomen possessively. There was no denying how she felt about Alejandro any longer. When had she fallen again? When he'd found her with the photo album? When he'd looked at her with such naked need in the suite at the Villa de Musica?

Or had she never stopped loving him?

Not that it mattered how or why. She loved him. Love wasn't something you turned on and off like a faucet, however much she might wish it so. She was in love with the man who'd ruined her. And she was carrying his child!

The nights were the worst. So lonely. She hated sleeping alone in her bed so much she'd finally dragged a blanket to the couch and now slept there. She missed Alejandro's big warm body, his intense lovemaking, the rare smile that changed his features and bound her heart.

He obviously did not feel the same. He hadn't called, hadn't followed her, hadn't even written an e-mail. He wasn't tortured by sleepless nights and memories. The only thing she'd received from Spain was a severance check from Ramirez Enterprises.

She was on her own now. She'd returned to New York to pack up her apartment, and then she was on her way to London to take a job with the Cahill Group.

But with a baby on the way? They'd made a baby together. It was a miracle, an amazing, beautiful miracle. *Oh, Alejandro, I want you to know. I want you to love us.*

Rebecca swallowed. She didn't know how to be a mother. She'd always been busy with her career. She had friends with babies, but she didn't understand how they knew what to do. Her own mother would certainly be no help. The woman didn't have a maternal bone in her body. What if Rebecca didn't either? How could she possibly put a baby through the sort of neglectful existence she'd endured?

She drew in a shaky breath. It rattled out again and ended in a sob.

She had to tell Alejandro. For a moment she considered pretending the baby was someone else's. But she couldn't do it.

Not after Anya. He'd loved her, and he would love this child too, no matter how much he hated the baby's mother. But how to tell him and make sure he didn't try to take their baby away from her? Because she had to acknowledge it was a very real possibility. He hated her so much he would have no qualms about ripping her baby away and making her suffer.

And she would *never* allow that. This baby was hers, and she loved it more than she'd ever loved anything in her life.

She wasn't telling him today. Probably not even tomorrow. She'd tell him when she'd figured out how to deal with him and let him know in no uncertain terms that he wasn't taking their baby away from her.

The next few days were a blur. Between doctors' appointments and preparing for the move to London, Rebecca didn't have much time to herself. The movers would be here tomorrow, and she would fly the day after that. It was all so fast, but that was how she wanted it.

She'd stopped at the bookstore on her way home and picked up two books about pregnancy and one on mothering. Who knew they had such things? But thank the Lord they did, because she would need all the help she could get. She still hadn't figured out how to integrate this new life inside her with the one she knew—long days at the office, endless meetings and business trips—but there had to be something in these books that would help.

She thought of the evenings when she'd used to sit at the window and wait for her daddy to come home. Her mother, if she noticed, would say, "Your *père* is working, *ma belle*. He will be home when he can. Now, go play and stop your moping."

How could she do her job and make sure her child didn't feel as lonely as she had? Because she couldn't imagine this baby sitting at a window and waiting for her to come home. She would not let it happen. Her baby would know it was loved, cherished. Somehow she would make everything work. She had to.

Bernadette, the daytime door attendant to her building, rocked back and forth on the balls of her feet and smiled as Rebecca approached. Her blue uniform was always crisp, her smile always ready. Rebecca would miss the woman's cheery greetings.

"Miss Layton, good to see you. How's the move going, hmm?"

"It's a pain, but I think I'll survive," she answered. Her days had been so busy that she was behind on many of the things she'd wanted to accomplish, but she made a mental note to give Bernadette an extra-large tip and a gift before she left.

Bernadette leaned forward, her eyes flashing. Rebecca grinned. What manner of hunk had the woman seen now? Bernadette was always talking about the good-looking men in the building, or the ones who'd strolled by during the day. It was one of the highlights of her job.

"Supreme eye candy alert," she said. "A foreign type. Got out of that limo there and entered the building not more than five minutes ago. Bet he's on his way to that beauty queen's digs."

They had a former Miss Something or Other in the building, which seemed to fascinate Bernadette no end. Any time a good-looking guy went inside, she was convinced he was headed for the woman's apartment. She was probably right.

"How do you know he's foreign?" A little twinge of sadness hit her as she pictured Alejandro's incredible smile. Whoever this guy was, he couldn't compare, she was certain. No man could.

"Oh, honey, I can spot 'em a mile away. But he was on the phone, and it wasn't English he was talking. Smelled like money too, let me tell you." She wagged her head back and forth. "Mmm-mmm, I'd sell my soul to the devil himself for one night in the sack with that guy. He'd never know what hit him."

Rebecca laughed and left Bernadette to her daydreams about Miss Whatever's potential suitor. Taking one of the books out of her bag, she flipped through it while she waited for the elevator.

So much to know about babies. Unconsciously, her hand drifted over her abdomen. She smiled when she realized what she was doing.

"We have a lot to learn, you and I," she said to her baby. It didn't matter if the baby couldn't understand her yet; it comforted her to talk to her child. *Her child.* Those words still gave her a little thrill. And, funny enough, she no longer felt so alone in the world, knowing she had a life growing inside her. They would be okay. Somehow they would be okay.

She hummed a little as she walked down the hallway toward her apartment. A familiar scent seemed to linger in the air as she reached her door, and a trickle of alarm buzzed between her shoulder blades. It wasn't a heavy cologne smell, but a scent that came from expensive clothes and a certain brand of soap. Her heart pounded into her throat as she shoved the key in the lock and pushed the door open. She closed it behind her, slid the chains in place, and let out a shaky sigh.

What was the matter with her? Alejandro was *not* here. He couldn't be here. He had no reason to be. He didn't know about her pregnancy. And though he'd had her followed once before, he had no reason to do so now. He was finished with her. No investigator was lurking outside her building, sending reports to her gorgeous Spanish lover.

To the father of her child.

Rebecca shivered. Her senses were heightened due to the hormones rocketing through her system. The man visiting the beauty queen was simply cut from the same mold as Alejandro—rich, handsome, and possessed of impeccable taste. He eschewed cologne and used imported soap. So what?

She set her bag of books on the coffee table and went into the kitchen to get a glass of cool water. There were boxes everywhere. She surveyed the open loft, the amount of work yet to be done. Despair crushed down on her.

Though the Cahill Group was paying for her relocation, it didn't help her in sorting through her things before the movers arrived. She had to keep busy or she'd go crazy.

The doorbell buzzed and she sighed. Janine from down the hall had mentioned a get-together in her apartment this afternoon, but Rebecca didn't feel like going. Still, it was just like Janine to try and talk her into it—especially when she was leaving in two days.

"Just a minute," she called when the bell buzzed again. When she reached the door, she checked the peephole out of habit.

The man standing in the hall was definitely not Janine.

Her breath shortened, her heart plummeting to her toes before shooting through the roof. How could she deal with him? Why was he here? What would she tell him about the baby?

Tears flooded her eyes as she folded her hands over her belly protectively. No, she wasn't ready. If she didn't say anything, maybe he'd go away. What in hell was Alejandro doing in New York? Maybe he'd had her watched after all? Maybe he knew everything? Cold fear dripped down her spine.

"I know you're in there, Rebecca. Open the door."

CHAPTER TEN

REBECCA closed her eyes. That voice, the crisp Spanish inflections. The sound sent a wave of longing through her. And fury. How dare he show up *now* and demand she open the door to him? Where had he been a month ago? He should have been here, apologizing, begging her forgiveness. *Right.*

"Rebecca—open up or I'll kick it in."

She'd like to see that. The door was steel. And yet he was making enough noise that any second doors would start popping open up and down the hall. Worse, she believed he really would try to batter her door down if she didn't answer. She yanked it open, but didn't undo the chain.

Alejandro stared down his nose at her. His arrogant, rotten, deceptive nose.

And he looked every bit as delicious as he had over a month ago. He wore Armani, of course. The tailored gray suit made him look elegant and commanding. Every inch the captain of industry. He was so amazingly beautiful to her eyes. Any second her heart would crack wide open, and she'd be spilling her secrets to him.

His gaze raked over her. "You are unwell?"

Did she look that bad? Her doctor had said she was healthy, if a little underweight. Alejandro had probably moved on to some elegant, gorgeous woman who simpered and put up with his moods. She felt dowdy and unattractive just thinking about it. And heartbroken.

"I'm fine. What do you want?"

"I wish to talk with you."

"Start talking."

He nodded at the door. "Can I come in?"

"No."

He pushed a hand through his hair, blew out his breath in annoyance. "It would be easier to let me in, would it not? Or do you prefer your neighbors hear what I have to say?"

She had no idea what he would say but, no, she didn't want her neighbors to hear it. She shoved the door closed and slid the chain back. Besides, her stomach chose that moment to roil. All she wanted was to sit down and get this over with. She jerked the door open and turned her back on him, going over to sit on the couch and fold her legs beneath her. Hostility was her only armor. She prayed he would not see beneath it.

He came inside, his gray gaze coolly assessing his surroundings. He seemed unsurprised she was moving. Of course. He probably knew everything about her job with the Cahill Group. No doubt he saw it as a betrayal that she would work for Roger, but what else was she supposed to do?

"You look unwell," he said again as he strode into the living room. His hands were thrust in his pockets. He was so tall, so imposing. And he was standing in her apartment, his presence reminding her of all they'd done together. Her heart throbbed with anger and hurt.

She shook her head. "It's nothing. What do you want?"

"You didn't cash your severance check."

Rebecca blinked. "You came all the way to New York to say that?"

"No. I came to meet with Layton International's board."

She swallowed a wave of tears. He was here for business, not for her. It seemed so strange to hear something about her company from him. A board meeting that she wasn't a part of. Hadn't known about.

"Just tell me what you want and get out," she said wearily. Her brain had gone numb. She couldn't deal with him—couldn't begin to imagine telling him about the baby she carried. When she got to London and got settled in she'd give him the news. He'd be angry, but this was her body and her pregnancy and she'd do things her way.

He reached into his jacket and pulled out an envelope. When he tossed it onto the coffee table, she eyed it warily. "If that's another severance check, you can keep it. I don't want your money."

Perhaps if Roger hadn't hired her she would have been forced to cash it. But now that he had, she had no intention of taking a dime from Alejandro. He'd once called her greedy. Let him wonder why she wouldn't accept money from him.

"It's not."

Rebecca heaved a sigh and leaned forward to grasp the envelope. Maybe if she opened it he would leave. Sadness washed over her, but she pushed it away and ripped the packet open to stare at the contents.

Dashing a hand over her cheeks to wipe away her tears, she tried to sound flippant. "I should refuse, but I won't." She clutched the deed, more touched than she wanted to be. She wasn't going to take his money, but she would take this. One day she would give it to their child.

"No, La Belle Amelie is yours."

"I'll pay you for it. Just give me time to put together the financing."

"No."

Rebecca sucked back tears, forced a laugh. She didn't know how to respond, so she resorted to flippancy. "Honestly, Alejandro, the sex *was* pretty good, but I doubt it was worth quite this much."

His mouth opened, then closed as his gaze fixed on something lying on the table. His head turned, as if he was trying to read—

She scrambled for the bag of books she'd knocked over reaching for the envelope and shoved them back inside. Before she could stash the bag beneath the table Alejandro had ripped it from her grasp.

His expression was a mixture of horror and rage as he yanked a book out and stared at the title. Eyes hot with emotion pinned her like a bug. "What is the meaning of this?"

She considered for about half a second telling him the books were for a friend. But she couldn't do it. This baby was his too, and, God help her, she still loved him. She wanted him to know—wanted him to be happy about it. And she was terrified at the same time. Terrified he would be angry, that he wouldn't believe her, that he might try to take the baby away.

No. She would never allow that. Never. He'd already taken the one thing that had meant the most to her. He would not do so ever again.

"Surprise," she said softly, her throat as dry as noon in the Sahara.

Soul-deep fear riveted Alejandro in place. Pregnant? She was *pregnant*? He shook his head to clear it. No, this could not be.

"How did it happen?" he said, his voice very cold and controlled.

Her expression crumpled a little, then hardened as if she were determined not to show any weakness in front of him. "The usual way, I imagine. We certainly had enough sex, don't you think?"

"You are telling me you're pregnant." It was a statement, not a question.

"Yes, Alejandro. I'm pregnant."

"How do you know the baby is mine?" She'd left him five weeks ago. Plenty of time to dupe some other man into believing she cared for him. Roger Cahill, perhaps? The man was only about twenty years her senior—still perfectly capable of being her lover.

Her face whitened. She shielded her abdomen with a hand. "How could you ask such a thing? Of course it's yours! The doctor estimates seven weeks."

Alejandro dropped the book on the table and raked a hand through his hair. *Dios.* If this baby were really his, how could he go through it again? How could he live each day wondering if it would be the day his baby would die?

Anya. Her little body turning blue, the trip to the emergency room, the frantic efforts to revive her. *Dios, no.* Her eyes haunted him to this day. He would never survive it a second time.

Hurricane-force emotion whirled inside him. Which was the easier to digest? Rebecca sleeping with another man so soon after she'd left him—which would require the doctor to be wrong about the dates—or the knowledge her baby was his and might very well be vulnerable to the genetic defect that had taken Anya's life?

Solving the baby's parentage would be easy enough to do, though he very much feared it was unnecessary; she was telling the truth. He went over to where she sat on the couch, her expression one of hurt and misery. She tilted her head back to look up at him.

He would not be moved by what he saw in her face. "You said you were taking the pill. Did you lie? Did you do this on purpose, thinking it would gain you Layton International?"

She shot up from her sitting position, but he was too quick for her. Grabbing her wrist, he prevented the slap she tried to deliver. Her blue eyes reflected hurt and surprise. Awareness shot through him at the contact of skin on skin, though it was only his hand on her wrist. He wondered if she felt it too. What would she do if he lowered his head and kissed her?

He wanted to. The compulsion shocked him.

She jerked free and moved out of his reach. "You can be so vicious, Alejandro. Why do you always need to think the worst of people? Sometimes things just happen."

He rolled a shoulder irritably. "I'm a wealthy man, *querida*. It wouldn't be the first time a woman thought to gain advantage by claiming I'd fathered her child."

Her jaw went slack.

"I have had one child, Rebecca, in spite of what you might think. Fatherhood is not a responsibility I take lightly."

"I'm glad to hear it, for our baby's sake. But I am—*was*— on birth control. It was a new prescription and it obviously didn't do the job it was supposed to do."

He took his mobile phone from his pocket and called the airport, giving instructions to ready his jet for takeoff.

"What are you doing?" Her voice sounded strained.

He ignored her.

"Alejandro?" The sound was sharper this time.

He pocketed the phone and prepared to do battle. "We are returning to Madrid tonight."

She folded her arms beneath her breasts. He ignored the arrow of heat knifing into his groin. Had her breasts gotten fuller? *Sí*. As if she wasn't beautiful enough already. Need washed over him. To strip her slowly, to lick his way from nipple to nipple, to drop lower and taste her before thrusting hard into her—he very much wanted to do all these things, and often. For a month he'd thought of almost nothing else.

"Have a nice flight," she said. "Glad you could stop by."

He bared his teeth in a smile he knew she couldn't mistake for a friendly overture. "I do not use the royal we, *amor*. You are coming with me."

She paled. "No. You aren't taking this baby away from me, Alejandro. I'll fight you with everything I have."

"And what would that be, Rebecca?" He stalked closer, satisfied when she backed away. He was too furious to play games with her. "I have more money and more resources at my disposal than you could ever hope to muster in a year of phone calls to all your former contacts. You *will* accompany me."

Her throat worked. "Why are you doing this? I have a job in London. I have a life—"

"Your life is with me now. You will pack a suitcase, *inmediatamente*, and come with me."

"This is America, Alejandro. You can't kidnap me and force me onto a plane. We have laws against that."

He laughed. Cute of her to try and dissuade him with the threat of the American authorities. And completely useless. He would do anything—no matter how ruthless, no matter how underhanded—to win this battle with her.

"Nevertheless, you belong to me. You will cooperate, or I will make sure you never see this child again after it is born. I will use any means necessary to win. Do not mistake me."

Her breathing grew faster as she battled some emotion. Tears, no doubt. But he would not be swayed if she lost control. He knew he was being harsh, but icy sharp fear had him in its grip. He would protect this child at all costs. He would never, ever allow Anya's fate to strike again. This baby would be tested within an inch of its life. So would he. And so would Rebecca. He would leave nothing to chance.

"Why do you have to be so cruel?" It was little more than a whisper.

The barb pricked him. But he had no use for misguided attempts to imbue him with guilt. "Life is cruel. Better to face the bull head-on, *sí*?"

She sank back onto the couch, her breathing irregular. The

hairs on his arms prickled. *Dios*, she'd had trouble breathing once before—when he'd upset her.

He dropped to his knees in front of her, gripped her shoulders. "Breathe, Rebecca. All will be well. Come with me and I will take care of you both. I promise you."

She dropped forward until her forehead was touching his, pulled in deep breaths. He cupped her jaw in both hands, smoothed his thumbs over her cheeks. "Shh, *mi querida*, don't fight. Think of something happy, yes?"

"Easy…for you…to…say—"

"Kittens," he said. "Kittens are happy. Or puppies. *Sí*, think of these things. I will buy you a puppy. Or a kitten. Or both. Just be calm," he said softly, caressing her slowly, rhythmically. His heart battered his ribs as he worked to soothe her. *Because of the baby—it is only because of the baby…*

"You will *not*…take…my baby. Not—"

"No." What else could he say? It was imperative she be healthy for their child.

"Your…word."

Cold conviction dripped down his spine. He knew what he had to do, though it filled him with dread. "You don't need my word, *amor*. You will have my name."

How could she possibly marry him?

A week later Rebecca was still wondering how she'd agreed to get on that plane and return to Madrid. She'd been terrified when he had threatened to take her baby away by fair means or foul. After what he'd done to get Layton International, she did not doubt he was capable of anything.

But even that hadn't been quite enough to tip her over the edge. No, it was the way he had touched her so sweetly, the way he had soothed her with his beautiful, sexy voice. His fingers on her skin, sending shards of sensation through her. Giving her his strength, helping her get through the panic.

She'd loved him so much in those moments that she'd have agreed to move to Mars if he'd asked her to. Worse, she had been able to deceive herself—briefly—that he loved her in return simply by the sweetness of his touch.

It certainly *had* been self-deception, because he hadn't touched her since. She did not know if he ever would.

Rebecca pressed her temples against the headache flaring to life. She'd quit her new job, followed him to Spain like a lovesick puppy, and he'd barely spoken to her. He was probably still laughing at how easy it had been to convince her.

But it *was* the best decision for their child. She knew it down deep. Alejandro would be a good father, a fierce, protective father. His child would never be an afterthought in his life. She was comforted by that knowledge.

For herself, however, a lifetime of heartbreak lay ahead. He'd gone to extraordinary lengths to get her company, yet the real punishment would be in living with him and loving him when he did not return the feeling.

How would she endure it?

She would simply have to. But she could never allow him to know the power he had over her. While she could trust him with their child, she could never trust him with her heart. It would be a lonely existence, but she would survive it. And once their child came along she would have someone to love, someone who would love her unconditionally.

Unexpectedly, Alejandro arrived home that afternoon to collect her for her doctor's appointment. She protested that she could go alone, but he would hear none of it. Because of what had happened to Anya, she didn't fight him over it. He had a need to be there—a need to be involved and understand everything that happened with her pregnancy. He wanted to protect the baby. If it helped him feel somehow in control of the future, she wouldn't stop him.

The appointment was routine. Alejandro was sensible enough about her wish not to have him there for the pelvic exam, but he returned immediately after. They both had blood taken for the genetic testing Alejandro insisted on having, though the baby couldn't be tested for heart defects until much later. The doctor assured them that if they both were fine, the baby most likely would be too.

Later, when they were in the car on the way back to the villa, Alejandro said, "We need to set a date for the wedding. Have you called your mother?"

Rebecca turned to look at him. She'd been watching the people on the sidewalks as they passed by. She didn't know what to say to him anymore. He was like a stranger to her. When they talked it was about the baby or the wedding; nothing more. And that was only sporadic.

"She hasn't returned my call yet."

He looked surprised. Rebecca shrugged. She was accustomed to her mother's shallowness by now. "She's probably shopping. Or skiing."

Disapproval hardened his expression. "Do you want to wait so she can be here for the ceremony?"

She picked at a thread on her cardigan. "It's not necessary."

Silence. Then, "My sister wants to meet you."

"I'd like to meet her, too." He'd always spoken with affection for his sister. She was nervous about the prospect of meeting Valencia, but curious as well.

"She is arriving soon for a short visit. We can be married while she's here, if that is agreeable."

Rebecca fiddled with her bracelet as she digested this information. He hadn't mentioned his family at all since she'd returned. "Does she know about the baby?"

"*Sí*, I have told her."

Which meant his sister knew why they were marrying so quickly. "And your parents?"

"They will know soon enough."

She wasn't sure what to think about why he hadn't yet told his parents. "What will they think about you marrying me?"

He gave her a significant look. "They won't care. They are far more interested in their own lives than in mine or my sister's."

She heard the bitterness in his voice. She hadn't forgotten what he'd said to her in the car the night they'd returned from his parents' party. And after her brief time in Juan and Carmen Ramirez's company she knew it was probably the truth. They reminded her of her own mother: selfish and self-absorbed.

"They will not be at the wedding?"

His laugh was sudden and sharp. "You don't want them there, believe me. They would somehow manage to turn it into a personal drama where they occupied center stage."

"You had a lavish wedding before," she said. "I believe even the King and Queen attended." She'd looked up the photos on the Internet. Alejandro had been spectacular, his bride gorgeous—but neither of them had smiled much.

"There is no time for this kind of wedding," he said coolly. "You would be big with our baby by the time we married. We will have a quick civil ceremony and be done, *sí*?"

She pushed her hurt down deep. It wasn't that she wanted a huge wedding—she just wanted this to be about something more than a marriage of convenience to him. She also wanted to understand why he'd married his first wife, since he claimed not to have loved her.

Something he'd told her tickled her mind. "You said the night of the anniversary party that your father wanted to chase me away five years ago. If he cared who you married then, why not now?"

Alejandro sighed. "It wasn't you specifically, Rebecca. He wanted me to marry my brother's fiancée."

"I don't understand."

"My father arranged a marriage for my brother. It was a

matter of family honor to him. When Roberto died, it fell to me to keep the agreement."

"Your brother died before you met me. If you were to marry her in his place, then you were already engaged." She felt tears pricking her eyes. Stupid hormones. This was old news.

Alejandro's brows slashed down. "No. I had no intention of marrying her, in spite of my father."

"But you did anyway. Did our sheets even get cold before she moved in?"

"You left *me*, Rebecca."

She lifted her chin and met him dead in the eye. "It took me almost a year to see someone else. Yet you were married and expecting a baby by then."

It was hard to admit the truth, but why hide it any longer? He acted like he was the one who was wronged. What about her? She *wanted* him to know how difficult it had been for her.

His look was intense, curious. "You did not take a new lover? Why should I believe this?"

"You can believe what you want, Alejandro." She lowered her eyes, toyed with the hula girl charm on her bracelet. "I've never been the sort of woman who falls into bed with whomever strikes my fancy. Not that there's anything wrong with it, but I always had to be careful."

Alejandro stared at the top of her head. All this talk about marriage was closing a vise around his neck. He had every intention of marrying her, of binding her to him so he had legal rights to his child, but the thought of it always made anger burn low in his gut. He would marry her, but he didn't have to enjoy the prospect. Sometimes he wondered if he'd been expertly maneuvered into it. He tried not to consider that possibility very often.

But what was this about being careful who she'd slept with? Her attention was firmly fixed on the gold bracelet she wore. He wanted to reach out, clasp her arm and make her look at him. But he did not.

"What do you mean, *querida*?"

"My father. Layton International," she said, never looking up.

He thought back to how upset she'd gotten when he told her he'd had her investigated. Suddenly it made sense. And he thought that if Jackson Layton were here now, he'd throttle him. "Did your father have you watched all the time?"

Her head snapped up. Tears glinted in her eyes. Something tightened in his chest. He reached up to rub absently at the spot, realized what he was doing and dropped his hand again.

"He might have. I don't really know any longer." She laid her head back against the seat, closed her eyes. He found himself thinking how fragile she looked. She'd been almost a shadow of herself when he'd seen her in New York last week. Since returning to Spain he'd put Señora Flores to work feeding her. She had more color in her cheeks, and she was starting to fill out a little bit. Soon she would be big with his child. The thought made him possessive.

"Why would he do this to you?"

She took a deep breath, let it out again. "Because I was a girl, Alejandro. He wanted a son to leave the business to." She looked at him. "He thought I would be weak, that I would lose my head over a man—because that's what women do, naturally."

"Not you," he said, and meant it. One of the things he'd always been impressed with was her sense of the hotel business. They'd spent hours talking about every aspect of the business when he had still been new to it. And after he'd taken her company he'd watched her in the boardroom, reviewed her management of Layton International, and realized who'd really steered the company into a freefall. The only weak Layton had been her father.

"He had cause to think so," she said quietly.

"Because of me?"

"No, someone else."

Something very like jealousy sliced into him. "You were in love?" She'd told him she loved *him*. He'd believed it until she'd betrayed him. But to think she'd loved someone else, really loved him? He had an urge to slam his fist into something.

"It was a couple of years before I met you, the summer I was twenty," she said. "Parker Gaines was very sophisticated, very suave. He was a con man—though I didn't know it, of course."

She bowed her head, spoke to her lap. "My father wanted to test me. Or so he said. He hired Parker to 'breach my defenses' as he put it. I was young enough and—" she laughed bitterly, brokenly "—lonely enough to believe Parker's lies. He seduced me, claimed to love me and stole money from me. Worse, he got the combination to the safe in my office. He stole documents, checks, plans for future developments. Father was livid."

Alejandro seethed with fury. *Dios*, had her father been insane? He did not doubt for a moment that she spoke the truth. She was too devastated, her fingers trembling as she talked, her voice breaking on the name *Parker Gaines*.

"Why would your father do this?"

She shrugged, as if it didn't mean anything, but he knew that was far from true. "He wanted to teach me to be ruthless. He called me to his office after I'd discovered the extent of Parker's theft. And Parker was there, drinking Scotch and smiling like he'd won the lottery. He'd recorded our conversations, played back some of the juicier ones for my father while I stood there and tried to defend myself." She sucked in a shaky breath. "God, it was humiliating. But I learned my lesson. I was very careful who I let into my life after that."

She was supposed to be a spoiled heiress, not this ravaged woman pouring out her private pain to him. Alejandro didn't know he'd reached for her until he gripped her hand in his, felt the small bones and cool skin. "I'm sorry that happened to you, *querida.*"

Though he would never say so to her, he was also glad her father was dead. It saved him the trouble of killing the man himself.

She didn't say anything, just nodded, her head turned toward the window. When her shoulders shook silently, he squeezed her hand. Nothing more. Though it went against every instinct he had not to drag her into his arms and hold her.

Why had she told him those things? Rebecca splashed cool water on her face and looked at her red-rimmed eyes in the mirror. Was she insane? He'd been horrified, like any rational person would be, but he'd viewed it more as a curiosity outside his sphere than as something that touched him personally. He'd been kind, but no more.

What had she expected? That he would enfold her in his arms and kiss her tears away? Take her to his bed and make love to her? If she'd hoped for a connection with him she'd sorely miscalculated. She had to be careful, had to keep her feelings hidden. She would not give him that kind of power to hurt her ever again.

When they had arrived back at the villa he'd wasted no time getting away from her. He'd gone into his office and shut the door. She didn't blame him. It was a pitiful story, but not truly tragic in the way losing a child was.

Rebecca pressed her hand to her stomach, her heart fluttering at the thought. "You will be well, little one. I know it," she said. "Your daddy is big and strong, and you will be strong just like him."

For the rest of the evening she didn't see Alejandro. He was still in his office, door closed, when she returned from the kitchen and Señora Flores's wonderful *paella*. She could hear him barking out orders to someone on the other end of the telephone line.

Though she didn't remember going to bed, it was dark when she opened her eyes. She was floating, falling, her back landing on cushiony softness. Something covered her. Blankets?

"Alejandro," she breathed, knowing even in sleep who had moved her. She reached for him, wound her arms around his neck. "You are here," she said. "With me."

"Why were you on the chaise, Rebecca? It cannot be comfortable for the whole night."

"Bed's too big." She yawned.

"You have to sleep in the bed. It is better for you."

"Stay with me."

Did he groan? "I cannot," he said, gently pulling her arms away from his neck.

She was waking up by degrees, her mind becoming more alert. Alejandro was here, now. She'd been so lonely without him. Was it wrong of her to want him? To want to feel needed by him, even if only for a short while?

"Why don't you want me?" she asked, unable to keep the hurt from her voice.

"I don't want to hurt you."

He sat on the edge of the bed. She reached out, trailed her fingertips along his jaw. She could see him in the dim light from the moon—the hard lines of his face, the outline of his big body silhouetted against the pale wall behind him.

"You've already hurt me," she said softly. "What's one more time?"

"Go back to sleep, Rebecca." He kissed her palm and placed her hand over her heart.

She thought his hand ghosted over her hair, but she couldn't be sure.

CHAPTER ELEVEN

WHEN Alejandro told her they could marry while his sister was visiting, she didn't realize he meant that very afternoon. He'd presented her with a prenuptial agreement that morning. Somehow, after what she'd told him about her father and Parker, it hurt that he would shove a legal document at her that basically said he didn't trust her and ask her to sign it.

And, truthfully, it wasn't just about the agreement. She understood that a rich man—or woman—had to protect assets. But when she loved him so much, when she wanted him to love her in return, it simply drove home the fact this marriage was convenient, a means to an end. It was about the baby, not about her.

He'd watched her without speaking while she read it. It took a while, since her vision kept blurring.

"You do not wish your lawyers to see this first?" he'd asked, when she kept rereading the same clause.

"I can read a contract, Alejandro." And she could—but when this was about her life with the man she loved, about their future and their baby, it took longer to digest all the legalese. Finally she'd signed it, then excused herself. He'd let her go easily enough, and for that she was grateful.

Now, the four of them rode to the registry hall together. Valencia and her husband Philippe, who'd been able to get away from his business at the last minute, talked and laughed the entire way. Even Alejandro laughed from time to time. He clearly adored his sister. He was almost a different person with her around.

Rebecca could see why. Valencia's personality was infectious. She was a kind, happy person, and she loved her husband to distraction. Rebecca watched the other couple enviously. If Valencia loved her handsome Frenchman, then Philippe worshipped the ground his wife walked on. Their children, whom they'd left in France with his parents, were their pride and joy. It was a blessed existence they shared. Rebecca could only hope for a fraction of their happiness once her baby was born.

The ceremony was conducted in Spanish, with a translator for her—required by law—and was over quickly. Though she hadn't been in Spain the requisite amount of time to marry a citizen, Alejandro had somehow got around that detail. It was good to be rich and famous, apparently.

Valencia hugged her tight after it was over. "I am so glad my brother has you," she said in thick English. "You will make him happy. He deserves happiness, yes?"

Rebecca smiled tremulously. "Yes, he does."

Though he looked, to her, as if he'd be happier anywhere but standing in the registry office with a new bride. Fortunately his discomfort was not apparent to his sister or her husband. Philippe clapped him on the back and congratulated him profusely, and Valencia hugged him and whispered something in his ear.

After the wedding, they spent the afternoon shopping for baby furniture. Valencia was excited, Philippe marginally less so, but Alejandro wore a look of stony reserve. She imagined that shopping for baby things so soon, when they'd been married only a couple of hours and she didn't even look pregnant, was hard on him. He must surely be thinking of the last time he'd picked out cribs and bassinets.

She wanted to go to him, wanted to take his hand and squeeze it the way he'd squeezed hers when she had told him about Parker. Eventually, when they'd strolled into yet another store featuring yet more cribs, Rebecca found herself beside him. She put her hand into his and gave it a quick squeeze, before joining Valencia, who was cooing over sleepsuits and piling them into a basket.

By the time they arrived back at the villa after dinner, it was late. Valencia and Philippe retired to their room, and Rebecca decided to say good-night as well. Alejandro stopped her when she started up the stairs.

"We are in the master suite, *mi esposa*. It would be odd for us not to share a room now, *sí*?"

Blood thundering in her ears, she followed him to the room where they'd made love for the first time in five years. He stopped in the door and let her go through first. If she'd anticipated him carrying her over the threshold, she would have been disappointed. As expected, the memories assailed her as soon as she walked inside. She could see the bed in the room beyond the living area. Had she gotten pregnant there? Or had it happened in Dubai?

Fifteen minutes later, Alejandro still hadn't spoken. He showed no signs of heading into the bedroom any time soon. She remembered last night, how she'd so pitifully asked him to stay. How he'd refused. So now what?

Finally, she couldn't stand the silence any longer. "How are we to share a room together if you don't want to be in the same bed with me? Shall we play a game of tic-tac-toe to decide who gets the bed and who gets the couch? Or maybe you should just let me return to my own room."

He looked up from his seat on one of the leather couches flanking the television. He hadn't turned the TV on, had just sort of sunk wearily onto the leather with a glass of sherry and a dark look.

"The servants will talk, *querida*. Besides, I want to share a bed with you," he said. "Very much."

"But last night—"

"Last night we were not married." He spat the last word as if it were hemlock on his tongue.

She folded her arms and leaned against the arm of the opposite sofa, bemused. "Why did that matter? We've obviously spent the night together before." She pressed her hand to her stomach. "I have proof."

She tried to be lighthearted, but he didn't laugh. His gaze raked her from head to toe.

"You look tired," he said. "Why don't you get ready for bed?"

She slipped onto the cushion facing him. He was snappish because of the memories he'd had to endure today. "I'm sorry you had to go into all those stores. I know it must have been hard for you to look at baby things."

The black look on his face didn't change as he tossed back his drink. "I have a better idea," he said, rising to his feet. "Why don't we get ready for bed together?"

Before she knew what he planned, he was pushing her back on the couch, unbuttoning the cream silk dress she'd gotten married in, his lips following the gaping trail of buttons down between her breasts.

Sensation rocketed through her, so much more sweet and sensitive now that she was pregnant. She tried to concentrate, to focus on him. She knew what he was doing. Avoidance. Only this time he couldn't order her out of his sight. This time he had to shut her up with his mouth, his body.

Was it wrong to be happy about his methodology? Eagerly she went for his shirt, and he captured her mouth, thrusting his tongue inside to tangle with hers. He tasted like sherry, sweet and silky, and she shoved the shirt from his shoulders, her control slipping away with every caress, every breath.

"Alejandro, oh, I missed you…"

"I need you, Rebecca," he said seconds later.

Butterflies swarmed in her stomach as she kissed him again, fusing her mouth to his almost desperately. He'd never said that to her before. Not like that. *Want*, yes. *Need*, never.

He removed her dress while she shoved his trousers off. Underwear disappeared, and then there was nothing left between them but skin—damp, hot. She wrapped her legs around his waist as he rocked his hips against her. He stopped short of entering her body and she whimpered.

"I don't want to hurt you," he said, his eyes wildly searching hers.

"You won't. Make love to me. Please make love to me, Alejandro." Silently, she said the words she couldn't say: *I love you.*

Then he was thrusting deep inside her, their bodies rising to meet each other in perfect harmony.

Rebecca awoke sometime in the night, aware she was alone in bed. A light came from the living area. She searched for something to put on, found Alejandro's shirt. The tails went halfway down her thighs and she had to roll the sleeves several times. It smelled like him. She pulled the fabric over her nose, inhaled deeply.

Alejandro sat on the couch, a photo album on his lap. She stopped short, her heart thudding into her throat. But he looked up at her, and the movement prevented her from backing away, pretending she hadn't been there at all.

He didn't look angry. Emboldened, she went over and sat beside him, leaned her head against his shoulder. She didn't speak. Neither did he.

"She trusted me," he finally said. "I failed."

Rebecca climbed to her knees beside him, put her arms around him, leaned her head against his. "It's not your fault. It's no one's fault."

He didn't say anything.

"I went to tuck her in," he said a long while later. "She was blue. Her body was swollen with the fluids her heart couldn't pump. The doctors couldn't save her."

She stroked his hair. "I'm sorry."

"I cannot do it again."

"You won't have to." Her heart ached so much she thought it might burst.

"You do not know that," he said softly. "You cannot know it."

She took his hand, placed it over her abdomen. "I do," she said fiercely. "I won't let it happen."

"I have said the same thing," he replied. "But there are some things even I cannot control."

Something was wrong with him. He didn't feel right. He'd been on the edge of something for days now. Alejandro threw his pen down and swore violently. All he wanted to do was return home to the villa and make love to Rebecca. He should be over this compulsion by now, but it showed no signs of evaporating.

He'd told her about the night he'd found Anya. He'd never told anyone but the doctors. Never wanted to. He couldn't tell her, however, that he'd blamed *her* for the pain he'd suffered. It didn't seem right with her sitting there beside him, holding him, their baby growing inside her and her swearing she would not let the same thing happen again.

Did he still blame her? He couldn't be sure. One more thing that was wrong with him.

He'd had to force himself to come to the office today. He could work at home, but he'd gotten dressed and taken his Aston Martin Vanquish from the garage. Zipping through the streets of Madrid, he'd tried to concentrate on all he needed to accomplish.

It had worked for a little while, but now that he was at his desk his mind was wandering again. *Focus.* The hotel in Dubai was finally about to begin construction. Though it had been weeks since he'd uncovered his corporate spy, it had still taken time to disentangle the web and get everything straightened away with the Dubai authorities.

His reorganization of Layton International was proceeding. He always felt a little pang of guilt when he reviewed the progress. Absorbing the company had been a good move, but the difficulties he was experiencing with management made him long for the days when Rebecca had been in charge. She knew that company like she'd been born to it. He allowed himself a smile. Indeed, she *had* been born to it. Literally.

He'd considered more than once asking her to come back, but he couldn't sort out his feelings about it well enough to do so.

Was it a sign of defeat? Weakness? Was it tantamount to admitting he'd been wrong?

And what about the baby? Would work be too stressful on her pregnancy? Could she manage the hotel business and a baby too? A very male part of him wanted to lock her in the house and keep her there, but he knew from personal experience that whether or not a woman worked had nothing to do with her ability as a mother. Caridad had had nothing but time, and she'd failed miserably. His own mother was self-absorbed. Apparently so was Rebecca's.

He hadn't missed the disappointment on her face when her mother had finally called. The conversation had been short, to the point, and over without Rebecca saying more than a dozen words. Valencia had chattered endlessly to him about his marriage—she'd whispered that she liked Rebecca very much—though he could have done without it. He thought women liked to talk about those things. It seemed as if Rebecca and her mother did not.

Madre de Dios, he was married. If someone had told him

two months ago that not only would Rebecca Layton be pregnant with his child she would also be his wife, he would have never have believed it. Life was very strange sometimes.

His secretary came in with some paperwork, and he turned his attention to accomplishing something today other than thinking about his wife. Several hours later, when he'd spoken with his man in Dubai, negotiated a new contract in Russia and approved an impact study for a proposed site in India, he felt he'd done enough work to justify returning home. Perhaps Rebecca would be wearing that little bikini he'd bought her. She'd protested that she'd soon be too fat for it, but he'd bought it anyway.

There was nothing sexier than his wife lying beside the pool in her hot-pink bikini. Especially when she then let him take her into the house and peel it from her body as he kissed his way over every centimeter of her satiny skin.

He phoned down to the valet to have his car brought around. When he stepped outside to climb into the sleek gray car, reporters were waiting for him. He didn't think too much of it at first. Long after his years in the ring were over, the newspapers still seemed to find his life fascinating. Now that he'd so recently married they tended to shadow his and Rebecca's public appearances. The attention would die down soon enough.

"Señor Ramirez, is it true you systematically destroyed Layton International through an untraceable chain of subsidiaries? That you duped Jackson Layton into the acquisitions that led him into debt and contributed to his apparent suicide last year?"

Alejandro felt as if someone had kicked the ground out from under him. One minute he was standing firmly in place; the next he was searching for a foothold. "I acquired Layton International legally," he stated evenly, though he was seething inside. "You may check all the filings for your answer."

"But you owned the only bank that would lend him money. Was that a sound financial decision? Or calculation on your part? What does Rebecca Layton think about these revelations?"

"You mean Rebecca Ramirez," Alejandro said, in a voice very like a growl. Oh, he knew *exactly* what Rebecca thought. Exactly the lengths she would go to in order to do him harm. How had he ever thought she might be falling in love with him? Everything she did, every caress and kiss and sweet sigh, was nothing more than a lie.

She wanted to embarrass him, wanted his reputation to be damaged and his business interests to suffer. Did she think he would be forced to part with Layton International? That she would be waiting to snap it up? Did she think she could possibly win this battle?

"No more questions," Alejandro barked, before getting into the open door the valet held. He gunned the powerful engine and raced out onto the *paseo*. Traffic was heavy, but he barely noticed.

He was going to enjoy this confrontation. He'd been so close to falling off the precipice, to caring for her once more. Thank God she'd shown her hand. Finally everything made sense to him again. He had a purpose, a driving goal, a reason to lock her up and throw away the key. And when the baby was born he would be cutting his treacherous wife from both their lives.

"Thank you for the tea, Señora Flores," Rebecca said. The other woman smiled and dipped her head in a nod before retreating to the kitchen. Rebecca couldn't help but grin. She had been convinced, when she had first arrived, that Señora Flores hated her. Now the woman took pains to pamper her.

She sat at a table on the terrace, beneath the bougainvillea,

and studied the fat book that the decorator Alejandro hired had
compiled. She'd wanted to paint the baby's room herself—
wanted to order fabrics and toys and pick out her own rocking
chair. Alejandro had insisted it would be easier with a professional's help. But the woman he'd sent understood Rebecca's
urges and had made a book with many samples to choose
from. She'd also recommended combinations that went well
together.

It was, Rebecca thought with a sigh, far easier than her
plan had been.

"What would you like, my baby?" she said, flipping pages.
"White wicker? Mahogany? Oak? Will we need pink or
blue?"

They would not know the sex for many weeks yet, though
she was secretly hoping for a girl. Little girls' clothes were
so cute. And, since Rebecca was new at this mother thing, she
figured she would understand a little girl better than a little
boy. Perhaps the next one would be a boy.

A boy with Alejandro's smile.

A movement in the doorway caught her eye and she looked
up. "Alejandro!" she exclaimed, jumping up just a little too
excitedly. Damn, did she have to be so transparent? Surely
the man knew she adored him, in spite of her best intentions
not to give away the secret?

He looked stormy. Stony. Furious. Her steps faltered.
"What's wrong, Alejandro? Did something happen at work?
Is everything okay?"

He took two strides toward her, gripped her upper arms and
glared down at her. "Is something wrong at work? You know
very well something is wrong!" he thundered. "*Dios*, how did
I ever fall for this act of yours again?"

He thrust her away and she wrapped her arms around
herself, stared at him in shock. She could still feel the imprint
of his fingers, the pain of his grip. Her stomach lodged some-

where in the vicinity of her toes. Her heart was sinking like a lead weight. Her limbs refused to move. *Oh, God.*

Even the birds had stopped singing. Señora Flores appeared in the doorway, disappeared again. Or it might not have been her. Rebecca wasn't sure because everything was blurry.

Breathe.

She had to get a grip on herself, had to control her emotions for the baby. "Tell me," she said very calmly. "I want to hear it from your lips."

He raked a hand through his hair, spun back to her. "As if you don't know."

"Tell me!" she screamed, suddenly angry and—and *offended*! That was the word she wanted. *Offended.* How dared he?

His nostrils flared, his chest rising and falling hard. As if he'd run all the way here. As if he'd scaled a mountain to get to her. No doubt he had. An evil, ugly mountain of his own design.

"Do not get worked up," he ordered. "Think of the baby."

She dashed tears from her cheeks. "Or kittens and puppies. Anything but the nastiness in your mind."

"You went to the press," he said, stalking closer again. Whirling away. "You told them your father committed suicide and that it was *my fault*! You want to ruin me, Rebecca. You want Layton International back by any means necessary, *sí*? Well, you will not get it!" he roared. "I will *destroy* it first."

"Suicide?" She could only stare at him as she tried to process it. "What are you talking about? It was a single-engine plane crash. There was a pilot."

"Do not pretend you don't know! You are the one who told them this! You tried to make it look like I did something illegal—like I am a criminal. Just a lowly bullfighter who dared to aim too high, right?" He stopped his pacing and glared at her. "This, combined with the Dubai accusations, will make my shareholders think twice, yes? Ramirez

Enterprises is in for a rocky quarter, thanks to you. But it will not work! You will *not* win!"

Rebecca sucked in a breath, surprised it wasn't shaky or short. Strong emotion buffeted her, threatened her, but she held steady. She would not panic over this. Over him. Not ever again.

"So this is what you think of me." It was a statement, not a question. "You're more worried about a dip in stock prices than you are about me or our baby."

"No, *you* are more concerned with getting your precious company back. You are selfish, Rebecca. Selfish and manipulative. You planned this all along. You didn't take your pills, you got pregnant on purpose, and you faked a panic attack to get me to marry you!"

Icy calm wafted over her, chilled her down to the bone. Inside, her heart bled. Outside, she was detached. So cold it frightened her. She could see with such clarity now. She'd been right about him. The man she loved was controlled by the angry, grief-stricken, suspicious man before her now. She loved him too, but she could not live with him.

"Then why did you marry me if you didn't want to?" she demanded. "No one held a gun to your head. We could have worked out visitation, if you wanted it."

"Visitation? This is *my* child."

"Are you sure?" As soon as she said it, she regretted it. The raw pain on his face told her she'd stabbed deep. But she was furious, hurt, and she wanted to hurt back.

His face was dark. "If not for the timing, I might doubt it."

She swallowed a bubble of hysteria. "Because I am a slut, of course. I'll sleep with anyone for advantage, right? My God, you make me sick." After everything she'd told him, everything she'd felt and believed. It was too much to process. She didn't even bother gathering up the sample book. She just headed for the door.

"Where are you going?"

"Away from you."

"You cannot hide from the truth, *mi esposa*," he said nastily.

She turned back to him. He was a big blur in her field of vision. She swiped her tears away, shook her head. "But you can, can't you? You do it quite well."

CHAPTER TWELVE

ALEJANDRO did not feel any better. In fact he felt worse. After his confrontation with Rebecca he'd thought he would feel exhilaration, triumph, all the things he usually felt when he'd won a fight. Like he could conquer anything.

He *always* felt like he was bursting with life and energy when he won.

But not this time.

He sat in his study and blinked at the computer screen. Señora Flores brought him the drink he'd requested, dropping it on the desk with a thud and marching away without bothering to wipe up the splashes that had landed on the mahogany. She was angry with him for yelling at Rebecca.

He focused on the news headlines he'd been reading. It was there—the sensational story about Jackson Layton's suicide and Alejandro's part in pushing the man over the brink. He'd had all his phones diverted to an answering service hours ago. Reporters would be calling nonstop. Hell, there were probably a few camped outside his gates.

Rebecca had accused him of hiding from the truth. The charge stung, though he knew she was wrong. Why did her barbs prick at him when *she* was the one who had lied and cheated?

He put his head in his hands, stared at the wood grain, the

way a drop of moisture was beginning to stain the surface. Odd how just that little drop could change the wood—the color bleaching out, the grain showing clearer, the visible blotch on what had once been a perfect surface.

What if he was wrong? What if the perfect surface of what he'd thought was true had a blemish? Why would she wait weeks to feed this story to the press?

He thought back over the last few weeks—thought of everything he knew about her. Nothing she had done, if he truly examined it from all angles, showed calculation. Someone with an agenda would have had a better plan. Did it make sense to get pregnant on purpose, but then leave the instant she learned he'd owned the bank and resorts? Wouldn't a woman with a plan to get her company back pretend not to know what he'd done? And wouldn't she plant misleading stories to the press far earlier?

Anyone could have brought this story out now to try and discredit him. Someone with a grudge over the Dubai contracts, in fact. Cahill? He'd been the one to send Rebecca documents, and he'd be just crafty enough to hold a story until it would do him the most good.

Alejandro sat there for a long time, not touching the drink, not moving. Just thinking.

Finally, he lifted his head. *"Maldito sea."*

He shoved himself to his feet, sought her out. But every room he went into was empty. His heart began to pound a drumbeat in his chest, growing faster with each successive room.

Señora Flores met him in the foyer when he came full circle. She did not look happy to see him. "Señora Ramirez, she has gone."

The best thing about being Señora Ramirez was that she could walk into the Villa de Musica, demand a room for the night, and no one would blink. She knew Alejandro would track her down eventually, but at least she'd have a few hours' peace.

Not surprisingly, the room the staff put her in was the suite, with all its memories. Just her luck.

She'd cried a bucketload earlier, but she was startlingly out of tears now. She couldn't even muster a whimper. She went into the bedroom they'd once shared and sank into a chair by the window. Below, traffic was moving steadily. Across the street, a man and woman argued. She could tell because she could see their arms waving back and forth. And then they were kissing.

If only her problems were solved so easily.

She would ask for a divorce. There was no other way. She would not live with him—not as cold and unforgiving and suspicious as he was. If he wouldn't divorce her, she'd insist on her own place. A house nearby, or an apartment. They would live separately, but they would parent their child together.

And how is that going to work, Rebecca?

She pushed a hand through her hair. She didn't know, and she didn't have the energy to think about it right now. She just sat and stared and planned random scenarios, none of them truly viable.

Her respite didn't last long. An hour, maybe two, and then she heard the chime announcing someone had entered the room.

"Rebecca."

She didn't even glance at the entry. She'd felt his presence before he'd spoken. The soft, sexy timbre of his voice stroked her abused senses. She was far too weak with this man.

"I want a divorce, Alejandro."

"No."

She bolted up from the chair, faced him across the room, her arms rigid at her sides. She'd never felt more like doing battle in her life. "I will not stay married to you, living in that house, putting up with your abuse. You wouldn't know the truth if it fell on top of you, so don't you *dare* come in here with the idea you're going to force me to go back with you. Not tonight, Alejandro. Maybe not ever."

"*Sí*, I agree."

Her eyes narrowed as she watched him. He looked a little haggard, as if he'd been working hard and hadn't had enough rest. He wore khakis and a dark button-down shirt, and he looked so delicious she wanted to press her mouth to the hollow of his throat and taste the saltiness of his skin.

Folding her arms beneath her breasts, she turned her head away. "You agree to a divorce? So quickly?"

"That is not what I said." He came into the room, shoved his hands in his pockets and went to the window. Close to her, but not too close. She would have to take at least three steps to be beside him.

"Then what are you saying? Because I'm too drained to figure it out."

"The truth, Rebecca. It has been staring me in the face."

She let out a heavy sigh. He wasn't making any sense.

"Will you sit?" he asked. "I want to say things."

"Fine." She went over and sat on the edge of the bed— away from him. He leaned against the windowsill, as if he realized she would not welcome him moving close again.

"I found Parker Gaines," he said softly. "I did it the night after you told me about him."

Her heart suddenly felt like it was beating in a sea of molasses. "Okay," she said, stupidly.

"He is in a California prison for embezzlement."

Was it wrong to feel satisfaction at the knowledge? "Good."

"Yes, I thought so as well. It saved me the trouble of killing him for you."

"Alejandro—"

"No," he said, holding up a hand to silence her. "I would do this gladly. You need only ask. When he gets out in twenty years I will challenge him to a duel."

In spite of herself, she grinned. Not much, but still a grin. She tilted her head down to hide it.

"Are you laughing at me, Rebecca?"

She wanted to, but she shook her head.

He sighed. "Ah, well, I am not so amusing."

He didn't say anything for so long she looked up to see what he was doing. He was staring back at her.

"I know you did not give the story to the press," he said gravely.

If he hoped that news would make her leap up and throw herself in his arms, he was mistaken. "And? Did you hire someone to tell you this? Find the real culprit so you could no longer blame me?"

"No, I did none of these things. I just know."

She did laugh this time—and it was as bitter as acid. "How can you suddenly just *know*? It's not like you, Alejandro! You've done something and you're lying to me about it."

He moved with a speed that startled her. When she would have scrambled away, he dropped to his knees in front of her, gripped her hands. "I know because of many things, *amor*. I know you are not capable of this kind of deception. It's too calculated, too cold—"

She tried to wrench her hands away, but he wouldn't let go. "But this is exactly what you've been accusing me of all along! I'm cold, calculating. I'll sleep with anyone for anything, I make bargains on my back and—"

"Stop," he ordered. "I was wrong."

She searched his eyes, looking for deceit. "I don't understand you," she whispered.

"Can you forgive me for the things I've said? The things I've done?"

"I don't know," she said honestly. She stared at their clenched hands. His dark ones gripping her paler ones. "You've hurt me too many times. I'm not sure I can take that risk again. Or that I want to."

He let her go and she pulled away, stood up and moved out of his reach, while he remained kneeling by the bed. He dropped his forehead on the edge of the mattress, stayed that way for several moments.

Her heart slammed her ribs at seeing him like that. She didn't understand it, didn't know why he would go to such lengths. Had she missed some sort of Spanish law about mothers getting full custody of children in divorces? About foreigners married to Spaniards for less than a month? Did he need her to come back so he could take their baby away?

She pressed a hand to her abdomen protectively.

"I blamed you," he said. "That's why I did it."

"What?"

He looked up. "For Anya. I blamed you."

Horror coated her in iciness. "That makes no sense, Alejandro. How could it be *my* fault?"

He got to his feet, began to pace. "My father arranged for my brother to marry the daughter of one of his friends—a man he owed money to. When my brother died, my father wished me to honor the agreement. I have told you this, *sí*?"

She nodded, not quite sure where he was going with this.

"But I did not want to marry her. I wanted to choose my own wife, in my own time. So I refused. And then you ran because you thought I was engaged. I tried to explain this to you, but you did not believe me. Nor did I believe that you ever really loved me once Cahill pulled my deal. So I agreed to marry Caridad. She had all the right qualifications: bloodline, wealth, beauty. It was a marriage of convenience, and I was satisfied. She would be the perfect wife for me."

He blew out a breath, raked his hand through his hair. "I

was wrong. When Anya was born Caridad didn't seem to care. She was always distant and cold. This did not bother me until she was the same with our child. I knew I had made a mistake."

He stopped and faced her. "The night Anya died, Caridad was in Milan. She was unreachable for many hours. And when I did track her down she refused to come home until the next afternoon, because there was nothing she could do for Anya."

Rebecca's heart squeezed. She wanted to wrap her arms around him, but she was frozen in place. "And you blamed *me* for this? Why?"

"I chose to marry her because you left me, Rebecca. Everything that happened to me and to Anya happened because you left."

Resentment and sorrow mingled, burned deep. Her throat hurt as she forced the words to come. "You had a choice, Alejandro. There is always a choice. Just like my father had when he chose to pursue the Thailand acquisition. It is not your fault he was there, or that he got on that plane. He made his own choice. Just as you did. And had you *not* married Caridad you would have never had the joy of Anya. You wouldn't have suffered the pain, but you wouldn't have had the beauty either."

"I know this now. You have made me see it. You have made me see many things about myself I do not like," he finished quietly.

"Why are you saying this to me now? How do I know you won't blame me for something else, or accuse me of betraying you again?" She shook her head. "I don't want to take a chance and have it blow up in my face."

He drew in a sharp breath, let it out in a rush. "*Dios*, I must learn to let go, yes? You said the world will still move without me forcing it, so I have to take this leap. With you, Rebecca. I cannot do it alone."

Her lungs felt tight, but it wasn't panic closing in on her. Did she dare to hope? Or was he simply saying he would try better at their marriage? "Tell me what you mean, Alejandro. You have to say the words so I can be sure I understand you clearly."

"I am saying I wanted to marry *you* five years ago, Rebecca. I cared for you. It has taken me much thinking to realize the truth. And the truth is that I would not have been so angry you left had I not loved you."

Tears pricked her eyes. "You're saying you loved me when we were together before?" She could scarcely believe it. It was what she'd wanted then, more than anything. To be loved in return by the only man she had ever lost her heart to. But did he truly mean it? Could they get past all the hurt and anger between them?

"I loved you then. I love you now." He closed his eyes and bowed his head. "I am terrified of this love."

She knew why. "Because you don't have power over it." For him, the loss of control would be devastating.

"Sí," he replied, suddenly looking at her with such tenderness she thought her knees would buckle if she weren't already sitting down.

"I'm not sure what to say, Alejandro." But her pulse was racing and her body was humming with energy.

"Say you love me too."

She couldn't deny it. She had no wish to. "I never stopped."

"Madre de Dios, gracias," he offered skyward. "Does this mean you will forgive me?"

"I'm working on it. I need time."

He looked disappointed, but resigned. "You will tell me when?"

She nodded. She thought he might leave her alone now, but he shoved his hands into his pockets and turned to look out the window. She didn't know how long they stayed like that—

him looking outside, her sitting in the chair, thinking about everything that had happened. She wanted to believe him. She wanted to go to him.

And yet—

Each time she'd opened herself to him in the past she'd been hurt. She looked at his profile, his proud features, and realized just how hard this had been for him. To tell her everything, to admit he was wrong, to declare he loved her. If he could take that chance, couldn't she?

Rebecca got up, and he turned at the movement. She went and wrapped her arms around his neck and he caught her close, buried his face in her hair. They stayed that way for several minutes, not talking, just holding each other. Finally she pushed him back just a little, so she could look at his gorgeous face. Yes, it was a leap, but she had to do it with him. She had to trust him with her heart and soul.

"I think I forgive you now. I love you, Alejandro. I always have."

He kissed her so sweetly she could have cried. *"Mi corazón,"* he whispered. "You have enslaved me. I fought you but I did not win."

"Are you sorry?"

His smile lit up her world. "There are no losers in this game, *mi amor*. I am, finally, your willing slave."

She gave him a wicked smile as she reached for his belt. "I can think of a few commands for my slave."

"I had hoped you would say so," he said fervently.

Life, Rebecca decided, was about to get a whole lot more interesting.

EPILOGUE

REBECCA emerged from the limo after her doctor's appointment and headed into Ramirez Enterprises. The appointment had been simply routine now she was closer to her due date. The genetic testing had revealed months ago that their baby would not be at any higher risk than was usual.

The receptionist greeted her with a smile as she strode into the lobby. She stepped into the private elevator and let the operator send her to Alejandro's office. The business was as strong as ever. Once Rebecca had united with Alejandro for a joint statement to the press about her father, the speculation had died down and the rumor had disappeared.

Further, when Alejandro had announced she was joining Ramirez Enterprises as the lead consultant to the hotel division, share prices had taken off. And she had no qualms about charging him an exorbitant fee for her expertise, husband or not.

Alejandro looked up from his desk. "I thought you were working from home today, *mi amor*?"

She shrugged. "I have already completed the projections for your next big project. Besides, I wanted to see you."

One eyebrow lifted. "Dare I hope why?"

"You may hope."

He came around the desk and pulled her gently into his embrace. "I can hardly get my arms around you."

"Alejandro, no woman likes to be called fat. Shame on you."

He laughed. "You aren't fat, *mi amor*. You are radiant."

She lost herself in his kiss. A second later, he seated her in a cushy chair. He put his hands on either side of her, tilting her back. "So tell me," he said, his lips ghosting over hers, down her neck, back up again. "What did the doctor say?"

"Veronica is perfectly healthy. I too am healthy as a horse. And just about as big." Rebecca frowned. How the man still found her attractive, she would never know.

"Yes, but can we still make love so close to your due date?"

"You really want to?"

He took her hand, pressed it to his groin. "What do you think?"

Rebecca sucked in a breath. *Oh, my…* "I think you need glasses."

"I think I adore you. I need you, *mi amor*."

"It would be cruel of me to deny you."

"Oh, indeed."

"Lock the door."

"Consider it done."

When he returned, he pulled her with him to the leather sofa and took her in his arms again. He gazed into her face with a look so serious it took her breath away. "You have made my life more wonderful than I ever thought possible. I am truly blessed."

"Alejandro," she breathed, "you are my everything."

And then she proved it to him.

A month later, Veronica Rebecca Angelica Rivera de Ramirez made her long-awaited debut—much to the delight of her parents. Eight months after that Rebecca was pregnant again—with twins. Life in the Ramirez household was never boring, but it *was* filled with love and laughter—and a few kittens and puppies.

* * * * *

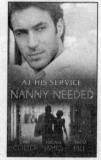

The World of Mills & Boon®

There's a Mills & Boon® series that's perfect for you. We publish ten series and, with new titles every month, you never have to wait long for your favourite to come along.

Blaze®
Scorching hot, sexy reads
4 new stories every month

By Request
Relive the romance with the best of the best
9 new stories every month

Cherish™
Romance to melt the heart every time
12 new stories every month

Desire™
Passionate and dramatic love stories
8 new stories every month

Have Your Say

You've just finished your book.
So what did you think?

We'd love to hear your thoughts on our 'Have your say' online panel
www.millsandboon.co.uk/haveyoursay

- Easy to use
- Short questionnaire
- Chance to win Mills & Boon® goodies

Visit us Online

Tell us what you thought of this book now at
www.millsandboon.co.uk/haveyoursay

YOUR_SAY